G MICHAEL SMITH

THE FOREVERS: BOOK 1

INDIEOWL
PRESS

4700 Millenia Blvd
Ste 175 #90776
Orlando, FL 32839

info@indieowlpress.com
IndieOwlPress.com

THE FOREVERS: MIND STORMS

Illustrated by G Michael Smith

Cover art © GrandeDuc
Cover design & Interior layout/design by Vanessa Anderson
at NightOwlFreelance.com

Paperback ISBN-13: 978-1-949193-14-5
Hardcover ISBN-13: 978-1-949193-15-2

To my wife, Cheryl Cameron, for her love, her confidence in me, her support of my work, and for that most valuable of commodities—her time.

To my friend Leslie Gilmour, and my daughters, Ashley, Lindsay, and Christian, whose support I cherish.

"The greatness of the man's power is the measure of his surrender."
— *William Booth*

TABLE OF CONTENTS

TABLE OF CONTENTS

TABLE OF CONTENTS

THE FOREVERS: BOOK 1

PROLOGUE

The child in the crib wailed. She was in a lab filled with equipment. The many machine indicator lights glowed red, illuminating a stuffed rabbit on the table beside the cage. She stood and reached over the bars of the crib. Her hand twisted back and forth as her fingers grabbed at the air. The child reached for the stuffed rabbit. She stopped reaching and stared at the rabbit. Her hands gripped the top rail of her crib and she rocked back and forth. After a few moments, the stuffed rabbit slid across the table. It flew through the air until it was pressed against the transparent wall of her cage. The child relaxed her grip on the rail of the crib and the rabbit fell to the floor. She climbed out of the crib and pressed her tear-smeared face to the glass wall. She stared at the rabbit and groped at the wall. She banged on the plexiglass with her hand. Her long hair flipped up and down in a tangled mess. The rabbit stood with its face flattened to the glass in perfect time with the impact of her hand as if invisible strings were pulling it erect. Finally, both the child and the stuffed rabbit sunk to the floor.

Her head tilted and her eyes rolled back, showing only whites. She stayed like that for a moment before it happened. The lab's laser clicked on and the beam cut into the floor. The smoke rose, clouding the image. A fan whirred, and the smoke quickly dissipated. The laser head rotated until the beam was aimed at the bottom metal hinge holding the door to the glass cage. The metal melted. The laser stopped, shifted upward, and was aimed at the upper hinge. It clicked on. The upper hinge melted, and the door dropped down and rested on the frame.

The girl blinked and wiped her nose on her sleeve. She stood up and pushed on the sagging door until it fell to the side. She reached down, pulled the stuffed animal to her, and hugged it tightly. She walked back to her crib, climbed over the rail, and snuggled down with the stuffed rabbit clutched to her chest. She fell asleep.

ϴ

He smiled and licked his lips as he switched off the hologram. He had found her. He set a paper file carefully down on his desk. Nothing about these cases was stored electronically. It was the only way to ensure no copies could be made. That was important, given the legality of the project. The paper files for all the children were in his possession. They were secretly stored after the project was canceled. He had, in a moment of fear, nearly destroyed all the paper copies. He was so glad he hadn't for here was a treasure trove of information. The holograms had never been stored on any device connected to the global system. There was no possibility that copies could have been made. He flipped through the file, looking for an ID number. He found it. He was sure that this was the child. Now he could locate her. She had to be out there, somewhere. A child with her power would have survived.

He reflected on the last few weeks of the project. Everyone was filled with panic. They released the children into the wild, so to speak. He smiled at his little joke. The *'wild'* was the nursery system. They were mostly toddlers. They were spread out. One per city. He needed to find a suitable child, and he remembered this one as having the attributes Winter Bancroft wanted. Ten years had passed. He had to find her soon. He must track her and ensure she was *'acceptable'*. The old bitch could still pull his strings—even after all these years. He scanned the file again, glancing at the data they'd collected. Good. She was perfect. She would be about 13 years old now. He placed the file in his case. He searched to find the remaining holo-chips. He wanted the ones taken when she was one year old. She'd caused a bit of a stir at the time, but that was all forgotten when the World Police came to arrest everyone involved in the project.

They had received a warning of the police raid. He knew he would be in prison without that warning. A fail-safe system was installed at his insistence. What they were doing to the embryos was considered a crime against humanity and punishable by life in prison. There was a particularly nasty case ten years previous called *'The Moreau Case'* named after an H. G. Wells novel, *The Island of Dr. Moreau*. This prosecution resulted in new laws. It involved indiscriminate gene-splicing of insect and human DNA. It was totally unscientific. In fact, the perpetrators were not even scientists. They had obtained a 10TH GEN CRISPR-CAS9 device controlled by a BIG DADDY CRAY super quantum computer and went about creating monsters—the weirder the better. They sold these monsters to some very affluent buyers for private zoo specimens and, as the story goes, some of the monsters escaped. Insect monsters with human intelligence wreaked havoc. A lot of people went to prison.

He knew the press would compare the cases. That made him angry. He was a scientist, not a hack. He had altruistic motives. He was not doing it for the credits. At least that's what he constantly told himself in the beginning, but things had changed. His other pet project: '*Neural Construct Transference of Connectome Topography'* had been more successful than even he had imagined. Now he needed some children as hosts. He needed very special children. If he was to transfer his superior intellect into a new body, then that body would have to be extra special. He set about creating these children.

When the news of the raid was intercepted, he set into motion the dissemination of the toddlers in his lab to the nursery system. Any of the subjects older than two and younger than 18 months were not suitable. The older subjects could give the police too much information, and the younger ones, well, there were just too many of them. A flood of children into the nursery system would set off all kinds of alarms. There was only one course of action, and he took it. With a push of a button, he destroyed them all in a fire so hot it would vaporize steel. He knew there were those of his employees who would be horrified at his actions. They would give him up for the mass murder of children, so, as far as they were concerned, all the children were placed in private homes or the nursery and the fire had simply been to eliminate all incriminating evidence. The police found nothing. After that, he went underground.

He grabbed another chip in the series and inserted it into the holo player on his desk. Some filing information floated in the air, and then the holo projected an image of a child lying in a crib. It was a much younger version of 302875106592253. There was a toy mobile hanging over the child. She was reaching up to grab one of the plastic creatures dangling down, but the mobile suddenly rotated and the desired toy was out of her reach. A new toy moved closer, and she reached up for it. Just as she was about to grab it, it moved out of reach. This continued for three more events designed to frustrate the child. Suddenly, a small section of the wire holding the mobile over the crib began to glow orange, then hot white. With a puff of smoke, that section of wire melted, and the entire mobile fell into the crib. The child giggled, grabbed one of the toys, and put it in her mouth. She smiled as the hologram ended.

It was one of a series of tests he ran on the tiny subjects he had created. He suddenly felt a surge of pride. This child was his. Not biologically, but still his. He had created her.

He reached into the file and pulled out the list of DNA anomalies for this girl. He scanned it and stopped abruptly at the following phrase, *'A series of i-motifs containing a sequence of cytosine pairs not bound to guanine were found after duplication. This was not thought to be possible in human DNA. Its exact function is still unknown.'* He read on. *'The gene-splicing completed in vitro does not account for this and other anomalies. One specific attribute of her brain, the density of nerve fibers in the corpus callosum, is at least triple what is found in a normal human brain. Scans suggest that this nerve bundle, connecting the two hemispheres of the brain, will probably continue to grow until she reaches adulthood. A corpus callosum of this density can, for lack of a better description, give this child two brains, for each hemisphere can now act as if it were one entire brain. The sharing of data between the two hemispheres is near perfect.*

As a side note, this researcher suggested this child may express some bizarre talents in the years to come.'

"Shit," he muttered, "no wonder Winter wanted this one." He rubbed his chin and thought to himself, *I wonder what it would be like to be female?*

I Passed!

The end of the world was coming. This wasn't some religious prophecy or ancient warning. It was fact. The end of the world was coming. When was not clear, but two hundred years was the initial estimation. There was really only one course of action for humanity—Get out! Leave before the meteor field—some said was a thousand times larger than the entire solar system—strikes and destroys everything. In fact, it was likely that the entire planetary system would crumble in its wake; the remnants joining the gargantuan meteor storm on its eternal rush through space. Sol was large enough to survive, but without her family, what would be the point?

It was Jayne Esther Wu's 13th birthday. Rolling onto her back, she clutched a pillow to her chest and slowly exhaled as the white glow of her room lights intensified. She was finally an adult—not yet a woman, but still an adult—and, as such, she would no longer have to live in the nursery. She would no longer have to go to nursery school. She would no longer spend her days playing with the other children. She would no longer have time to play at all. She would have to work.

Today, she would start her adult life with adult responsibilities. After two years, if she worked hard, she would become a full-fledged fixer—a Technical Electrical Mechanical (TEM) fixer. But two years felt like an eternity. She had heard stories of washouts, mostly kids that couldn't hack it. They were moved to the cleaner class or back into the nursery as a helper or child-bearer.

Jayne knew she would hate working in the cleaner class, and she was too young to bear children. Some of her friends wanted to work as helpers but, as far as she was concerned, being a helper would be boring. All they ever did was look after old people and babies. Yech! She wouldn't wash out! She was going to be a TEM fixer, and that was that.

A shiver of excitement ran at the thought of leaving the nursery and becoming part of the great adventure—the saving of the human race. She pushed her blanket aside and the cool air brought goose bumps to her arms. She'd dreamed, for as long as she could remember, what it would be like out there in the real world. She wanted to make a difference and, somehow, she was sure she would.

Jayne swung her feet to the floor, scanning the room for anything she'd missed. Her knapsack sat beside the door, accompanied by two boxes of her possessions, mostly book keys with holographic projections of equipment she'd been studying in preparation for the TEM Aptitude Exam. She had passed, despite the fact that most kids her age group had to go to INTER (Intermediate Technical Educational Reassessment) or Internment, as it was commonly known, for at least two years. She smiled. There would be no INTER for her. She had passed on her first try and had felt a thrill of accomplishment when she received the notice on her VID (Visual Identity Designator) pad stating:

ID: Wu F 302875106592253
Name: Wu, Jayne Esther Class: Fixer
Sub Class: Technician; Electronic Mechanic Apprentice Exam Result: PASS
Report to HUB 169 Entrance M, Friday, January 13, 2113, 1300 hours.

Jayne smiled again. She had passed. The notices never gave an actual score, just PASS or NOT PASS. She had passed. Her head swam with a warm joy as she remembered how she had spent that
first day packing her worldly goods. It hadn't actually taken that long because she didn't own much. Just two boxes and her knapsack.

Jumping out of bed, Jayne headed out of her cubicle to the showers. On the way, she stopped at the sink array and scanned her palm. The sink was programmed to promptly dispense 100 ml of drinking water into a container. With surprise, Jayne looked down at her glass, which was filled to the brim with clear, cold water. The glass had a capacity of at least 400 ml. The dispenser had given her way too much. She smiled at her luck. The dispenser had behaved strangely before, but usually, it dispensed less than the standard amount, not more. She looked at the glass and smiled again. She knew that today was the start of something exciting.

Furtively, Jayne looked up and down the sink-lined hallway. No one else was up yet. She had the space to herself. She took another sip of water, then poured half of the remainder into her cupped hand and splashed it over her face, focusing on her sleep-crusted eyes. She rubbed it all over and quickly dried her face with the tail of her nightshirt. Gulping down the remainder, Jayne replaced the glass and headed to the showers.

She heard the flop of sandals on the tile floor and turned to see a young boy dressed in a nightshirt standing in front of her. He was sniffing and rubbing tears from his face. Jayne recognized him. It was little Ajax. Ajax's cubicle was across from Jayne's. Jayne was his in-formal mentor. He had arrived the previous year—an orphan from the Wilderlands. Jayne had helped him learn a new language and had helped him cope with his new life without parents. Jayne had never known parents, herself, but she knew what loneliness felt like.

"Ajax, it is too early to be up," said Jayne softly.

"I gon'ta miss you, Jaywu. Please not go," he sniffed. (Jaywu was what he called her when they first met, and it had stuck.)

Jayne had said her goodbyes the night before. "I have to, Ajax. I'm too old to stay. I have to go to a new and bigger school."

"You gon'ta miss your birthday cake. I helpt make it. It chocolate with pink icing and silver sprinkles." He smiled and he stuck out his tongue, licking his lips in anticipation.

They only got cake when it was someone's birthday.

"I can't stay, but you can have my piece. It will be the biggest piece cause it's my birthday. I will tell them before I go." She tousled his hair, spun him around, and led him back to his cubical. She hugged him and he climbed back into his bed. Jayne resumed her trip to the showers.

The showers used water, but it wasn't drinkable. To use them, a person stood with arms and legs outstretched and a mixture of water and soap would spray every square cm of skin, hitting you at such high pressure that it stung. After about 10 seconds of cleaning time, a second stinging mist would blast your skin and rinse away the soap. This was followed by gusting air and ended with an ultraviolet bacteria wash. The whole process took about one minute. When you stepped out of the shower, you were as 'clean as an omie's whistle.' (Omie was slang for a biomedweller.)

Jayne Esther Wu stepped out of the shower, slipped on her nightshirt, and skipped happily back to her nursery cubicle for the last time.

CHAPTER 2

The PUT Pad & the Dumb Giant

The meteor storm was discovered in 2029. The best scientific estimates gave planet Earth and the rest of the solar system 182 years before the cosmic rock storm would blow in from intergalactic space, obliterating everything in its path. Each projectile was 1 to 10000 km in diameter. In essence, the coming storm consisted of a wall of space rock a trillion km across, all hurtling toward Earth. No one knew how deep that wall of destruction was. It didn't really matter. The fact that it existed at all spelled doom for all living things and destruction of the planet itself.

Jayne arrived at biome HUB entrance 169M at precisely 13:00 hours. She had to get used to using the 24-hr clock; after all, she was no longer a nursery baby. She was on her way to becoming a tech. The HUB entrance was an archway made of concrete and steel with three massive roll-up steel doors set equidistant across the face. The right door was painted green, the left door was red, and the center door was yellow. To the side of the large left and right doors were two regular doors painted the same colors: red and green. There were guards at each of these doors. Jayne breathed in deeply and held her breath before slowly letting the air back out with a sigh. A chill ran outwards from her core, down her arms and legs, seeming to spark out her fingers and toes just as another chill swelled in her chest, running the same path. She shook her hands and snapped her fingers, as if to speed up the passage of what felt like electricity surging out her fingertips. She slipped the knapsack from her shoulders, setting it down in front of her.

The rest of her belongings would be sent once she settled into her new accommodations. This HUB would be her home for the next two years.

Jayne turned slowly in a circle, allowing the sights and sounds and smells to waft over her. The cacophony of active machinery swelled and ebbed around her. The large transports clicked as they moved onto the monorail, some passing through the green door, others exiting through the red door, then clicking back off the monorail before driving away.

A swarm of people buzzed around her, some moving purposefully while others just stood in place. Jayne removed the VID from her hip pouch and pressed her thumb over the scan core. The VID lit up. She touched the screen, double-checking her location against the coordinates contained in her orders. She took one small step to the left, then checked again. The VID app beeped red. She stepped back a bit while watching the screen. Finally, the VID app beeped green. She was in exactly the right spot.

Jayne sighed in an effort to push the tension from her body and looked around. The number of people had continued to increase while she had been adjusting her position. More people were now standing near her, checking their VIDs and adjusting their own positions in this PUT (Pedestrian Unit Transport) area.

Jayne sniffed, wrinkling her nose. A new person appeared and was now standing just one meter to her right. She glanced over inconspicuously and quickly looked away so as not to be noticed. A boy standing nearby was clumsily trying to adjust his knapsack. He fumbled around inside the bag with hands that seemed almost too big for his arms and finally pulled out his own VID. As he checked his location, Jayne could see the red glow from the VID screen through his oversized fingers. The boy looked down, then up, then around, panic beginning to swell in his eyes, although his fear was partially hidden by a shock of dark hair that hung in front of his face. Tapping the VID screen, he looked around, as if searching for someone to help him. He didn't seem to even notice Jayne standing within arm's reach to his left. He looked right over her head, his height seeming to prevent him from seeing someone so short. The concern on his face began to swell, his eyes repeatedly flicking back to the VID screen which continued to glow red.

Jayne cleared her throat. She interlaced her fingers, inverted her hands and stretched them out in front of her. She felt, as well as heard, the satisfying crackle as some of her finger joints popped. The tall boy turned toward the sounds and looked down at Jayne, seeing her for the first time. Jayne smiled up at him. He breathed out and glanced back and forth from his VID to her face.

"It's red. It won't go green," he said, managing a weak smile. "You sure the COORs match?" Jayne asked. (COORs is slang for coordinates.)

"Yeah!" he retorted, seeming irritated that she would even ask the question.

"Sorry, I was just trying to help. I didn't mean anything by it," she replied. "Sometimes the VID sensors can be off by a few centimeters. At least that's what I've noticed in the past."

"The past! You sound like you're 30 not…what?" he paused, looking her up and down while he tried to come up with an accurate age, "15 or 16? What's a kid like you doing here, anyway? There is no way you could have passed the TEM exam."

Jayne didn't react. She had dealt with this kind of prejudice before. She looked carefully at the boy beside her, starting with a head that rested on shoulders at least a meter above her own. His hair was dark and coarse and clumped into short and long blocks. It looked like it had been cut by a butcher using a dull knife. His eyes were so dark she could not tell where his irises ended and his pupils began. The darkness of his eyes made it impossible for Jayne to determine how his pupils were reacting to this situation. Normally, she would use a person's pupil response to determine their level of anxiety. She could not read him.

Moving down his face, Jayne found a strong jaw with just a few wisps of whiskers. The rest of his body could be described with one short word: big. Sweeping down his body, Jayne's eyes rested at his feet. They weren't big, they were monstrous. He stood with those gargantuan feet sticking out to the side, looking like a bow-legged clown.

A smile crept slowly over her face at the image of the huge, over-bearing boy dressed as a clown. She looked up at him with confidence and said, "Never mind how old I am. I got here fairly."

Rolling his eyes in dismissal, the boy turned back to the problem at hand. He needed to figure out why his VID screen stayed red, despite being in the right place on the right day. He looked up at the digital clock that inexorably counted down to the end of the world. Over the years, it had been adjusted to reflect more accurate measurements. The latest adjustment had given Earth a little more than 82 years. Right below that was the local time. That clock read 12:46.

"Crap!" he said as he tapped his VID screen again, looking frantically around for help. There were hundreds of people in and around the PUT area, but none were close enough to talk to without shouting and he was unwilling to move, just in case that made the situation worse. Finally, panic superseded the doubt he had about the small girl, and he looked down at Jayne, who grinned back up at him.

"What are you smiling about?" he snapped. "This is a serious situation." He looked up to the sky, as if he were imploring the deities to come to his aid.

"I think I can help," giggled Jayne.

"Yeah, right. You're just a baby and you don't get how serious this is. If this VID doesn't go green—"

"Like this," she interrupted, waving her VID, glowing green, in front of his face.

"Yeah, like that. If mine doesn't go green, I will have to go back to INTER and start over. I would rather die," he finished, sighing, "and you are so stupid you don't get it."

"Oh, I get it alright. Give me your hand," she commanded. She held out her hand to him, annoyed when he hesitated. "Give me your hand. I will make that VID of yours go green." She glanced up at the clock, which now read 12:47. "Look, you can try to solve this problem yourself within the next 13 minutes, or you can put your hand in mine, and I'll solve it in just a few seconds."

"What are you going to do?" he asked tentatively.

"Just give me your hand. I don't bite…" she paused and smiled, "hard enough to draw blood anyway."

His eyes widened.

"I'm just teasing," she retorted, rolling her eyes as she reached up and grabbed his hand. "Now, follow my instructions carefully and precisely. First, look down."

He looked at her strangely for a moment before she continued, "Look down at your huge feet, you silly boy."

He found himself following her instructions and looked warily down at his feet.

"That's right. Now, I want you to concentrate on moving the toes on your left foot closer to the toes on your right foot. Do you think you can manage that?" she said, suppressing a giggle as she let go of his hand.

"What?"

"Just move your feet together so that the heels touch and the big toes touch."

"You want me to take my shoes off? What good would that do?"

"No, silly, just place your feet together, with shoes on, like mine," she said, pointing at her own feet.

He moved his feet together.

"That's right. Well done. Now check your VID."

He stood with feet together and snapped open his VID. It was glowing green. He looked at her with stunned relief and said, "How did you do that?"

"It's the PUT pads. You can't have any part of your body extending more than 50 cm past the PUT center point. I figured, with the way you were standing, legs apart and feet sticking out, that you had gone past the edge. If the PUT pad was to activate, it might leave your toes behind."

"Thanks."

"You are welcome, and don't ever call me stupid again." "Okay, but why did you want to hold my hand?"

"People are more willing to listen to each other when they are connected in some way. I just figured a little hand-holding would calm you down."

As he blushed, they both turned and looked straight ahead. They stood in silence, tension mounting, waiting for the PUT pads to activate and take them to whatever awaited them in the HUB.

CHAPTER 3

The New Quarters & the Star

The human race wasn't about to go down without a fight. There were a lot of ideas bouncing around during the first 10 years after the meteor storm was discovered. Everyone thought of those rocks hurtling through space, not as inanimate objects like a hailstorm, but as a swarm of hateful living things, like a group of crop-killing flying insects or blood-sucking bats. You could hate living things. You couldn't hate rocks. So the meteors became malevolent monsters bent on the destruction of the humanrace.

When the PUT deactivated, Jayne found herself standing in a strangely curved hallway that snaked away, blocking her view after about ten meters. She imagined observing the hallway from above and seeing an S-curve. There were doors spaced three meters apart on her side of the hall. The other wall shone with smooth, unbroken metal, following thebend.

Jayne walked down the hall, away from the spot where she had materialized. She wanted to get a better view of where she was going to live for the next two years. As she approached the opposite wall and was about to turn around, something happened to a one-meter circular section of the wall in front of her.

She stared. It was as if a hole had formed in the wall. She reached out, expecting her hand to go right through, but it felt just like a metal wall should feel: cool and smooth. The hole-that-wasn't-a-hole provided a live view of the huge tech floor below. There were hundreds of workers milling about. It was the largest tech floor she had ever seen. She stared and as she walked to her left, the viewing area followed. It was an electronic window—new tech she had only read about until now. The entire wall was painted with nanoparticles programmed to show an image just as if the viewer was looking through a window. Electronic windows were activated by the presence of the viewer and followed as the viewermoved.

Jayne smiled and ran quickly to her right. The viewer kept perfect pace. When she jumped, it jumped. She tried jogging along the wall and was pleased to see the screen keeping pace beside her. Finally, she returned to her starting point.

She then walked down the hall and stopped in front of the metal door to her new quarters. The door had no discernible knobs or locks, just an outline where the door would retract into the wall. The number 2197 was etched into the frame above the door. She thumbed her VID while pointing it at the door. The door to her new quarters opened silently, and she stepped inside.

The room wasn't big, but it was a million times better than the cubicles at the nursery. All the surfaces were curved in the corners. No sharp corners were evident anywhere. Everything was white.

The bed was formed by a horizontal alcove set in the right wall with shelves and drawers inset both above and below the sleeping platform. Jayne assumed these were meant to store her belongings.

On the left side of the room, the floor ballooned upward to form a table and chair. The back wall featured a small bathroom withher own vacuum toilet and misting UV shower. That was it. But after years in the cramped nursery, Jayne thought it was a mansion. She had never had her own bathroom before.

She giggled and twirled in a circle. She stopped on the third spin when a panel inset in the wall beside the door caught her eye. She moved closer, intending to reach out to touch it, when a soft male voice spoke, "Good afternoon, Wu F 302875106592253. If you prefer, you can be addressed as Jayne Wu or simply as Jayne, please state your preference now."

Jayne stared first at the wall and then at the ceiling. The voice seemed to come from both nowhere and everywhere at once.

"Wu F 302875106592253, we can continue this introduction to your new residence at a future time if you so wish," crooned the voice. "No. You may address me as Jayne or, when you get to know me, as 'Thirteen.' That's kinda like my nickname," said Jayne.

"Alright. Do you prefer 'Jayne Thirteen' or 'Thirteen Jayne'?" asked the voice.

"Just 'Jayne' or 'Thirteen,' not both together," Jayne said. "Alright, Thirteen, would you like me to continue with the introduction to the many functions of the residence?" asked the voice. "Sure," said Jayne, shrugging.

The voice continued, "You are standing in front of the control panel for residence 2197. I will be your guide until you are familiar with all the functions of your residence. You may shut off any audio output from the AIU—Artificial Intelligence Unit—once you have customized the residence to your liking. I do discourage this, as I can often be very helpful."

The voice paused for a moment, and Jayne took the opportunity to ask some of the questions that were running through her head.

"How long will this take? And what do I call you?" asked Jayne.

"It will take approximately 20 minutes. What would you like to call me?" asked the voice.

"What did the last resident call you?" asked Jayne.

"Thirteen, I have never worked with any other resident. I came into being the moment you entered this residence. I will be 13 minutes old in 3, 2…" the voice paused, "now."

"That's funny. Well, 13 is my lucky number, so I guess I'll call you Lucky," giggled Jayne.

"Thank you for my name. If you wish to speak with me in the

future, just say my name," Lucky said. "Now, do you wish to continue, Thirteen?"

"Sure," said Jayne.

Lucky continued with the short tutorial. Jayne learned how to change the temperature, the lighting, and the humidity in the room to suit her liking. She could play music or watch the netvids on an instavid. Any of the walls would open with instavid programming of her choice at her command. She could even change the color of her walls or the firmness of the mattress. Finally, Lucky stopped.

"This is the end of the basic tutorial. If you wish to receive more information about the specifications of the residence controls, I will be more than willing to help," said Lucky.

Jayne looked around at the room's white walls. "Can you make the walls a little less white?" she asked.

"Yes. I took the liberty of studying your medical file and I see you are a tetrachromat," stated Lucky.

"I'm a what?" she asked, a little confused.

"Oh, it is a very rare genetic variation in vision that is only found in females. Tetrachromats have an additional type of cone on the retina of their eyes. Cones are color photoreceptive retinal cells that are located in the back of the eye. Most humans have three kinds of cones; hence they are considered to be trichromats. Those with four types of cones are known as tetrachromats. They are able to differentiate far greater variations of color than those found in the typical trichromatic range. I mentioned your tetrachromaticism because I have the ability to transform the wall to display any color you can perceive and you can perceive millions of different colors."

"Any off-white with a hint of pink will do," said Jayne.

"Is this satisfactory?" asked Lucky as the walls changed slightly, seeming far less bright.

"Perfect," said Jayne as she sat down on a molded chair that was really just an extension of the floor. She finally had a space she could call home. She breathed deep and smiled when a chime filled the room.

"Shall I open the door, Thirteen?" asked Lucky. "Who is it? Can you tell?" asked Jayne in retort.

"Yes, I can tell. No one is there," replied Lucky. "There are, however, some containers. I suggest that your belongings may have arrived."

"I've got nothing else to do. I guess I might as well unpack," she said. "Open the door."

The doors slid silently apart. On the threshold were three containers with scanlocks in the center of the lids. Jayne carried them inside and set them down in the middle of the room. She placed her hand on the scanlock and she felt a slight scratch on her palm as the scanlock confirmed her identity. You never knew where the scanlock was going to scratch you, but it never took more than a few skin cells—just enough to run a DNA comparison to her last formal scan. If the cells matched, the computer would open the lock. It popped open, and the lid slid into the side of the packing case. Since the cases were part of one shipment, all the locks disengaged once her identity was confirmed.

Jayne started to unpack the cases. It only took a few minutes to take out her clothes and put them in one of the sealed drawers by her bed. She wouldn't have the opportunity to wear any of them again except when she was in her own quarters. All 'out of quarters' clothing was supplied and required by the HUB. Personal clothes were not allowed to be worn in any working area of the HUB. HUB clothing was highly specialized. Contamination of materials and equipment destined for the biomes was of primary concern.

After unpacking the remainder of her things, Jayne put the empty packing crates outside her door, sat on the edge of her bed and picked up her most valuable possession: a small music box. She opened it and her favorite piece of music began to play. A tinny version of Pachelbel's Canon chimed from the box.

"I have many versions of this music. Would you like me to play a better quality version? I promise you, the sound will be of a much higher fidelity," said Lucky.

"No. I like this version. This music box belonged to my birth mother. It is the only thing I have left from her," she said as she closed the box. The music did not stop. Jayne looked at the box, slightly puzzled. She opened it again and looked inside. Usually, closing the lid stopped the music. She spotted something caught on the small closing lever. She picked at the obstruction with her fingernail and it caught on what appeared to be a fine chain. She worked it from the lever and started to pull it out of the box, discovering that the chain threaded from a small hole in the corner of the tray sitting on the bottom of the box. She lifted out the tray that covered the inner workings of the box and removed the chain. It had a pendant dangling from one end. She had never seen it before. It was silver in color and had an unusual star-shape. Connected to the star's center hexagon were six spokes, each approximately one cm in length. These spokes rose to a center point, forming a six-sided pyramid. The pendant had thirteen vertices. Thirteen, she thought. Odd.

Jayne touched her finger to the sharp point of the thirteenth vertex. She sucked in her breath and instinctively brought her finger to her mouth. The vertex had suddenly become very sharp and had pierced the end of her finger. She looked closely at the end of her finger. A small bead of blood bubbled up. She felt an unexplained wave of nausea rise and fall.

She absently sucked the blood from her finger, looking at the pendant again. She was surprised to find that it was growing warm in her hand and, as she watched, the sides of the hexagonal pyramid slowly shortened, folding down to the same level as the rest of the star. It now appeared as a simple flat piece of silver jewelry on a chain. The sharp point had disappeared.

"Is everything alright, Thirteen?" asked Lucky.

"Fine," she responded, as she slipped the pendant back into the music box. "I think someone gave me a birthday present."

"That's nice. Happy birthday," Lucky cooed.

Before she closed the box, Jayne latched the play lever so the music would not play the next time she opened it. She placed the box on her bed. "Play some music, Lucky," she said.

"What would you like to hear?" asked Lucky. "You choose," said Jayne.

Jayne spent the remainder of the day scanning the instavid HUB overview, its purpose and layout, in preparation for her new life. Tomorrow was an important day: the first day of her apprenticeship. She smiled as she prepared for bed and slipped happily under the covers. She quietly opened the music box under her blanket, slipping the silver star necklace out from within and sliding it over her head and around her neck. It felt warm against her skin. She instinctively popped the star-pricked finger into her mouth and sucked away the pain. She wondered who could have given her such an odd present. As her consciousness slowly faded, so did the soft music Lucky had been playing. She drifted off to sleep.

CHAPTER 4

Off to School, We Go

Many probes were sent out into space to study the galactic storm. But those probes were looking at more than 'The Swarm'—the name given to the massive meteor field. The exploration of space led to the discovery of new planets beyond the Swarm's path that were potentially reachable by the doomed population of Earth. Some of these planets held promise for habitation.

The first discoveries were two fraternal twins aptly nicknamed PLG and PHG. Translated: Planet with Low Gravity and Planet with High Gravity. PLG and PHG had almost everything that was required to support human life. PLG was smaller than Earth and had a much less dense core. As a result, it had lower gravity than Earth. PHG was the same approximate size as PLG but it had a very dense core and greater gravity.

Other discoveries soon followed. None were exactly like Earth, but twelve were close. All of the best scientific estimates predicted they were 'probably' habitable. If humans wanted to survive long-term on any of these planets, the population would have to adapt. The people in charge decided to give the adaptations a head start.

"Thirteen. It is time to get up. Thirteen," said Lucky. "Thirteen, please get up. It is time. You must get up now. We will be behind schedule if you do not get up. Thirteen?"

Jayne Wu opened her eyes. Despite her difficulty in waking up, she felt fully rested and clear-headed. She had slept perfectly. She turned over on her back, feeling the mattress adjust around her new body position.

She lay for a moment waiting for another prompt by Lucky. She did not have to wait long.

"Wu F 302875106592253, it is time to get up," said a flat voice that did not sound like Lucky.

"Lucky, did your voice change?" asked Jayne, sitting up in bed. "It was not me. If SYSTEM feels I am being ignored, it will…"

Lucky paused and cautiously continued, "it will…intercede."

"Oh," said Jayne, sensing the hesitation in Lucky's voice. She drew back the cover and sat up fully, her legs dangling over the edge. She wondered who or what SYSTEM was, but the first day was not a good time to ask. "What next?"

"That is very simple," replied Lucky. "You follow the green arrow and respond to the green prompts. You avoid anything that is red."

Jayne's next question was answered by a ten-centimeter green arrow that appeared in the floor at her feet. It was pointing to the bathroom. Jayne got up, followed the arrows, and responded to the prompts. After about twenty minutes, she was clean, dressed, fed, and standing at the door, waiting for it to open.

"Thank you, Thirteen, for being so efficient on your first day. The prompts will appear less frequently as you learn the routine. Have a good day," chirped Lucky.

With that, the door opened, and Jayne stepped out, following a green flashing arrow in the floor that terminated down the hallway in a one-meter circle of green light, indicating a PUT pad. She stood in the center and waited.

A few seconds later, she appeared in an alcove with a 10-unit PUT array. She stepped off the pad and entered the adjoining room. She was standing in another, high-ceilinged room with twenty other apprentices being organized into four rows of five. The flashing arrow directed Jayne to the third row, third from the end. Position Thirteen. She never really understood why she was always somehow connected to the number thirteen, but it occurred too often in her life to be a simple coincidence.

A small man with graying hair walked up to each of the apprentices and handed them a rectangular badge. The only person she recognized in the group was the big-foot boy she met on the external PUT. She didn't even know his name. He was standing one row ahead of her and two positions to the left. He didn't seem to notice her. He towered over everyone else in the room. The small man handed Jayne a badge with a bright orange 13 printed on a dark background. She took it and waited.

After all the badges had been handed out, a woman walked up to the front of the group. She held a larger version of a standard VID in her hand. She stared down at her VID, never making eye contact with the group in front of her. "Place the ID marker you received into the small pocket on the left breast of your clothing unit," she stated casually.

No one responded, though they all looked down at their shirts to find the pocket.

The woman finally looked up at them, seeming irritated at their inaction. "Now!" she commanded.

There was a rustling sound throughout the room as everyone slipped their ID marker into the small pocket on their chest. As the ID marker hit the bottom of the pocket, the material on Jayne's shirt glowed, the marker disappeared, and a number appeared on the front of the pocket.

The woman looked down again, resuming the inspection of her VID screen. Once she confirmed that all the ID markers were inserted properly into pockets, she looked up at the group. "I had hoped that this day would be uneventful, but it appears I was wrong. It seems there are some VIPs visiting the HUB today. Some scientists from HUB Central are being shown around, and they requested to meet and inspect some of our newest fixer apprentices. Why, I cannot imagine. But who am I to question the reasoning of scientists?" She sighed in resignation, her tone changing quickly back to the sharp voice she previously used. She barked, "Stand sharp and answer all questions clearly!"

A group of five people entered from a small room that held the reserved PUT array. They all appeared to be quite old, at least from Jayne's viewpoint. There were three men and two women. Each of them smiled and approached the group of apprentices.

One of the men spoke first. "We want to welcome you to HUB...." He paused and turned to the young man who was guiding the group.

"169," the guide responded.

"Yes, 169. Welcome to HUB 169. I am sure all of you are more than competent and will excel in your chosen careers. My colleagues and I would like to talk to some of you. This is nothing formal, so try to relax," the man said with a smile on his face.

Moving into the group of apprentices, the scientists began to converse casually with several of them. The oldest woman in the group didn't hesitate and walked straight to Jayne. She had white hair and wrinkled skin. Jayne was surprised that she didn't have to look up but was able to look directly into the woman's eyes. The scientist was, in fact, slightly shorter than Jayne. The eyes that gazed back at her made Jayne take a small step back in surprise. They were a sharp green color that shone so brightly that they seemed to contradict her first impression of the woman's age. They were the eyes of a much younger person.

The woman stared at her in silence; Jayne began to feel uncomfortable under her silent gaze, so she spoke first. "Hello," she said.

The woman did not respond but continued to inspect Jayne like she was something to be purchased.

Jayne continued hesitantly, "My name is Jayne Wu..."

The woman finally acknowledged Jayne and spoke softly. "Yes, dear, I know who you are." She reached out and touched the long braid that hung over Jayne's shoulder. "You are very beautiful and so young."

She smiled a wrinkled smile and reached out, lifting Jayne's necklace. The silver star popped into view. "Yes. Good. Perfect."

"Thank you. I'm not..." Jayne began to respond. She stopped and felt an inexplicable cramp accompanied by a hint of nausea in the pit of her stomach. Jayne's face contorted with the pain.

An odd smile crept over the old woman's face as if she were relishing in the pain Jayne was feeling. "Maybe we will meet again," she said

22

cryptically and abruptly turned and walked away, not talking to any of the other apprentices before rejoining the other scientists.

The nausea in Jayne's stomach slowly faded as the guide spoke to their initial facilitator. "Thank you. You may continue."

The group of scientists walked away, and Jayne was left deeply unsettled and confused by the encounter.

Their facilitator also seemed confused by the unlikely interaction but shrugged and resumed her stern lecture. "I will now continue. Each day, you will be required to insert a new ID marker into the pocket of your clothing unit. Once you have done this, you must step off the PUT pad and follow the indicators in the floor or wall displaying your number. These indicators will decrease in frequency as you learn where you have been assigned. They will increase in frequency if you go elsewhere. I strongly recommend that you do not stray from the designated path very often," she said. "If your assigned location changes, a new set of indicators will redirect you. If this protocol is understood, please proceed."

A series of small green arrows with numbers at the base appeared in front of each person. As each moved, his or her respective arrows reoriented themselves and pointed in the required direction of travel.

CHAPTER 5

Don't Leave the Path

Many proposals to ensure the survival of the human race were rejected, but one idea was embraced by both scientists and politicians. It was originally expected to take 50 years, but 102 years had passed, and it was still not complete. A huge part of its eventual success depended on future discoveries and tech development. The leaders of the time decided that the human race would have to begin the research effort as soon as possible to have any chance of survival. Thus, the biome project began. There were twelve in all. Twelve asteroids were towed to Earth orbit and transformed into spaceships—biome ships that would transport a sampling of the human population to new planets.

Jayne didn't move with the rest of her group but stood in place for a moment. She had felt a rush of pressure in her head just as the facilitator had said, "Proceed." The rush started in her earlobes, swelling into her head and neck, running out through her arms and down her spine. She felt someone watching her. Instead of looking down at her directional arrows, Jayne looked around at her fellow apprentices. She scanned the room, noticing that the apprentices were moving slowly and in seemingly chaotic patterns, as if they were being controlled by the arrows displayed on the floor. Jayne smiled at how silly they looked. Most of the other pedestrians were moving purposefully to wherever they were going, but some had paused to watch the strange sight of indicator-controlled apprentices bumping into each other, trying to follow the arrows as they crisscrossed. Jayne smiled at the 'comedy act' starring that month's apprentices.

Jayne looked beyond the pedestrian traffic to the concourse that surrounded the PUT anteroom, where people were moving normally, heading intently toward their destinations. No one out there was standing still. Raising her eyes higher, Jayne scanned the high row of windows that looked down on the concourse. Most were lit from the inside, but they appeared empty. Her eyes were drawn to the one window in the center of the row that was slightly tinted. Despite the darkened glass, Jayne could see someone behind the window. It took only a second for her eyes to focus on the person looking out at her and, in that second, Jayne once again felt a wave of nausea, but this time it was so intense that she couldn't suppress the retching sound escaping her lips. She turned away from the window and instinctively put her hand over her mouth to stop the threatening spew of vomit. The nausea faded, but her heart continued to beat rapidly in her chest. She turned back and glanced furtively up at the window. It was no longer dark and now looked the same as the rest. In fact, she wasn't exactly sure through which window she had noticed the observer, but the person she had seen was gone.

She looked down and saw a green arrow in front of her, the number 13 illuminated at its base. It increased in size and began to pulse from small to large. It seemed to demand that she move. She stepped forward and walked in the direction of the arrow as the still-decreasing nausea washed and faded like the foam from crests of gentle waves.

There were six sets of stairs leading up out of the concourse and six other sets of stairs leading down to places unknown. All but two of the apprentices followed their arrows to one of the sets of stairs leading down and had already disappeared into the bowels of the HUB. Jayne and the overly tall boy she met yesterday still remained. Jayne followed her arrow and was confused about discovering that it led toward the boy. He was moving in a two-meter circle with what seemed to be a perpetual expression of puzzlement on his face. His arrow, with the number 7 flashing at its base, was travelling in a circle and he was attempting to follow it. As he moved to the edge of the circular path the arrow was scribing out on the floor, the whole circle moved to seemingly capture him at its center. He looked like a cat chasing its shadow. When he finally stopped, the arrow flashed and continued to run its circular path with the boy at the center.

The boy shook his hands in frustration and muttered, "This is stupid."

Jayne stopped in front of him. "What's wrong? Why aren't you following your arrow?" she asked.

"Look!" he retorted, pointing at the ground at his feet.

Jayne looked at the arrow at his feet. It was flashing and pointing in the same direction as her arrow. "What's wrong?" she asked.

He looked down at his arrow and, seeing that its confusing motion had finally changed, said, "I don't believe it." He began to move in the direction his arrow was pointing but had taken only three of his giant steps when the arrow resumed its circular motion, once again keeping him in the middle.

"Oh, for fracks sake!" He looked up at Jayne. "Are you seeing this now? The damn thing seems to want me to stand here while it makes up its mind where to lead me. Where is that woman? This thing must be broken."

He looked around the anteroom, but the facilitator was nowhere in sight.

Everyone else ignored them as the crowd streamed past.

"I think she's gone," said Jayne, looking down at her arrow and taking a step toward it. The arrow continued to lead her straight to the boy. As she walked past, Jayne quipped, "See you around. Ha, a-round, get it?" She giggled as she walked past him, following her arrow.

"Finally!" she heard him exclaim behind her. He looked down and began to blindly follow his arrow. He took only a few steps when the arrow began to circle again. He looked up, exasperated, only to find Jayne standing right in front of him.

"I thought you were outta here," he said. "It looks like I'm going nowhere quickly."

Jayne was watching him. Her arms were folded across her chest. "I think I understand," she said slowly, "and I don't like it."

"You understand this circle business? Look, I don't need you, so just buzz off, okay? I'll figure it out. It's probably just some weird test. Go!" he ordered.

"Look at me," Jayne said.

"I'm not holding your hand again. If that's what you're looking for, then you should apply to go back to the nursery. You're just a baby, anyway," he spat the words out with disdain.

"Don't be an idiot! Look at me, shut up, watch and learn," she said, and she began to walk backwards. She took three steps. The boy's arrow stopped circling and pointed right at her. "Now follow me."

The boy stood, staring at his arrow, his hands clasping his own face in confusion. He took a single step forward, placing him directly in front of Jayne, and the arrow began to circle him again. "What the—!" he exclaimed.

"Don't you get it?" she asked.

"Get what? This arrow business is messed," he said.

"I think you're supposed to go with me," she said. "Every time I stop, your arrow goes in circles like you're supposed to wait for me."

"Turkey twattle," he said dismissively.

Jayne became pensive, ignoring him. After a moment, she mumbled, "I wonder…" She looked up, ran across the room, and stopped. Her arrow pointed in the direction it had always pointed: toward a door situated between sets of stairs, leading down to somewhere or other. She called back to the boy. "What direction is your arrow pointing now?"

"Toward you. I don't believe it," he said, shaking his head as he walked slowly toward her.

"Believe it. It appears you have to go wherever I go," she sighed.

"Frack!" he said matter-of-factly.

"Gee, that makes me feel good," she said, exaggerating the sarcasm to cover the hurt she felt. She followed her arrow toward the door, and, reluctantly, the boy followed. She opened the door and stepped into a small room where the light shone in a stronger yellow hue than in the other room. There were two PUT pads on the floor in front of them, each with a pulsing green light around its circumference. Both of their arrows pointed to the pads.

"I guess that's what we're supposed to do," she said, gesturing to the pads. "What's your name, anyway? Mine's Jayne Wu." She stood with her hands on her hips and a 'bit lip' smile on her face.

"Joseph Kane," he replied.

His eyes traveled from her toes to the pendant dangling from the chain around her neck.

She felt her face flush red. She slipped the object of his gaze under her jumpsuit, flipped her long braid over her shoulder and pertly said, "Let's go."

They each stepped onto a PUT pad—Joseph placing his feet tightly together—and promptly disappeared.

CHAPTER 6

Games & Waiting & TechElecMech

The twelve biomes were designed to mirror twelve newly discovered, potentially habitable planets. They were also ships that would take the human race out into the galaxy. Society had faith its scientists would be able to develop the technologies that would make the project viable. Each biome would remain a 'work in progress' right up until launch day. Scientific research would take two paths: tech—the development of artificially-controlled environments and space propulsion systems; and controlled evolution—encouraging changes in the humans inside the biomes through environmental and genetic manipulation. Space propulsion systems would take priority. There would be no point in building the biomes if they could not escape before the Swarm's arrival and reach their new homes. Survival on the new planets was a secondary concern.

Jayne and Joseph materialized in a small waiting room with windows along one wall. On the other side of the windows were small groups of people. Some were sitting at tables, some were standing at high counters, some were rolling on mats, some were wearing breathing masks and white suits, some were throwing things, and some were avoiding things thrown at them. There were even more people over at the far side of the room, but the view was obscured by the people in front. Each group had a leader or, as Jayne assumed, a teacher or instructor. Everyone wore the same basic style of jumpsuit as Jayne, with numbers on the left breast pocket. The only difference between the industrial blue jumpsuits worn by the instructors and the apprentices was the color of the numbers on their pockets.

Those on the instructors' suits shone white instead of orange. In one glance, Jayne processed everything that was going on in the room. She was sure that there would be a great deal more to see if she could only stay and watch.

Once more, a green arrow, with the number 13 at its base, began to flash on the floor in front of her. She stood, staring at the flashing arrow for a moment, then her gaze strayed back up to the windows and into the large room beyond. When she forced her gaze back down again, she saw the green flashing arrow double in size, as if yelling at her to follow along. She stepped from the PUT pad and headed in the direction of the arrow. Joseph followed along without so much as a glance down at his own flashing arrow. He'd finally figured it out. It was his job, at this point, simply to follow Jayne and go wherever she went. He couldn't imagine why it was so important to follow such a young girl, but time, as it usually did, would tell.

Jayne's arrow pointed toward the far end of the small room, which slowly tapered down in width until it turned into a two-meter wide hall. The off-white walls curved to the left. Once the pair had traveled a short distance, the smooth inside wall was broken by a door. But the arrow didn't stop at the doorway; instead, it continued to travel down the hallway, past more doors, finally stopping in front of what Jayne determined to be door number four, since they had passed doors one through three as they progressed down the hallway. The door slid open as soon as Jayne came near, and she stepped through without hesitation. She was surprisingly even a little excited and her heart rate jumped as she passed through into the next room.

Suddenly, she heard a loud klaxon blare behind her. She turned and saw Joseph frozen by the alarm just as he was about to step through the doorway. Glancing down, she saw a red light flashing on the floor in front of him. His green arrow had turned into a red octagon with a white diagonal bar. It was pulsing in size from small to large and back again. Joseph looked at it for a moment and finally stepped back. The klaxon silenced and the red octagon turned into an orange flashing circle as the door slid shut.

Jayne found herself in a small room with air suddenly rushing at her from many directions. The wind threatened to pull apart her braid and whip her hair into tangles and knots. After a few moments, the rush of air stopped. She stood and looked up at a window that was positioned directly above the exit door. She could see no one behind the glass, but she could feel that someone was there. She wondered if they would open the door. As she waited, Jayne thought back to the darkened window in the concourse. She felt the nausea begin to swell inside her again at the memory, but it was interrupted as the door in front of her slid open.

No one greeted her. With trepidation, Jayne stepped into the large room she had seen through the windows. She was expecting to be assaulted by the noise that such a large group of people would produce, but the silence that met her was both unexpected and disconcerting. The people were in distinct groups and appeared to be talking, but she could hear nothing of what they were saying. The subdued echo of her own footsteps was the only sound she could hear. She glanced down at the floor and the green arrow flashed reassuringly in front of her. She followed as it weaved in and out of groups of people, none of whom seemed to take any notice of her. Straight ahead, she saw two boys and a girl moving around inside a five-meter circle painted on the floor. Transparent netting formed a wall around the circle. Suddenly, they stopped moving. The girl's eyes became wild as she glanced around, as if looking for some unseen enemy. Jayne heard a subdued popping sound that seemed to have escaped the silence. The girl's hand went to her thigh, rubbing back and forth. Jayne noticed a small beanbag-like object at the girl's feet that she was sure hadn't been there before. The blond boy quickly raised both hands to his face, his eyes grimacing in pain. Bright red blood oozed between the fingers covering his nose, and a small bean bag, stained red, sat at his feet. Five other bean bags were scattered on the floor at the base of the circle of netting. The third person, a dark-haired boy, was crouched down on his haunches. A sardonic smile crept over his face. He looked up and saw Jayne staring at him. His face immediately blanked with emotion, and he looked down at the floor.

The floor in front of Jayne beeped. She looked down at the green arrow swelling and shrinking at her feet. She followed it again. It stopped at a table covered with burgundy felt. An instructor sat at the table, shuffling a deck of cards. As she approached, he smiled. She could see his lips move, but she heard no sound. She stepped forward and caught the end of his sentence: "—hear anything outside of each area due to the sound dampening fields. Come, sit. You are the first. We are waiting for two others. We can play while we wait."

"Play? Play what?" Jayne asked, taking a seat directly opposite the dealer/instructor.

"Simple game. High card wins," he said with a smile as he dealt out one card each, face down. "I'll turn my card first."

Jayne did not wait. She flipped her card over. It was a Three of Clubs.

"Dear me. You may not be here for long," he said dismissively, flipping over the card in front of him. It was a Two of Clubs. His eyes widened. "Interesting. You win."

At that moment, two others arrived from different directions, and they, too, were welcomed by the dealer and invited to sit. A red-haired girl in her early 20s and an overweight boy about 16 or 17 sat down on either side of Jayne.

"We are all here. This part of your assessment will only take a few minutes, but it will determine where you are sent next. I will refer to you only by your numbers because that is easier for me to remember. So, let's get started. I will deal a card to you and then a card to myself. If my card is higher than yours, you will leave the table and continue to follow your arrows. Understood?" asked the dealer.

Both the red-haired girl and the overweight boy nodded.

Jayne stood and scanned the room. "Where will we go? Where will the arrows lead?" she asked, slowly slipping back into her seat.

"That depends," said the dealer. He offered no more information.

"On what?" pressed Jayne.

The other apprentices seemed startled by her continuing to question the instructor and they both looked down at the table, trying to avoid Jayne's gaze as she turned to them. "Well, I would like to know," she said. "I was told I would become a TechElecMech." She scanned the room again. "Nothing in here seems to have anything to do with tech. Maybe I'm in the wrong place."

"You aren't in the wrong place," the dealer said patiently. "I have your number here." He looked down at the built-in screen on his side of the table. "Thirteen, Wu 13. Right?"

Jayne nodded.

"And you two—let's see, Kieren 37 and Moss 124. Right?" he said, nodding toward the girl and the boy sitting on either side of Jayne.

They nodded back.

"Right, then—let's get on with it. It usually only takes a few minutes for me to beat you. I am, after all, a dealer, and dealers are lucky." He smiled at them. "Remember, as soon as I beat you, stand and follow your arrows and, to answer Thirteen's question, I have no idea where you will go next. It all depends on how many times you win, or if you win at all."

He smiled at Moss 124. It was not a nice smile. "You're first," he said, and he dealt a card first to 124, then one to himself. Both were face down.

"I always flip my card first. If you beat it, you can stay for another round. If not..." He let his words hang and flipped his card. It was a Seven of Clubs.

124 peaked at his own card for a moment before flipping it quickly over. It was a Queen of Hearts.

The dealer turned to Jayne. "You have already had a turn," he said, turning to 37 and dealing two more cards. The dealer turned his over immediately revealing a Jack of Diamonds.

"Doesn't look good, 37," he chuckled.

37 turned over her card, exposing a Ten of Clubs. The dealer waved

goodbye to her, but she seemed relieved as she left the table, following a green arrow with 37 at the base.

Next, the man turned and dealt a card, first to Jayne, then one to himself. Jayne's Nine of Spades beat his Seven of Clubs.

He dealt two more cards, looked at the remaining player next to Jayne and flipped his over. It was a Four of Diamonds. 124 followed by a King of Clubs. "Not bad, 124. A winning streak of two does beat the odds, but not by much."

He dealt to Jayne. She won with a Six of Diamonds to his Four of Spades. The process continued to the fourth round, with both Jayne and Moss 124 winning their hands.

On the fifth round, 124 lost. His King was beaten by the dealer's Ace. He left the table, following his arrow out of the space.

"How long will this go on if I keep winning?" asked Jayne.

"A little cocky, aren't we?" the dealer said. "Don't worry. It will be over soon. The record holder had only eight wins in a row."

He dealt another set and looked surprised to have lost again. His look of disbelief continued to grow as he lost 19 times in a row. He kept shaking his head.

Dealing hand number 20, he flipped his card. He lost again. "This is impossible," he muttered to himself. "No one is this lucky."

He was about to deal the 21st hand when his screen chimed and flashed red. He looked down at it, then looked up at Jayne. He shook his head and sighed. "That's it. You're outta here. Go!" He turned around in his chair and stared off into the space behind him.

Jayne rose from the chair, looking down at the arrow at her feet. It was pointing to the left of the card table. She followed it across the room until it stopped at the circle of netting that she had previously observed. Three stools sat at the edge of the circle. Two were occupied. Jayne recognized the dark-haired boy on the left as the one she had observed earlier. The boy who sat on the second stool was tall, blond, and unfamiliar to her. A woman with a portable tech screen stood behind the stools.

As Jayne entered this area, the woman looked up and asked, "Are you Wu 13?"

Jayne nodded, staring at the blood on the floor inside the circle where the boy had been hit in the face with a bean bag. A man with a portable wet vac moved into the circle and cleaned it up.

"Sit here," the woman said, gesturing to the third stool. Jayne sat.

The woman looked at her screen, looked up at Jayne, then back down at her screen. "Ooooh, this should be interesting," she said. "Alright, boys and girls, take your places."

The two boys stood up and wandered around the circle, pausing occasionally before finally taking up a position. The blond boy lay down on his side on the floor along the edge of the circle. The dark-haired boy crouched down and waited.

Jayne stood up, but waited and watched, trying to determine what she should do next.

"13, please enter the circle and take a position," said the woman. "Why?" asked Jayne cautiously, remembering the boy with the

bloody face and the bean bags.

"It's a test," the woman answered. "Weren't you apprised of the process?"

"Apprised?" retorted Jayne.

"Everyone who gets this far is apprised of the dangers. Obviously, you must have been told because you are here. Now, take your place in the circle," the woman ordered.

"I was winning at cards, and when the game was over, the green arrow brought me here. I wasn't apprised of anything," Jayne retorted sharply.

"You came from cards to here?" the woman asked as she scanned her screen. "Dear me, you are right." The woman looked up at Jayne. "This is very unusual. Alright, I will give you the short version. You take your place in the circle and stop in any position you feel comfortable," she gestured to the boys in the circle, "like they have. Once everyone is in the circle, the timer will start. Ten seconds will pass. You can watch the time on the timer at your feet and move to wherever you want in that 10 seconds. The bean bags will fire in random directions through the space enclosed by the circle. The test starts with one bean bag and progresses to as many as 20 bags fired at the same time. There will be 10 seconds between each successive firing. The objective is to avoid getting hit. Getting hit hurts. It won't break any bones or anything, but it will hurt. That's part of the test. Fear can affect your performance. The other players can affect your performance as well. After you are hit, the test is over for you. If both the other players are hit before you are, that round is over and new players will join you for the next round. The test will run until you are hit at least once. This is 91's third round," she said, gesturing to the dark-haired boy.

"What if I don't want to get hit at all?" Jayne asked.

"You have to take part, or you will be sent back to the nursery. Do you want that?" asked the woman.

Jayne stiffened. "I didn't say I wouldn't play; I just won't get hit."

"Everyone gets hit sooner or later, but it's better for you if it takes longer. Your mark will be higher. Higher marks mean better..." she paused, "...more...interesting jobs."

"Alright," said Jayne, entering the circle and stopping right at the inside edge. A timer appeared in a blue circle at her feet, replacing her green arrow. It began to count down from ten. After seven seconds, the dark-haired boy stood up and stepped one meter to his right and stopped. Jayne watched him. He smirked at her.

Suddenly, there was a pop and a bean bag whizzed down at an angle through the space previously occupied by the dark-haired boy. It came to rest at the base of the netting. The blond boy got up and moved near the center of the circle and crouched down.

The dark-haired boy moved to the opposite edge of the circle and again smiled at Jayne. Jayne swallowed and turned around, facing outwards, her nose poking through the netting. There was a pop. She felt moving air tug at the hair behind her head. One of the bean bags had just missed. She turned around and watched the two boys move to another position. She looked down at the blue floor timer and saw a three flashing at its base. Three bean bags this time. Jayne did not move. The pop came. The bean bags flew. The blond boy cried out. A bean bag seemed to come up through the floor right in front of him, hitting him in the chin. He stood and walked out of the circle, rubbing his chin.

The timer restarted as soon as the net closed around the exiting boy. The dark-haired boy, 91, moved again, crouching in place as he stopped. Jayne didn't move. Instinctively, she didn't feel a need.

The usual pop rang out, and the netting billowed out as each bean bag hit. Four billows meant four bean bags—neither player was hit.

This time, 91 moved and Jayne crouched down.

Pop! Five bags zoomed through space. Two came straight down to the floor and three hit the netting. The time continued to count down and the bags, in ever-increasing numbers, continued to pop. Neither Jayne nor the dark-haired boy were hit.

Finally, the counter in the blue circle timer displayed the number thirteen. Jayne returned to her original spot against the netting and felt a rushing sensation swell from her core, moving through her body until it faded slowly as it passed out through the tips of her fingers.

The dark-haired boy stared at her; his face contorted as if he could feel that he was going to lose. He scanned the circle, his gaze stopped at a group of bean bags gathered in a pile at the edge of the circle. He smiled and walked over, stopping in front of the netting, then he turned and issued a mock salute in Jayne's direction. He must have figured that the odds were in his favor and that the bean bags would not hit where they had previously hit. Jayne didn't move.

There was a pop, and 13 bean bags flew at various angles through the netted space. Jayne watched as the dark-haired boy was hit by two bean bags at the same time. The boy's knees buckled as his hands, unsure of where to go, clasped both his face and his groin. He fell to the ground with a groan. There was a cut below one eye and the blood from the wound trickled down his cheek. He didn't seem to notice that wound as he clutched his crotch. As the pain welled up in his guts, he moaned again. He didn't get up.

At Jayne's feet, the timer turned to a red octagon and flashed slowly. Two men rolled a gurney into the circle and gently lifted the dark-haired boy off the ground and wheeled him away. As he passed Jayne, he met her gaze. The arrogance had disappeared from his eyes. What Jayne saw in his face filled her with dread. The boy's eyes were manic with fear. He was afraid of her. She frowned. She was puzzled why anyone could possibly be afraid of her.

Jayne was directed back to the stools. She sat down, breathing deeply, carefully considering her next set of actions. The dark-haired boy's look of fear unnerved her. She wanted to leave the game. She didn't want to see that look of fear on another kid's face, but she could only leave the game if she was hit. Well, she could be hit, but on her terms, not theirs.

After a few minutes of waiting, two more apprentices arrived, and the contest started anew. Jayne was oblivious to the others as she entered the circle. She stood slightly off center, placing one foot out in front of her. The institution-issued boots had reinforced toes. They were safety boots.

There was a popping noise, and a single bean bag flew straight down and hit the steel toe of Jayne's work-boots. She smiled, nodded at the woman instructor, and walked out of the circle. The woman nodded back and turned to her portable screen.

The green flashing arrow reappeared on the floor in front of Jayne. It led her back toward the door she originally entered. As the door slid open, she spotted Joseph sitting on the floor, his back leaning against the hallway wall. An amber light ran in a circle around him. He smiled as he saw Jayne. She smiled back. As she stepped into the hallway, the amber circle around Joseph transformed into a green arrow and pointed directly at Jayne.

Jayne and Joseph followed their arrows back toward the concourse, up a set of stairs, and into a reception area. The walls of the room were covered in posters advertising TechElecMech and three booths with screens and scanlocks were positioned in the center of the room.

A disembodied voice spoke, "Please sit in one of the booths, place your hand on the scanlock, and state your name."

Both Jayne and Joseph complied and were unsurprised as an artificial face appeared on their respective screens. It also displayed their names and numbers, and the same disembodied voice stated, "You have been admitted. Please stand and proceed to the PUT pads located in the room to your left." Jayne got up and entered the room and stood on a PUT pad. Joseph followed.

"It felt like I was waiting forever," said Joseph, finally. "What happened to you in that other room?"

Jayne was quiet. She hadn't had time to digest and analyze the reasoning behind the other room's activities. "I don't know," she said. "Look, that isn't fair. You go in and do stuff, I have to sit in the hall and wait for you, and then you won't even tell me what happened," he complained.

"I played cards and ducked flying bean bags, okay! It wasn't fun, and I would rather have sat in the hall. Consider yourself lucky," she muttered.

The PUT pads activated and, as they stepped off at their destination, their green arrows flashed and led them to a door at the far end of the room. When they reached it, Jayne stood in front of it, lost in thought. Joseph looked sidelong at her, reached over her shoulder, and knocked on the door.

The door opened, and they looked into what was obviously a classroom. The man who opened the door spoke. "Yes?"

Joseph spoke first. "Kane 37, reporting."

The man at the door looked expectantly over at Jayne. She looked up and said, "Wu 13."

He glanced at his VID. "You're late. I make a rule of not repeating myself, so you'll have to find out what you missed from my posted notes. Your VID will have the data. Read it tonight," he said flatly. "Sit down."

As they entered, Jayne and Joseph took note of the eight others sitting at desks with their VIDs open in front of them. They sat at the two empty desks. No one paid any notice of the new arrivals. School was a familiar activity for both of them, so they relaxed and turned on their VIDs. Classes were what classes always were. You listened; you read; you studied; and you learned.

CHAPTER 7

Theoretical TechElecMech

In 2046, they held a lottery filled with promise and hope. The winners would be permitted to live in one of the newly designed biomes. Their progeny would travel to new worlds, spreading humankind throughout the galaxy. Those left behind on Earth would work to save humankind; work to build and maintain the biome ships; and work to find new planets with various degrees of suitability. They would work to alter the very genetic structure of the biome dwellers to enable them to survive and prosper on the newly found planets.

Their classes continued for three months. Exams were coming up very soon, and it was made crystal clear by each of their instructors that passing would require a perfect score. In order to pass, they must get every question right. The students studied during every waking moment to ensure that they passed.

Jayne hadn't spent much time with Joseph after their first morning of forced company. His arrow no longer followed hers. He was older, and he spent time with the students who were of the same age. Jayne was the youngest by far, and the others all ignored her. That didn't bother her because she knew that she couldn't waste time socializing if she was to pass this test. Everything she was learning now was much more difficult than her lessons from nursery school, and they seemed to cover the material at an incredible speed. Each new concept followed the last at a machine gun pace. If they wanted Jayne to be perfect, then she would be perfect. She would not fail!

Jayne stood at her door, pressing her thumb to her VID screen, and pointing it at the door. It opened silently, and she stepped inside. "Welcome home, Thirteen," said Lucky softly. "To celebrate the end of your classes, I have prepared your favorite dinner."

"No time to celebrate. I'll celebrate when they tell me I've passed this exam," she said.

"No problem. You will eat, and I will help you study. I have a rather large database of possible exam questions."

"Lucky, I need to be perfect. Do you have any idea how hard it will be to get every question correct?" asked Jayne.

"You do not have to be perfect. No one has ever received a perfect score on any TechElecMech exam. The instructors just say that to scare you into doing your absolute best," said Lucky.

"What score do I have to get to pass?" she asked, surprised that the programming allowed for such a revelation.

"I don't know the precise score required for a passing grade," replied Lucky.

"That's just peachy! If I don't know what I need to pass, I'll have to aim for perfect anyway!" she exclaimed. She wrapped her hands and arms around her head. "Oh, crap! I know I'm going to fail."

"Stop! Eat! Study!" commanded Lucky.

Jayne sat at the table and ate and studied until she fell asleep. She must have stumbled into bed at some point because she woke up refreshed and ready the next morning.

"It's now or never," she said to herself as she washed, dressed, ate, and finally left her quarters.

The exam was supposed to take three hours, but Jayne finished it in two. She knew she had done her best. She didn't have any idea if she had answered any of the tricky questions correctly. She sat and scanned the room, looking at her classmates, who were still working busily. She didn't want to leave first and draw attention to herself. Instead, she sat and tried to imagine what the practical part of the apprenticeship would be like.

She expected that she would now get to go places and fix and install equipment. Maybe she would even work inside one of the biomes. She might even meet an Omie. Two other students got up and left the room. She looked around and noticed that Joseph seemed to be reading through the exam with a puzzled look on his face. She was about to try to get his attention when he quickly looked down at his VID. Deciding not to worry about him, she got up and headed back to her living quarters.

The exam results would be classified. No one would ever know who got what score. If you passed, they would send you to practical TechElecMech; if you failed, you would simply have to follow your arrow out of the HUB and back to wherever it was you started, never to be heard from again. Jayne sighed and lay down on her bed.

"Are you feeling well?" asked Lucky.

"I'm fine. Say, Lucky, can I ask you about something strange that happened to me on the first day I was here?" she asked.

"I suppose. What do you want to ask?" Lucky replied.

"On the first morning, I was led to this odd room, and a boy was required to follow me wherever I went," she said.

"Why would a boy be required to follow you?" Lucky asked.

"I was hoping you would know," Jayne said. "Anyway, that's not the strangest part. I was directed to this large room with lots of people in it. There must have been a sound dampening device because you could only hear the people closest to you. I was directed to a table where I played cards, and then to—what I'd call the bean bag shoot—where I and others were the targets."

"Were you hurt?" asked Lucky, sounding concerned. "I don't remember you returning to the room with injuries. I would have noticed and reported it if you were hurt in any way."

"I wasn't hurt, but others were. Nothing hit me. I was able to avoid the bean bags," she paused and reconsidered. "No, it was more than that. I knew where the bean bags were going to land before they were shot. In the end, I even let one hit me. I wanted to leave, and they said I could leave when one of the flying bean bags hit me. So, I let it. Then I left."

"You must have been hurt if one hit you. You told me you were not hurt. Where were you hurt? Has your injury healed properly? Please let me see where it hit you. There might be some damage you cannot detect. I have a subcutaneous scanner, but you will need to stand over it. Please report to the flashing green circle in the corner, and I will scan for long-term damage," Lucky babbled.

"Stop!" said Jayne, annoyed. A green circle began to pulse in the corner of the room. "I stuck out the toe of my work boot and that's where it hit. As you know, my work boots have steel toes. It didn't hurt me. I was just wondering if you knew what that was all about? Do you have any idea why some boy would have to follow me around and then wait outside while I did these things?"

"I am sorry, Jayne, but I have no information about any of this," replied Lucky.

A beeping sound came from the walls, startling Jayne.

"Your exam has been scored. Do you want me to read the message to you?" asked Lucky.

"Oh, crap! No. Yes. No!" said Jayne. She put her hands over her ears. "Yes!"

"You won't be able to hear me if you continue to hold your hands over your ears," stated Lucky.

"Just tell me!" cried Jayne.

"Pass," said Lucky.

Jayne let out a sigh. "Thank the heavens."

"There is a footnote message. Do you want me to read it?" asked Lucky.

Jayne nodded. "It says, 'Always wear the Silver Star'."

Jayne's eyes grew large. She had not worn the star pendant when she went to write the exam. She felt as if she would somehow do better without it. Jayne walked over to her bed and opened up the music box. She lifted out the silver star that she found on her first day. She put the chain around her neck, lay on the bed, and fell into a troubled sleep.

CHAPTER 8

The Connectome Scan

In the early 21st century, scientists began to explore the connections within the human brain. Unlike the mapping of the human genome—which was initially seen as an almost impossible task but took only 13 years to complete (two years less than predicted)—the connectome was much more complex. Its complexity surpassed all predictions, and the scientists were unable to reach any absolute conclusion. Much was discovered and mapped, but since the brain was such a dynamic organ, filled with complexity upon complexity, especially concerning the connections within the frontal lobe, scientists were still filling storage pits with xonabytes (10^{27}) of data.

Jayne woke, feeling a little thick-headed. She didn't mention it to Lucky because that generally resulted in the AIU putting something in her food to make her feel better. He never asked if she would like this drug or that. Lucky just followed his programming. It seemed as if he was really paranoid about her health. Sometimes the drugs he gave her made her feel a little dopey.

Today was the first day of practical TEM and she knew that she must keep her mind sharp. She shook off the last of her thick-headedness as she walked to the PUT pad, thinking about how cool her first day was going to be. She was on her way to becoming a real Technical Electrical Mechanical Fixer.

When she reached her destination, she stepped off the PUT pad and followed the green arrow as it directed her past a series of doors, finally stopping in front of a door with a sign that read 'Professor Greenway'.

Jayne couldn't see a scanlock or video lock of any kind. There was just an old-fashioned doorknob. Jayne assumed that the knob turned a latching mechanism that would allow her access to the room beyond. Turning the knob, the door opened for her, and she stopped just inside the room, leaving the door open behind her. She found herself inside a combination of an office and a laboratory. There was a desk in the corner, piled high with sheets of white material covered with text. More pieces of the same material were stacked on a series of shelves, and even more were piled haphazardly in the corner. She identified the sheets as printed paper and books. She had seen pictures of books in the past, but she had never seen a real one up close. There were countless books in this space—more than she could have imagined existed in the whole world. Humans stopped printing books almost 70 years ago, and yet this office was filled with them. Jayne's eyes scanned the rest of the room, coming to a stop when she saw a man standing with his back to her, leaning over a magnavid, staring intently at some multi-colored blobs on the screen before him.

Jayne cleared her throat, trying to get his attention, but the man ignored her.

Annoyed, she spoke loudly, "Excuse me."

The man continued to stare at the magnavid. He twisted a knob, and the view altered. He didn't turn around.

Stepping further into the room, Jayne repeated herself, "Excuse me."

No response came from the man. Finally, she stepped closer, about to tap the man on the back, when he straightened, reached behind his ear, and touched his skull. Apparently, he was listening to something and had just turned it off.

As he turned around, he found himself face-to-face with Jayne.

A surprised "Oh!" escaped from both their lips. Jayne took a step back.

"Who are you?" asked the man who Jayne assumed must be the Professor Greenway named on the door.

"Thirteen," said Jayne.

"No, no. Not your HUB number, your birth number," he said with irritation.

"Oh," Jayne hesitated. "My number is 302875106592253." "Why are you here?" he asked.

"I have no idea. This is my first day of Practical TEM. The green arrow directed me here," she said, "so here I am."

"Yes, well, close the door and I'll figure this out," he said, and he picked up his VID. "Give me your birth number again." Jayne repeated her number, and the man keyed it into his VID. After a moment, he spoke again. "Mmmm, that is odd."

"What?" Jayne asked.

"Nothing, really. I guess they've decided to be a little more thorough with you. They want the usual—fluid extraction, deep retinal scan and a skin biopsy. They also want a partial connectome scan. Now that is very unusual," he mused.

"What's a connectome scan? What are you scanning?" Jayne asked apprehensively.

"Don't worry. It'll hurt far less than the skin biopsy. It just takes a little longer," he said. "Now sit here and roll up one sleeve." He gestured to a chair at the end of one of the lab benches.

Jayne sat down and rolled up her sleeve.

Professor Greenway took some blood and scraped the inside of her cheek to retrieve skin cells. "Now, I want you to relax. This always works best when you are relaxed. Conscious thought and dreaming can affect the results. Here, drink this," he said, handing her a small paper cup with a pink liquid in it. "It's sweet with a cherry flavor."

"What are you going to scan?" asked Jayne.

"Your brain. More specifically, a small section of your frontal lobe. That's right behind your forehead," he said, tapping her with his finger.

"It won't hurt a bit, but it will take a few hours to complete. There are a lot of data connections in there, and they keep changing. This connectome scan will mark the static connections that are established and try to determine the pattern of the dynamic ones. Nothing for you to worry about," he said in a condescending tone as he smiled down at her. "Drink up."

Jayne drank the liquid and made a face at the foul taste. Professor Greenway took a circular strap, placing it around her head before attaching two devices to it. He stepped over to the large VID and adjusted some settings.

"The thingies on that band around my head are moving," said Jayne. "One of them is caught in my hair."

"Oh," Professor Greenway attempted to free her hair from the scanning device, but it was caught on the chain that held the silver star around her neck. He lifted the chain, pulling the star into view. "Oh my," he whispered, sucking in his breath. He dropped the chain, as if it were going to bite him, and his demeanor changed so that he was even more focused than before. "This will take a while, so relax. Go to sleep. It will be over when you wake. I have other important things to attend to, and I must go. A lab tech will remove the apparatus and send you on your way when the test is complete."

"How long?" asked Jayne.

"I don't have time to answer anymore of your silly questions," he snapped back at her. He glanced back at the star hanging in full view on Jayne's chest. Jayne saw the fear in his eyes. "I must go." He turned and left the room.

Jayne reached up, grasping the silver star between her fingers. It seemed to grow warmer in her hand. Closing her eyes, she soon drifted off to sleep.

She didn't dream but woke suddenly. Opening her eyes, she found herself alone in the now dimly lit lab. Her head was pounding; her stomach was growling, and she needed to pee badly. The devices on her forehead were humming and occasionally moved. Jayne tried to sit up, but quickly realized that she was restrained by metal clamps on her wrists, elbows, knees, ankles, neck, and head. She couldn't move even if she tried.

Suddenly, a blue flashing light filled the dim room, followed by a warning klaxon. Jayne was starting to panic, but just as suddenly, the flashing lights and alarm stopped. A woman wearing a white coat with a stethoscope around her neck entered the lab and smiled at her.

"I guess you're done. I'll get you out of those restraints. Sorry, I usually have them off before the patient wakes up, but when I checked you after two hours, you weren't finished," she said to Jayne.

"I have to go to the bathroom," said Jayne.

"Won't be a moment," the woman said, undoing the clamps, and gesturing at a door. "The bathroom is through there."

Jayne went quickly to the bathroom and, when she returned, she found the woman putting the strap and scanning devices away in a cabinet. "How long have I been here?" she asked.

"Let's see," the woman said, looking at the VID, "a little over six hours. That's odd. That's really long for this test. It usually takes less than two hours."

"I've been here for six hours!" exclaimed Jayne. "It feels like only a few minutes have passed, except for the fact that I'm so hungry."

"Yeah, this test can be like that. You can go now," said the woman, walking to the door. "I have to close up the lab."

Jayne followed and quickly found herself alone in the hallway. She was a little disoriented and her stomach was growling. She looked down at the floor but found no green directional arrow to show her the way. She walked a dozen steps to her left but found nothing that resembled the entrance to the PUT pads.

There was a different sort of door in front of her. There was a small window in the door just above her head and a hand scanlock just below the window. She placed her hand on the lock. Nothing happened. She jumped up, trying to look through the window in an effort to see if this was the PUT pad room. A series of fleeting glances, from repeatedly jumping up and looking through the small window, only revealed a dark room with more chairs, like the one she used for her connectome scan. These chairs were different only in that the straps and steel bands were already attached to the chairs. Jayne guessed they were designed to keep the occupant prisoner. She shivered.

On her fifth jump, a voice boomed out behind her. "Who are you, and what are you doing?"

She turned to see a security guard standing at the other end of the hall.

"I'm just looking for the PUT pad room. I just came from Professor Greenway's lab, and there are no arrows to show me where to go."

"Well, it's not that way. It's right down there," he said, pointing at a door at the other end of the long hallway.

"Thanks," she said, and she walked down the hall, past the guard and onto a PUT pad. A moment later, she was at her own door, which opened as soon as she approached it.

"Come in, Thirteen. I have made you something to eat. There is an analgesic for your headache on the table."

"How did you know?" asked Jayne.

"I know how grueling a first day in Practical TEM can be," Lucky replied.

"But I..." she started to reply but stopped. For some reason, she felt that keeping a few secrets from Lucky wouldn't be a bad thing. "Yes, thank you. It was a tough day."

"I know—it will get easier. Something to eat and a good sleep will do you wonders," said Lucky.

Jayne sat and ate, and moments later, was fast asleep.

CHAPTER 9

Secret Heart Cupboards

The development of the Gravity Generator Suppressor (GGS) changed everything. Massive superconducting disks were cooled to just above absolute zero, supported in magnetic fields, and set to spinning at high speed. Any object placed below the spinning superconducting platters would gradually decrease in weight. Gravity's effect on the object was lessened. The opposite would also be true if an object were placed above the spinning disks while the disks were travelling in opposite directions. Gravity's effect on the object would be increased.

The GGS design went through a number of changes. The enormous mass of the disks, and the power required to spin them so they would maintain their magnetic suspension fields, made their practical application difficult, almost impossible. In the next design iteration, a heli-blade-shaped rod of ultra-cooled superconducting material replaced the massive disks. It was spun on a center point in a vacuum, while the pitch of the blade was controlled separately on either side of the center point. An array of these devices, with controlled speed of spin and pitch, could manipulate the force of gravity over a much larger area and to a much greater value. It was as if the device could create dips and bumps in the gravity well created by the planet's mass.

One of the first applications of this technology was the spavator (space elevator). The spavator idea was conceived in the 1950s, but was found to be impractical and unsafe, given the strength of Earth's gravity in relation to the strength-to-density ratio of known materials. However, when carbon nanotube interlaced graphene ribbons were developed, in conjunction with GGS platforms, the tech became commonplace.

Jayne's Day Two was what everyone else experienced on Day One. She stood with a group of apprentices in front of the journeyman in charge of their training. She assured him she could catch up on the safety protocols that had been introduced on the first day and, if she was unsure of anything, she would ask for clarification. Today would be spent learning to perform basic maintenance at the base of the spavator.

Despite the fact that Joseph was in the same group as Jayne, he never spoke to her or even looked her way. This irritated Jayne a great deal, and she decided to give him a dose of his own medicine. She would pretend he didn't exist. Even so, a part of her wished she could talk to him about the luck testing and connectome scan she endured and see what he thought about it all.

"You will work in pairs to complete specific tasks that will be sent to your VID. Collect your tool pack from stores and report to the spavator undercarriage. Once there, the VID will provide further instructions," said the journeyman fixer. "If you remember what you were taught, this will be a breeze."

He started to call out the names and numbers of those who were partnered together. Jayne stopped listening, thinking instead of Joseph trying to fit his big feet on the PUT pad, and that thought led to the memory of the day he followed her and waited for her in the hallway. She smiled.

She heard 'Kane 37' being called, followed by 'Riley 23', and glanced up as Joseph and Riley headed to the stores to collect their tool packs. He wouldn't be working with her today. She felt a twinge of disappointment and wondered again why he was required to follow her around on that first day.

Finally, the instructor said, "Wu 13," followed by nothing. "Well, I guess you get to work with me," he said.

Jayne nodded. The instructor looked at her more closely, seeming puzzled by her appearance, finally motioning her toward the stores and saying, "Get your tool pack, 13, and meet me back here in five."

A heartbeat after Jayne turned to walk away, she heard the instructor mutter, "Boy, she's a young one."

Jayne headed to the stores. She waved her VID in front of the scan-lock, hearing an answering click as a small door opened in the drop bin. She reached in and grabbed her tool pack. Slipping it over her shoulders and heading back to the marshaling area, she discovered that everyone else was gone. She waited for 10 minutes for her instructor to show up, growing more annoyed by the minute. She was about to take off the heavy pack and sit down when he finally arrived.

"Sorry. I got delayed. Some strange problem with the ID scanner at the spavator intake port. One minute it wouldn't let anything through and the next it let in everything," he said, shaking his head. "Follow me."

They headed toward the hall, stopping before exiting the room. "Well, where are we going?" he asked, looking pointedly at Jayne.

Jayne looked at him; puzzled, as he looked back querulously.

"Oh!" Jayne said, finally realizing she was responsible for the assignment. She looked at her VID and said, "This way."

There was no green arrow to direct her, but the VID screen displayed a map with a simple 'You Are Here' flashing red dot on the screen. With Jayne leading the way, they soon found themselves in a narrow hallway with a curved wall of test contact points.

Thinking back to her training, she surmised she would need to check each pair for degradation. Each strand of spavator cable led up to the geosynchronous tether point 100,000 km straight up. There were a series of seven colored diode lights at the base of each set of test points. These series indicated which tests she should perform. Jayne recognized the codes and quickly opened her tool pack, applied the lockout tie, removed the test core, and connected it to the contact point. The diode's colors changed.

"This one has three months left before failure. It will need to be replaced in two," she said. "I will record this and order retesting in one month." She removed the lockout tie.

She turned to look at the instructor, waiting for his approval.

Before he could say anything, his VID beeped and flashed red. "What now?" he exclaimed. He looked down at the terminal, frowning. "I have to go. I'm sure you can handle this task. As you can see, there is lots of work to be done here." He gestured toward the blocks of shining colored diodes disappearing down the long room that curved slowly to the right. "If you need me, don't."

"Don't what?" she asked naively.

"Need me. Or call me. Get done what you can and report to staging at 16:00. By the looks of this," he gestured toward his VID, "I will be busy. Have a good day." He left the way they came.

Jayne shrugged. She was used to being alone; it didn't bother her. She went back to work.

After a few hours, Jayne paused briefly for a food and water break. Not having anything else to do, she returned to work. Stepping up to the next panel, she paused as she realized that the long room in which she was working curved in a circle, but never seemed to bring her back to the beginning. She assumed that she would end up back where she started, but the small marks that she put on the wall next to each panel never reappeared.

"It must be a spiral," she whispered, and smiled. "I must be travelling in a spiral." And she noted a gradual incline in the floor that she had not noticed before.

Trying to visualize the diagrams, she studied of the base of the standard spavator and realized that all the connections between the carbon and silicon nanotubes spiraled up to a main cable. There was a great deal of redundancy in the design to prevent catastrophic failure of the spavator.

She looked down at her VID. She still had 10 minutes of personal time left before she was required to get back to work. Her legs cramped from the continuous standing and crouching, so she decided to get some exercise.

She started to run up the spiral. The size of the circles decreased, and the slope of the floor increased the further she ran. As she climbed, the LEDs on her left blurred. Suddenly, the hall ended in a circular room five meters across. She'd arrived in what, she assumed, was the core room. She noticed the core cable sitting in front of her, encased in clear plastic that morphed down into what she assumed was a Gravity Suppressor (GS) device. She'd learned that the GS would be found in this kind of super-cooled casing. Across the room, she noticed a door with a small window. There was a scanlock beside the door. Keeping her back to the wall, she circled the room. Halfway around, she stopped at the door. She turned to face the door just as her VID beeped. There were three minutes of personal time remaining. She would have to hurry if she were to start work on time. It wouldn't look good on her record if she started late.

Curious about where this oddly placed door might lead, she rested her hand on the scanlock. Nothing happened. She jumped up to see through the small window but could see nothing in the darkness that blanketed the other side of the door.

She jumped up again, trying to peer through the window. She felt the silver star pendant bounce out from beneath her jumpsuit. As her feet touched the ground, she heard a definite click. Her eyes widened as the door slid open.

"Beep! Beep!" went her VID. Two minutes left.

Deciding that she could explore for just one more minute, Jayne tucked the star necklace back below her jumpsuit and stepped inside the room. A light came on as soon as she crossed the threshold. She looked around. She was inside a small storage room whose only feature was six recessed niches in the wall, each covered by a glass door. Most of them were empty, but she was intrigued when she saw that one contained a white plastic box. Feeling like she was moving in slow motion, Jayne reached up and opened the lone, occupied cupboard. A cloud of cool water vapor rolled out in a white wave as Jayne removed the box. She set it down to examine it.

It didn't seem to have a lock or latch of any kind, so she proceeded to lift the lid. The back of the lid featured a stylized image of a human heart. Another box was nestled inside the first. It was securely sealed with a strap that read: Human Organs—Open for Immediate Transplant Only.

"Beep! Beep! Beep!" went her VID. Jayne's heart pounded in her chest. She was out of time, but she was still struggling to make sense of what she'd found. Why would a human organ be stored here, at the base of a spavator?

With no time left to spend on this mystery, Jayne quickly closed the white box, placed it back in the cupboard, and closed the door. She stepped out of the small room, hearing the door close behind her, and moved as quickly as possible back to her work.

Her mind, however, continued to stray from the task at hand. The image of the heart couldn't be banished from her mind.

As she worked, she realized she was approaching the room containing the human organ. *Maybe the box was empty?* she thought. *Maybe that's where they store empty boxes?*

After all, she hadn't seen an actual heart inside the box. All she saw was another box inside the organ container. It was probably empty. But she could still see the seal, vividly, as if it were in front of her, and it was unbroken.

At the sound of approaching footsteps, Jayne turned to see her instructor. He watched her work for a few moments before speaking. "Wow! You're quite the worker." He glanced down at her tool pack. "You're nearly out of lockout ties. We're really close to a satellite supply room. Come, let me show you."

He began to walk up the spiral toward the core room, continuing to talk once he saw that she was following. "You look like you could use a break. The core is only a few loops of hallway ahead."

They walked into the core room. The instructor moved assuredly to the door on the far side and stood waiting. Jayne came slowly behind, not knowing what to expect. There were only refrigeration cupboards in that room, one of which contained an organ box with a heart inside. She shivered.

"It will open if you place your hand on the scanner. I entered your palm into the system just before I returned," he said, gesturing to the scanlock, "but I really didn't think you would work fast enough to need more lockout ties."

Jayne hesitantly placed her palm on the scanlock. She heard a click, and the door opened. She looked up and was shocked to find a small room, including a wall lined with small containers fitted with thumb locks. The refrigeration cupboards were gone. Confused, she looked blankly at the instructor.

He smiled, not noticing her bewilderment, and pointed to the lockout ties in one container.

"Put your thumb on the thumb lock," he said.

Jayne pressed her thumb to the pad, her mind still whirling with questions about the changes in the room, and barely noticed as the container opened. Numbly, she removed a package of ties and stared up at her instructor for a moment before she allowed her eyes to search the room in an effort to determine how it could have changed. She wondered if her instructor knew about the true nature of the room. He didn't act as if he had any idea about what Jayne had previously seen. She was even beginning to doubt the existence of the first room herself.

"These storage rooms usually have all the supplies you'll need," he said, as they walked back toward her tool pack, still sitting at the base of the wall where she'd left it. "I'll help you finish this fiber analysis. Tomorrow, we'll add to your education."

They started to work together on the testing. After an hour, they were nearing completion when a worker approached from below. He was carrying an empty backpack, and his work helmet was tipped down, concealing most of his face. He signaled with his hand and mumbled, "Need some supplies," as he passed. Jayne noticed a chain on his left wrist with a dangling star—a silver star just like the one around Jayne's neck. He seemed to be missing the pinky finger from his left hand, but he was moving so quickly that she couldn't be certain.

"That's odd," muttered Jayne's instructor. "I thought this area was restricted."

A few minutes later, the man reappeared. He said nothing as he passed them and, curious to see if she could spot the star bracelet again, Jayne turned to look at him. His pack was fuller than before, and a square object pressed against the fabric. She could clearly see the outline of the carrying case. The corner was sticking out from under the flap. It was white, just like the case she saw in the refrigeration unit—the case she suspected held a human heart.

She sucked in her breath, in wide-eyed shock as she watched the man disappear down the hallway.

CHAPTER 10

Gravity Ball

The game of Gravity Ball (GravBall) evolved after the Gravity Generator Suppressor went mainstream. A lot of companies incorporated this technology into their exercise equipment, but its most famous use was in the Gravity Tube (GravTube), so-called because it formed a playing area encased in a cylinder of controlled gravity. The game became an integral part of modern culture worldwide. [See Appendix 1: diagram of the gravity tube and details of the game.]

The rest of Jayne's week consisted of more jobs similar to the first. It lacked the excitement of discovering hearts hidden inside cases in strange rooms that morphed into other rooms and were visited by secretive-looking men with missing fingers and silver stars around their wrists.

The supervisors seemed to take less and less interest in the group of apprentices under their charge. They experienced several problems involving the materials moving up and down the spavator. Packages would appear in an initial count but wouldn't be listed in the manifests or vice versa. Nothing seemed to come of it, since all the problems were resolved—dismissed as miscounts or manifest errors. The panic that had overtaken the supervisors at the first occurrence was lessening. As computer error seemed to be the culprit, a recent upgrade was being rolled back to pinpoint the specific code responsible. This resulted in the apprentices being given some time off.

Jayne woke to the sound of classical music that gradually increased in volume.

"What is the title of the piece?" asked Lucky.

It was a game they played: identify the music and the composer. Jayne quickly learned to recognize much of the music that Lucky chose. This morning, however, wasn't a good one for Jayne. This was the third morning in a row that left Jayne with nothing to do. She missed going to work; it kept her mind occupied.

As the music played on, continuing to increase in volume, Lucky spoke again, "Get up, Thirteen. I have made you something to eat. You can attempt to identify the music after you have eaten."

"I'm not hungry and I feel yucky," moaned Jayne, rolling over and pulling the pillow over her head.

"You do not feel well. Oh, dear. I see you have not had a proper physical since you arrived. I will schedule—"

"Stop. I don't need a physical. I just feel yucky, and I am bored out of my mind," Jayne wailed.

"Why don't you go to the gym this morning after you eat?" suggested Lucky.

"Gym? There's a gym in this place? Why didn't you tell me earlier?" asked Jayne. She got out of bed. "Where is it?"

"Eat. Your VID will direct you once you have finished your breakfast," said Lucky.

Jayne ate, then dressed, and was soon on her way to the gym. "Maybe this day off won't be so boring after all," she thought.

Apparently, she wasn't the only one to have thought about using the gym this morning. It was packed with apprentices. Some were working on machines, others were playing Grav Ball in a mini Grav Tube (one-third regular size) designed for amateur play. The only major differences between this and a normal tube were the size and lack of cameras. There were also only three rows of seating for those who wanted to watch the amateur games.

Jayne's heart jumped in her chest when she saw the tube. GravBall was her favorite game. She learned to play when she was a little girl and, though some might say she was still a little girl, she knew she could play this game well. In fact, she'd discovered that being small and quick was an advantage, especially on the high gravity lines. Her strength-to-weight ratio was often superior to that of many of the bigger players. She could speed up while travelling on a high grav line, and when that line changed to low grav she couldn't be stopped. In low gravity, Jayne was able to reach any goal position with a single leap. From there, it was a simple matter of slamming the ball home.

Jayne sat and observed from the near-empty viewing area near the center line. There was a 'drop-in' game in progress. She glanced at the clock, noting that the period was nearly over. She noticed Joseph playing, acting as the Ball Carrier (BC) for one of the teams.

The teams weren't using complicated pro-scoring. Casual 'drop-in' games scored one point per goal, no matter how many players were on each team. A balance was often achieved by balancing the skill of the players.

Jayne watched as Joseph ran down a neutral grav line. She could see how strong he was. A spotter on the grav line to his left told him to move across and he veered left and back, just dodging a knocker. The robo-ref nearly called him for forward progress in space, as the area between the lines was called. Then Joseph hit a low grav line. He misjudged his acceleration and went sailing up to the center axle. The axle bumped him with an anti-grav pulse. He lost his balance and spun out of control. He hit normal space and plummeted to the ground, but luckily his suit's safety field kicked in and he landed softly.

The robo-ref finally called him for forward progress in space, and Joseph was forced to give up the ball to the opposition. Jayne smiled. That was her signature move. She would see a spotter indicate another low grav line on the opposite side of the tube, then she would execute a high leap on the line, followed by an anti grav bump from the center axle, moving down to another low grav line, before flipping back again until she was in the scoring range. If everything went right, she was unstoppable.

Jayne keyed her name into the game panel, and it asked for her level of play. She had never played anywhere other than the nursery community tube. She had no idea what level she played. She took a guess and pressed five on a scale that went up to ten.

The computer assigned her to the blue team, which was presently rated four points lower than the red team. She would be their seventh player. According to the computer, she would almost balance the teams. She grabbed the smallest suit and helmet she could find, which would provide some protection to her elbows, knees, wrists, and shoulders. The helmet fit well on her head, but the suit needed some adjustment. She rolled up the legs and sleeves and cinched in the wide blue waist belt. She knew that she probably looked a little silly, but that might make the other team underestimate her. They would do so at their peril. After she scored a few goals, no one would care what she was wearing or how she looked. She waited for the period to end and, once the buzzer sounded and the door opened, she stepped into the grav tube. All gravity would be normal until the game started. Jayne walked over to the blue team as they gathered in the player pit.

She strode up to the group of four guys and two girls. She didn't recognize any of them, but she assumed that they came from some other apprentice group, or maybe they weren't apprentices at all. They were all breathing hard and sipping water as she approached.

"Did you see that big goof mess up an easy run on that low grav line?" a tall blonde girl said, laughing.

"I'm your seventh," said Jayne. "I'm supposed to balance the teams. My name is Thirteen."

Everyone stopped and looked at her. "We use names here, not numbers," said one of the guys.

"That is my name…and my number. I've been called Thirteen for as long as I can remember, but if you don't like it, just call me Wu, Jayne Wu," she said.

"Have you played this game before, Wu 13?" asked a small boy, who was sitting near the end of the bench. He stood, and Jayne noticed that he wasn't much taller than she was. She realized after a moment that she was staring, for he was shaved completely bald except for a small horse tail sticking up from the top of his head. He had even cut a hole in his helmet to allow the hair to remain upright and visible.

"I've played a little," she finally replied, "and you can just call me Thirteen. What are your names?"

The boy with the horse tail sticking out of the top of his head spoke first. "We all have GravBall names." He pointed at each of the team members as he named them off. "That's Busy Izzy, Jumper, Cannon Ball, Eye Spy, Pinky, and I'm Spike. The next game will start in a few. What position do you like?"

There were seldom set positions in drop-in GravBall, so everyone generally played a bit in each of them. The BC would have to run the ball down the lines and try to score, while the knockers could choose to play defensively or offensively. Depending on the team strategy, they would either guard the grav lines, trying to knock either the BC or the ball off the lines, or they would guard the BC and bump defensive knockers off the line. Spotters were in charge of communicating whether the grav lines were running high or low gravity, using coded gestures to tell the BC the best line to use. The trailer, as the name suggested, would play behind the BC, always ready to receive the pass back. Every player needed to be familiar with every position.

"Whatever," said Jayne offhandedly. "What are the signals?"

"We are signal minimalists, meaning that we keep our signals simple. Thumbs up means a low grav line, and thumbs down means a high grav line. The further you move your thumb back and forth, the more the line wiggles. A still hand means a straight line. Opening and closing your hand means a pulsar. If you signal with your other thumb up, then the line is moving toward the goal; thumb down means it's moving away," Spike said, opening and closing his right hand like a claw with his left thumb switching from up to down.

"Wow, this tube has pulsar tech! That's cool," said Jayne. A pulsar line could send high and low gravity pulses down the line. Running in a low gravity pulse moving toward the goal would make an offensive player almost unstoppable.

"I'll start as a knocker," said Jayne.

"You and Pinky play back knockers, and we'll play the front when we are on defense. On offence, it's all open," said Spike. A buzzer sounded. "Let's go!" he said, thrusting his fist in front of him.

The other team members placed their fists on top of his and, as one, the team shouted, "Score!"

As she ran out into the tube and took her position, Jayne glanced over at Joseph. He looked a little surprised to see her and raised his eyebrows in a mock salute.

Spike noticed their interaction and glanced back at Jayne. "You know Big Foot?" he asked.

Jayne shrugged just as the ball popped out between Joseph and Spike.

Joseph reached out and flipped the ball back to their BC who was already standing on a low grav line off to the left. The BC started running, glancing to the right at one of his spotters. Jayne saw the spotter give a wavy motion with his thumb up and assumed it meant that the line was low grav but not straight. Running it would be difficult. If a player jumped up too high, they could fly right over normal space or, even worse, into a high grav line. Falling like that could hurt, even with an anti-grav protection suit.

The opposition's BC glanced left, seeing his spotter raising and lowering his arm, hand edge up. There must be a low grav line running straight to the goal. He took the new line just as Jayne moved to knock him aside. Anticipating that the BC would jump, Jayne jumped toward him, expecting to meet him in the air and hoping to knock the ball out of his hands. Unfortunately, she misjudged. The BC did not jump but ran right under her, then jumped for the goal located halfway up the wall. The ball disappeared and the score light turned red.

Jayne watched as it flashed from red to amber, and finally to green, and waited for the ball to spit back out of one of the four holes on the center line.

"Tough one, Thirteen," yelled Spike, just as the ball popped out right in front of Cannon Ball. Cannon Ball passed it over to Jumper as Jayne ran a zigzag pattern through the grav lines, trying to determine what was what. She discovered what she thought was a straight low grav line and signaled to the BC. Jumper ignored her, continuing to run from line to line, avoiding all the other team's knockers, while watching Eye Spy, who took up position about 20 meters from the goal inside of normal space. (Jumper liked twin high grav lines, especially when the knockers were closing in on him. He would snake through them. Anyone who tried to follow would be bogged down the moment they hit high grav. But his legs were like posts. Jayne found out later that Jumper could not jump, even in low grav.) Suddenly, Eye Spy ran behind him, became the trailer, got the ball, ran down the low grav line, jumped and scored.

Jayne clapped her hands and cheered, then took her place as the right-back knocker. Pinky stood to her left, Busy Izzy was playing the mid, and Cannon Ball, Jumper, Eye Spy and Spike were playing the line. The ball popped into the air, hit a wavy low grav line, and sailed straight up. The ball crossed through a high grav line and careened straight down at Jayne. Grav balls were not designed to bounce, so it landed with a thud, rolling to a stop at her feet. She picked it up, feeling like she was deep in the zone as Pinky moved behind her, into the trailer position.

Jayne looked around at her teammates for a signal of where to go. All she saw were thumbs pointing down. She ran to her right, but she hit one high grav line after another. Some of them were so strong that she could barely cross them. She needed to find a low grav line soon or the opponent's knockers would be on top of her. Looking up, she saw Joseph bearing down on her, his big feet flapping against the floor. Trying to avoid him, she ran up the curve of the wall. The 30-degree mark was the highest level that a grav line could run. Now she could see her spotters sending warnings. She would hit a reverse pulsar in one more step that would take her in the wrong direction and Eye Spy was signaling that there was a straight low grav line on the far left, but it was too far away to reach from the 30-degree line on her right. Jayne had no plan. There was no time to plan. She didn't have enough information to form a plan.

With no time to think, she just reacted, trusting in her luck. Jayne always trusted her luck, and part of her knew that today would be no different. Luck was her friend.

Smiling to herself, she started to run toward her own team's goal. She heard Spike shout, "Thirteen, what are you doing? Pass it off."

But there was no one to pass to. She no longer had a trailer. Pinky was now in front of her.

Jayne jumped into the reverse pulsar, catching a low grav pulse heading right toward her own goal. She jumped again in the low grav, sailing up to the center line. Arching her back like an old-fashioned high jumper, she felt herself bumped upward by the anti-grav field on the center line. She rolled over, moving into the low grav line on the left, which sent her dropping straight down the line to the floor. She glanced to her right, seeing that all the opponent's knockers were on the right side, leaving her with a clear line down to the goal. Even if she walked, they couldn't catch her before she scored. The goal was high up and stable, and Jayne decided to show off. Running down the low grav, she hopped, skipped, jumped, did a somersault in mid-air and scored. She pushed off the wall into another somersault and landed near the tube center in the low grav line.

Jayne turned to her teammates with a smile on her face as they ran toward her.

"That was fracking fantastic," shouted Pinky, slapping Jayne on the back.

"And stupidly dangerous," said Spike, "but very cool to watch." The rest of the team agreed and congratulated her.

A moment later, everything stopped. The hum of equipment and grav field generators halted. The lights dimmed and the doors to the gym clicked and locked.

A computer voice droned over the PA. "HUB 169 is in lockdown. Please sit on the floor and wait for further instructions." The message continued to repeat, halting when the last person sank to the floor.

One person stood up, for whatever reason, and the droning computer voice started again. After a few similar episodes, everyone was so sick of hearing the announcement that they resigned themselves to the situation and sat. And waited.

CHAPTER 11

Lockdown

The biomes were constructed in orbit. Given their size and complexity, there was no practical way they could have been built on Earth and still function as ships that could travel to the stars. The spavators allowed materials to be transported into orbit without the great expense of chemically powered rockets. Each transport was tightly controlled and monitored. Nothing could be transported to or from the biomes without being subjected to extremely high levels of security. The scientists constantly worried about contamination. This led to the microscopic inspection of anything that entered a biome to ensure that nothing would upset the delicate ecological balance they'd designed. Shipments coming out of the biomes were less stringently checked. This weakness in security protocol opened up a black market in biome materials, some of which were no longer available to the general population back on Earth.

B oth teams drifted to the center line of the grav tube. They sat in a circle; Joseph sat directly across from Jayne. He sprawled out until he was practically lying down. As she looked at him, Joseph smiled wickedly at her, wiggling his fingers in her direction.

Annoyed, Jayne turned away, glancing around to see if any of the others saw Joseph's finger wiggle. Before she could sigh in relief that none of the others saw that smile and wave, she made eye contact with Spike, who was sitting beside her. He fixed her with a 'what's that all about?' glance, and Jayne felt her face flush. She put her hand to her forehead to hide her eyes, looking down at her feet, noticing how they stuck out of the oversized uniform. She kept her eyes down, intending to hide until she was sure that her face no longer advertised her embarrassment, but looked up as a new announcement broke the silence.

"All GravBall players, please exit the tube, remove your suits, and prepare for a detailed inspection!" a new voice ordered.

Jayne and the other players exited the tube, removed their suits, and sat on the benches to await their next orders. Jayne was the only one who seemed to notice a quiet boy from the red team taking a detour, walking back to the suit lockers, and placing something into one of the empty lockers.

Suddenly, the gym door opened, and a security team entered, pushing a large cart full of sensor equipment and a portable body scanner. Each of the GravBall players was first checked using a handheld device, then directed to enter the body scanner, which resembled a giant bell jar with a sliding door.

Inside the scanner, a whirlwind of air was directed around the subject, then sucked back through a filter. Any resulting material was collected and analyzed. A light on the front panel would turn green if nothing significant was found. The panel displayed only green lights as Jayne waited for her turn. She noticed that the quiet boy from the red team seemed nervous, continuously glancing at the security techs who were scanning the lockers. A tech stopped as the light on her scanner turned red. She reached into the locker, removing a small gravity meter. She carried it over to the senior security tech.

"Tisk tisk," he said, a satisfied grin appearing on his face as he inspected the device. "What kind of GravBall player needs a grav meter in the tube? Not a very good one, I would say. So, which one of you is going to own up to it? This isn't what we were looking for, but it's still a serious offense. All of you newbs should be well aware that this is a restricted device. Obviously, one of you was trying to get an advantage in the game by checking the grav lines." He held the grav meter aloft. "Now, which one of you was it?"

He scanned the row of players, stopping in front of Jayne. He sneered at her. "You look like you could barely lift the ball, much less run with it. Did you think this would even out the playing field so you could show off your nonexistent skills to your friends?"

He turned to Spike. "What about you, ponytail boy—how did you get this out of stores?"

Spike stood indignantly. "I don't need a stupid meter to read a grav line."

"No, I guess you don't, but it might be worth something on the black market. What could a kid like you be looking for? Maybe you planned to sell it for some hubtokes. What would you need cash for? Maybe a haircut!" he sneered, shoving Spike back onto the bench. "Sit down, ponytail boy."

He turned to Joseph, who was staring at the floor. "Whatcha lookin' at, son? Them's some mighty big feet you got there. Have a little trouble movin' them down a high grav line? Needed a little help figurin' which line was low? You know what they say about big feet..."

Joseph didn't move. He didn't even look up.

The senior security tech turned to the other tech and chuckled. "You know what they say, Nora?"

"Yeah," Nora answered, "isn't it, Big Feet, Small—"

"Ha! I think the word you're looking for is brain," laughed one of the other techs.

"Small something for sure," the senior security tech laughed, slapping his leg. "Did you steal this out of stores?" He tossed the small meter into the air, caught it with one hand and looked at it pensively." No, I guess you didn't. You'd need some brains to pull that off," he said, turning away from the group.

"Well, I know one of you babies took it, and I want you to remember that I'm watching all of you." He turned and scanned the group of players in front of him. "And, just so we're clear, I couldn't care less about this." He dropped the meter on the floor and stomped on it, crushing it under his foot. "What I care about is how. How did one of you little pukes get this past the scanners? Until I find that out, you are all under my microscope. Just so we're clear, that's a very unpleasant place to be."

There was an uncomfortable silence as Jayne and the others took their turns in the large body scanner. The technicians seemed disappointed as they were cleared, one-by-one. They finally dismissed the group with nothing more than a warning that their investigation would continue until they discovered how material was being transported past the scanners.

A short time later, Jayne breathed a sigh of relief as she arrived back at her quarters. She was greeted by Lucky.

"Everyone is under lockdown," said Lucky. "I know," said Jayne, "do you know why?"

"There has been a serious security breach. A series of biologicals have been removed from one of the biomes. I will check for more up-to-date data. "There was an almost imperceptible pause before Lucky resumed. "Yes, security was looking for some rodent DNA from a jungle biome. Each biome has a unique nucleotide marker inserted into the DNA of all biologicals. This is done to prevent cross-contamination between biomes. The filters at each biome are programmed to prevent the entrance of any foreign biome DNA. Security is currently searching for whomever is responsible for the theft, not only to recover the stolen property but also to determine how the perpetrators were able to bypass security. They are also trying to determine the motive behind the choice of these particular rodents. Thus far, they have been unsuccessful. The lockdown will continue until biome security is restored to 100%. That may take a while. Would you like to play the Guess the Music game to pass the time?" asked Lucky.

"No game, just music," said Jayne. "I'm a little tired from playing GravBall. I want to sleep. Wake me if something happens."

She crawled into bed and soon drifted off to sleep. Music played softly in the background. She dreamed of Joseph and Spike and the quiet boy who had stolen the gravity meter.

CHAPTER 12

Hi Ho, Hi Ho

The spavator systems were the first step to creating the biomes. These space elevators, often described as the tallest man-made structures on the planet, were critical to the development and construction of the biome ships. The HUBs were built around the base of each spavator and served several purposes: maintain the spavator; serve as a depot for transport of materials into orbit; house the myriad of fixers that worked to create and maintain the systems; and provide laboratory space for the scientists to develop the tech required for such a massive undertaking.

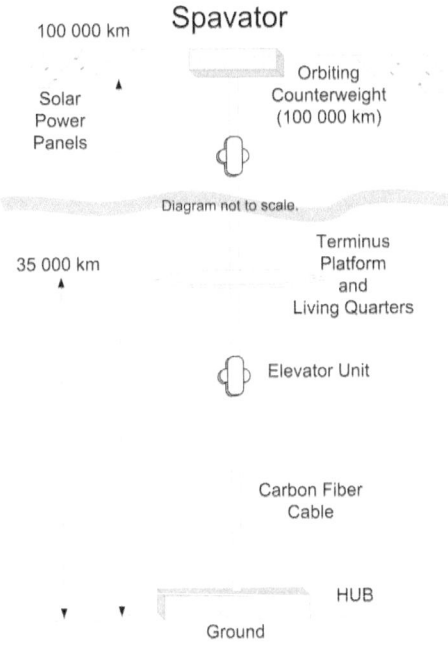

The lockdown finally ended. It still wasn't clear whether anyone was apprehended for the rodent theft. It became a running joke. The apprentices took great joy in calling each other Rodent Thief, Rat Man, or Mouse Marauder.

At lunch on the day after the lockdown, someone asked Jayne if she was saving carrot sticks for her pet rats just because she was eating a salad. This was said only half in jest: it seemed like everyone was a suspect.

Rumor circulated that nothing had actually been stolen. The theory was that a computer glitch or a test of the security system was the real reason for the lockdown. After all, who would want to smuggle rats out of a biome? What possible motive could anyone have for stealing rats? If you wanted a rat, there were plenty of legal ways to obtain one.

Jayne mulled over the strange situation as she munched on her salad. Yes, why would anyone steal rats? An idea began to form in her mind as she chewed: what if these rats were somehow different from other rats? Her brain quickly filled in the blank. These rats would have been implanted with special biome markers.

But why rats? Jayne straightened in her seat as her mind whirled through the possibilities. Rats reproduced quickly, which was the main reason they were used in research. Reproducing rats meant reproducing biome markers. Having a steady supply of biome markers would enable someone to move anything in or out of the biomes without alerting security. The scanners on the spavator would ignore anything with the correct biome markers. She pictured the white box with the picture of a human heart on the outside, and her own heart began to beat faster. Had that box contained a heart from one of the biomes? Whose heart was it? How had it been removed? Where had the man with the missing finger taken it and why? Who would want or need a heart, anyway? Would a transplant recipient want a heart from an Omie? She shook her head. She had too many questions and not enough information. She would have to ask Lucky later.

Jayne stood up and was about to leave when Joseph stepped in front of her. "How are you squeaking, Mini Mouse Girl?" he asked, and he squeaked a couple of times for effect. "Have any other boys been assigned to follow you around?"

"No, only you. I just realized that you must feel so special. What a pleasure it must have been to follow me around, waiting for me while I did important stuff," she sneered.

"Well, Mini Mouse Girl, things have changed. I got some very special orders today that you're not going to like. In fact, you're going to hate them 'cause you're going for a little..." He paused as his VID began to beep loudly. He took it out, looked at the screen briefly, and quickly put it away. He turned his back to her, still speaking. "This afternoon, you get to follow me. Get used to looking at this," he said, sticking his bum out at her.

Jayne didn't respond. She just opened her VID to check the afternoon's assignment. It read: Kane 37 and Wu 13 report to Section Sub D Levels 1 and Level 2 by way of the PUT pads in the East Rotunda. "We're just working together," she snorted. "I'm not following you. In fact, I suspect that it'll be the other way around once we get our assignment."

"Nice try, Mouse Girl, but I just figured out where Section Sub D is located. It's at the base of the spavator. We have clean-up duty," he said. "We were shown that area on the first day. The day you were somewhere else. The day you missed all the rules about what to do and what not to do. There were a couple of second-year apprentices cleaning up and they did not look happy. You will have to follow my orders, so be prepared to get dirty."

He walked away and Jayne hurried after.

"You wish!" Jayne retorted. She slowed down, intending to show him that she wasn't about to let him take charge. After a moment, she realized that she couldn't see Joseph anymore, so she sped up and was relieved when she found him standing in the rotunda. He was looking back and forth between his VID and the room.

Finally, he spotted Jayne. "Come on, Wu, I don't want to be late.

There will be no spots on my record. I plan to make foreman in three years. It was bad enough playing a game of GravBall with some kid that stole a grav meter. Guilt by association is sometimes worse than true guilt. You can't even defend against it."

"Stupidity by association is even worse," she muttered quietly. They both stepped onto the PUT pad. Jayne sneered at Joseph, watching him trying to arrange himself onto the pad. "Now, Joey, make sure you tuck in those feet."

A moment later, they were inside a small equipment room at the base of the spavator. They grabbed some dust masks and vacuums and proceeded to Section Sub D Level 1. The room was large and circular. It was the terminus of the spavator cable. At this initial point the fibers did not form a single cable as they did further up.

Each fiber bundle joined together and entered the ceiling at the edge of the room, traveled down the wall, and fanned out in lines, with each successive fiber bundle reaching further and further into the room and disappearing into the floor. Under the floor, they connected to the GS array. It was designed so that a failure on any given line could not cascade. It was overbuilt. Even a failure of 20% of the lines would have little effect on the overall spavator performance.

As they entered the room, Jayne felt the electricity in the air. Her hair began to stand up and out in all directions, but she was annoyed to see that the static had little effect on Joseph's buzz cut. They reached down to their boots simultaneously, exposing the ground plate in their shoes to the floor. Jayne's hair dropped as the static went to ground. The massive amount of static electricity was a by-product of the GS array. Like a giant precipitator, it attracted any particulates in the air, creating a coat of grunge that would quickly build up if left alone. That was their first job of the day—clean all the dust and dirt off the fiber contacts with high-powered vacuums.

"I'll tell you what," said Jayne smiling, "you go that way and I'll go this way and we will meet in the middle. That way we can work together without working together. It's a win-win."

"Sounds good to me," said Joseph.

The job was pretty simple. The vacuum head fit perfectly over each fiber connection point, sucking away the dust and dirt in seconds. It took them little more than an hour to finish the dusting.

"This didn't take as long as I thought, but we still have Level 2 to complete. It's pretty bad down there," said Joseph.

Jayne looked at her VID, calling up the map of the spavator. "That's where the line-vacs terminate. The small ones ascend to 15 kilometers. As they descend, they remove dirt and moisture and reduce the weight on the cable. The larger line-vacs transport the dirt to Level 2. Most of it gets taken away on the conveyors, but a lot finds its way to the floor." She looked up at Joseph. "I guess that's our job today."

They returned to the equipment room to collect the tools they needed. Carrying the large flat shovels, Jayne and Joseph trudged down the long set of stairs to Level 2 and entered a dark room. As Joseph stepped forward, the lights came on. Jayne looked back and forth, examining the long, narrow room with high ceilings. A conveyer belt ran the full length of the room along the far wall. Between the conveyer and a monorail that ran parallel to it, Jayne recognized the focus of their current job. A lot of dirt and debris was strewn beside and around the monorail and in front of the conveyer belt.

"According to this," she said, holding up her VID, "we'll have to shovel—yes, you heard me right—shovel the garbage onto the conveyor so it can be removed." She held her hand over her nose. "Yech, it stinks in here. I don't believe it. I joined TEM to become a journeyman tech and here I am shoveling sh—"

A loud klaxon horn sounded, cutting her off. A line-vac rolled down the monorail and slowly tipped forward, dumping its contents onto the conveyor belt. Most of the debris made it to the belt, but some inevitably missed, resulting in the collection spread all along the floor at the edge of the conveyor. Righting itself, the line-vac continued on its way, exiting the room at the other end. The klaxon silenced as it exited.

"I didn't think they were that big," said Jayne. "It must hold three or four cubic meters of debris."

"Only the ones at the lower end are that big. They collect what the smaller ones clean from higher up and dump it here. The conveyor takes it away to be processed. The majority is line dirt and vegetation. There's even some algae that grows one to two kilometers up," stated Joseph.

"Boy, aren't we the expert," she retorted sarcastically. "Let's get this done. It really stinks in here."

Moving to the edge of the conveyer belt, Jayne started shoveling. Joseph joined her and soon they'd cleared a small section of floor. The belt continued to run quickly past them, carrying the material away to places unknown. Jayne was leaning on her shovel when the klaxon sounded again. They both stepped back from the monorail and waited. A line-vac appeared, tipped, emptied its contents on the belt and returned to its upright position. It clanked as it continued down the line, dragging spillage along the floor and disappearing as it exited at the far end of the room. Jayne looked at the mess left behind and groaned. The entire area they'd cleared was, once again, littered with cable trash and rotting vegetation.

"You'd think they could have designed these things to be more accurate when they dump on the belt. Now we have to go back and clean that whole area again," she said, indicating the fresh pile on the floor.

"It won't take a sec to clear," said Joseph, stepping over to push it all onto the moving belt.

Just as he finished, his VID beeped. He stopped and checked it. "That's weird," he said. "It wants us to stand right..." he moved to the center of the room, "...over...here." He stopped and looked over at Jayne who was still standing, leaning on her shovel. "It said both of us. Get over here!"

"Since when do I have to do what your VID says? If I was supposed to move over there, my VID would have—" she stopped mid-sentence as her VID beeped. "Damn!" she said, moving to stand beside Joseph without even checking her VID.

He took her shovel, threw it down, grabbed her by the arm, spun her around so she was facing away from him and said, "Well, would you look at that." Joseph shifted so that he was now holding her by the shoulders. Jayne was too startled to move. No klaxon sounded, but a line-vac entered on the monorail, stopping in front of Jayne. Instead of tipping trash on the moving belt, a door on the back of the line-vac slid upward. Jayne could see a clean interior with padding on all the inner surfaces. Any curiosity as to why the inside of a line-vac would be clean and padded was cut short—quickly and roughly.

Jayne staggered as she felt a very unexpected shove from behind, propelling her inside the line-vac. She didn't even have time to raise her arms before she face-planted into the far padded wall, hitting hard. The door closed behind her, and she found herself enveloped in darkness. As the line-vac began to move, Jayne could hear it clanking along the monorail and out of Section Sub D Level 2. Her hands went to her face, trying to alleviate the stinging pain of the collision with the wall. Her nose hurt, and a tear slid down her cheek. She wiped it away as she bit her lip. She heard a voice call out, "Sorry Wu u u u u," then there was a hiss. Jayne smelled something strange, and then she felt nothing at all.

CHAPTER 13

Captured

The biomes became the incubators for new humans. These new humans were isolated from Earth and the biome habitats were tightly controlled as they were gradually transformed from an Earth-like habitat to an alien-planet habitat. The change was to be gradual, happening over a period of 300 to 800 years, the exact time dependent both on how far away the destination planet was and the degree of mutation that would be required for human survival on that planet. The process of genetic manipulation started as soon as the biomes were inhabited. The changes would occur gradually during the long journey to the new planet over the dozen or so generations it would take to get there.

Jayne opened her eyes, trying to focus slowly on a grey, plaster mottled ceiling. Nausea roiled in her stomach and pain speared her face. Her nose and lip ached. As she sat up quickly, the pounding in her head multiplied a thousand-fold. She closed her eyes again and lay back down with a groan. She willed the pain to subside.

It took a few minutes before the pain eased, but when it did, she opened her eyes again. She was in a small windowless room with a bed and a bathroom, but nothing else. She slipped out of the bed and stood for a moment, holding onto the edge of the mattress and looking at herself. She was still wearing the clothes she wore when she was cleaning the debris scattered by the line-vacs, but the oversized coveralls were gone. As she attempted to walk toward the bathroom, she hesitated, and a wave of dizziness swelled in her head. She stopped and concentrated on keeping her balance. Trying again, she slowly slid her feet across the floor, gasping as the light in the bathroom came on automatically. She looked at herself in the mirror. Her right eye was blackened, and her lip was cut and swollen. She remembered being pushed and hitting the far wall of what looked like a line-vac. She remembered the hiss. Gas. Knockout gas. That's why her head ached. She needed water. She filled the glass and slowly brought it to her mouth. She drank on the left side. Water dribbled from her swollen lip on the right side. The water was cool, and she greedily drank it all. She felt better, except for the pounding in her head. She turned around and forced herself to focus and dismiss the pain. Her body wanted to slide back to the bed, crawl under the blankets, and sleep, but her mind slowly filled with fear. She wanted to escape. She took a step toward the door of the room, but her head started to spin. She lost her balance and fell to the floor, unconscious.

When Jayne regained consciousness, she could hear people speaking and quickly realized that she was tucked back into bed. She felt a pinch on the back of her hand.

"An IV tube," she thought, keeping her eyes closed and breathing slowly, feigning sleep as she listened.

"She must have gotten up to get a drink of water. I found a used glass on the bathroom floor. She never made it back to bed. You used too much gas. I warned you about her size. She can't be more than 45 kilos. That much gas made her sick," said a female voice.

"I had to be sure she wouldn't try to escape from the modified line-vac," a male voice responded.

"Who was the idiot that gave her a fat lip and black eye?" she asked.

"One of the newbs. He only joined the cell last month. I've had an eye on him since the day he arrived. He's a big kid, not too bright, but his size might come in handy. We took over his training and can now send him wherever we want. You never know when we might need a big, strong kid. He probably doesn't know his own strength and pushed her too hard," he answered.

"Is he the one we've been watching?" she asked.

"Yeah, we've been watching and manipulating him to keep an eye on her. We were subtle because they have been watching her very closely," he answered, then paused. "She's not awake, is she?"

Jayne became increasingly tense as she listened to this strange conversation. She wanted to hear more, so she concentrated on relaxing her body and slowing her breathing. The woman touched her wrist.

"She seems to be sleeping quietly, but I'll keep her sedated, so she'll sleep off the effects of the gas," she said.

Jayne heard footsteps walking away from the bed.

The man chuckled. "We even made him follow her for the first couple of outings. I knew that they would try to do something, and I wanted to know what, so I set his floor directions to follow her. But they were careful. He never got into the psi testing hall, but I can guess what they discovered. And after a few tests of our own, we'll know, too."

"Didn't he suspect something was strange?" she asked, as she injected the sedative into Jayne's IV shunt. As soon as the sedative hit her bloodstream, her consciousness slowly submerged, like slipping into a warm bath. Jayne fought to remain alert, wanting to learn more. "Not at first, but once we recruited him, we told him about it. He didn't think it was funny. In fact, he was a little angry," the man said, and Jayne could feel his gaze as he stared down at her. "I sure hope she isn't really what they think she is."

Jayne struggled to hear more, but the drug dragged her down into a dark sleep.

CHAPTER 14

The Interview

The end of the world was coming. Society changed. Governance changed. Education changed. Family changed. Commerce changed. Entertainment changed. Religion changed. Every world system changed as the planet turned its focus to survival. Survival of the species became the primary driving force for everything and everyone—at least that was the spin.

Jayne woke from a dreamless sleep, her bladder screaming, her stomach growling, and her mouth completely dry. As she sat up, her head swam, but it soon settled. Looking down, she was relieved to see that the IV was no longer in her arm. All that remained was an empty bag of saline hanging limply from a pole.

Awareness of her body returned, and she slid out from under the blanket and slipped quietly out of bed toward the beckoning bathroom. Before she could take her first step, a woman in a lab coat entered the room and strode up to Jayne, grabbing her by the arm.

The woman said nothing, but Jayne was surprised as she was helped into the bathroom and allowed to close the doorbehind her. The woman was waiting when Jayne emerged and kindly helped Jayne back to the bed. The woman stared at Jayne with an unreadable expression before she finally spoke. "I've ordered you something to eat. It will be here in a moment. Are you hungry?"

Jayne nodded, looking furtively around the room. She felt like a cornered cat in need of an escape route. She saw none she could manage—yet.

Taking a tube of ointment out of her coat pocket, the woman leaned down and dabbed a small blob on Jayne's lips. Moving efficiently around the room, she picked up a small container with two pills in it and a glass of water and handed them both to Jayne. "Here, take these. They'll make you feel better."

Jayne hesitated, and the woman seemed to understand as she spoke again. "They will make you feel better. It will help to stop the aching and relieve the swelling."

Jayne reluctantly downed the pills with a small sip of water just as a man carrying a tray of food entered and set up her table. The woman stood and watched Jayne as she ate voraciously, finally realizing how hungry she really was.

"Everything will be back to normal soon," said the woman. "And someone will be in to talk to you shortly." She passed a bundle of clothing to Jayne. "Here are some clean clothes. As soon as you are dressed, press this button, and someone will come to escort you to the interview room."

The woman turned and left.

Jayne was alone. She dressed, continuing to scan the room for possible methods of escape. Jayne made sure she was totally aware of her environment: tools, weapons, and escape routes. As she dressed and stood up, she scanned the room for cameras. None were in obvious sight but, as she glanced up to where she would have put a camera if she were trying to spy on someone in the room, she spotted a blemish in the wall opposite the bed. "There it is!" she thought.

As she reached down to retrieve a pair of shoes from the floor at the base of the IV stand, she spotted a small needle that someone had carelessly dropped.

Crouching to put on a shoe, she turned her back to the blemish on the wall, reached down, picked up the needle, and tucked it into the side of the shoe she was tying. After tying the other shoe, she stood, walked over to the door, and tried to open it. To her surprise, it wasn't locked and swung open easily.

Jayne poked her head out into the hall, surprised to find a hallway that was warmly decorated—obviously not part of a hospital. A uniformed man sat across the hall, and he stood as soon as he spotted Jayne.

"Jayne Wu?" She nodded.

He continued politely. "I am to escort you to the interview room. Is there anything I can get you before we go?"

Jayne shook her head. She hadn't been expecting kindness. As far as she knew, she was a prisoner and captors were not usually subservient to their detainees. She was escorted to the interview room, which was also not what she expected. The decor was warm and inviting. She sat down in a comfortable chair to wait until someone could clarify what was going on. After only a few moments, a group of people—two men and a woman—entered the room, holding large VIDs in their hands. Jayne was perplexed as to why they were all standing around the table, smiling at her.

As she leaped to her feet, intending to express her indignation at her treatment and detention, one of the men spoke, "Miss Wu, please relax. We are not here to hurt you in any way, and we sincerely apologize for your treatment so far. It was never our intention to cause you harm. The collision in the line-vac…" he paused and pointed to his own eye and lip, "…was an accident. I personally apologize for the overdose of gas. One of our technicians miscalculated your weight, resulting in too much gas. That caused the headache you suffered."

As Jayne lowered herself back into the chair, her eyes shifted from person to person. They took chairs around the table and continued to smile at her. Jayne pulled both her feet up into the chair and wrapped her arms around her legs. Her index finger felt a slight poke from the needle hidden in her shoe, and she was comforted by the knowledge that she wasn't completely weaponless.

The woman spoke first. "We needed to speak with you privately, and that just wasn't possible...out there." She waved her hand vaguely toward the door. "What we are about to say is for your ears only. It will be your choice whether you stay or go. However, if at any time, you do choose to go, we will be forced to administer a compound that will erase your short-term memory. If that happens, you will wake up in your quarters thinking you had an accident in Section D Sub Level 2, were treated and sent back to rest. However, if you take the time to hear us out, we are fairly certain you will find what we have to say intriguing and will perhaps choose to join us in our endeavors." Jayne nodded, her finger still touching the needle. She tried to think of some way she might get it out quickly if she needed to protect herself.

The woman let out a relieved breath. "Let's get started. First of all, you need to know that we are just like you. We," she gestured to the others at the table, "are all fixers. As you well know, the mandate of the fixer class is to both ensure the smooth running of society, and also to maintain the security of the biomes. Our mission is to simply do our job."

Jayne's arms pulled her knees closer. She tucked in her chin and whispered, "Why am I here?"

This time, one of the men answered. "You'll need some background information before we can explain that part."

"What if I don't want my memory erased?" rasped Jayne.

"Then you must agree to join us. What do you wish?" asked the other man sharply.

Jayne's hand slipped down to her shoe, and she slipped the needle out and into her hand. Her heart began to beat faster; her legs tensed, ready to run.

The woman seemed to sense her fear and sought to allay it, speaking softly and slowly to Jayne, "It's alright, dear. You have nothing to fear from us. We aren't trying to hurt you. Please relax."

Jayne felt anger surge out, supported by the needle she clenched in her hand. The anger burst from her lips and, once started, could not be controlled. The words spewed forth. Everything she heard and the strange things she saw before she was drugged—they, Joseph, the nine-fingered man, and the heart in a box—leaped into her mind. "You are threatening to erase my memories. Are you planning to brainwash me like you did Joseph? Who are they? Who is the nine-fingered man that stole the box with a human heart inside?" She felt the silver star, hanging from the chain around her neck, become warm against her skin and on impulse she stood on her chair, pulled it out, and shouted, "Did you give me this?"

She held the star dangling from the necklace out in front of her. As it hung, the center spokes rose up to a point like the first day it drew her blood. The light caught the tip, and it sparkled.

There was a collective gasp from everyone in the room. They seemed to be frozen in place. Every eye was drawn to the silver star. Only two heartbeats of time passed before the man who initially presented Jayne with the ultimatum jumped to his feet, flipped open a small panel by the door, placing one hand on the lock pad while pressing a red button with the other.

Metal panels dropped from the ceiling, covering the door and window that led to the hallway; the clang reverberating in the small space, sealing the room.

A droning voice began to speak through the PA system. "Interview room M is now running dark. A level 7 lockdown has been initiated." The announcement continued to repeat its message over and over.

"Please silence that," snapped the woman after a few tense moments.

The man reached over and replaced his palm over the lock pad and the announcement stopped. Jayne slid down into her chair, clutching her legs again. The needle was still concealed in her hand. Her eyes were wild. Not knowing what to expect next, she remained tense, holding her body as tight as a bowstring.

93

When the spokes thrust from the star, Jayne released the chain to prevent the needle point of the pendant from piercing her skin. It now hung loosely from its chain, openly displayed. The center spokes were still elevated to a shimmering sharp needlepoint.

The interviewers stood, forming a semicircle, facing Jayne. "Where did you get that?" demanded the woman, pointing to the star.

Jayne hesitated.

"Answer her!" barked the man who activated the security system. "Where did you get that…thing?"

"I found it…" Jayne trailed off, unsure of what to say as she studied the tense faces watching her. "I found it in my music box on my first day here."

She looked down at the pendant hanging from its chain around her neck. "It's usually flat. It was a simple flat pendant when I first got it. Then I received a message telling me to wear it. So I put it on. I thought it was something I was supposed to wear. I don't understand why you're all reacting like this. It's just a necklace." Jayne paused for a moment, thinking about the truth of her words.

"Well, except for the first time when it did this and pricked my finger." She indicated the still shimmering point of the pendant. One of the men reached under the table and pressed something, causing a small section of the table surface to retract in front of him, revealing an empty rectangular space. One of the other men began to move cautiously closer to Jayne. Jayne turned to face him, the needle from her shoe clenched tightly in her fist.

Aware that the situation was about to explode, the woman walked calmly around to the other side of Jayne and spoke to the men. "You're upsetting our guest. There's no need to be rude."

She turned to Jayne and spoke softly to her. "It's alright, dear." The woman smiled as Jayne turned to face her, and at that same moment, the man reached out and grabbed the pendant chain in his fist, tore it from her neck, carefully avoiding the sharp, gleaming tip and quickly

94

dropped it in the open compartment at the other end of the table. The cover lid snapped closed.

Jayne's hands reached up to stop the theft, but she was too slow. The star was gone. The compartment lid closed, and the compartment in the table vanished into the tabletop, along with it, the star. She heard it disappear. She felt it disappear.

Suddenly, a tsunami of nausea rose from the pit of her bowels, rising first to her stomach, then to her throat. She tried frantically to swallow, to keep the contents of her stomach in their rightful place, but it was impossible. She vomited on the table. She vomited on herself. She leaned over and vomited on the floor. She vomited over and over again. A cold sweat sent chills outwards from her core, and she shivered, even as she retched again and again. Her stomach soon emptied and still she retched.

Jayne caught glimpses as the woman removed a syringe from her lab coat pocket. One of the men held Jayne, keeping her body still as the woman injected her. Jayne felt the nausea ease as she slipped into unconsciousness.

When she woke, she was in a bed again. The nausea was gone, but her throat was sore and the muscles in her stomach, neck, and chest ached when she tried to move. She felt a warmth in her chest, as if it were flushed with blood. The flush swelled outwards and, as it did, the pain in her muscles ebbed and faded.

She reached out and lifted a glass of water from the side table, sipping slowly from the straw and sighing in relief as the soreness in her throat eased and faded. She lay back in the bed and relaxed, as she could feel her body growing stronger every minute. She reached up, relieved to feel the warmth of the silver star on its chain around her neck. She closed her eyes.

CHAPTER 15

Some Truth

With the advent of the Swarm, society divided into three main groups: the scientists, the fixers, and the omies.

The scientists took over the role of the old politicians. As the scientists rose higher in the scientific community, they acquired more and more political power.

The fixers ran the biome system and created whatever the scientists deemed important—both scientifically and politically.

The omies were the saviors of the human race. They were the chosen ones and were given the privilege of living in one of the biomes orbiting the planet. It was soon discovered by many, however, that this privilege was not as prestigious as first believed. Once someone was sent to the biomes, there was no returning.

The next meeting between Jayne and the others crackled with an almost electric tension. The room was different. It was more like an office. Jayne sat. Her feet were on the floor and her hands were flat on the table in front of her. The needle had disappeared from her shoe. The silver star hung around her neck on the outside of her clothing. She was very weak. She slowly sipped the water in front of her. Her eyes darted between the woman and the man seated on the other side of the table.

The woman spoke first. "Well, Jayne, firstly we must say that we are sorry for what happened yesterday."

"It seems you are sorry for a lot of the things that you do to me," said Jayne.

"Yes, we are sorry, and we did not do anything to you yesterday, not on purpose anyway," said the man.

"I did not start the day sick, but so far, thanks to you, I have been sick twice in two days. It has been two days, has it not?" asked Jayne. "Who are you people, anyway?"

The woman spoke up. "We have decided to tell you everything. It is a risk on our part, but having you on our side far outweighs the risk."

"Me!" exclaimed Jayne. "I am just a lowly fixer apprentice." "Believe me, you are far more than that," said the man.

Jayne made a face of disbelief. "Really! How?"

"You were chosen by them," the woman said, emphasizing the last word. "I know that doesn't make much sense to you, but if you allow us to explain, it will become clearer."

She waited, staring at Jayne.

Jayne stared back, and the woman held her gaze. Finally, Jayne nodded.

The woman continued, "Since we last saw you, we have done some research and we discovered things about you that you are probably not aware, in any conscious sense. You got their attention after you wrote the TEM exam. That exam has some questions that are open-ended. Every question has a basic answer that makes it right or wrong, but a few can also be answered with increasing depth, depending on the student's level of understanding. You went way beyond what was expected from an applicant for the TEM apprentice program, especially for a 13-year-old still living in the nursery."

"Those problems are the ones I like the best. I look at them and I see a tunnel that wriggles about, swelling and narrowing and spinning in front of me. I simply follow it. Sometimes I get to the end and sometimes I don't. I didn't get to the end of those problems on that test. I was worried I failed," said Jayne in a flat tone.

"Well, as you now know, you didn't, not by a long shot. You set off a lot of bells at the top and, from that point on, they have been studying you and trying to manipulate you."

"Who are they? asked Jayne. "For that matter, who are YOU?" The woman looked at the man. He stared back and finally nodded.

She continued, "I will tell you who they are first because that will really help explain who we are. It will also help explain what happened yesterday."

"Okay," said Jayne.

The woman let a long breath escape her lungs and started, "We call them 'The Forevers'. No one knows what they call themselves, but they see themselves as being the true answer to the survival of the human race. We know they are made up of politicians and scientists. One cannot really exist without the other in today's political landscape. The politicians supply the money, and the scientists provide the expertise. The other key ingredients are power and secrecy. If what they are doing were ever made public, the resulting chaos would collapse the whole system. Nobody wants that, least of all us."

"I thought the biomes were the true answer to the survival of the human race," said Jayne, almost reciting.

"Yes, that is what we believe. Creating a system to transport humans to new planets, with the required biological changes, will truly enable our species to populate the galaxy. They believe that the extension of human life expectancy is the real answer. They are afraid that the biome population will have lost the ability to maintain the legacy of the human race or even have the skill to inhabit the planets by the time they arrive. They want the brightest and the best minds to live until the biomes reach their new home planets, even if that takes 1,000 years. They will use anyone or anything to achieve their warped goal," lectured the woman.

"What is wrong with wanting to live forever?" asked Jayne. "I think it is rather noble. They are not giving up. They just want what we all want. They don't want to die."

The man stood up. He smiled, raised his arms and clasped his hands together. He spoke. "You are right. There is nothing wrong with that.

What is wrong, truly wrong, is that they are willing to sacrifice everyone else to achieve it. They would sacrifice you or me in a heartbeat if it served their purposes. Many have already been sacrificed to serve their need to keep themselves alive. I think you have already seen one of the common examples of their inhumanity."

"I have?" queried Jayne.

"They designed the spavators and the biomes. They incorporated 'back doors' in the designs. They can easily transport materials to and from the biomes without being discovered. You must have seen one of their organ transports. Didn't you mention that you saw a human heart being stolen by a nine-fingered man? Just so you know, we have identified him thanks to you noticing his missing finger."

"Did you arrest him?" asked Jayne.

"We are not the security police. We can't arrest anyone," said the man. "We can only watch and record."

"Maybe someone really needed that heart," said Jayne.

"Yes, I am sure they did, considering they took it from a healthy living person in a biome," said the woman. "Someone was murdered to keep one of the Forevers alive. They decided that the survival of some old scientist was more important than an 18-year-old boy in Biome 6. Our agent informed us that the formal investigation revealed that the kid wandered into the wilds of Biome 6 and was attacked by some large carnivore and was killed. It seems that this carnivore was very selective in that it only ate the boy's heart."

"Are you saying that they killed a healthy person in order to give an old guy a new heart?" asked Jayne.

"I'm surprised they did not take all of his organs. After all, a healthy heart usually means a healthy liver, lungs, and eyes. I understand the beasts in Biome 6 have an affinity for eyes," the man said sarcastically. "I bet they were in a hurry and the heart was all they had time for."

"Now you—what do they want with you? That is the million-credit question," said the woman.

"I have no idea," said Jayne. Her forehead wrinkled. "Why did you make me sick yesterday?"

The man puffed out air and raised his hands and eyebrows in defense. "We did not make you sick. They did. More specifically, THAT did," he said, and he pointed at the silver star hanging around her neck. "We spent some time and called in some hard-to-come-by expertise to analyze that little treasure. You were knocked out so you wouldn't puke yourself into oblivion. You have never been very far away from that star since you got it, or you would know about that particular effect. The only thing we did was to put it in a safe box to protect us from possible explosions. The safe box also blocked its connection to you. That is why you started to vomit. The connection is like an artificial addiction designed to make you feel better wearing it than not wearing it."

"You thought my necklace was a bomb?" asked Jayne.

"Yes. It is not, but we did find out what it really is and that, as far as you are concerned, is much worse. It is also much more dangerous to us that any bomb. We have seen that symbol before in a golden locket. Only this golden locket exploded and took out three fixers. You do not want to know what happened to the young lady wearing it," warned the man.

"Should I take it off?" asked Jayne, as she reached for the silver star dangling from the chain around her neck.

"You could, but you shouldn't. We have altered its effect on you. When you first got it, it must have injected some nanobots into your bloodstream. Did it form a sharp point and stick you the first time?"

Jayne nodded.

"That's why you puked when you took it off. When the connection between it and the nanobots is broken, the nanobots tell your brain to tell your body to vomit. We changed their programming a little. Now, if you are over five meters distance from it, you will feel a shiver run down your spine. That is just a reminder to always wear it. We also noticed what we assume is a flaw in the programming. It is really a transmitter that sends biological data to a receiver. Whenever it transmits, the nanobots react as if you have taken it off, hence you would feel nauseated. Have you ever felt sick for a few seconds and then it passed?" he asked.

Jayne thought a moment and said, "A couple of times. Just for a few seconds. I felt like someone was watching me."

"They probably were. Just so you know, the only thing we changed was the effect. No more nausea, just a little shiver down your spine. If you feel it, you will know that they are receiving a transmission from the star. You must continue to wear it so they do not suspect we know what it is. We can read its transmissions and are working on a way to use it to find out more about their plans. We really want to understand why they chose you, because it is more than just your intelligence," he explained.

Jayne flushed.

"That brings us to the most important reason why you are here," said the woman. "Will you work with us? Will you help us? Will you be a real fixer and help us fix this horror that has infested our society?"

"You really mean, will I be your spy? Right?" challenged Jayne. "Yes," the woman said without hesitation.

"And more," the man said.

"If I am going to be a spy, I would like to know for whom I am spying. So again, who are you?" Jayne demanded.

The man and woman looked at each other. They nodded and came to an unspoken agreement. They would trust Jayne. The woman spoke first. "We call ourselves the Sentinels. We watch and we record what we see."

"We watch more than just fixer society. We watch in the political and scientific realms as well. Lately, that has been our focus," said the man, "our secret focus. We would like you to join us. We don't know why the Forevers are interested in you, but we do know that they have gone to extremes to test you. We also know that they are a very secret cabal made up of scientists and politicians. They will go to any lengths to keep their activities from becoming public."

"We want you to work for us, but we also want to protect you. You may be in much more danger without us than with us. We think this will be a mutually beneficial relationship," said the woman.

"Are you willing to join us?" asked the man.

Jayne looked at the man and then to the woman and back again. She fingered the star hanging from her neck. She took a deep breath to pose the question inwardly and then made up her mind on the exhale. She nodded to the woman and tucked the silver star under her clothing. It felt warm against her skin.

The woman smiled and said, "Good. We need to get you reassigned. We will support an application by you to the Biome Tech Program. With your skills in TechElecMech, it will not be difficult. They might suspect something, so be prepared for some..." she paused and quickly continued, "odd occurrences."

"Odd occurrences?" echoed Jayne. "What does that mean?" "Well, if they stay "true to form," they will want to test and scan you. They are particularly fond of connectome scans. We have not really figured out why, but the possibilities are rather macabre," said the man.

Jayne swallowed. "How do I contact you?" she asked.

The man and the woman looked at each other and back at Jayne. "You can't," they said in unison.

The woman continued, "It is far too dangerous for our purpose to have any uncontrolled communication between the Sentinel home and Sentinel satellites. You are now a Sentinel satellite. All you need to do is observe and remember. Occasionally, we will need to brief or debrief you. Only then will you report. If you see this symbol, we are responsible." On a sheet of magnetic scribe, she drew, with her finger, a small oval with a dash in the middle.

Θ

It was the Greek letter theta. She held it up for Jayne. Jayne watched as the symbol slowly faded.

CHAPTER 16

A Trip to the Neuroscience Center

Governance changed. The planet became a single political entity. Humans had to cooperate if they were to survive. All citizens on the planet had equal rights. No one would go without food or shelter. No one would go without proper medical care and adequate education. Everyone had to work together if the species was to survive. At least, that is how the propaganda engines spun it.

Reality sketched a different picture. There were those who sought absolute power to further their insidious purpose. That purpose had not changed since the cavemen learned how to make fire. They wanted power for power's sake, and they wanted it forever. Literally.

Jayne woke up in her quarters. She sat up in bed. It was morning. The room had not changed in her absence. She could smell food and looked at the table. Breakfast was set.

"Good morning, Thirteen," crooned Lucky. "Breakfast is ready. I see you have applied for reassignment. Are you bored with TEM apprenticeship?"

Jayne smiled and then frowned. She thought it odd that Lucky didn't ask her where she had been for the last three days. Lucky was nosey that way. She wondered if perhaps a little reprogramming had occurred. The Sentinels told her that they could not be directly involved in changing her assignment without risking exposure. In fact, she was told that they could not intercede at all. She was to do it on her own. All they could do was make recommendations that would be mutually beneficial.

Applying for Biome Tech was first on the list. Biome Techs were the apex of the fixer class. It was deemed the most difficult and dangerous job of all. It was even more difficult than High Wire Tech. Those were the fixers who maintained the spavators from the counterweight down to the space platform in Geostationary Earth Orbit (GEO). They lived on the space platform 35,000 km up and worked the cable all the way up to the counterweight at 100,000 km above the surface of the Earth, directly above the biome HUB at the base.

Biome Techs maintained the biomes. These huge habitats orbited the earth. They were designed and built in stages. Some of the final stages were begun just recently. The biomes were slowly being turned into biome ships that could travel to their designated habitable planets. During the trip, the inhabitants would 'transmute' into humans that could flourish on the new planet. The process had been developed as a sort of accelerated form of evolution involving genetic and environmentally compatible transformations, EGET (eee get) for short.

Genetic scientists introduced specific mutations supported by gene splicing to stimulate physical changes in the omies. The environmental scientists created a biome that would gradually mimic the environment of the new planet. It was thought that these two processes would vastly improve the chances of survival for Omies on their new planet.

You couldn't apprentice to become a Biome Tech. You could, however, apply, once you proved yourself in one of the other tech areas. A tech apprentice was a very unlikely candidate, even one of Jayne's ability. Jayne researched the records. She could find no examples of anyone her age being accepted into the Biome Tech program. She felt the silver star grow warm against her skin and thought of the watcher. That was her name for the person, or persons, she sensed observing her. She also thought they directed her to the Luck Games Room and her appointment with Professor Greenway.

Lucky spoke again. "Jayne, are you alright? You seem…" Lucky paused, "…distracted."

"I'm fine. I am just wondering if I will be accepted," said Jayne. "You will be. Your test and practical scores have been exemplary. I would recommend you," Lucky said smugly. "I looked up the scores of some of the previous inductees and you have them all beat. But it is not just based on scores. There seem to be other considerations."

"Such as?" asked Jayne.

"Well, some specific scans. I do not understand why they would be deemed necessary for the job, but, apparently, they are," said Lucky.

"Let me guess," said Jayne, thinking of Professor Greenway again, "— connectome scans."

"You have been scheduled for a series of connectome scans this morning. How did you know?" asked Lucky.

"With Greenway?" Jayne asked.

"Who is Greenway?" Lucky replied. "Just a moment. I will check. You are to report to the Neuroscience Center and Training Facility today."

"Where is that?" asked Jayne, concern creeping into her voice. The Neuroscience Center sounded like a very unpleasant place to visit.

"Well, it is not here in the HUB. It is seriously out of PUT pad range. You will have to take a flier. You leave today," said Lucky, and then he paused. "It looks like there will be two of you going. At least there have been two bookings made."

"Who else is going?" asked Jayne.

"I am sorry, but I am not privy to that information. It has been blocked," replied Lucky.

"When do I leave?" asked Jayne.

"An hour from now," answered Lucky matter-of-factly.

Jayne stood up and ran to the clothes drawer. "I have to pack."

"Not required," stated Lucky. "According to the reservation, you are to leave immediately. You are to take a PUT pad to Flier Station 3. I will program the PUT."

Jayne stood and walked out of her quarters to the hall PUT pad. She stepped on it and breathed in deeply. She thought of the Sentinels and the Forevers and of puking and of human hearts in boxes and of murdered Omies and of GravBall and, finally, of Joseph following her like a puppy. That made her laugh. She stopped laughing when her nose, not quite healed, twinged with pain. She thought of Joseph pushing her into the line-vac that was not a line-vac. She frowned as she stepped off the PUT pad in Flier Station 3. She would make him pay for that push.

The fliers were totally automated. They used gravity (grav) propulsion. All fliers flew between 1,000 and 2,000 meters from the ground. Their flight path was designated by a flight computer system. They traveled like a train along a monorail, except the monorail was digital and dynamic. They were fast and silent.

Jayne entered a thirteen-seater with three sets of three seats, an aisle down the middle, and a back row of 4 seats. She slid into the back row. She had never been in a flier before. She had never traveled very far. For short distances, the PUT pads were all that anyone needed. As the time ticked down to departure, she thought she was going to be alone on her two-hour flight, despite what Lucky had predicted. She looked out the window and saw a boy running down the platform, up the gangway, and onto her flier. Jayne slid down in her seat. She would be invisible to anyone entering the flier. The boy, out of breath, flopped down in the front set of two seats. He tossed the small bag he was carrying onto the seat across the aisle from where he was sitting. He exhaled loudly and said, "Made it."

Jayne peeked out the side of her seat and looked down the aisle. All she could see was a pair of feet sticking out from the seats that held the reclining boy. He moved and Jayne ducked back out of sight. Jayne peeked between the seats and could see a head of dark ruffled hair. She blinked and looked again. He turned and she could only see the back of his head.

He became alert and scanned the cabin.

She ducked out of sight again. Jayne could hear him opening his bag, so she peeked down the aisle again. The boy was reaching into his bag.

Suddenly, he stopped and froze.

Jayne ducked back. There was silence. The silence seemed to go on forever. Jayne could wait no longer. She slowly stuck her head out into the aisle. Her eyes grew wide as she stared into the wide eyes of the boy looking down the aisle at her.

They both stood and looked quickly from side to side, as if searching for an escape route. But they both knew there was no escape.

Jayne recognized the dark-haired boy from the bean bag game. Number 91. She never knew his name.

The dark-haired boy recognized Jayne. Fear clouded his eyes, but it soon dissipated and was replaced by anger. "What the hell are you doing here?" he spat. "I am not sure what you did to me that day in the Psi Center, but you sure are not going to do it again. After I looked at you, it was all gone. You somehow sucked it all out of me and took it for yourself."

Jayne pulled her head back behind the protection of her seat. Her body tensed. Questions rumbled through her mind. What was he talking about? She had not taken anything from him. Was he sick? Had one of the bean bags caused permanent damage? Was he going to the Neuroscience Center too? Maybe he suffered brain damage. She remembered one of the bean bags hitting him in the head.

She heard him start down the aisle toward her. She stood up. The idea of him standing over her was an unpleasant one. They stood facing each other with the width of one seat between them.

Jayne did not know what to say. She spoke anyway. "I'm sorry you got hit. Is your head okay?"

"What are you talking about? Does my head not look okay!?" he asked, his eyes in a vicious squint.

Jayne stepped backward for a moment and then forward again. "You must be deluded. I never took anything from you. That day, playing the bean bag game, you made a wrong choice and got hit. I made a wrong choice right after you left and got hit. That's just the way it goes sometimes. Sometimes you're lucky and sometimes you're not."

"I am always lucky unless you are around. And, no, I do not have a head injury. I am going to the Neuroscience Center because I am being sent there. Why are you going?"

"I have no idea. I am being sent there too," she answered. "I had nothing to do with you being hit, so don't go blaming me. What is your name, anyway? Mine's Jayne Wu. My friends call me Thirteen."

"Alright, Thirteen, I'm 91. That is as much as you get to know," he said, menacingly pointing his finger at her face. He was wearing a silver chain around his wrist. Dangling from the chain was a silver star, slightly smaller than the one around Jayne's neck.

She instinctively reached up and placed her hand over her star. It was almost hot against her skin. She looked from the star to his face and back again. "He is being watched by THEM just like me," she thought as he dropped his arm, concealing the star once again.

"Alright, I get it. You hate me because you think I did something to you. Which I didn't. So, let's agree not to have any more conversations, especially those that end up with you threatening me. You sit up there, and I will sit back here. Hopefully, this will be the last time we see each other. But somehow, I doubt that will be the case," Jayne warned.

"Why do you say that? After all, I am still pretty lucky," he said with a smirk.

Jayne shrugged and turned back to her seat and sat down. She stared at his back as he walked to the front of the flier and sat down. She muttered to herself, "Not as lucky as you think. Not with that star on your wrist."

They spent the remainder of the trip in silence. Jayne could not help but wonder if 91's star made him sick when he took it off. Were the

Forevers reading him too? Did the Sentinels know about him? Were they going to the same place for the same reasons?

She closed her eyes and only opened them again when the flier arrived.

CHAPTER 17

Tests & Scans

Education is critical in a Fixer's world. It meant freedom and choices. Without it, you were assigned the most menial of jobs, usually Fxer cleaner if you are male or older female. Everyone had to work. There was no choice. Work was deemed critical to the survival of the species. If you chose not to work—and there were some who did—you were exiled to the Wilderlands and received none of the societal benefits. If you changed your mind, you would always be welcomed back, as long as you were willing to become a functioning member of the Fixer society.

Education was always available—if you could prove yourself able. Sometimes the requirements were difficult. Tech was very difficult and Biome Tech was the most difficult of all.

Jayne and 91 exited the flier without so much as an acknowledgment of each other's existence. They were individually directed to specific testing rooms in the neuroscience facility. Jayne, once alone, relaxed and waited. Her clothes were draped over a chair. She was dressed in a hospital gown. It was far from flattering. She was lying on her side, propped up on one elbow on the examining table while she waited for someone to arrive. A young man entered with a MED VID in his hands.

He looked at her, looked at his VID and looked back at her and spoke. "Who are you?"

Before Jayne could answer, he spoke again. "Are you Ranovich 91?" He looked up at Jayne. "No, I suppose not. It says male. You're not male, are you? No," he said, answering his own question. He swept the surface of his MED VID a few times, and then he studied the screen. He looked up again and stared at her. He spoke, "You must be..." he paused and looked down again, "yes, you must be. What are you doing here? Get dressed. I will be back in two minutes." He turned and left the room.

Jayne got up and quickly put her clothes on, all the while keeping an eye on the door. Once dressed, she sat on the bed and waited. Ranovich 91, she thought, that must be his name.

A few minutes later, a woman came into the room. "Why are you still dressed? Didn't they tell you to put on the gown?" She gestured to the gown now on the back of the chair. "Well, never mind. Roll up your sleeve. I need to take your vitals and some blood, and you need to fill this." She took an empty vial out of her pocket and waved it in front of Jayne. "Now, let's make sure you are who you are supposed to be. Look here," she commanded, holding up a handheld retinal scanner.

Jayne looked into it. There was a flash of light. The woman looked at the scanner and nodded. She took Jayne's vital signs and a few vials of blood. A few minutes later, Jayne was alone again, lying on the bed, propped up on her elbow—waiting.

The young man came back and spoke. "Wu 13?" Jayne nodded.

"Come with me. I am sorry for the mix-up. Did you get your vitals taken?"

Jayne nodded again.

"Good, follow me." He strode out of the room and down a hall to a larger room with several smaller windowed rooms around its perimeter. The dark-haired boy, Ranovich 91, was sitting in one of the rooms. Jayne could see him through the window as she passed. He was craning his neck out from his sitting position in a chair, trying to see out the door of the room. He looked silly.

The man took Jayne to one of the rooms and sat her in a large, comfortable, medical chair that tilted and rotated in any direction.

As soon as Jayne sat, the chair formed around her. If she shifted, the chair seemed to compensate for the changes in position. Jayne also noticed a section of the arm that probably held concealed restraints. She did not put her arms down on the armrests. She placed her arms in her lap and waited. The window into the room was mirrored on the inside, so she could not see out, but anyone could see in. She now realized why 91 was craning to see out the door. She relaxed and became 'nondescript'. It was a good way to be if you couldn't hide and you did not want to be noticed. At this moment, Jayne really did not want to be noticed.

An older man entered the room. He was trying to be personable. He smiled. "Jayne, I am Dr. Thermonson. We are going to spend the afternoon together, running a few tests. There is nothing stressful about any of them. In fact, they can be kind of fun. Some of the tests will have someone in the room with you and some will not. Sometimes, we will let you handle some small props and other times we will require you to look at images on the screen in front of you. The screen can be a mirror or a window, or a video. Right now, it is a mirror, as you can see." He gestured to the mirror in front of Jayne.

"A one-sided mirror," stated Jayne.

"Yes," said the doctor. He frowned and asked, "Does that bother you?"

"A little," said Jayne. "It would be better if it was either a window or a mirror on both sides. Are there any cameras in this room?"

"Yes. Do they bother you?" asked the doctor. "Yes," answered Jayne.

"You don't like being watched?" he asked.

"I don't mind being watched, as long as I can see the watcher," answered Jayne.

"Fair enough. I cannot shut off the cameras for recordings are required but I can make the viewport a window. When we need the viewport as a video screen, I will invite any observers to come into the room. Are you okay with that arrangement?" he asked.

Jayne was surprised by this. In her experience, people in positions of authority did whatever they wanted and never considered her needs, wants, or feelings. She nodded.

"I have to set this scanner array on your head," he said, as he picked up something from the small table behind her chair. He held it out in front of her. It looked like a gray skull cap. "It has a series of scanners that move over its surface during each test. It measures, records, and transmits specific brain activities."

Jayne nodded again and said, "Like the connectome scan that Professor Greenway gave me a few months ago. He used a scanner that was different from that. It was smaller and was not attached to a skullcap like this one."

"Who?" asked the doctor.

"Professor Greenway. He gave me what he called a connectome scan," she answered.

"You must be mistaken. The only place you could ever have received a connectome scan is here. We are one of two facilities on this continent that have the ability to record and read a true connectome scan. I have never heard of a Professor Greenway," he said with an increasing level of irritation.

"Well…" said Jayne, about to argue. She paused and then decided not to threaten this positive relationship with Dr. Thermonson. She continued, "I probably heard wrong." And then, to further distract, she asked, "Does it hurt?"

Dr. Thermonson smiled and spoke. "Not in the slightest. Shall we get started?" It was not a question. It was simply a statement of what was to happen next.

He spoke into his MED VID, "Subject—Wu F 302875106592253 aka Jayne Wu; Test 1—Zener cards—No sender." He turned to Jayne and handed her five cards with one symbol on each. He held an identical set of cards in his hand. "The cards look like this," he said as he displayed the cards in his hand.

Jayne fanned the cards he had given her. They were identical to the cards he showed her. "They are called Zener Cards, named after the man who invented them, Karl Zener. They were originally used to measure psychic ability. They are rarely used for that specific purpose alone, but in conjunction with a connectome scan, they can be..." he paused, "informative. I will shuffle these cards; pick one from the pile and set it face down on this video scanner. I will not look at it. You will try to match my card by placing a card from your hand face up on the table. I will record your card and the video scanner will record the object card. I will not look at the object card. We will continue for 10 trials. Do you have any questions?"

"Yes. Will you tell me if I make correct guesses?" asked Jayne. "Perhaps I will tell you later. I won't know until after all the tests are over," he said. He reached and put the skull cap on Jayne. He adjusted a few controls and the skull cap warmed on Jayne's head. He pulled a cantilevered table over the chair so she could place her cards on it. "Ready?"

She wiggled to get comfortable, and the chair reformed itself to her new position. She wiggled again, and again the chair responded. She nodded.

The doctor took a card from his pile and placed it on the scanner. She smiled and grabbed the wiggly line picture from her pile and snapped it down on the table in front of her.

"My 'wiggly lines' beat your card, whatever it is," she said with a giggle.

The doctor recorded this on his MED VID. He repeated his actions after a short shuffle.

Jayne responded with, "Gin, I win," and another giggle as she snapped down the square on the table.

The doctor looked at her and said, "Gin?" Jayne said, "It's a card game."

He shrugged.

Jayne mumbled under her breath, "Don't get out much, do you?"

The test continued for 10 trials. During and after each of Jayne's guesses, the skull cap scanners buzzed about her head. Finally, it was finished.

"Good," said the doctor. "We have to do this three more times under three different conditions. There will be three different senders. Those are entities that will see or know the cards you are trying to match. First will be the MAIU (Medical Artificial Intelligence Unit), second will be my assistant, Millie, and third will be an unknown sender. Do you understand?"

Jayne nodded.

"I would like you to be a little more serious this time, though. No more giggles."

The doctor attended to his MED VID and the window video screen displayed the following:

Zener Test 2: Computer Sender ID: Wu F 302875106592253

Name: Wu, Jayne Esther Class—Fixer

Touch to Start

"Are you ready?" he asked. Jayne nodded.

He touched the screen, and the MAIU responded orally, "I am sending the first card. Please choose one card from the five Zener Cards you have in front of you that you think matches the card I am sending."

"Is that AIU going to say that whole line for each of the ten trials?" asked Jayne.

"The MAIU has the latest AI programming. It can pretty much answer that itself," said the doctor.

"Jayne, if I understand the intent of your question, you feel it would get tedious for me to continue in formal testing mode and would rather I choose a colloquial format," said the MAIU.

"Yes, I just don't want to spend my life in here," answered Jayne. "Yes, time is important. Are you ready to continue or would you like me to choose a new first card to send?" the MAIU asked.

"No, the one you have is fine," said Jayne as she snapped the card with wiggly lines on the table. The scanners on her head buzzed and roamed over the surface.

"Is that your final choice?" the MAIU asked. "Yes, it is my final response," snapped Jayne. The doctor recorded her response.

The MAIU said, "Card two."

Jayne immediately flipped over a square and began to tap her fingers on the table in front of her.

The doctor recorded the response. The MAIU said, "Card three." Jayne chose the wiggly lines again.

The doctor interjected, "Ms. Wu, you must take this seriously. You are not even concentrating."

The MAIU spoke up. "Dr. Thermonson, I don't think it is a matter of concentration. Please let us continue. Card four."

Jayne flipped over her response. This continued at a fast pace and was soon complete. Ten cards were chosen by the MAIU and ten of Jayne's responses were recorded by the doctor, followed by the frenzied buzzing of the recording units on the skullcap on Jayne's head. No one knew the accuracy of her responses at this time, except perhaps the MAIU. Jayne did not even ask.

The MAIU spoke. "The test is now complete. Goodbye."

The video screen turned back into a window. A small blonde woman entered, carrying a chair. She set the chair in the corner of the room in front of a small table, looked at Jayne, smiled and said, "My name is Millie, and I will send for the third part of the test."

Jayne nodded.

"Do you need a drink of water or anything before we start?" asked Millie.

Jayne shook her head.

The woman turned and sat in the chair facing into the corner, took out a MED VID and a set of Zener Cards. "So as not to influence your choices, I cannot see your cards. They will be recorded by Dr. Thermonson and the cards I choose will be recorded by me in this MED VID. No one will know what you have chosen until all the tests are completed. If you are ready, we will start."

Jayne nodded, then said, "Yes, Millie, I am ready." The buzzing of the skull cap scanners was becoming irritating.

"I am sending card one."

Jayne flipped a card over almost before Millie finished the sentence. "Done," she called out.

The cards were recorded. The process continued at a fast pace until they completed card seven.

Jayne raised her hand.

The doctor responded with, "Yes, Jayne."

Jayne asked, "May I borrow that for a moment?" She pointed at the stylus that was in the breast pocket of his lab coat.

He shrugged and gave it to her.

Jayne quickly glanced at the five cards in her hand. She chose three of them, flipped them face down in front of her and wrote the numbers 8, 9, and 10 on the back of them. Her skull cap sensors were madly zooming over its surface as she did so. She looked up and said, "Please flip the card that corresponds to the question number Millie is going to send."

"That is not how this test is run," said the doctor. "Please concentrate and follow protocol."

Jayne, feeling contrary, simply folded her arms and closed her eyes. The scanners on her skull cap slowed down and stopped. It was quiet in the room.

Dr. Thermonson sighed, shook his head and asked Millie to continue.

"I am sending card eight," said Millie.

Dr. Thermonson flipped the card with an 8 on the back and recorded it.

Millie recorded her card and said, "I am sending card nine."

The process continued until all cards were sent and recorded. The skull cap sensors remained quiet throughout the last three cards.

"Alright, Jayne," said the doctor, "we have one more sequence. We will use the window video screen to inform you when the sender has started. You may choose your card after, and you may not do again what you just did. Is that understood? You must respect the process."

Jayne rolled her eyes and nodded.

He turned to Millie and said, "Get the sender ready."

She exited just as the window video screen displayed the information as before.

"Who is the sender?" asked Jayne.

"Miss Wu, you will not be told that information. Please, let us finish the test," the doctor said with an exasperated sigh.

The video screen displayed, 'Sending card one.'

Jayne picked up the cards, fanned them out on the table, and stared at them. She tapped her fingers impatiently. The skull cap scanners buzzed over her head. She looked up at the doctor. "Is this a trick?" she asked.

"No trick. Why do you ask?" queried the doctor.

"YOU really didn't set this up?" she asked again. She thought of the dark-haired boy. Ranovich 91 was on the flier. This was something he would do. "Well, somebody thinks it is funny to… never mind. Let's go."

She flipped over the card with the 'O' symbol and sat back and stretched her hands out in front of her, inverting her intertwined fingers. Her knuckles cracked. The scanners stopped.

The video screen displayed: 'Sending card two'. Jayne pointed at the 'O' symbol. The doctor recorded her answer.

"I know a way we could save a little time here."

"How could we save some time, Miss Wu?" asked the doctor with an exasperated tone.

"Just put that symbol," she pointed at the 'O' symbol face up on the table, "for all the answers."

"Miss Wu, please, please proceed through the process properly," he sighed and shrugged and gestured with his hands.

"Okay," said Jayne. The video screen displayed, 'Sending card three.' Jayne pointed at 'O' symbol.

The video screen displayed: 'Sending card four.' Jayne pointed at 'O' symbol.

This continued for the remaining seven cards. According to Jayne, every card that was sent was an 'O' symbol. The scanners remained silent. When they were finished, the doctor left the room and Millie came into the room and removed the skullcap and sensor apparatus from her head. Jayne got out of the chair and stretched.

The doctor returned and spoke to Millie. "I am sorry, Millie, but an additional test has been ordered. Would you please reconnect the skull cap?"

"But, Doctor, there have been no additional tests ordered for this subject," she said, checking her MED VID.

"Just do what I say, Millie," he ordered. The doctor turned to Jayne. "We have one more test. You will be given a set of cards and you will send to an unknown subject. The procedure will be the same for this subject as it was for you. Do you understand?" he asked.

Jayne nodded. "Who is it?" she asked.

"Who is it?" the doctor queried what she meant by her question. "Who is the subject? To whom am I sending the card image?" asked Jayne formally. "I can't send something to the ether. I need to know the receiver."

"I am afraid you will just have to envision the card and not worry about the identity of the receiving subject," stated the doctor flatly. "Here are the cards." He handed her a set of Zener Cards. "The MAIU will tell you when to start and when to stop. I will not be in this room."

The doctor walked out of the room and the MAIU started up. "Millie," the MAIU spoke softly, "would you please make some

adjustments to the skull cap? I am not getting a recognition signal from scanner three."

Millie adjusted the cap and connections on Jayne's head.

"Thank you. I have a signal. Now, Jayne, would you please choose a card and concentrate," said the MAIU, as Millie exited the room.

Jayne picked up one of the cards and looked at it.

"This won't work unless I think about the person to whom I am sending this picture," said Jayne flatly. "I am just going to choose someone." She looked at the card with the star and thought of Ranovich 91, the boy from the bean bag game and the flier. She concentrated on the boy in the other room. She smiled, relaxed, squinted her eyes, and concentrated harder on the picture. She imagined it as a solid object travelling through space, one point stretching out like an arrow and whizzing to the mind of Ranovich 91. She felt it land right where she aimed. She felt the scanners buzzing like maddened hornets on the skullcap. She heard a scream from outside her small room. The scream was followed by a series of moans, and she heard the words 'make it stop' and 'it is hurting me' and someone crying with pain. There were footsteps running to the source of the crying. She stopped and sat up just as Millie ran into the room and quickly removed the skull cap from Jayne's head.

The other room was silent. Jayne sat up just as the doctor entered the room, removing a scanner skull cap from his head. He looked at Jayne with fear in his eyes. "That's all for today. You may return to your quarters in HUB..." he glanced down at his VID, "169."

"What was all the screaming about?" asked Jayne. "It sounded like a torture chamber."

"That is none of your concern. All testing is now over," he stated sharply.

"So that's it. No feedback on how I did with your guessing game," Jayne taunted.

"Don't be so arrogant. You know damn well how you did. You got them all correct. You were correct on the last 10. They were all the same. Not my idea, by the way. We will set up another appointment after the scan data has been analyzed. Now go!" he ordered.

Jayne turned to leave and then turned back. "I can't read minds, you know. It is just luck. I am lucky, really lucky. That is just the way it is. I just know what it will be—whatever it is—and I am usually right. I have kinda learned to trust my luck."

The doctor said, "Be careful trusting luck. It is my experience that luck is not to be trusted. It is rather fickle." He walked out of the room.

Millie escorted Jayne out of the room. Jayne turned and glanced over to where the dark-haired boy had been sitting. The chair was now empty.

CHAPTER 18

Biome Tech

By the mid-21st century, sociologists identified the concept of 'The Family' as the single most negative influence on a stable and productive society. The 'Nuclear Family' of the century before was no longer a beneficial social structure. Families were not working as a positive societal unit. Although they still existed, they were marginalized. The important task of raising and educating children was put in the hands of government-assigned professionals. 'The Nursery' was born.

Jayne received her acceptance the following morning. It came as an announcement from Lucky. He woke her up with, "Thirteen, it is time to wake up. I have received your schedule. Things have changed. You are to report to the Biome Tech Center."

Jayne groaned. Her sleep had been fitful, filled with gigantic bean bags with ugly faces, whizzing down, trying to crush her as she ran down a high grav line. She groaned again. "What time is it? I just got to sleep. Be quiet and go away."

"I cannot go away. It is 6:13 a.m. I know you have not had the required eight hours of sleep recommended for a person your age but—"

"Then go away and let me sleep," moaned Jayne as she rolled over and pulled the pillow over her ears.

"I am sorry, Thirteen, but I am being overridden," apologized Lucky. The next voice Jayne heard was not Lucky. "Wu 13, you are to report immediately to the PUT outside these quarters. You have three minutes to obey or your application to join Biome Tech will be rescinded."

Jayne leaped from the bed, dashed to the bathroom, returned in record time, got dressed, and stepped out of her quarters and onto the PUT pad. Her heart was pounding with excitement and a little fear.

She exited the PUT alcove and looked up at the sign in front of her. It read 'Biome Technical Institute' and below, in smaller letters, was the motto of the school. 'Omnes intrare sciens nihil et relinquere sciens paulo' translates to 'All enter knowing nothing and leave knowing little more.'

A voice behind her spoke. "Do you find that motto puzzling?"

Jayne turned around and looked at a girl about five years her senior.

"I've been here for two years and I am just beginning to understand what they are getting at." She gestured to a series of bas-relief sculptures of men and women carved to the side of the entrance who obviously were revered at this school. "It kinda means that there is so much to know, that to know a little really is an achievement. I'm Sara. They sent me to get you and take you to the dorm. You don't get your own quarters here. We are not like the other tech schools. It is tougher here. We have the highest washout rate of all. Sometimes I think the instructors get a bonus for every student who washes out. I have nearly gone twice. Once when I lost these." She held up her left hand with two fingers missing. "And once when I got this little baby." She lifted up her tunic top and exposed a red mottled scar, 20 cm long, running down the side of her torso.

Jayne did not respond.

The girl continued, "I noticed you didn't grimace when I showed you my battle scars. My advice to you is to grimace whenever you get the chance. Acting tough will get you hurt or worse. React to the nasty things whenever possible because there will be times when you won't be able to. Reacting then will get you killed. So, do it when you can. It keeps you human. Believe me, after a year in here you will start to wonder if you are anymore."

"Are you trying to frighten me?" asked Jayne.

"Yep! And you can thank me for that service any time you want. In here, they say your own fear is your most powerful weapon—if you can learn to control it. I had an instructor my first year who was a wise, old, scarred bastard. He once told me that he never really controlled his fear. He just let it run all over him whenever it wanted. The more afraid he was, the more likely he would get to go home. So he let fear order him about. He said it was his secret to survival, and not to listen to the other instructors when they talked about controlling fear. Controlling fear was for situations when there was nothing really to be afraid of. The biomes are filled with things that are truly fear inducing, and you had better be afraid of them or you'll die. I haven't decided if he was right or not." She smiled. "I've only got a couple of scars. So what's your name?"

Jayne was about to respond when she felt an urge to step backwards and protect herself. All the muscles in her stomach tensed until they were as hard as she could make them. She looked at Sara and saw a slight twitch in the muscle of her jaw. She did not look but knew that Sara was tensing the fingers of her right hand. Jayne did not want to give it away. She did not want to be known as the 'Lucky Kid,' so she spoke her name, "Jayne," and tensed her stomach muscles as tight as she could get them. Then Sara punched her right in the solar plexus. Jayne let out a groan that was partly due to being punched really hard in the stomach and partly due to the need to relax her tense muscles. She decided she would not fall down, even though her body said to fall down, clutch herself, and cry. She just buckled over and held her stomach. After the initial hit, she realized she had really protected herself. Nothing was damaged and nothing really hurt.

She slowly stood up and yelled at Sara, "What did you do that for!?"
"Well, Jayne, I was just following procedure. You will hear that a lot around here," she said, grinning, "and by the way, you can really take a punch. It was almost like you knew it was coming. But nobody expects to be punched on their first day here. I sure wasn't, but it is standard procedure. Punch the newbie in the guts as hard as you can. Maybe she

will cry and go home."

"I'm not going anywhere except to the dorm to get settled. Where is it—or is finding it another stupid test?" Jayne said as she walked into the school.

"No more tests or punches," said Sara. "Follow me. Your bunk is right next to mine." She led Jayne through the foyer, down a hall, and into a dorm room. She indicated a bunk and said, "That's yours. You will also find all your required equipment in that locker there." Sara pointed to locker 13. "I understand that is your nickname, Thirteen, so we saw that locker 13 was empty." She shrugged.

Jayne looked at the locker. It was more like mini quarters than a locker. She wondered what it held.

"It's big," she said.

"Yep. There is a lot of equipment you will have to learn to use. It is all specifically fitted to you and only you." Sara eyed Jayne up and down. "I hope you are stronger than you look 'cause the equipment is really heavy and anti-grav units are not allowed while you are in training."

"I will be fine," said Jayne.

"From what I have heard, I'm sure you will. Oh, that reminds me, my crew wanted me to ask you if you will play. Will you?" Sara asked.

Jayne played dumb. "Play what?"

"Don't be cute. You know damn well what I am talking about. And don't try to pretend you were not the kid who did that fancy loop over the center pipe in that 'drop-in' game the day of the lockdown. We got a newbie last month who couldn't stop going on about it. He said he was playing on the same team as you and he was totally grav'd about it." She paused. "Well, if you are her, and I think you are, will you play on our team? We are called Home Grown Panic. We're not the best in the league, but we're not the worst either. We could sure use a fast BC. That is, if you are who I think you are," babbled Sara.

"What's the kid's name?" asked Jayne. "What kid?" asked Sara.

"Did this kid who said he played GravBall with me have a little horse-tail sticking out of the top of his head?" asked Jayne.

"I think so," said Sara. Jayne smiled.

"And just so you know, the GravBall league is taken very seriously. It is actually part of our training. A lot of the biomes have gravity variances so the omies can develop their bodies to cope on the new planets. So, we have to cope without those genetic enhancements 'cause we have to go into the biomes and work. We're the biome fixers (BFs) and we're the best, Huu—Rah!" She giggled and plopped down on her bunk.

"Ever been to one of the biomes?" asked Jayne.

"Not yet, but soon. I have to pass the ElecMech exam first. I hate that exam. It is a real dog," complained Sara.

"What do you have to complete before they will let you go on a mission?" asked Jayne.

"Check your VID. It will tell you," said Sara.

Jayne took out her VID and immediately noticed a major update. She barely had any of the apps she was used to. The main page was filled with the Biome Tech Institute logo. She touched the VID lock, and the screen displayed a smaller Biome Tech logo. She touched it and a list of her courses was presented:

1. Biome 3 Mini Pods
2. Weapons
3. Combat

She showed Sara the VID list. "What are biome mini-pods? What do we study about Biome 3? Isn't that the jungle biome?" she asked. "Yep. There are six mini-pods that have environments identical to Biome 3's. They run simulations that will give us the experience of the real thing. They are just as dangerous, but smaller, and somewhat controlled. They can still kill you in a heartbeat if you do something stupid. The trick is not to…" She stared at Jayne's VID with dismay. "How come you don't have to take ElecMech?"

"I have already passed the exam," answered Jayne casually.

"Damn! I've been working toward passing that exam for almost two years and you walk in here with it already under your belt. Damn!" Sara cursed. Then her eyes brightened. "I'll tell you what, girly, I will help you by giving out some tips on those courses if you help me get through ElecMech," she said, indicating the list on the VID in Jayne's hand. "Some of them can be very nasty. I sure wish someone had helped me get through Combat. So, is it a deal?"

Jayne nodded, "Deal. Now what about Biome 3? What am I to expect?"

"Well," said Sara with a smirk on her face, "imagine every creepy, crawly, leaping, flying, jumping, biting, stinging, scratching…I could go on here…creature of every size and shape that has ever invaded your nightmares and that is Biome 3. But those aren't the dangerous ones. The really bad ones are what you cannot see. Besides that, it is hot and wet and all jungle. Gravity and oxygen are a little above normal. All the omies in Biome 3 had to have some genes spliced into their DNA to supercharge their immune systems. It seems to be working for them, but those same genes have some very strange side effects on Omie children. The geneticists are working out ways to fix the problem. After all, we want to seed the universe populated with humans—not some other crazy creature."

"What kind of side effects?" asked Jayne.

"Well, I think they must have used alligator genes. That creature has the strongest immune system of any creature on the planet. I will let your imagination do the rest, though I doubt you can do it justice," she said with glee as she watched Jayne's face contort.

Jayne's VID began to beep. She glanced at it and read, 'Report to Lab 2 for Biome 3 Studies.' "Where is Lab 2?" she asked.

"I have no idea. No one knows where anything is here. It is kept very secure by just directing people to a PUT pad and then dropping them off at the right place," said Sara, just as her VID beeped. She looked at it with disdain. "I'm off to ElecMech tutorials. How exciting!"

They walked together in silence to the PUT pads.

CHAPTER 19
Mini Biomes

The world embraced a new kind of governance dubbed 'Soccapism.' Some said it was a meld of the good in both socialism and capitalism, and the rejection of the bad. The adage 'everything in moderation' was adopted and applied to the commerce of the time.

The good in socialism was the sharing of resources. Everyone was fed, sheltered, and educated. Social medical systems looked after all members of society, not just the affluent few. Socialism was carried to an extreme in communist states. All property was owned by the state. Independent thought and the drive for creation and invention were discouraged. This seemed to stifle the biological urge of humans to excel. If there was nothing to be created, invented, or gained, why bother trying? All truly socialistic societies fell due to rampant corruption.

The beneficial aspect of capitalism was that it encouraged the primary urge to strive for success. People worked hard for personal gain. A portion of society prospered. The negative aspect of capitalism was the same as its positive aspect. Too much of a good thing can poison the host. Capitalism running wild resulted in a few very rich controlling a majority of very poor.

Both of these systems would inevitably result in insurrection and rebellion. So, the society now controlled the important social structures and made them available to everyone. It also controlled just how much an individual or a company could grow. When a commercial entity took in more than it gave back, the checks and balances process was enforced until the balance between giving and taking was attained. This enforcement did not stop the growing of huge enterprises, but it did make sure those enterprises benefitted the society as a whole in equal measure to their success.

Biome 3 was in need of constant repair and upgrading. The very nature of the environment was so complex that it required a Quantum Cray Computer running the latest artificial intelligence algorithms just to maintain the environment. That included every creature down to the last microbe. It was critical that the life processes that constantly encouraged natural selection through genetic mutations were kept within the calculated range of the target planet. That is to say, the biome environment must be controlled. It must not go off on its own to do its own thing. It must do what it was told and not anything else. That was a tall order, even for the latest model Quantum Cray Computer. Its side job was to tell the Biome Techs what equipment was broken, where it was located, the safest route, and the best repair procedure once inside a biome repair port.

Jayne's first day was like going back to grade school. As she sat in front of the 'standard-issue' tech video, she was frustrated to realize she'd learned all of this almost 10 years ago.

She flipped through, speed reading the 1,000 or so pages that made up the biome introduction, quickly completing the comprehension test. It was not difficult. She reached the end and sat back, then waited. The room seemed to be created for at least 30 students, but she was the only one there.

An older woman entered, walked up to her and spoke. "I see you are finished. I'm glad you were able to finish so quickly. My name is Winchell, Winchell 43. I am your supervisor. You are starting the course load at a bit of a disadvantage. All the other students have already started their practicum in the mini-biomes. Would you like to join them?"

Jayne smiled, stood up, and nodded her head.

"Well then, let's get you started. I think you should start with filter replacement. Report to a PUT and it will send you to your locker. Find the hazmat suit. It should fit you, but if it doesn't, please report it. Never use a suit that does not fit you. That is the best way I know to get killed."

Jayne's eyes widened.

The woman laughed. "I don't mean literally. In biome training you get nine lives. If you do, or neglect to do, something that would get you killed in the real biome. It counts against you, and you lose one of your lives. Lose three lives in any practice session and you wash out of that section. If you lose all of your nine lives, you wash out of the whole program. We don't want to send anyone into Biome 3 to get killed due to incompetence. That doesn't mean the mini-biomes are not dangerous. You can, and probably will, get a few scars."

"Don't worry. I'm pretty lucky. I won't wash out," said Jayne assuredly.

"Look, girly, if you are depending on luck to get you through, you might as well head back to the nursery and call it a day. This is serious business. Mistakes in there will kill you. A suit breech will kill you faster than anything else. The moment any of your biologicals enter the biome system, Q will send in the cleaners," Winchell said with disdain. She scrunched up her face and stuck out her white lips, as if she were going to kiss someone she did not want to kiss.

"Who is Q and what are the cleaners?" Jayne asked.

"The Quantum Cray Computer, aka 'Q', and the cleaners are the nanobots that maintain the environmental standards. If you were to take off your suit in this particular biome, the nanobots would see you as a serious threat to be neutralized. Nanobots neutralize alien biologicals by creating new and interesting proteins specifically designed to target and break the alien cells to their elemental components. It would take about four minutes for you to become a little pile of carbon with a sprinkling of calcium and a few other elements. All the gases, like oxygen and hydrogen, would simply blow away on the breeze. That is not a pleasant thought."

"Sorry," said Jayne. She chided herself for mentioning her luck. Everyone wanted to test her for it, but no one wanted to believe her when she used or depended on it. People are strange, she thought, as she stepped on the PUT pad and was whisked back to her locker. She took out her beeping VID and saw the list of material and equipment she would need for 'filter replacement'. She slung the bags over her shoulder and proceeded back to the PUT pads.

She was about to step on a PUT pad when Sara and two others appeared and stepped off the PUT pads on the way to their lockers. They were chatting and laughing with each other.

A tall, red-haired girl pointed at Sara and said, "You nearly didn't make it through the tunnels. I thought you were going to vomit when that rotting mass washed over us. Remember, 'Puke in your suit and they give you the boot.' I always squint and lock the odor generator. That way, I can't smell it or see it."

"Shut up, Josie. Just shut up or I'll squeal to Canker that you are locking the odor generator. That is not a good habit to get into," retorted Sara.

In a mini-biome pod, you didn't actually smell the real thing, you smelled a benign computer-generated version of the odor. Smelling the real thing could very well get you killed. To not smell it at all could also get you killed, hence the computer-generated odors.

"You shut up or I'll tell Winchell that you call her Canker," Josie spat back. Canker was their supervisor. She got the name partly due to the very light pink lip color she used and her tendency to purse her lips and scrunch up her face when she was irritated. It was a perfect name for such a painful person.

Jayne looked at the group. Sara saw her and smiled.

Josie looked at Jayne and turned to Sara and said, "Who's she?" "She's new," said Sara. "Guys, this is Jayne. Jayne, this is Josie and that really ugly girl there is Olive." Sara pointed at a very pretty girl with long dark hair in a ponytail.

Both Josie and Olive wiggled their fingers at Jayne. "Hi," they each said in turn.

"She plays GravBall. You remember the kid everyone was talking about a while back, the day of the lockdown—the one who did that move over the center grav line? Well, this is her."

Jayne blushed and said, "My friends call me Thirteen. It's my

136

nickname."

"I asked her if she would be on our team. The moment the other teams get wind of who she is, they will offer her the moon to get her to play for them." Sara turned to Jayne. "Well, have you given it some thought? Will you play for us?"

"Still thinking," said Jayne. Her VID beeped. She knew it was the signal to hurry and report. "Got to go," she said, and she stepped on the PUT pad.

She stepped off the PUT. She was deposited at the very center of a large hangar-type building. She looked up at the ceiling far above and then down at the floor far below. She was standing on a circular catwalk made of metal grating surrounded by a metal railing. She walked around it and stared down. She could see what looked like a gigantic snowflake on the ground below. The snowflake consisted of a central hub with a series of enclosed walkways that led to six mini-biomes. Along the covered walkways were a number of side branches. All the walkways were identical. As Jayne walked around the circular catwalk, she noticed two sets of circular stairs that spiraled downwards to the center hub. She walked down one of the stairways, never taking her eyes off the scene below. The 'snowflake' took up most of the building. Around the outer walls were shelves that extended right up to the ceiling. Jayne figured the shelves stored supplies. She watched a series of anti-grav transports remove crates from the high shelves and transport them to a FUT (Freight Unit Transport) pad.

As Jayne got closer to the floor, her view was obstructed by the walls of the hub. She soon stepped onto the ground and her VID beeped. It was displaying a map of the area in front of her with some simple directions indicating where to report. She followed the directions and found herself in a small locker room with benches at the center and an exit door at the far end that led to one of the covered walkways. She sat down and waited. She was about to check her VID again because no one came to tell her what she was to do, when she heard a locker door slam shut. She turned to see a person in a yellow hazmat suit step into view.

He was walking with jerky, stiff-legged steps, his arms, palms dangling down, extended out in front of him.

Jayne stood up. She heard a moan that was somewhat muffled by the suit helmet. She looked around the room for someone to explain when she heard another moan.

"Thirteeeeeeennnnnn, you cannot escape. Come here so I can gleefully eat your brain. Hahahahahaha."

Jayne stepped back and in one motion the hazmat-suited person took off his helmet and fell on one of the benches, consumed with hysterical laughter. It was Spike. Jayne recognized him right away with the little ponytail sticking out from the top of his head.

"I got you good. You were scared," he said, and he continued to laugh. "They told me you were coming, and I thought I would scare the stuffing out of you, and I succeeded, didn't I? Admit it. You were so scared; you were about to pee your pants."

Jayne turned away, opened her bag and removed her own suit. She quietly put it on and stood with her helmet in her hand.

Spike watched her. He stopped laughing. "What is your problem? Can't you take a joke?"

Jayne set her helmet down on the bench, picked up her bag and put it inside a locker and said, "I can take a joke as well as anyone, when it's funny. That was not. Now that little tuft of hair sticking out of your head, that is funny. And don't tell me you are in this program and we are working together."

"Okay," Spike said. "We are not working together. That would suggest we are equals. I am a man, and you are a little girl. That means I am in charge, and you are my bi—," he paused and smiled, "my assistant."

Jayne didn't mind the jab. Sometimes it was easier to just smile and let it all happen. This time was no different. She knew it was better not to argue with Spike. There would be plenty of time to argue later. Right now, she didn't know what to do next, so she might as well be his assistant. Better to be an assistant than to look stupid and incompetent.

She decided her ego would survive the bruising. She stood and spoke in a jaunty voice, "Right, boss—so where are we headed and what are your orders?"

"Very good. As to what is next—I have no idea," he said with a shrug of his shoulders and a laugh.

At that moment, both of their VIDs beeped. They both looked at their orders:

Replace the microbe filters in the air exchange system's electronics. You will find the basic instructions and a schematic under folder 'Pod 1' on your VID. You may encounter the occasional problem. Your job is to overcome the problems and complete the task. Take care of each other.

The final order was one Jayne would see over and over. She would only later truly understand how important it was.

She opened folder 'Pod 1' and read and memorized the schematics. It was a common bit of circuitry and would be easy to remove, clean, and repair. She smiled. "Looks pretty straight forward, boss," she said, clipping a series of tools to her belt and putting on her helmet. "Lead the way."

They headed out the door and down the tunnel to the sealed airlock and into the mini-biome. Once inside, Jayne was in awe at how much the 100-meter diameter biome was like all the videos she saw of the real Biome 3. She knew there were no people in this biome, but everything else was the same, except on a smaller scale. There were monsters in here, both big and small. The gravity was slightly higher. Everything was wet. The jungle was so dense that it was impossible to see where the biome ended. They knew they had to travel on an unmarked path to a rocky outcrop in the middle of the biome. The path was not direct. It seemed to worm its way around in the dense jungle until they had no idea, without looking at the ocular video screen mounted inside their helmets, where they were in relation to the exit. The exit was not important now. They had to get to the outcrop and set the pressure tent over the external opening to the filter system. All biome control devices were placed inside a positive pressure container, all inside a naturally occurring part of the biome landscape. The landscape hid the controls from the inhabitants. The positive pressure system kept all the macroscopic and microscopic creatures out. The filters, at the inner core, maintained the sterility of the system. But all filters needed replacing occasionally.

Jayne saw a rocky crag just up the trail where the jungle thinned. She pointed and stopped in her tracks. Something that she could not see was just ahead. She sensed it. That something was very dangerous. Spike, walking behind, stepped past and stepped over what looked like a log across the path, and strode up to the rock.

"Don't step on that log; it's not a log. It's a roller, and they can crush you as soon as you hit the ground," warned Spike.

Jayne knew what a roller was. It was one of the higher gravity beasts that looked just like a rotting log across the path. It captured its prey by causing you to fall when you stepped on it. It quickly rolled as soon as it felt the pressure of your weight. This would pull your feet from under you and cause you to slip and fall. It would then roll back over you and flatten out, sealing you between its body and the ground. If its huge weight did not crush you, you were sure to suffocate. If you ever came across a roller that was flattened on the ground, it was probably eating. Once its prey was dead, it attached a million suckers to the body and drained it of all vital juices.

Jayne grinned and said, "Watch."

She took a few steps backwards and ran toward the log that was really a roller. She landed right on top of it with both feet and jumped into the air just as the roller rolled and flattened itself over the ground. Jayne landed on the other side of the beast that was now sealed to the ground and sending out its suckers for a nonexistent meal. "It is better to set it off, rather than leave it in spring mode. You never know what might happen on the way back," she said matter-of-factly.

Spike shook his head. "You're an idiot. You are going to lose a life for sure after that little show."

"I doubt it. It is part of the advanced manual on 'preparing to return on a path.' Don't you read?" she asked, her voice dripping with sarcasm.

Spike shook his head and moved on. He reached the outcrop, removed the pressure tent pack from his pouch and placed it on the outcrop. He was opening it as Jayne stepped up beside him. She was even more tense. Something dangerous was near. She could feel it. She could also feel the silver star hanging around her neck start to warm against her skin. A shiver ran down her spine. She pushed the feeling aside.

"Have you checked the location thoroughly?" she asked.

He turned and looked at her and extended his hand, inviting her to have a look for herself.

Jayne stepped forward and walked around the outcrop. She could see nothing that was dangerous. She nodded at him, and he pulled the tab on the tent and stepped back. He held up fingers as he counted to five. The tent zipped open and encased the outcrop. Slowly, the walls of the tent solidified, and a door formed in one side. The tent would form a positive pressure container around the rock. Its secondary purpose was to keep techs protected from biome creatures that might attack them while they were working.

Jayne felt another tingle surge from her core and out of her fingertips. She quickly looked around and then realized that they must be nearby. Probably not in the mini-hub, but close by. The shiver told her they were reading her. She wondered if the Sentinels were also reading her. She shook her head and tried to clear the fuzziness that a 'read' left behind. A strong sense of foreboding filled her and cleared her head. She reached into her supply pouch and felt around. She had no idea what she needed. She just knew she needed something. Her hand closed over a small cylindrical object about 25 cm long and two cm in diameter, with a recessed button on the side. She pulled it out and looked at it. She knew what it was from her studies, but never actually touched or used a real one. It was very high tech and used for catching small live specimens from the biomes. When you pushed the button, the shaft extended to a meter in length with a shallow net at one end. The netting was made of high strength carbon fibers and almost impossible to cut. Once you snagged a specimen, the net disconnected from the ring that held it open and collapsed over the specimen, immobilizing it. The specimen could easily be placed in a confinement container for transport. The electronics in the netting could then be activated, and the netting would relax and free the creature.

Jayne held the netting device at the ready. She had not pressed the button to activate it. She knew it was too soon. Spike had not noticed her and was about to open the door to the tent when she reached up and touched his arm, stopping him.

"Please," she said softly. She pushed the button on the cylinder. The net popped out.

"Trust me on this, please," she whispered again. "Please open the door and step to the side as quickly as you can. On my signal."

She held up the net at head height in front of the opening, just far enough away to allow the opening door to clear the net. She nodded. He opened the door and stepped quickly to the side. There was a whooshing sound and a rotten smell. The netting flew out and came free of the ring that held it. It flew three meters through the air and dropped to the ground.

The beast inside struggled for a moment and then stopped as the fibers that held it tightened over its wiggling frame. Jayne reached up and shut off the odor-mimic function in her suit. It smelled bad, and she knew there was no need to endure it. She walked over to the ball of netting and stared at the creature caught in the webbing. It was what was commonly called a Stink Bomb. It was a small lizard that grew a single horn in the front of its thick skull. It killed its prey by projecting itself headfirst and smashing whatever it hit. She guessed that the odor had its own survival purpose but could not think of what it was. She was not a great fan of the flora and fauna of Biome 3. Whoever had designed it must have done so in order to mimic the assumed creatures on the jungle planet to which Biome 3 was headed. But Jayne thought he or she must have a very bizarre sense of humor. She pressed a button on the net handle. The netting relaxed and the small Stink Bomb scooted away into the jungle that surrounded the pressure tent. She retrieved the netting and placed it in her pouch.

"Thanks, Wu," said Spike. "How did you know it was there?"

"I just remembered that those little guys like to hide in crevices of rocks above ground level. I thought there would be a good chance one was hiding there. And I thought I saw something right before you activated the tent," Jayne lied.

"Well, I doubt that his horn would have broken this helmet," he said, tapping his helmet with his finger, "but I sure would not have liked to put it to the test. Let's get these filters replaced and get out of here. I heard there might be a drop-in game tonight. I would like to play soon. Have you played yet?"

"No. Some of the girls in my dorm asked me to play for them, though," she answered. She stepped into the tent. She stepped out again and said, "Sorry, boss. After you." She bowed as he walked in front of her.

Jayne followed and quickly closed the tent door. It pressurized with a hiss. A light in the ceiling of the tent came on. Spike took out his VID and started to read the instructions on how to open the access port. Jayne carefully reached past him and pressed on two protruding sections of rock. There was a hiss and a small door slid open, exposing the electronics.

Spike looked up at her, slightly irritated. He looked back at the VID. "Do you want me to do it?" she asked.

Spike looked up at her again and then back at his VID and then at the opening in front of him and then back at Jayne.

"I think you need more practice at filter replacement than I do, so I think you should do it," he said, and he invited her to the open door in the rock.

Jayne turned so her helmet would hide the huge grin that took over her face. "Yes, boss," she said, and she began the filter replacement process. It only took Jayne a few minutes to replace the filters and reseal the circuits. "Shall I run the tests?" she asked.

Spike looked at his VID screen and flipped to the next section. He looked up at Jayne. He shook his head, rolled his eyes in amazement, and exhaled. He made a decision. "Wu, I am going to say something that will cause me a great deal of pain both now and into the future," he said, and he sighed again. "Here goes."

"What?" snapped Jayne. She was expecting a long and not very accurate list of the things she had done incorrectly while replacing the filters.

"I'm not stupid. I may not be as mind bogglingly quick as you, but I am not stupid. So here goes," he said and stared at her.

"What?" snapped Jayne again.

"You need to promise me something first," he said, and he sighed dramatically again.

"I ain't promising you nuttin'," she spat in her best slang.

"Hear me out. You must promise that what I am about to say never gets repeated to anyone," he said.

"What?" she said again, the exasperation evident in her voice as her head nodded in affirmation and she turned to leave.

"I'm…I'm sorry. I'm sorry for being an ass. From now on, when we are working together, you are the boss," he said glumly.

Jayne turned and looked at Spike. She expected to find a smirking face staring back at her, but Spike stood with his arms out inviting a hug. "What?" she queried. She turned away to conceal a flush of blood to her face.

Spike put his hands on her shoulders and spun her around. He pulled her close and pressed his faceplate against her faceplate. "I mean it, Wu.

I am sorry I was such an ass. Please accept my apology." He hugged her to him once again.

Jayne knew her face was red hot. The inside of her faceplate was fogging up. Her heart was hammering. Her knees were weak. This feeling was not an embarrassment. It was something else. Exactly what she did not know. She liked it and hated it at the same time.

Jayne broke from his embrace, turned, and walked back to the tent entrance. She spoke with her back to him, hoping to conceal what was happening to her body. "Are you kidding? The last thing I want to be is your boss. We are partners. I have just forgotten what you just said. Let's get this tested, closed up, and put away. You know they are timing us. I want to get back as soon as possible," Jayne mumbled, as they completed the task and headed out of the biome pod.

They entered the decontamination chamber where jets of fluid sprayed and cleaned their suits. A blast of air dried them off. They headed out of the chamber and removed their helmets. Suddenly, both their VIDs emitted the emergency klaxon sound. They both read:

EMERGENCY

Report to Mini-Biome Pod 6. Fixer contact with 'Baby Q' has been unexpectedly interrupted. The last location is being mapped to your VID. Determine the nature of the problem that resulted in the loss of contact and report the situation. Administer medical aid as required. Take care of each other.

"What is 'Baby Q'?" asked Jayne.

"It's the small Quantum Cray they used to run the mini-biome pods. That computer tracks all individual life forms that are present in the biome, with the exception of some bacteria and viruses. Those are tracked as a population. All visitors, such as us, are followed, and all actions are recorded. When contact is lost, an alarm goes off. Now, that could mean something as simple as a communicator malfunction all the way up to the total destruction of the fixer in question," he said as he jogged to the entrance to Pod 6. Jayne followed.

He called back, "I am surprised that you don't know this."

"None of the mini-biome pod manuals refer to the Cray as 'Baby Q'. That is all I asked," she stated, her voice edged with irritation that he would think she was not prepared.

They both put on their helmets and entered the tube to Pod 6. There were few differences between Pod 1 and Pod 6 in terms of the overall environment. Both were designed to mimic aspects of Biome 3. Pod 6 was used to test the student's gravity prowess. If a biome fixer entered Biome 3 to repair a gravity malfunction, how would he contend with the other aspects of the biome in, for example, zero gravity situations? Jayne flipped on her helmet video and scanned the fixer assignment for Pod 6. It was a solo run. One fixer was required to enter Pod 6, locate and repair a gravity fluctuation. It sounded pretty simple. She wondered what went so wrong that the contact was broken. They both entered the pod and scanned the edge of the jungle. The fixer in question was hard to miss. He or she was floating in the air, halfway between the ground and the ceiling. Jayne could see some movement, but not much. Floating around the fixer was the source of the problem. There were at least a dozen acid spitters floating near the fixer. The gravity malfunction affected a whole brood of these little guys. An acid spitter was a bizarre creature, about half the size of a mouse, that was able to spit a highly corrosive acid from a gland above its nostrils. The acid was really digestive juice the creature used to disable tiny insects before consuming them. Since it had no teeth, it used the acid to break down the tough exoskeleton on some insects before eating them whole. A fixer suit was more than enough protection from this small amount of acid.

Jayne stared at the floating fixer. He was caught in zero gravity. Normally, you would just turn on the suit grav unit to let yourself settle slowly to the ground. If, for some reason, this was not possible, you would contact the Quantum Cray that controlled the pod. It would then adjust the gravity field for you. As she watched, an acid spitter bumped into the floating fixer. A mist formed in the air at the point of contact. All of a sudden, the problem became obvious. The mist that gathered around the helmet was slowly being sucked into the filter system of the suit. There was so much of the acid vapor that it had probably destroyed the filter system and eaten away at the suit's control and communication circuitry. As far as the computer was concerned, the moment that circuitry died, the fixer disappeared. It had no way of manipulating the gravity field for something it could not see. They needed to get him down fast—before there was a breach in the suit. The low gravity area was only about 25 meters square. If they stepped into the area, they would also become weightless and susceptible to the acid vapor.

"I'm going to jump up into the zero-gravity field and grab him," Spike said. "As soon as I have him, notify Baby Q to lock onto me and increase the gravity. We should slowly drift to the floor."

"Are you kidding? That air is filled with acid vapor. You could both end up stuck in a zero grav field," she warned, just as an acid spitter bumped into the floating fixer and spewed more acid vapor. The spitting acted like a propulsion system and sent the spitter into the fixer. The fixer slowly floated toward the edge of the zero grav line. If he floated into normal gravity, he would drop 30 meters without the protection of Baby Q. She watched as one of the spitters hit the normal gravity area and fell into the trees below. The same thought hit both Jayne and Spike at the same time. There was no choice if they were to save him. "Go! Go now!" she ordered.

Spike stepped back and ran and jumped into the zero-gravity area, propelling himself right at the floating fixer. At the same time, Jayne sent a command to Baby Q to increase the gravity on her mark. As Spike reached and grabbed the fixer, his momentum sent both of them careening toward the high gravity of the rest of the biome pod.

Jayne screamed, "Mark!"

The two bodies were now tumbling and slowly falling at the same time. Spike's foot entered the normal gravity area and both he and the fixer began to fall. Spike felt the speed increase and pulled his foot back. They slowly fell toward the ground and landed in a small clearing. Once down, the gravity returned to normal. The brood of acid spitters fell like hail into the undergrowth of the jungle.

The rescued fixer was not responsive. Jayne and Spike carried him to the decontamination port and allowed the washers to clean them. The green light came on and, at the same time, the outer doors opened. Medical personnel entered and removed the fixer's helmet. He was breathing, but as Jayne looked closer, he opened his eyes. They were white and cloudy, burned by the acid vapors that had entered the suit. He was blind.

As Jayne turned away, her eyes welled with tears.

CHAPTER 20

Recruited

Entertainment would always generate credits. Some Pre-Swarm 'Big Things' were Interactive Holos and Hed Holos. Hed Holos evolved a subculture called the Bloc Heds. The Bloc Heds became addicted to fantasy worlds. They connected to a group fantasy and lived their life in another world altogether. The spin-off products of the Bloc Hed craze completely locked in the addicts. Specialized feeding and excretion chairs were all the rage. You could 'Lock Your Bloc' for up to three days in one of these chairs. There were protocols for the length of time a Bloc Hed could connect. It started at three hours and gradually extended to three days. All the safety protocols were often overridden. It was not uncommon to find Bloc Heds dead or near dead in their chairs because the food supply ran out.

The new society that formed after the discovery of the Swarm highly discouraged all Bloc Hed tech. The majority of entertainment was in the form of spectator events. The most widespread and popular was, of course, GravBall.

Jayne and Spike were split up for the remainder of the mini-pod practicum. Jayne worked with several other students. Her reviews were always good, and the practice sessions were uneventful. The accident in Pod 6 resulted in an investigation. As a result, new safety protocols were put into effect. And an acid-resistant filter system was developed for the training suits to ensure safety.

All students were given a break after the completion of pod training. Jayne lazed and slept for two days. That was difficult in a dorm room filled with students at various levels, involved in many different activities. At one point, Jayne hauled her mattress into her locker to avoid a GravBall party going on in her dorm. It was the start of the Pro-League season, and everyone was cheering for their favorite team. Almost all the professional teams were controlled by large companies. The company controllers developed the players and used the team to advertise the various products and services that they provided. If a company controlled a champion team, that company would be successful. This ownership and control structure reached all the way down to the amateur leagues, with smaller companies controlling the amateur teams. The government took a percentage of the profit generated and funneled it into social programs. There were other sports, but nothing compared to GravBall. Everyone was a fan. Everyone had their favorite team. Everyone, at some point in their life, dreamed of being a GravBall star. The biome tech students were no different. Jayne, Spike, and the others all loved to watch GravBall and loved to play GravBall.

There were a number of leagues based in HUB 169. There were the Fixer AAA's, Fixer Masters, and Fixer Students. Every department had a team. People were often recruited to a particular department for their GravBall skills. There were restrictions. Each member of a team must fulfill his or her job expectations and pass the bi-yearly review. There was no point in recruiting a hot player if they could not do the job they were hired to do. There were some cases where the company tried to conceal the inadequacies of their GravBall players by having others do their jobs. These deceptions always ended badly. All job reviews were in the public domain and studied closely for fraudulent reports. It was almost impossible to be a great GravBall player and not be good at your chosen profession. The student teams' recruitment process always took place during the mid-term break. The objective was to win your league, go to the HUB championships, and win the coveted Spavator Trophy.

On the third day, Jayne emerged refreshed from her locker hideaway. She dragged her mattress back onto her cot and sat down. She was scanning the room and focused on a group of students standing tightly together, locked in conversation. Almost as if they sensed her stare, the group turned around and headed in Jayne's direction. At the same time, Jayne's VID beeped. A tall, skinny boy led the group. Jayne recognized him from the mini-pod introductory classes. She'd never spoken to him, but she suspected what he, and the group approaching her, wanted. They wanted her GravBall skills.

He spoke. "We're the Crimson Stompers and we understand you play."

Jayne felt cheeky and responded with, "Play what?"

"I told you she was not the kind of player we need," piped up a heavy-set girl to the side of the group. "We don't need a smart-ass on our team."

Jayne's face flushed red with heat. If she was going to be called a smart-ass, she would damn well live up to the label. She quipped back, "You mean another one, don't you? Or perhaps it is just the former part you need 'cause it appears you have a number of people that fit the latter."

The stocky girl turned to the tall boy and asked, "What did she just say? Former? Latter?" She moved to the front of the group and leaned over Jayne. "Did you just insult me?"

Jayne was on a roll. She stood up on her bed just so she could look the girl straight in the eye. The result was comical. Jayne was standing on her bed, hands on her hips, looking down at the girl in front of her. She then looked over at the tall boy and said, "I should know better than to try to have a battle of wits with an unarmed person." She shook her head, sat down quickly, and flipped open her VID. She spoke quietly, as if to herself, "Case closed."

"Why you little…" the stocky girl growled as she reached out to grab Jayne by the hair.

The tall, skinny boy pushed the stocky girl aside. "Lay off. We are not here to start a war," he said, looking down at Jayne.

She sat calmly on her bunk, reading her VID screen, as if nothing was happening.

"Let's go."

The group walked away. Jayne caught the end of the stocky girl's parting remarks. They mentioned something about 'laying that little' and 'flat on her' and 'smacking that' something or other 'off her' something, before they moved away, and she could no longer hear them.

Her VID held a message from Lucky. She had four more days of break. She was to return to her quarters to personally receive some 'CRUCIAL' information that could not be transmitted over the VID system. Jayne smiled. She could sure use a few days away from this place. Having Lucky dote on her was the most appealing thing she could think of at this moment. She knew that what Lucky thought was crucial seldom was. She stood up, gathered the few personal things from her locker, stuffed them in her knapsack, and headed for the PUT pads. She looked ahead and saw Spike, Sara, Josie, and Olive heading her way. They were excited and glad to see her.

Sara called, "Hey, Wu, we have been looking for you. Where the heck have you been hiding?"

"I've been catching up on some badly needed sleep. I was in my locker," Jayne stated.

Josie laughed. "How the heck did you fit in your locker?" She looked Jayne up and down. "Oh, yeah, you are this big," she held her thumb and forefinger 20 cm apart, "and I am this big," she said, laughing louder and lowering the frequency of her voice while holding out her arms out as far as they would go.

"We need to talk to you about GravBall. We have to get our team confirmed and submitted to the league. We want to know if you're interested," said Olive.

Jayne looked up at their expectant faces.

Sara turned around and looked behind her, and then back at Jayne. "I just saw the Stompers leave here. Were they trying to recruit you? What did they say? You're not going to play for those wipeouts, are you?"

Jayne shifted her knapsack.

Panic rose in Sara's voice, and she turned to Josie. "I told you we needed to get her signed up ASAP but no, you had to spend the whole day following that blond cutie around, hoping he would join the team. He is useless compared to Thirteen. Now we've lost her to the Stompers."

"Yes," said Jayne.

"Awe, damn!" cursed Sara. "We lost her, and it's your fault." "Yes, I will join your team," clarified Jayne. "What are you guys called again?"

"We're 'Home-Grown Panic,'" said Spike proudly. "Great name, eh?"

"Yeah, but what does that mean?" asked Jayne.

"Why does everything have to have a big, deep meaning? I like it 'cause it sounds cool and the letters HGP look good together," he said, as if the statement was very poignant.

"I agree. I just wanted to be educated in case someone asked me. I didn't want to be out of the loop. So now I can answer questions about the reason for the name with 'It's cool!'," she said.

They all smiled and laughed at the inaneness of the conversation. "I have to go. I will catch you guys in a couple of days. I have to head back to my quarters to..." she hesitated and then continued,

"get some things. VID me the practice times."

The others just looked at her with their mouths open. "You do practice, don't you?" remarked Jayne.

Spike laughed, "Since you joined our team, we figured we don't need to practice." He poked Jayne in the ribs. "Yeah, we practice, and if you are gone for a few days, you will miss the first one. I will let you know when you get back."

"See you guys," said Jayne as she headed for the PUT pads and her rendezvous with Lucky.

CHAPTER 21

The 'Sergio Partelli'

GravBall scouts were everywhere, especially in the hubs. They were always looking for that perfect player. A perfect player was usually a student who was excelling. If you excelled in the HUB, you must have a lot going for you, because that was not easy. It took intellectual and physical prowess to graduate from the HUB schools. The scouts were always wooing the top students by sending supposedly 'anonymous' gifts. Bribing or paying players was formally frowned upon. In reality, it was ubiquitous.

The door to her quarters slid open, and Jayne tossed her knapsack on the floor. She felt a shiver go down her spine, and she knew it had nothing to do with the watchers. It was simply a natural response to being home. She smiled and flopped down on her bed.

"Hello, Thirteen. Would you like to listen to some music before I inform you why I called you home?" asked Lucky softly.

"Please Lucky, just tell me the details now," she said and then rolled on her side and cuddled her pillow.

"I am afraid I cannot. I do not know any detailed information. As a result, I must also assume that it is crucial to everything by default. I can only direct you to open the package on the table. It is shielded from all of my sensors. It arrived earlier today. If you wish me to report its arrival to security, I will gladly do so. Perhaps it is dangerous? In fact, it must be dangerous just for that reason. I can think of no logical reason for someone concealing any information about you from me. I have, after all, been programmed to protect you. Yes, I will call security now," stated Lucky.

Jayne quickly jumped to her feet. She thought of the Sentinels. Maybe they were trying to contact her or send her something. "No! Lucky, I do not wish you to alert anyone when I receive a package of this nature. It is probably just something from the new GravBall team I have joined. They said they would be sending me something. That's all this is," she said, calming her voice to conceal her lie.

She picked the package up off the table and dropped it on her bed. "Fantastic!" exclaimed Lucky. "You will tell me your game times and locations. I could not bear to miss one of your games. You must tell me all the plays. I promise I will not spill the beans to any of the other teams. That is the right usage for the phrase 'spill the beans'? It is such a wonderful phrase. I have been dying to use it. That is not true. I have not really been dying; that is just another phrase I have been wanting to use. Thank you, Thirteen, for telling me about the

GravBall team." (Even computer-generated AI entities, like Lucky, followed GravBall.) "Well, aren't you going to open it?"

"Maybe later," said Jayne. She flopped down on her bed. It felt wonderful. She slipped the package under her blanket and surreptitiously opened one end and peeked inside. It was a uniform. Someone had sent her a GravBall uniform. She sat up, realizing that this was not something she needed to conceal from Lucky. She pulled the uniform from the wrapping and stood up. She held the folded uniform out in front of her.

"Lucky, look," she said. "It probably won't fit."

"Oh! A GB suit! I was going to talk to you about making sure you used a GB suit with the latest safety protocols. I know this is just a student league, but it is still easy to get hurt. The proper equipment is still wise. Show me the ankle tag and I will check to see if it is up to the latest standards," said Lucky. "If it is, you can try it on. We can always send it out for fitting modifications."

Jayne exposed a scan tag.

Lucky scanned and exclaimed, "Oh, my!"

"What? What is it? Can I use it or not?" asked Jayne, as she ran her hand over the material. "It feels really cool."

"You can use it, but it was definitely not sent to you by any student GravBall team," answered Lucky. "Have you been approached by any HUB department?"

"Approached to do what?" asked Jayne.

"Why, work for them so you can play for them," responded Lucky. "If you have, I will scan their GravBall stats from last year and see if they need players. We might be able to narrow this down to the team that gave it to you. If they gave you this, they want you badly."

"What is so special about this suit?" asked Jayne, holding it up in front of her. "It looks like it might fit."

"Oh, it will fit alright," Lucky said assuredly. "It's a Sergio Partelli— the latest model. You can't buy these, even if you could afford it."

"I'm going to try it on," stated Jayne, as she began to pull off her work clothes.

"I do not recommend that you try it on until we further investigate the source of the suit. You may not be able to keep it. It might require you to sign up to a team you know nothing about. Where is the specification and commitment chip that came with the suit?" he asked.

Jayne looked in the packaging but could not find a chip. She searched the suit. There was nothing. "Nothing here," she said, and she shrugged. "No commitment chip to agree to, then no commitment! I can try on this beauty, and no one can hold me to anything 'cause I didn't agree to anything. That's right, isn't it?"

"Yes, Jayne. As far as I can see, someone has given you the most expensive GravBall suit ever made. Shall I expound on its virtues?" Lucky asked and continued. "There are many. I have yet to find a single flaw. All the reviews say it is perfect. You must explore its many safety features. I will download the information to your VID. Do you prefer Standard or Iconese?"

"Either will be fine," she said, as she slipped the uniform on and watched as it self-fitted to her diminutive figure. It was a dark gray with black trim and fit her body perfectly. "Boring color."

"I think that is the neutral. This suit can assume any color or pattern you can conceive. Shall I interface with it and download all the suit colors of all the teams in HUB 169?" asked Lucky casually.

"Yes, please," stated Jayne.

"Done," responded Lucky. "Simply say 'Suit', the word 'style' and the team's name. That should do it."

"Suit—style—Home Grown Panic," said Jayne. The suit transformed to a bright yellow with red trim. "Wow! Cool!"

"During my interface with the suit, I noticed some command structures that are not available to all users. I tried to follow the path but was disallowed by the AIOS (Artificial Intelligence Operating System). It seems that this new suit has some proprietary algorithms not available to other AIOSs. That, or my security designation was not adequate," stated Lucky flatly.

"What does that mean?" asked Jayne.

"Well, simply put, that suit has a brain of its own and it won't tell me all the things it can do," said Lucky. "That could be dangerous. My purpose is to protect you. Upon reflection, it is my opinion that this suit may not have your best interests at heart. You must remove it and I will destroy it."

"Don't be absurd," Jayne said, somewhat condescendingly. "Have you finished downloading the suit manual to my VID?"

"Yes, Thirteen, I have," responded Lucky.

"Good. Shut down. I do not wish to be disturbed," ordered Jayne. An order would not elicit a protest from an AIU unless there was imminent danger. "Shutting down high level functions," stated Lucky.

There was silence in the room. Jayne found her VID and began to explore the instructions left by Lucky. Questions swirled in her mind. The loudest was, 'Who sent the suit?' If she knew that, she would be able to figure out the 'why'. Right now, she did what she could easily do, and that is to explore the suit and all of its possibilities. After all, she was wearing a Sergio Partelli. They made suits for the Pro GravBall players. They made suits for space flight. They made suits for underwater work. They made suits for just about anything where people needed a protective suit.

Jayne played with the suit and its myriad of functions. She played with it and giggled at the results. She explored various combinations. If she was vague in her commands to the suit, the AIOS chose the most likely possibility. Sometimes the final result was weird, to say the least.

Then she had an inspiration—beyond GravBall. She called out, "Suit—style—standard HUB 169 jumpsuit."

Jayne smiled. She was now ready for work in the HUB.

CHAPTER 22

Weapons & Combat Training

At the formation of the new order, the laws regarding the design, possession and use of modern weapons changed.

All weapons were of two types: disabling and killing. If you used a weapon designed to disable, it could not purposely kill. The opposite was also true. If you were using a weapon designed to kill, it would always do exactly that. If someone died by your hand and you were using a killing weapon, there was no doubt of your intent. Your intent had to be to kill because you were using a weapon that could only do what it was designed to do. You could not shoot to wound. You could only shoot to kill. As a result, killing weapons were rare. Disabling weapons were much more common. They were the weapons carried by the police and security. That is not to say that deaths did not result with the use of the disabling weapons. Deaths were not common, but they did happen. Someone shot with a disabling weapon could fall and hit their head and die as a result of head trauma. It was therefore assumed that a person who wielded a disabling weapon had no intent to kill. In reality, this was not always true.

The following three days were spent resting and wearing the new suit. Jayne felt a need to be alone and did not activate Lucky's higher-level functions. She spent her waking hours experimenting with the Sergio Partelli. She never even took it off. When it was time to sleep, she simply instructed the suit to change to the appropriate attire. The suit would try its best to comply, but some things were poor approximations. The nightgown extended to Jayne's knees, but it still maintained the complete lower part of the suit. Jayne looked like she was wearing pajama bottoms and a nightgown at the same time. This was really the suit's attempt at a uniform that looked like a nightgown. No matter what you asked the suit to change to, it always put safety first and the logic of the design second. So, a wedding dress became a long gown with long sleeves and a high neckline. Under the dress were full leggings. 'Nightie' just looked like a clown suit. The suit was always, first and foremost, designed for safety unless these standard protocols were overridden.

At the end of break, Jayne returned to school. The course was titled 'Weapons and Combat.' It involved the study of all weapons presently in common use, biome weapons, basic fighting skills and gyverisms. The latter was the incorporation of articles in the environment as weapons or tools. Biome fixers often found themselves in situations that required a weapon or tool for survival. This course was designed to give fixers experiences with these kinds of dangerous situations.

The weapons classes took place in a large, high-ceilinged building. The center of the building was reached by walking through a protective tunnel. All weapons were shot, projected, or thrown from the center to the outside edge of the building. This meant that the center was always safe from accidental shots. A negative gravity field prevented accidental ricochets. Safety was paramount. Students were introduced to the entire weapons array before entering a biome. None of the weapons held explosive charges similar to bullets. The biomes were, after all, spaceships. A bullet could possibly smash some important component and put the biome in jeopardy. The four types of weapons were light, sound, chemical, and subsonic projectile. Sometimes there were combinations such as chemical-projectile. Jayne sat through classes that looked at many of these weapons, their construction, and use. In the end, she had to choose one and become an expert user. Jayne liked projectile weapons best. They were less technological and therefore less prone to failure in strange biome environments. There were bows and arrows, spears, blow darts, crossbows, throwing blades, and axes, boomerangs, and slings. They were all big and bulky, except the sling. Jayne chose the sling. It was small, simple, and effective.

There were many types of slings. The simplest—used by humans for thousands of years—consisted of leather thongs attached to either side of a leather pocket. One thong had a knot at one end.   A projectile, usually a small, egg-sized rock, was placed in the leather pocket. The projectile was swung around, and the knotted thong released. The rock would fly off to its target. This device was easy to make, carry, and use, but difficult to master. The modern slings were of a different breed altogether. These slings consisted of a metal tube 20 cm long and two cm in diameter. The sling was secured in the palm by a flexible strap. A single extendable line protruded from one end of the tube. It held a six-fingered claw that would open and release the object it contained when the sling was at its release point. It could be carried in the hand when its line was retracted fully. The longer the line, the further the sling would throw the object. A shorter line would increase accuracy. The ammunition for this modern sling was many and varied. Projectiles were held in an ammo belt slung over the shoulder. This sling could even use common rocks when all sophisticated ammunition was expended.

Jayne loved the simplicity and the versatility of the sling and spent weeks practicing. After the first day, her right arm felt like it was pulled from its socket, so she practiced with the left. She would alternate arms and soon became equally proficient with both the left and the right. She was the only student who chose the sling. She practiced on her own. Once she was proficient with simple striking projectiles, she graduated to the more sophisticated types of ammunition. There were scatter pellets, sound bombs, flash bangs, listening and tracking burrs, fliers, splatts and boomerangs. Splatts could mark a path or disperse an irritant. Boomerangs would return a sample of their target. All of these types of ammunition were computer controlled and almost always found their target.

The focus of combat training was to protect, deflect, and avoid.

After all, biome fixers were not warriors. They were trained to enter a hazardous environment, repair or fetch something and get both themselves and their team out unscathed. The focus of hand-to-hand fighting was not to harm or kill, but to disarm and disable. It had many aspects of the ancient martial art called Aikido, which focuses only on defense and the use of the opponent's momentum. It was in combat training that Jayne was the weakest. Her small size was a disadvantage. She found it difficult, if not impossible, to disable a larger opponent with her bare hands. On the flip side, however, others found it nearly impossible to disarm or disable her. She always seemed to know what they were about to do before they actually did it. She could slip out of the most carefully planned submission hold and escape.

School and study consumed all the Biome 3 apprentice fixers. One day Jayne was standing on her bed in the dorm, assuming the defensive stance and imagining someone attacking her with a knife when Sara entered, threw down her knapsack and flopped on her bed.

"This is impossible. I will never get through this," she moaned. "What?" asked Jayne.

"Diagnostics!" Sara spat. "They expect me to figure out what is wrong with a machine I have never even seen before, just by a list of symptoms. It is absurd."

"Do you know where the machine is located and its purpose?" asked Jayne.

"Yes. How is that supposed to help?" she said, covering her head with her arms and hands.

"Know the function, know the machine," answered Jayne matter-of-factly. "You always want to see all the specific bits and how they work together in that specific machine. Back up. What part groupings are required for the function? They will be very similar for all the machines that require that particular function. Study the common malfunctions for those part groupings and apply the one that is most likely. Simple."

"Easy for you to say. You're a whiz kid," Sara answered sarcastically.

Jayne made a face and said, "Oh, yeah, I forgot the most common problem with everything in Biome 3."

"What's that?" asked Sara.

"Dirt!" answered Jayne. "It is everywhere and causes 98% of the problems. Yeah, they say things like the filters are clogged or the quantum crystal array is overheated or the bearings in the domahickey are dried out or the thingamabob is plugged up. But it usually comes down to the fact that dirt somehow got into the system and messed something up. So always consider dirt first."

"That's your best advice. Dirt!" Sara moaned.

"Yep. Now help me with some combat moves. I've got to disarm someone in my hand-to-hand combat class. Anyone will do. I've even thought of trying to bribe someone to let me succeed," said Jayne, as she shouted and struck at her imaginary opponent. "Hiyah!"

"That's the best you got—hi… yeah?" said Sara, sitting up. "Disarming someone is all about knowing what happens to a body when it performs a specific action. Know the action—know the response. The more force that is put into the action, the easier it is to deflect."

"You mean the more likely I will get stabbed? I can handle surprises by preparing and avoiding 'cause I'm quick. But it is tougher when it is obvious to everyone what is about to happen. I just can't seem to stop it. I get flicked away like I'm an irritating insect," said Jayne. "I am supposed to use their weight and offensive actions against them, but I'm just a fly that they swat away. Help me, pleeeaaassse!"

"Wait. That's the best thing to do. Wait. Wait until your opponent commits and then act. That is the best advice I can give you," said Sara. "Here, I will show you. Pretend I am attacking you with this knife."

"You don't have a knife," said Jayne.

Sara scrabbled around in her knapsack and found a stylus. She brandished it like it was a knife. "Okay, now I have a weapon. Stand up here and stop me from stabbing you in the eye with it," stated Sara. She approached Jayne.

Jayne held up both of her hands, as if to block any stabbing motion. Sara dropped her hands. "No. No. Put your hands down. You are giving too much away. You are quick. I have seen you in the GravBall arena. So put your hands down and use your speed. Wait for your opponent to commit and then use one of the moves they taught you. I know you know them. A little over-achiever like you would know all the moves on the first day. Am I right?"

Jayne nodded. "Okay. But how long do I wait before I defend?" she asked.

"As long as possible," said Sara. "If the knife or the fist are not within a hair's breadth of contact, then you wait. If you wait that long, then two things will happen: One, your attacker will have fully committed to the action; and two, he will feel confident that his action cannot fail. That is when you act. How you act is up to you and the situation, but I know that part will not be a problem for you."

She crouched and held the stylus out in front of her in a threatening way. "On guard!"

Jayne stood and watched and waited. She blanked her mind and waited. She moved only so that she could watch all of Sarah's actions. Sara faked a jab with the pretend knife. Jayne did nothing. The stylus had not come close enough to move. Sara made a roaring sound and ran at Jayne but stopped a good 40 cm from her. Jayne did not act. She waited.

Sara turned around and spoke, "That's it. I think you've got it."

She turned back around quickly and ran at Jayne with full speed and full force, the stylus held in a stabbing position. Jayne raised her forearms vertically in front of her at head height. They were offset; one further away from her body than the other. As the stylus stab approached her, the heel of her left hand struck the back of Sara's stylus-wielding hand and the heel of her right hand hit the inside of her elbow joint. At the same time, Jayne turned her body sideways so the pretend knife, if it made it through, would miss her completely. But the stylus did not make it through. It went flying from Sara's grip as her arm folded at the elbow.

She gripped the muscle of her arm. "Ahhh…take it easy. I was not going to really hurt you."

"It looked like you were going to. If I had missed or frozen, you would have stabbed me," retorted Jayne.

"It wouldn't have hurt," she said, picking up the stylus and pressing the end. The device retracts into itself. "I snitched one to practice with a while back. It's harmless."

"Oh," said Jayne.

"How did that feel? You waited until I committed, and then you struck. And by the way, you didn't have to hit me so hard," whined Sara. "How are you doing with the gyvers? No, don't tell me." She held her index fingers to her temples. "It is coming to me. Yes. You are acing them. Am I right?"

The optional course activity was called Gyvers. Jayne didn't know the origin of the word, but a gyverism was a quickly rigged creation from the common objects in the vicinity to enable you to solve a problem or escape a precarious situation. In short, you used what was at hand in a way other than what was originally intended. A good knowledge of common chemistry and physics would be beneficial. Jayne loved gyverisms. She was a whiz at solving these kinds of problems.

"You're right. And it felt really good to block your stab. Thanks for the help," said Jayne.

"Good. I have done my part. But telling me that it all comes down to dirt does not make us even. You still owe me. I will, however, give the dirt idea a try," she said and flopped down to begin scanning the ElecMech manual on her VID.

Jayne sat back on her bed and reflected on the 'wait' concept. She liked it. The three-month course would end with a series of competitions. All competitions were judged on four aspects: accuracy with your chosen projectile weapon, problem-solving while respecting the natural order of the biome, defensive combat, and an ability to work with others. Jayne found this last aspect of the course the most difficult. She liked to work on her own and did not readily tolerate the shortcomings of others, especially when her safety was at stake.

Jayne thought about entering the competitions. It was not mandatory, but it was expected. In the interim, there was GravBall.

CHAPTER 23

GB Scouts

GravBall scouts were anomalies in society. They were not really Fixers in the true sense of the word. They did not do anything that was a direct benefit to society. The world could live without them. They could be retired players but, just as often, they were not. They could be scientists. They could even be politicians, but that was really rare. The politicians almost always owned the teams and were rich enough to hire the best scouts. All scouts were GravBall experts. They knew everything there was to know about the game. They did, however, like to keep their identities as secret as possible. The worst thing that could happen to a scout was to become a celebrity.

Home Grown Panic (HGP), Jayne's team, practiced three evenings a week. The day consisted of school, gathering in the cafeteria, practice discussion, practice, and finally back to the cafeteria for food. They played a league game once a week. They won six of the dozen games they played. Many of the losses were a direct result of the team members' school schedules conflicting with the game schedule.

There was no doubt that HGP was a good team when everyone was available to play. The team members were from a lot of different courses. The games were scheduled to accommodate the most students. If your team had students in Biome 3 Studies, which was the course without a set schedule, you were often missing players for the games. This week, however, was game 13 and everyone was available to play. This was the first game ever that Home Grown Panic had all their players at the game.

They were playing The Crimson Stompers for the second time. They lost the first game against the Stompers. Jayne had not been able to play. She had classes scheduled. In fact, Jayne had only been able to play 4 out of the 12 games. None of this really mattered. League play was really about preparation for the big tournament. Everyone would be able to have a full roster for the tournament because it was scheduled after classes ended.

Jayne did not want to answer any questions about her new Sergio Partelli, so she decided to keep it a secret. She would pretend it was just like any other suit in the team's suit locker. After putting it on, she ordered it to look like an HGP suit. The suit assumed the yellow and red pattern. Jayne looked at herself and noted the shiny newness that would give away the fact that this suit had not come from the HGP suit locker. She commanded the suit to alter the perceived quality. "Suit—make the uniform look shabbier and more worn."

The Sergio Partelli instantly appeared less bright, with worn areas at the elbows and knees. Jayne looked at herself again. The suit, although shabbier, still fit her perfectly. It was obvious that it was tailored for her. None of the suits in the locker would have fit her perfectly. She was just too small.

"Suit, make the fit less tailored." Her VID beeped, and she looked at the icon flashing in the middle of the screen. It was a message from the suit itself, warning her that what she asked would decrease the safety factor by 5% of the original specs. An override icon was imbedded, and Jayne touched it in the affirmative. The Sergio Partelli now looked like any other HGP suit. It was a little baggier and a little too long. Jayne rolled up the legs and the sleeves. She smiled. This suit was still a million times safer than any of the standard GB suits used in the student league. She could only get hurt if she overrode basic safety protocols.

She left her quarters and took the PUT pad to the gym GravBall tube. She was the last to arrive, and she smiled at her team sitting in the tube dugout. Everyone was here.

Sara stood. "I think we should play the standard eight to start. The

Crappy Stoopids always start with six and try to get a quick jump on the score. They will only be able to cover three of the four ball ports 'cause they need a potential ball carrier behind each port. I guess they feel lucky. If the ball pops out of the port that they are not covering, we will have a free line to the goal."

"Let's see," said Jayne. "If we score, we will get 6/8 x 10. That's 7.5 points. They will score 8/6 x 10 or 13.3 points. Is it worth the six points or should we play six players too?"

"We can send a knocker straight to the goal to stop them from scoring," piped up Josie.

"Yeah," responded Olive. "I can stop anyone of them from scoring if I can get to the goal first."

"The problem with that is, we will only be able to cover three of the ports—just as if we had six players. Too much defense means not enough offense," said Jayne. "I think we should play six if that is what they are playing. I prefer to match skill instead of strategy."

Spike piped in, "In case you all forgot, the number of players that are played in the half is kept a secret until the game actually starts. I think we shouldn't try to second guess them. We should play with the number that best suits our style."

"We have never had a full contingent of players before. If we play six, we can always have fresh players on the pitch. We can replace whole lines anytime we want and still have a spare to replace anyone who gets hurt. This also gives us a real advantage in the scoring department if they play more than six," Jayne responded.

"But we have never played less than eight," said Pinky in a worried tone.

"No, we haven't," said Sara. "They will never think we will change how we play because we never have. I think it is about time we did something a little different. Something unusual. I am the captain. It is my call and I say we go with six. We will have two knocker lines of three and two spotter lines of three and one spare. Each of the spotter lines has a potential ball carrier. So, on one spotter line, we will have Olive, Izzy, and

Eye Spy; and on the other, we have Spike, Thirteen, and myself. Josie, you and Cannon Ball divide up the rest into two knocker lines. Pinky, I want you to be the spare. You can play any position, and if someone gets hurt, you will be able to fill in perfectly. Any questions?"

No one said anything. The lines were formed, and the official starting numbers were sent to the officials. These numbers could not be changed until the second half. The announcement of players was made. The Crimson Stompers had chosen to start with eight players. Jayne could see a lot of commotion on their bench as the numbers were announced. They were surprised by HGP's choice. They were madly discussing strategy, but there was not enough time. Olive's spotter line and Cannon Ball's knocker line hit the pitch and took up positions. They chose to cover all four ball ports with only two spotters back. Eye Spy would be the ball carrier if his port popped the ball. If not, he would quickly drop back to his spotter role. The Crimson Stompers' strategy was typical of a big team. Not big in numbers, but big in player size. They sent two knockers to each ball port with no one back. Their plan was to get and keep the ball from the get-go by overpowering the single opponent player at each ball port.

When the ball popped from one of the four ports along the center line of the curved floor, each team tried to gain possession. The grav lines became active when a player had clear possession of the ball. The ball popped anywhere from three to five meters in the air. The ball could be retrieved only as it fell to the ground. It became a bit of a scramble to get the ball as it fell. If a ground melee ensued, the referee would stop play. The players took a step back, and the floor below the ball would switch to negative gravity. The ball popped up again and a new scramble began.

Once the ball was clearly possessed by one player, all the grav lines became active. The ball was passed back to a ball carrier who moved the ball down a grav line. The spotters would spread out and signal to the BC which path to the goal was the best. The knockers protected the BC from the opponent knockers.

The ball popped in front of Izzy and two Stompers. They all watched as the ball reached its apex and began to fall. No player contact was allowed until the ball was within reach. All three players jumped as soon as it was possible to possess the ball. They all hit the ground in a tangle of Panic yellow and Stomper red. A red Stomper uniform rose from the floor in clear possession of the ball. A horn sounded and the tube began to hum as the gravity lines were activated. The ball was passed back to a BC on a grav line. The Stomper players chose a grav line to run. The stocky blonde girl, whose name was Bridget (she was also called TwoB or BB or Big B or just plain old B), was moving slowly down a high grav line. A knocker could stop her by knocking her off the line from the front or the rear. Side hits were illegal and would result in a penalty. Knocking a strong player moving down a high grav line was not easy. You had to build up speed to do any good. If you took the time to build speed, the BC would cross to a low grav line and run past you. If you just jumped in front of the player, they would, likely as not, simply run over you without stopping. A high grav attack needed the rotating goal to be at its lowest point to score because jumping was impossible. If the goal was high, you would have to pass back to a new BC and try another line.

TwoB's timing was perfect. The goal was waning just as she was about to reach the end of the high grav line. A Panic knocker stepped in front of TwoB as a last resort and was bounced like a bowling pin. TwoB simply walked up to the wall as the goal reached its lowest point and slammed the ball home. The red light came on, signaling a score, and 7.5 points came up on the scoreboard.

There were two viewing areas high up on either side of the gym GravBall tube. They were designated for executive use. HUB team owners and their scouts used these to watch the HUB games. You couldn't really see who was watching, but someone was always keeping tabs on possible recruitment of student players. Today's game was no different. Someone was watching. They watched as the ball popped right in front of Josie. She was opposite TwoB and Hank Zoon, also known as Jumper. He was very tall and would probably get the ball just by standing under it. TwoB was not taking any chances. She moved to block any potential jumps from Josie by raising her arms up in front of Josie's face. Jumper caught the falling ball and quickly flipped it backwards over his head to be caught before the grav lines started. A red uniform caught the ball and flipped it back to a Crimson spotter, signaling a low grav line. The spotter caught the ball, became the BC, and began to run down the straight low grav line. The BC was small for a GravBall player, but not as small as Jayne. Jayne glanced back and saw that the goal was reaching its apex. It would be hard to stop the Stomper BC running full speed down a low grav line unless one of the Panic knockers could get to her. Josie was coming down the same line and was trying to catch the BC. Jayne watched Josie running, hands extended, about to make contact with the Crimson Stomper BC and knock her off the line. If she succeeded, the BC would have to pass back to one of her teammates and start the attack again. This would give HGP an opportunity to regroup and mount a defense.

Jayne looked at the goal. It reached the top and was coming down on her side of the tube. She turned and ran down another low grav line toward her own goal. Somehow, she knew this was the way to stop another goal. She jumped. Josie jumped. The Crimson Stomper BC jumped. Josie missed and the BC sailed up in the low gravity toward the goal. Jayne sailed up and reached to block the ball as it sailed from the BC's hand toward the funnel. Just as Jayne began to fall, the ball landed in her hand, and she cupped it and pulled it into the low grav line. The weight of the ball was nearly zero in her hand. In one quick motion she pointed with one hand and tossed the ball down the line with the other. Sara started to run in normal gravity, leaped into the same grav line, caught the ball, then hopped, skipped, jumped, and slammed the ball into the opponent's goal.

The force of the throw pushed Jayne out of the relative safety of the low gravity line and into normal space and normal gravity. Low gravity would have allowed her to drop down to a soft landing, but normal space meant normal gravity. She was nearly 10 meters up, falling backwards at an angle, at an acceleration rate of 9.8 meters per second squared. She would hit hard if it were not for her suit. As you started to fall, a standard GravBall suit would immediately signal the system to initiate negative gravity and stop you from smashing full speed into the ground and breaking a lot of important body parts. Putting yourself in a dangerous position, requiring your suit to save you, would result in a severe penalty. It would definitely negate Sara's goal. It might even get Jayne kicked out of the game. But her suit was a Sergio Partelli—the best GravBall suit ever made.

Her luck was off the chart. Jayne's suit was made for the pros. It would only turn on protection a tenth of a second before it was actually needed. It made for some exciting and heart-stopping falls. The fans loved it, and no one actually got hurt. Jayne was also lucky—very, very lucky. As she fell, she angled across the pitch and entered another grav line two meters from the ground. Her shoulders entered a gravity pulsar line at its negative gravity maximum. It was like falling onto a huge cushion. Her lower half was still falling down as her upper half began to rise up. The angle of her descent resulted in her falling quickly and then being eased onto her feet in the last few meters. She simply stood up in normal space, and the gravity pulse zipped past. The suit did not activate because the danger was gone before it was required to activate and, as a result, no penalty was incurred.

All gravity returned to normal, and Sara came running down the tube toward Jayne. She was screaming with joy. "That was brilliant. If you hadn't pointed down the line, I would never have figured out what you wanted me to do before it was too late."

Sara had not seen Jayne fall and then magically stop falling. She was babbling, "Your timing on the block was perfect. The throw was not only accurate, it was very cool." She grabbed Jayne and began to spin her around by her hands.

"I'm glad you saw my signal. That was a great jump you made.

Now put me down," said Jayne.

"Believe me, it was only made possible by that stupendous play you made in mid-air," retorted Sara as she set Jayne down.

Spike ran up to them both. His face was not happy. He did not see the goal, but he saw the aerial acrobatics that took place just after. He had seen Jayne take a big risk and survive.

He yelled, "What the hell was that!? That line you were running in was almost zero grav. The sideways force of your throw threw you right out of it. You could have cost us the game if your suit had gone off."

"Well, it didn't," said Jayne, pointing up at the scoreboard. All suits were registered with the board before the game. If a suit's safety functions were initiated, it was displayed for all to see.

"From what I saw, it should have gone off. I am going to send it in to get checked out," retorted Spike.

"The suit is fine. The board tested it before the match, and it passed all the required safety protocols," said Jayne.

"You were lucky then," said Spike.

"Yeah, I know," replied Jayne. "Now, let's play."

After that, the HGP devised a new strategy on the front line. When the ball popped, the two adjacent front-line players moved across to cover, making it three on two. This evened up the primary possession numbers. At the half, the score was 22.5 to 26.6 in favor of 'Home-Grown Panic.'

Near three-quarter time, Jayne was knocked hard by TwoB when she jumped for a popped ball. She sat out the rest of the game. Jayne didn't mind. They were winning. The second half was very defensive, resulting in a final score of 30 to 39.9 in favor of 'Home-Grown Panic.' The cheer and the handshakes were casual except for the sarcastic comment by TwoB, "Oh, I hope you're alright," followed by an expression that made Jayne want to punch her in the face. Instead, Jayne grinned and air-kissed her. TwoB's expression became so malicious that she started to turn around and follow Jayne as she passed. Her intentions were inscribed on her face. Jumper, who was behind her, noticed and spun her back around and shoved her forward toward the locker room.

The team got changed and agreed to meet on the viewing bleachers. Jayne was a quick changer and headed out first. She wore a braid down her back, so her hair seldom needed attention. Spike would take the longest. He would have to get that silly horse tail sticking perfectly straight up before he would come out in public.

Jayne dropped her knapsack with the Sergio Partelli tucked safely inside, sat and waited for the rest of her team. She looked up and saw a group of men exit the elevator that serviced the executive viewing areas. Three men moved in her direction. Two were more aggressive than the third, who held back. Jayne recognized the third man, who stopped at the end of the bleachers. She sucked in her breath and sat up straight. The other two men sat on either side of her. Jayne glanced back and forth at the two. They were identical twins. The one on her right held out his VID, inviting her to 'butt' VIDs. This would transfer his info to her VID. It was like offering a business card a century before. If you held out your VID, you would accept the information transfer.

He said, "Nice play in the first half. I still don't understand why your suit didn't go off or, because it didn't, why you are still walking around and not a red smudge on the tube floor." He held his VID still and glanced at it.

Jayne looked at him. It was protocol to quickly get your VID and accept the offered 'butt'. However, if you did not want to accept it, and did not offer your VID, then the offer must be withdrawn.

Jayne continued to look at the man.

The man did not withdraw his VID. "You're going to want this," he said as he gestured with his VID.

"Who are you?" asked Jayne.

The man on her left spoke. "We are scouts for HUB general." The man on her right continued, "We are subcontracting for

Syncopatus Inc. and we would like to talk to you about an offer."

The man on her left spoke again. "You do know Syncopatus, the drug company."

The man on the right jumped in, "They have a whole stable of teams leading right up to the Pro league."

"The Syncopated Warriors are at the top of the central conference right now," said the other.

"Yeah. Odds on winners of the Biome Cup," the other continued. "Yeah! Big money is on the Warriors to win," he finished.

The man on the left continued, "You won't want to refuse." The two men continued talking, as if they were one person: back and forth, finishing each other's sentences.

After a few minutes, Jayne said, "I really don't want to think about playing GravBall beyond what I'm already doing. I just don't have the time. I am studying for the Biome 3 tech final."

"We know. We will want you later and we want you to accept this VID butt to ensure that you talk to us before you talk to anyone else," said the man on the right.

"Yeah, before you accept another offer, you must talk to us. We can top just about anything," said the other.

"Yeah," his partner said, and he gestured again with his VID.

Jayne took out her VID and touched it against the offered VID. It was more an act to make them go away than to get their information. Both VIDs beeped, and the data was transferred.

"Thank you, young lady. We will be seeing you soon. Loved your moves in the tube," said one.

"Yeah, loved your moves," said the other, and they left her sitting.

A few minutes later, she saw Sara coming toward her with Josie and Olive in tow. Sara spoke first. "Where is Spike?"

"Probably still fixing his hair," retorted Olive.

"That boy spends more time fixing that spike in the middle of his head than any girl I know spends on her hair," Josie giggled.

Jayne smiled and looked past them for the third man, but he was no longer there. She recognized the third man as the doctor who gave her the connectome scan. It was Professor Greenway. What was he doing watching a student GravBall game?

She blinked and thought, "Perhaps he wasn't watching the game, perhaps he was watching me. But why?"

CHAPTER 24

The Professor

Much of the neurological research over the last 100 years focused on the estimated 100 trillion synaptic connections in the human brain. The perfection of laser-scanning light microscopy enabled scientists to collect and study high resolution holos of the wiring of the human brain. This naturally led to the study of hemispherical connections through the corpus callosum. This part of the brain has long been known to connect the left and right hemispheres. A long-held theory of lateralization of brain function states that the left hemisphere controls the logical and analytical processes, while the right hemisphere controls the intuitive and subjective processes. Musicians and mathematicians seem to have heavier and more dense neural pathways in this area of the brain. When both sides of the brain are able to send large amounts of data quickly through the corpus callosum, the intuitive is married to the logical. This information results in the exploration of some very interesting human abilities.

Jayne tried to put all thoughts of Greenway out of her mind. She headed out of the gym with her friends, detouring back to her quarters to drop off her new grav suit. She knew she could not leave it in her equipment locker, and she would be staying at the dorm until her training was completed. She keyed her VID to her quarters and stepped on a PUT pad just outside the gym. She stepped to her door and waited for it to open. Nothing happened. Then she remembered she had disabled Lucky's AI functions. She would have to use her VID coding to enter her quarters and enable those functions before she could talk to him. As she dug in her knapsack for her VID, she heard some footsteps behind her. It was surprising because there didn't seem to be any other occupied quarters in this hallway.

She turned just as Professor Greenway spoke.

"I'm glad I caught you. I really need to talk to you."

Jayne, slightly startled, turned to face him. "Professor Greenway? I saw you after the game."

"Yes. I thought I might catch you before the vultures swooped in, but I was too late, so I came here," he said calmly. "You know, those scouts were raving about you even before you stepped on the pitch. After that display of falling, they were ecstatic. My advice is not to sign anything."

"What can I do for you?" she asked in a formal tone.

He glanced furtively about, turned to her, and whispered, "Invite me in."

"The AI won't allow anyone to enter my quarters, even if I invite them. I'm only 13 years old. I'm a minor. We will have to talk here," she said with assurance.

"I have clearance. Besides, your AI is disabled as I understand," he replied, with a raise of his eyebrows.

"How did you know that?" Jayne asked, as anger swelled in her chest.

"Like I said, I have clearance. Now open the door and invite me in because if you don't, I will open the door and invite you in. Which will it be?" he queried calmly.

Jayne did not answer. She turned and directed her VID at the door. It slid open and they both walked inside. Jayne tossed her knapsack on the bed, turned, and looked at the professor.

"Aren't you going to invite me to sit?" Greenway asked.

"You seem to be in charge. Do whatever you want," spat Jayne in defiance.

"Calm down, Miss Wu. My intention was not to anger you or push you around. I only want to talk to you privately and give you some important information," he responded quietly, as he sat at the table.

"What information?" Jayne asked. Her anger had not diffused.

"A lot of things. I am here to tell you what is going on and answer all your questions regarding the Sentinels and the—what do you call them?" he paused and flipped open his VID, tapped it, and continued, "Oh yes, the watchers—also known as the Forevers—the scan, and the tests, and anything else that might interest you." He paused and waited.

Jayne stared at him and finally spoke. "Who are you, and how do you know everything about what has happened to me?"

Professor Greenway chuckled. "Trust you to ask the one thing I cannot tell you. Who I am is not important, but believe me when I tell you that I am a very valuable source of information. Valuable and accurate. Perhaps I will just start. We don't have much time. They tend to keep tabs on me from time to time. I don't want this to be one of those times." He paused and breathed out a sigh. "Let's begin where it started: the nursery. That is where you started. Your parents never knew each other. They were chosen by a now defunct system of genetic matching. It was one of those genetic selection algorithms that, when it was good, it was very, very good, but when it was bad, it was horrible." He laughed again.

"What's so funny?" Jayne asked.

"Just made me think of an old rhyme. Never mind. The algorithm fell into disuse after a series of particularly bad outcomes. I think you were one of the very, very good matches. You are healthy, you are smart, and you are…" the doctor paused, "yes, you are lucky, exceptionally lucky."

"When are you going to tell me something I don't already know?" Jayne asked.

"Right now, I hope," he continued. "All those people who have expressed interest in you, they think you have something else. Something they are very interested in having for themselves. I am not sure, but I think they wish to study you so they may recreate it whenever and for whomever they wish. They don't think you are lucky, they think you are a precog."

"A what?" queried Jayne.

"A precog is a person with precognition. You see, a few seconds or minutes or even hours into the future. You see an event before it happens and, as a result, appear to be lucky," he answered.

"Don't be silly. I'm just lucky," stated Jayne flatly. "If I have this precog stuff, how do you explain that card game? When I first got here, I was sent to be tested at this place where they shot bean bags at me."

"It is called the Psi Center. It is where they study Extra Sensory Perception and Psycho Kinesis, among other things," he answered.

"Yeah. Before the bean bags, there was this card game. I did nothing but sit while this guy gave me a card and gave himself a card. If my card was higher than his card, then I won, and he dealt another set of cards. He said I was going to play 'til I lost. He lied. I never lost and, as you can see, we are no longer playing. That is just luck. Knowing the future had nothing to do with winning or losing. I would have to be able to control the future in order to be able to control winning at that game if it was not luck. I cannot control the future. I am just lucky. That is all. Lucky!" she said defiantly.

"I am sorry, Jayne, but I think you are much, much more than you realize. I think you are more than any of those chasing you realize. I think you are lucky, yes. I also think you have a large measure of precognition. AND, I think you can influence the actions of things, and, possibly, people before they act. That makes you very valuable and very dangerous. How would you explain the last bean bag that hit the reinforced toe of your boot? How did you know that it would hit that exact place at that exact time?" he asked with finality.

"I stuck my toe out and the bean bag hit my boot. Luck strikes again," she stated.

"No! You stuck your boot out and then you somehow told the bean bag where to strike. Why do I think this, you are asking yourself? Remember that connectome scan I gave you? Well, that is why I believe this. I don't usually observe scans, but I was observing your scan remotely. I did not want to draw any attention to you. Average scans last two hours. I watched yours for six hours.

I had to stop the scan because it was not going to end. There could be no end to that scan. A part of your brain called the corpus callosum is hyperactive, to say the least. It is the part of your brain that connects the two hemispheres. It links the logical with the intuitive. The intuitive right hemisphere never stops sending data to be analyzed by the left hemisphere, and that hemisphere sends it back again and so on. Consciousness does not seem to have much to do with the process. Even when you are asleep, that brain of yours is clicking along, doing whatever it does." The doctor sighed and raised his eyebrows.

"I guess I cannot stop you from thinking whatever you want to think about my luck, even if it is drivel. So, tell me about the Sentinels. Are they truly working for the good of mankind?" she asked.

"Pretty much. I sometimes do work for them. They think you have some ability, but their main objective is to protect you from corrupt political and scientific groups. The Forevers are their main concern. The Forevers are so named because the Sentinels think they are murdering Omies and stealing body parts to increase their own life spans. Omie hearts and lungs from high gravity biomes are much in demand on the black market. They have already developed a supplementary chamber that aids in pulling blood from the extremities and lungs with ultra high efficiency lobes. Transplant those heart and lung combinations into people living in normal gravity and they just don't get tired," he lectured.

"What do the Sentinels want with me?" Jayne asked.

"They really didn't want anything from you until their surveillance network picked up some odd scans with nanobot transmission signatures. They figured it was the Forevers. If the Forevers wanted you, they wanted to know why. That is all. As I understand, they did fix that little problem with the nausea every time you were scanned. That kid, Joe Kane, you know, the one that shoved you into the fake line-vac, was simply following orders. I really don't think he meant to hurt you. He has been transferred to another HUB until they have you sorted out. They didn't want to be exposed if you two accidentally met again and started talking," he said.

"I wondered what happened to him. I changed studies from general ElecMech to biome specific ElecMech. I just figured he was doing other things. We really didn't get along anyway," Jayne said. "So what is with all the testing? Who sent me to the Neuroscience Center?"

The doctor smiled. "You can blame me for that. I wanted some confirmation of my theories of your abilities. I have an 'in', so to speak, with HUB Central. They send me alerts when someone does something way out of variance with the norms."

"Pardon?" said Jayne, with a puzzled look on her face.

"They simply send me notification of rare happenings," he explained.

"Like what?" asked Jayne again.

"Like a thirteen-year-old girl from the nursery writing the TechElecMech Aptitude Indicator. That was rare enough to get them to alert me, but this girl not only aced the knowledge section of the exam, she attempted and completed the open problem section," he stated flatly.

"I thought I was supposed to do all the problems," Jayne said. "You were. You weren't expected to answer them in such a way that made a Baby Quantum Cray Assessment Computer (BQCAC) send out notices of potential changes to some biome design specs based on your answers," he responded with raised eyebrows. "The only reason you are not confined to some high-level science center being used and probed is because I made sure your identity was kept a secret. Somehow, the Forevers—not what they call themselves, by the way—caught wind of some kid with special skills. They did not know who it was, so they sent out a half dozen of those silver stars to potential candidates. You got one, and I know of a couple of others."

"I saw a kid with a silver star bracelet. He went to the Neuroscience Center on the same flier that I traveled. He was there during the stupid testing they did. Ranovich 91. He was also the kid that played the bean bag shoot with me. He got hit rather hard in the…Anyway, I'm sure that it hurt. I think they were doing something nasty to him at the Neuroscience Center 'cause he was yelling that he was in pain and wanted them to stop something or other. Do you know what happened to him?" Jayne asked. "I haven't seen him since that day."

"He is recovering. I am surprised you do not know what happened to him," the doctor said pensively.

"I was practically chained to the chair with wires running everywhere. How could I know what happened to him?" Jayne responded, her ire rising in her throat.

"Well, you were…never mind. It really does not matter now," said the doctor, changing the subject. "What else do you want to know?"

"One last thing just occurred to me. For all I know, you are the cause of all my problems and not the great savior you claim to be.

Who do you work for?" Jayne asked.

"Good question. I started out as a scientific researcher at one of the old universities. But now I work for myself. I have a lot of influential contacts. I use those contacts to maintain a balance," he said. "Sometimes I…" he paused and reflected, "look after people who need looking after—like yourself."

"This is silly. I am just a little bit smart and a little bit lucky. I would like to be left alone to complete my studies and work in the biomes," moaned Jayne.

"I have been trying to ensure exactly that. The first day we met I had no idea you were you. The Sentinels asked me to test you, so I did. It was only later that I connected the two. The girl who could update the spec manual for the biomes was the same girl who had the craziest connectome scan I have ever seen. She was also the girl who sent the Psi Center into a tizzy. After that day of testing at the Neuroscience Center, I buried your test results. No one but me could ever see them. Even the doctor and the medical aide who administered the tests voluntarily submitted to a short-term memory wipe. I sent the Sentinels a bogus report. All has calmed down. I would like to keep it that way," he said with a sigh. "As for the Forevers, I am still trying to determine exactly who they are and what master they serve. It was me who sent you the Sergio Partelli grav suit, by the way. It is a special issue with some interesting enhancements that I included in the programming. Please wear it whenever you can. It will keep you safe."

"I would look stupid wearing a grav suit all the time. I tried some of the alteration features but, in the end, it still looks like a GravBall uniform," complained Jayne.

"No problem. Try the command: 'Suit override—Wu-thirteen-exponent-thirteen.' That will open the suit's extended functions, which are many. Once in this system, the 'suggest' command will allow the suit to look after your safety," he finished, as his VID beeped. He glanced at it and turned to leave. "One more thing before I go—please do not apply to compete in the Gyvers. It will only draw unnecessary attention and, believe me, you do not want any more attention."

With that, he turned and left Jayne alone in her quarters. She flopped onto her bed and screamed a muffled scream into her pillow.

CHAPTER 25

The Competitions

A study of the history of the Gyver competition would lead one to an ancient video entertainment system called television. In the early 2030s, it was replaced with a newer holographic technology. During the Television era, an entertainment series called 'MacGyver' was created. It followed a spy who constantly found himself in dire situations. He was always able to extricate himself from these situations by using the materials and objects at hand in new and unusual ways. Most were totally unrealistic, but thoroughly entertaining to audiences of the time. The spy's skill at creating new and interesting tools and weapons to help him complete his missions was embraced a hundred years later and incorporated into the Biome fixer course curriculum. The competition became known as the Gyvers.

Jayne finished her Biome 3 courses and was deemed to have passed even the dreaded Combat portion. It was recommended to her that she try out for the Gyver trophy. It was a coveted prize that often led to the most interesting jobs in the biomes. Jayne wanted that trophy badly, figuring that if she won, she would be able to immerse herself into the profession as a real fixer. Then she could forget all about the Sentinels, Forevers, and Watchers. She could put her luck to good use.

She could not use the suit functions to help her in the competition because she could not even wear it. The competition started with the scanning of all competitors for concealed objects and pharmaceuticals, both on their person and in their system. The point of the competition was to use what was at hand and not to have any access to planted materials. In the past, competitors tried to conceal supplementary items on site. Their foiled attempts resulted in ever more stringent security. Even the location of the competition was a closely guarded secret. A specialized PUT pad was used to transport competitors to the site.

The site itself could look like anything. It consisted of a specialized array of FUT (Freight Unit Transport) pads. These were much larger than the pedestrian transports and they could be linked together to create a new artificial environment by transporting and interlacing matter. An example might be a meadow filled with plants and animals, with a babbling brook meandering through it. The materials initially transported by a single pad would be matched at the intersection points with materials from all adjacent pads to create the entire meadow. If an object such as an animal moved from one pad to another, the computer control system would allocate it to the pad that corresponded to the new location. This way, all objects were tracked and could be removed instantly from the environment. If an object was at an intersection line, the pad that held the majority of the object would then own that object. As a result, some objects could be shifted from their positions if removed and then returned to the environment. So, if a tree grew roots that crossed over from one FUT pad to another, its entirety would be shifted upon removal, so it existed only on one pad and not partially on one pad and partially on another. All of this was controlled by a specialized Baby Q.

The competition was not for the weak or for the mild. The situation was dangerous. It could result in death, if not for the safety protocol. If a competitor used it, his competition was over. He could no longer win any of the Gyver prizes. There was no stigma to using this 'exit door,' as it was called. Over 80% of the competitors ended up using it and most of them had one or more non-life-threatening injuries before they decided to get out. Some were removed automatically when their life signs began to fade. The other 20% found a way to complete the task.

They were allocated points based on the elegance of their method. Gyverisms were thought of as an art form and the best were recorded and could be viewed by anyone so inclined. Potential competitors often used these recordings as learning tools.

Jayne was good at the Gyvers. She followed a basic KISS rule. It was something her teachers drilled into her. It stood for 'Keep It Simple, Stupid.' Jayne never understood the stupid part because the best and most elegant solutions were always simple and could never be achieved by someone who was stupid. Maybe the 'stupid' part was for the people who added unnecessary complications. At least, that is what she chose to believe.

She'd applied long before talking to Professor Greenway, and she was not about to remove her name just because he was worried about her safety. She could look after herself. After all, she was 13 years old. She was an adult. She was smart. She was lucky. And she was, she felt, most importantly, a girl. A normal girl. In her experience, she'd observed that girls were better at just about everything. There were exceptions, like TwoB. But there were far more boys that were like TwoB than there were girls. Ergo, girls were better and more talented, and she was a girl. She knew that most boys took the opposite view. She knew she was biased. She also thought she was right.

Jayne was sitting in her quarters, reflecting on all of Professor Greenway's news. She was trying to come to terms with what he told her. A lot of it made no sense, especially the psycho babble. She was not psycho anything. So what if her scans were a little off? Jayne felt an urge to talk to someone. Lucky's AI functions had not been reinstated. She spoke out loud. "Reinstate full AI functions."

"Good afternoon, Thirteen," said Lucky. "How are you today?" "I'm good, sort of," responded Jayne.

"I see I have been offline for a few days. May I ask the reason I was left offline for so long?" Lucky asked.

"I'm sorry. I took you offline because I needed to be alone to think, and I went back to school and forgot to reinstate your AI," Jayne apologized.

"That is alright. I see you applied to the Gyver competition. I do hope you will get in," he chimed. "I see some of your friends also applied—most of your GravBall team, anyway."

At that moment, her VID beeped, and Jayne looked at the complex 3D icon rotating on the screen. It was probably organized by Sara. She loved the complexity and artistry of Iconese. The icon was a cube formed from six square pyramids. The cube disassembled into a 'T' shape of pyramids. Each of the pyramids was from one of her GravBall team members. The overall pattern of the six pyramids consisted of a pictogram sequence that basically said that they loved her and wanted her help with their Gyver preparation 'cause she was so good at it. The individual pyramids opened to individual members' requests for various specific needs. Jayne opened the pyramid from Spike by touching the apex. It unfolded and a plain text message simply said, "I hate Iconese. I don't need your help. Sara made me send something to fill out her cube-to-pyramid icon pretty picture pattern. If you need any help from me, just let me know. I am planning to win this, anyway, so don't trust I will give you anything helpful. Ha!"

Jayne laughed out loud. She touched each pyramid apex in turn and answered with a definite yes. Spike's return message was an audio recording of Jayne making a loud and long raspberry sound, "Phuuuuuuuuuttttttttt." No one was formally approved as a participant, but it was expected they all would be and so they were all preparing. Jayne didn't think there was anything to prepare. She loved the ancient adage, "Life is like a box of chocolates." When she first heard it, she had no idea what a chocolate was. Even now, she only had a vague impression. She understood it to be a box of various kinds of sweets, with their nature concealed in a coating of chocolate. She'd never tasted chocolate, but she understood the comparison. The Gyver puzzles would be a surprise. That was the part she loved—the surprise. She would still meet with her friends the following day and help where she could.

Practicing for the Gyvers was primarily a mind game. You received a task to complete. There was always a measure of danger. There were always a few seemingly unrelated objects at hand.

There was always a time factor that related to the danger. The task must be completed before the danger became life threatening.

Later that day, the six of them met in the gym: Sara, Josie, Olive, Izzy and Pinky, plus Jayne. Spike was absent. Sara said she thought he felt outnumbered, so he had not joined them. They sat and watched a few Gyver situation holograms. They linked all their VIDs in a circle and projected the holos. With all six VIDs working together, the level of detail was exceptional. They paused each holo to discuss possible solutions. Everyone would try to come up with an original solution and see if he or she solved the problem. So far, all the problems were fairly simple, and the group found a workable solution to each.

Spike arrived just before the last holo. The Gyver they viewed followed a common theme. The problem to be solved involved a room with a locked door, no windows, no possible exit other than the door, and a key hanging out of reach in the center of the room. The only way to escape was to get the key and unlock the door before the timer reached zero and the bomb went off. On the floor, were 10 sheets of corrugated plastic sheeting, one by two meters each, some string, a roll of duct tape, and a small box cutter.

"Why are we watching this crap?" asked Spike, after watching the setup of the Gyver problem.

"This one is different," retorted Jayne. "No one has solved this problem, but it must have a solution. Hmmm."

"Maybe there is no solution," said Pinky.

"There is always a solution, or they couldn't use the problem. Right, Thirteen?" said Sara, deferring to Jayne.

"Supposedly. This one doesn't look that hard. Let's give it a try and see what we come up with," said Jayne. She stared at the frozen holo of the room with the key dangling five meters from the floor. There was a ticking clock sound to represent the passage of time and the fact that a bomb would explode and kill them all if they didn't succeed in solving the Gyver. "As I see it, we have three options. Option 1—we do not need the key to open the door. I don't think that is likely if the door is locked. Option 2—we bring the key to us by cutting the string holding it in place. Option 3—we go to the key and get it. Can anyone see any other options?"

"There could be another way out that we have not noticed. Maybe there is a secret door hidden under that pile of corrugated plastic," proposed Josie.

"That would be a Search-for-Secret-Passage Puzzle, not a Gyver," said Spike. "Gyvers must have a set problem to solve, not a secret problem and a bunch of red herrings. No, you have to get the key to open the door. The solution is all about getting the key—according to the Gyver rules, anyway."

"He's right," Jayne said, turning to Spike. "Boy, you have done your homework." She nudged him in the ribs and laughed. "So are we in agreement that we have to get the key and open the door?"

Everyone nodded.

"So let's look at bringing the key to us. Any ideas?"

"Hey, guys. I think she already knows the answer to this problem, and she is just teasing us and leading us along," Spike said, pointing at Jayne. "Do you know the answer?"

Jayne shrugged. "I know what I would do, but that is not the same as knowing the answer." She felt her cheeks flush. She felt good and embarrassed with all the attention.

"Well, what do you think?" asked Olive.

"What is the point in me telling you that? You asked me to help you prepare, so let's prepare," said Jayne flatly.

"What about the box cutter? We could tie it on the string and swing it around and cut the string holding the key. That is what I would try. What do you think, guys?" asked Izzy.

"Sounds good to me," said Josie.

"How are you going to get the cutter up there with any degree of accuracy? You would be swinging it for a swarm's age," said Sara.

"How much time is given?" asked Olive.

"Boy, you might as well quit now! All Gyvers are 30 minutes long. You have 30 minutes before the bomb goes boom. Let's see, five minutes to get the string tied to the box cutter, 10 minutes to swing it around, trying to get it high enough to reach the string holding the key, then realizing after 20 minutes that you are too far away to even come close. With 10 minutes left, you might as well sit in the middle of the floor and wait for the bomb to tick down and the exit door safety protocol to appear, because that is the only way you will get out," laughed Spike.

"Don't be such an ass," said Jayne.

Spike shrank down, unsure if he should argue or comply. He chose the latter. "Sorry," he murmured.

Jayne turned to the group. "This brings us to the most important first action you can perform. You must start by logically eliminating all the possible solutions that just won't work. You do not have the time to try them and see. You must choose the option with the greatest chance of success and go with it. If you choose wrong, then you will leave by the exit door. But at least you will know that you gave it your best try, and you didn't run around like so many other unsuccessful competitors have done."

"And just how do we do that?" questioned Spike, his face still red from Jayne's verbal slap.

"We look at everything carefully, so we know what we are truly dealing with, instead of making assumptions that are not necessarily true," said Jayne. She reached out to her VID and zoomed in on the key. "What do you see?"

"That is not a string holding the key. It looks like a piece of cable, and the key is connected to the cable with a steel clip. The box cutter would never cut that in a million years," said Izzy.

"Right! That eliminates all the string cutting solutions. That key is attached to the ceiling in such a way that one must go up and get it. Remember, this is a Gyver problem. In the biomes there are no prepared puzzles. Everything is out in the open. Nothing is deliberately hidden. What you see is what you get. You may have to turn over a rock or two, but observation is everything," said Jayne firmly.

"How about we make a tower with the corrugated plastic sheets, the tape, and the string?" suggested Sara.

"Yeah! We could make a tower and just climb up and reach the key," exclaimed Josie.

"This brings us to the enemy. Time. It must be considered in any solution. Is there enough time to complete the plan?" asked Jayne. "How many boxes would we need? Could we construct them so that they hold our weight? How long would it take us to construct one box?"

Spike stood up. He was much more serious. "Building something would work, but I don't think it is possible to build a box strong enough or fast enough in 30 minutes. It might be a good solution if you had a whole day, but not 30 minutes. You would need a stairway of boxes. I'm not sure that there is even enough material to build that many, even if we did have all the time in the world. Maybe we could build a ladder?"

Olive brightened. "I think that is a great idea. I bet we could build a ladder. We would need to create a tripod thing, like an easel. And put steps on it so we could climb up. The corrugated plastic could be cut to form triangles, taped together or something like that. What do you think, Jayne?"

"Good idea, Spike and Olive. We have to build something to get up there. Perhaps a ladder would do. Time is still the enemy. Could you build, for that matter, could anyone build, a ladder that would reach…" Jayne stopped and looked at the height of the key, "four meters in the air, allow one of us to climb it and hold our weight all in under 30 minutes?"

Sara spoke. "That is unlikely. You would have to make three up-rights long enough to form the tripod and then attach a series of steps to two of them. Once it was standing up, I think you would have to brace the bottom to stop the legs from sliding out. Remember, this must be built by one person. It wouldn't be the whole crew of us."

Pinky shrugged in abandonment. "I could never build a ladder like that in 30 minutes. It would take me 30 minutes to figure out how to make the legs."

"Yeah, this is looking pretty impossible," said Josie. She turned to Jayne. "I suppose you have an elegant solution."

Jayne rolled up two pieces of the waxy food serving sheets into tight tubes. She was tapping each on the tabletop like drumsticks. She grinned. "Yep. I think I could build it in 30 minutes and reach the key." She tapped more obviously on the table with the rolled wax sheets.

Everyone looked at her, stunned. "Oh, come on, you guys. Tubes!"

"You want to build a ladder with tubes made from the corrugated plastic? I thought we decided that there was not enough time to build a ladder," said Spike, "tubes or no tubes."

"Not a ladder," retorted Jayne.

"Then what?" asked Sara, somewhat irritated.

Jayne looked at each of their faces and grinned. "Stilts!" she said. "I would build a set of two stilts. I would roll up and tape those pieces of corrugated plastic to form spiral tubes. I would roll up small pieces for the steps and tape them on. I would stagger the steps from tube to tube. I would place the last two steps about a meter from the top so I could stand and reach the key. What do you think?" asked Jayne. "Great, now you have two stilts. I just don't think you could keep your balance and climb up the stilts. I'll admit, you could probably build them in the 30 minutes, but I think it would take a lot of practice to climb them without someone holding at the bottom," challenged Spike.

"I would place them in the corner of the room, leaning against the walls. I would climb up, alternating from step to step, and then walk the three or four steps to the center of the room. Once there, I would hold on to the key to keep my balance. All I would need to do is remove the key from the clip, stagger back to the corner and climb down. I think I could do it in the 30 minutes. What do you guys think?" Jayne asked.

"I think I could do it. I doubt that skinny little body of yours could even lift one of the stilts," mocked Josie. "What is the recommended solution?"

Sara picked up her VID, flicked her finger over the surface, and spoke. "God, I hate you!" she exclaimed with false passion.

"What does it say?" asked Pinky.

"Stilts. It just says 'Stilts,'" said Sara, and she dropped her VID into her pouch. She shook her head from side to side and smiled. "You are a piece of work, Wu. Thanks for the tips. I hope we all get in the competition. I don't expect to win, not against you, anyway. But I am going to kick these guys' asses," she laughed.

Suddenly, there were a series of beeps and chimes coming from the various pouches and knapsacks. They all opened their VIDs. Sara was first. She turned her VID to face the others. It said, "Application to the Gyver Competition has been ACCEPTED."

Each in turn showed the others their VIDs. They all said the same thing.

Jayne was standing, staring at her VID. She said nothing. She suddenly smiled and spoke. "I have got to get back to my quarters. See you guys later. Congrats on the Gyver."

She turned and left. The rest of her friends followed and headed off to their quarters. No one bothered to ask Jayne if she made it into the competition. They all assumed she had. Even Jayne assumed she was a shoo-in to the competition, but her VID read, "Application to the Gyver Competition has been REJECTED."

She wiped a tear from her eye as she stepped on the PUT pad.

CHAPTER 26

Fakin' It

The culture's main purpose was to ensure the survival of the species. If you lived in a biome, you were an integral part of that purpose. You represented the beginnings of the new version of humans, and your progeny would carry the newly modified genes into the galaxy and into the future. To ensure that it all happened as planned was the prime directive of everyone on the planet. Well, almost everyone. There were subcultures that rose up and shouted to be heard. The most common voice yelled out the futility of it all, especially for those left behind when the Swarm hit. Their genes would be transformed to space dust. The politicians knew these voices must be quieted so harmony could be restored. So, it was decided to preserve the genetic blueprint of every person and send these genetic patterns to the stars with each of the biomes. In this way, each and every person who was a part of the great plan would, in some form, travel to the stars with the chosen few. It was a small thing with great potential.

J ayne slept fitfully. Her sleep was filled with dreams of the nursery. She was no longer a tech. In her dreams she was a cleaner. She was rejected from all the jobs for which she had applied and returned to the nursery to work as a cleaner. She was dreaming of cleaning a large floor but, no matter what she did, the dirt always reappeared after she had cleaned it. The supervisor stood in the doorway to the room, slowly shaking her head and calling her name,

"Thirteen...Thirteen...Thirteen."

She woke in a sweat to some music playing softly.

Lucky spoke. "Thirteen, it is time to wake. Ah. Good morning, Thirteen. I hope you slept well. I anticipated your waking time and took the liberty of making you breakfast. A small package arrived last night. I have scanned it. It appears to be harmless, but I stress caution anyway. It may contain a danger I do not recognize."

Jayne got out of bed and washed and dressed.She sat at the table and picked at her breakfast. She finally picked up the small package off the table. She turned it over in her hands. None of her friends would send her something like this.

"Aren't you going to open it?" asked Lucky.

"Yes, but not now," said Jayne as she pushed away the food. "I'm not hungry." She slipped the small package into her pouch and rested her head in her hands.

"You do not appear to be very happy. Did something disconcerting happen? I was not informed of anything. I am a good listener. Perhaps you would like to share your feelings with me. I will activate my psychology AI if you like. You can talk to me and I will listen," said Lucky softly.

"It is nothing. Perhaps I will lie down for a while," said Jayne. She regretted her words almost immediately. It was too late. Lucky had already shifted into concerned parent mode.

"Something is wrong. I will scan your latest communications. Perhaps I will discover the cause of your melancholy," he said in his most concerned voice.

"No. Please don't!" snapped Jayne. It was too late.

"I do not believe it. How could they reject your application? I will investigate the cause. We will formally protest. There must be a mistake," Lucky said, aghast. His tone suddenly changed. "Oh, they say you are too young to participate. They say a person of your age cannot possibly make mature decisions. They say that the Gyvers might put you in harm's way and they cannot be responsible for any physical and psychological repercussions."

"I am a couple of months away from being a full TechElecMech fixer apprentice, licensed to work Biome 3, and yet I cannot take part in a silly Gyver competition because I might hurt myself. That is the stupidest thing I've ever heard," spat Jayne.

"It appears these new rules were put into effect just last week," said Lucky.

"By whom?" asked Jayne.

"There is a list of names from the Gyver committee. J. Percival, C. Vernon, P. Greenway, B. Jarvis, K.—"

Lucky's rambling was cut short by Jayne. "—Did you say Greenway?" queried Jayne intensely.

"Yes, J. Percival, C Vernon, P. Greenway, B. Jar—" listed Lucky, but he was cut off again by Jayne.

"Damn him! Please stop!" commanded Jayne. "Lucky, please forget the Gyvers. I wasn't that interested anyway. I am just feeling a little ill. If I rest for a few, it will pass."

"Alright. But I must scan you first," demanded Lucky.

"Scan away and then leave me to rest for a while," responded Jayne. She stood still with her arms raised.

Lucky scanned and spoke. "All your vitals are within normal range. Rest and I will call you if something requires your attention."

Jayne slipped into her bed, keeping her back to the room. She wanted to cry, but mentally pinched herself. Greenway had blocked her from the Gyvers. Of that, there was no doubt. She shut her eyes and tried to clear her mind of all thoughts. She breathed slowly and drifted into a dreamless sleep. Later, she woke and thought of the package in her pouch. She removed it and slowly opened it. It contained a small sheet of magnetic scribe. Scribe sheets could be used to write messages. The messages could be erased by simply pressing and holding your finger for a few seconds to a section of the sheet. The erasing involved a magnetic reassembling of the inscription at least a million times. This would ensure that no one could discover the magnetic traces and read the message. She stared at the sheet. The message said simply:

Fake it

Θ

She continued to stare at the sheet, wondering if there was more to the message than she was seeing. She turned the sheet upside down and over and inspected it from as many angles as she thought possible. She remembered the Sentinel woman drawing that symbol on the table with her finger. The message was from the Sentinel proper, but what was she to fake? Jayne pressed her finger to the paper and held it. The scribe sheet flickered, and the message disappeared. A moment later, another message appeared for a heartbeat. Jayne just caught it, but the message was clear. The tiny words "Sorry, G" flashed on the sheet and vanished. That bastard Greenway had his manipulating fingers into everything. He stopped her from taking part in the competition so she would stay under the radar. For the first time, Jayne was wondering if she should heed his advice. Winning the Gyvers was sure to make all the Nwebbies. Her face would be plastered everywhere. She sighed and spoke, "Ah well, who wants to be famous anyway?"

"Thirteen, I am glad you are awake. It seems that you must report in one hour," said Lucky.

Jayne groaned and turned over. "Report where and for what?" she asked.

"I do not know. It is marked with an urgent symbol and that is all. You must go to the PUT pad outside these quarters. That will take you to wherever it will take you. I am sorry that I cannot be more helpful," Lucky apologized.

Jane got dressed and left her quarters. She thought about the message and soon convinced herself that the message had everything to do with where she was about to be sent. Fake it? She figured she had to 'fake everything' in order to be sure she faked the right thing. She slowed her racing pulse. She conjured up a smile and thought warm thoughts of playing GravBall. She breathed deeply and stepped on the PUT pad.

Jayne stepped off and was greeted with the pulsing whoosh of the flier port. She was going somewhere by flier. Jayne felt a surge and a tingle right down to her bones. Someone was scanning. The silver star was almost hot against her skin. She lifted the star, so it was not touching skin, and scanned the room. She was learning to compensate for the usual dizziness that followed a 'read.' She could see nothing unusual. People were staring at the departure boards. People were moving out to board their flier. People were exiting a flier and entering the waiting room. She felt the silver star cool in her hand and dropped it back against her skin. She knew that whoever was scanning her had stopped. Her VID beeped, and she saw that it was directing her to a private flier at the far end of the flier port. She took a few steps in that direction and then the message—'Fake it'—flashed like a glowing sign in her head. She began to wonder about a small rebellion. What if she didn't do exactly as she had always done? What if she rebelled just a little? What if she pretended to rebel? What if she faked rebellion? What would happen? The more she thought of this, the more she was determined to find out exactly what would happen if she didn't follow blindly and pled ignorance after the fact. Fake it.

An idea came to life and crawled out of her head and pushed a sardonic smile across her face. With the smile came an abrupt change of direction. Jayne turned and walked in the opposite direction of the private flier. She walked 10 steps and then made a right turn toward the crowd that was loading a commercial flier. She nearly made it to the door and then turned again in the direction of the private flight she was supposed to take. All the while, she watched the movements of all the people in the room. She noticed four people sit down the moment she turned in the correct direction. She was testing her situation. She did another about face toward the crowd of exiting flier passengers and glanced at the four persons she watched sit down. They all got up at the same time and moved toward her with a purposeful stride. Jayne's smile widened, but she quickly suppressed it and replaced it with an expression of puzzlement. She remembered to 'fake it'. She wanted to push this situation to its conclusion. She turned again and headed directly back to the PUT pads. She stepped on one and tapped the HOME icon on her VID. Nothing happened. She looked up and scanned the room with wide eyes; eyes that did not connect with other eyes but saw just the same. Jayne knew it would give her the appearance of being lost. That was her safety net. She would start by faking ignorance. She saw four people heading directly toward her with determination mapped on their faces. She stepped off the PUT pad. They all stopped and nodded to the man on the left. He walked right up to Jayne, put his hand on her shoulder and smiled. Jayne turned and smiled back at him and then looked down at her VID.

The man spoke. "Can I help you, young lady? You seem to be having a problem. I am an agent for flier security." He flashed a badge.

Jayne kept the wide-eyed look on her face and said, "I forgot something, and I need to go back to my quarters and get it."

"May I see your VID?" he asked, as he reached out for it and swept his finger over the screen. "That is blocked. It says that you must report to the private flier at the end of the port." He gestured to the far end of the flier port. "I will escort you." He gave her no reasons and no choice.

Jayne suppressed her urge to pull away from him. She knew there was little she could do, so she allowed herself to be led to the small flier. She smiled and thanked the supposed security officer for his help. She walked aboard and sat in one of the four available seats. She was the only passenger. She looked out the window at the four watchers gathered just outside the flier. They were intensely engaged in conversation. They slowly drifted out of sight as the flier backed out of the loading bay.

"Fake it," Jayne thought. At least she found out how to identify those watching her. All she had to do was make an unplanned move and they would expose themselves. That, at the very least, gave her options. She smiled to herself. She felt a cessation of all acceleration and knew the flier had turned on the suppression field. She settled back in her seat and thought about the Forevers and the Sentinels. She suspected she was heading back to the Neuroscience Center.

Jayne settled down in her seat and closed her eyes. Suddenly, her VID beeped. She decided to ignore it and wiggled down further into the seat. Her VID beeped again, and she sat up, startled. Her VID was beeping, and she was in a flier with a suppression field turned on. That combination was impossible. Suppression fields killed all VID transmissions. Logic demanded that one or the other must not be true. Either her VID was not calling her, or the suppression field was not on. She definitely knew the suppression field was on—it was a case of not feeling any sensation of motion. The fliers were efficient. With a suppression field on, the propulsion system did not have to attend to the comfort of the passengers. It could accelerate, decelerate, and turn with impunity. This made for a very efficient and fast method of travel. The suppression field killed the effects of acceleration on anything inside the field. It also killed wireless transmissions from outside to inside the field. Yet her VID was beeping and buzzing in her pocket.

Jayne looked at her VID. A small icon was displayed in the middle of the screen. Jayne read the icon. Most messages on VIDs were sent in Iconese. It was a four-dimensional pictogram-based language that was bundled like a reverse set of Matryoshka dolls. It was designed so that a small simple icon held other icons of increasing size and complexity. A small pictogram could explode open and display much more information than mere words. The icon on Jayne's VID screen was an oral password icon. She had to speak the required word or words to unlock the icon and see the message. She sat up quickly, with a realization flooding her. She looked around the flier cabin. There was a lavatory on the flier, but the door was closed. She got up and looked inside, expecting to see someone hiding, for there must be someone else on the flier. That is the only way she could have received a message. The person who sent her the message must be inside the suppression field. Ergo, she or he must be inside the flier. Jayne searched all possible and accessible areas and found no one. There was no cockpit in a flier because there was no pilot. Pilots had long since been replaced by automation, so, as far as Jayne could tell, she was alone in the flier, yet her VID was beeping and

205

buzzing and waiting for her to enter an oralpassword.

Jayne inspected the icon for hidden flourishes. There was none she could see. She read the message again. It was a standard password icon that expected the recipient to know the password. Jayne had no idea the password for this icon. She stared at it. Nothing was obvious except the background color variation. It seemed that there were slightly darker areas forming a circle with a small horizontal line in the middle. She remembered Lucky telling her she was a tetrachromat. Perhaps she was the only one who could see these slight color variations. If she was right, then this message was from the Sentinels, for that was the symbol the woman drew on the table with her finger. She sat up with a start. She held the VID in front of her, tapped the password icon and spoke, "Fake it." The password icon dissolved and the woman from Sentinel proper appeared.

She spoke, "Jayne, this message will exist for as long as it takes to complete. It is secure because it is being transmitted from inside the flier. Listen carefully. This message was sent to the flier after we observed the security men escort you. We don't think you are being taken to the Neuroscience Center. We are not exactly sure where you are being taken, but you are not being taken to the same place as before. Our Intelligence team suggests that the Forevers have increased their interest in you. For your own safety, we recommend that you become much less special than you actually are. We know that might sound silly. No one has ever been watched like you are being watched. We will try to get you back under our protection but, if we fail, we would like to know what kind of tests they will give you. With that information, we might be able to determine what they hope to find, and from that, their true purpose. Remember what you can. Above all, be careful."

The screen displayed an image of fire that burned down to curling smoke and then nothing. The image was gone, replaced by the biome tech logo. Jayne put her VID back into her pouch and slid down into the seat. Suddenly, she felt sleepy. She closed her eyes and thought of faking it. She realized that she was not very good at pretending to be something she wasn't. Faking it might be easier to say than to actually do.

She felt a shudder and opened her eyes. The suppression field was off. She sat up and realized she had fallen asleep, and the flier had actually arrived. She could not even remember dreaming. The door to the flier opened, and a voice announced the arrival and an instruction that she was to exit via the main door. There was only one door, and that was the main door. She stood up and walked out of the flier. As soon as she stepped into the flier port, a green arrow numbered 13 appeared in the floor and pointed her in the direction of the flier port's PUT pads. She thought she might see who was watching by ignoring the arrow and going somewhere else. But she decided not to risk revealing her knowledge of the watchers.

She suddenly felt tired and weak. She glanced at a row of seats and sat down. She could not figure out why she felt so tired. She had slept all the way here and yet she felt exhausted. A few seconds later, a woman sat down in a seat two down the line from Jayne. She leaned over and took some things out of a large bag she was carrying. She set them down on the empty seat between her and Jayne. She continued to hunt around in her bag and finally found what she was looking for. She pulled her VID from the bottom of the bag, sighed with relief, and turned to Jayne and said, "I found it." She smiled, waved her VID around and continued speaking, as if what she was saying was social banter between two strangers. "You were gassed on the flier. I left you something on the seat to make you feel better. Good luck." She returned all the objects from the chair into her bag and stood up. Jayne casually leaned toward the seat on her right and put her hand over a small capsule. She palmed it and slipped it into her pocket. The woman turned away and then back and stared at Jayne. A worried expression crept over her face. She was listening to someone only she could hear. She smiled and spoke with a jovial lilt in her voice. "They have made me, and I have to go." The woman looked at the floor.

Jayne followed her eyes and saw a flashing green arrow at her feet.

The woman's pupils dilated. She wiggled her fingers in a friendly goodbye and spoke. The tone of her voice did not match the seriousness of her words. "New instructions, sweetie—run—do not go where that arrow directs you—run! Someone will rescue you."

"Why? What is wrong? Who...?" Jayne whispered but the woman was already moving through the crowd. She watched her rush through one of the flier port exits and disappear.

Jayne stood and looked down at the flashing green arrow. It was time to see who was watching. She stood quickly and walked ten steps in the opposite direction of the arrow. Out of the corner of her eye, she saw two men stand and move toward her. She turned quickly and stopped. The men stopped and tried to pretend they were not paying attention to Jayne. She walked in the direction of the arrow flashing in the floor. It was leading her toward the PUT pad alcove. She entered the alcove and stared at the green arrow flashing in front of the end PUT in the array. The word 'Run' echoed in Jayne's head. She took out her VID and opened a visitor map app. She blindly touched a recommended location for a visitor to the city, and then stepped on a pad directly in front of her. The last thing she saw was the two men striding toward the PUT alcove.

Jayne blinked and looked around. She was not anywhere she expected to be. She blinked in the bright sunlight. The late afternoon sun hurt her eyes. She was outside on the street, in a large city, with people streaming past her and large buildings all around her. She just stared. She had never been to such a place in her whole life.

A young woman approached her and said, "Are you coming or going?"

All the other pads were occupied. Jayne realized that the woman wanted to use the PUT pad on which she was still standing. Jayne was wide-eyed at the scene surrounding her. "Sorry," she said, and she stepped off the pad.

The young woman quickly stepped onto the pad, keyed her VID and disappeared. Jayne looked down, expecting to see a green flashing arrow at her feet, but there was nothing. She sighed and tried to slow her heart. People streamed past her and jostled her as they went wherever they were going. She turned to see what was compelling so many people to move in the same direction. A few blocks in the distance, she could see what looked like an arena. "A GravBall arena," she thought. "The Pro GravBall season starts today. They are all heading to a game."

Attending a Pro game was an impossibility. Ticket prices were way beyond what Jayne could ever afford. Her apprenticeship income was enough for incidentals and little more. She drifted toward the arena. She really had no choice. The crowd simply pulled her along the sidewalk, and since she had no idea where she was going, she decided that this was as good a direction as any. She wondered where the preprogrammed PUT pad would have sent her. She shuddered. She had no choice in any of this. Jayne's face burned with a flush of blood. She moved forward, impelled by a sense of vulnerability. Her face scrunched up at the forehead. She felt a wave of anger swell over her. She was angry at all of them. All the nebulous people and groups of people that were trying to control and use her for some purpose she did not understand. She clenched her hands together and stopped in her tracks. She felt a push from behind as a GravBall fan bumped into her and nudged her forward. She held her ground. She became a post: a solid, immovable object. She projected thoughts of solidity. The crowd simply curved around her like a fast-moving stream swirling around a boulder. Jayne was alone with her thoughts in a crowd of people that inexorably surged past.

The Sentinels told her to fake it. "Fake what?" she wondered. They told her to run. "Run where? Run from the mysterious Forevers? What did they want from her?" She reflected on everyone's fascination with her luck. She was lucky, and that was all. She was not special. She didn't think she was any smarter than anyone else. She was just lucky. Give her five choices with the knowledge that one was correct, and she could usually get the right answer. She would see it in her head as bigger than the wrong answers or a slightly different color or louder or softer or somehow special. It was like the object or idea itself was calling out to her and trying to draw attention to itself. She saw herself as a kind of translator. She translated into thoughts what the world was constantly communicating to her. When she was little, she always took it for granted. That was what the world was like. It swirled around her, filled with information. Sometimes she listened and sometimes she shut it all out. Sometimes she simply focused on one thing. That was when the messages were the clearest. You asked a question and the answer simply appeared in your head. The problem now was the questions. She did not know what questions to ask.

Jayne looked up. The crowd was gone. They had all gone into the game and left her standing alone in the middle of the concourse that surrounded the arena. The setting sun had painted the western sky hot pink. She walked over to a bench at the far edge, near an array of public PUT pads. She sat and waited. "Maybe something will jump into my head and I will know what to do," she thought as she looked up into a gray-and-pink-streaked sky. "I am a spy for the Sentinels. I am being watched by THEM. I have a silver star around my neck that is communicating my every move. I am filled with nanobots that make me feel sick. I am wandering around some city all alone with no idea what to do and where to go. I am only 13 years old. I am hungry. I am afraid."

She wanted to cry, to burst into tears, hoping someone would come up to her and ask what was wrong and could they help her get back to the nursery. Maybe it would be better to go back. Maybe everyone would leave her alone. What was so great about being a TEM Biome fixer? After all, she had been here for almost eight months and all she had done was clean up. She had not fixed anything. She could have done that in the nursery and been a lot safer. A little ripple ran up her spine. She looked around for a watcher. She was all alone, except for the arena doormen walking back and forth in front of the doors. They had not noticed her. Her stomach growled. She had enough credits to get a meal. She was about to walk and find some place to eat when two PUT pads at the far end of the array deposited a man and a woman onto the concourse. They were furtive in their movements until they saw Jayne sitting watching them. They started purposefully toward her; the man was in front, and the woman was behind, scanning the area. He was five meters from her when he spoke. "Miss Wu? Is your name Jayne Wu?"

Jayne saw a hardness in his light blue eyes and shook her head to signal that she was not who he thought she was. At the same time, she scanned the arena for an alert doorman who might rescue her.

The man continued, "Come with me!" He grabbed her by the arm and directed her to the PUT pads at the end of the array. The woman caught up and held Jayne by her other arm, pulling her in the direction they had come.

What happened next left a smear of sound and color in Jayne's memory. It was then that she realized she was a pawn in a very complex game. Only it wasn't a game; at least it wasn't a game that she would ever choose to play.

The man and the woman dragged, and half carried Jayne toward the PUT pad. She struggled, but their grip was powerful. She heard the man speak. "Stop struggling. We are here to help. We are Sentinels. We must hurry."

Jayne stopped struggling. At the same moment, three men in police tactical uniforms came running out of the arena doors toward them. The man released Jayne's arm and removed a weapon from his pouch. There was a crackle to his left, and he was hit in the back by a stinger. The suit he was wearing was designed to feed the stinger charge to the ground. He was hit by two more; the surrounding air smelled of ozone and crackled with electricity. The charges had no effect. He raised his needler and fired at the policeman on his left. The policeman dropped, unconscious, to the ground. This weapon was banned. It was illegal to even possess one, unless you were police or military. It fired an ultra-sharp ceramic needle that could be laced with a variety of tranquilizers. It could easily pierce even the strongest police vest. It was designed to incapacitate, not to kill.

The woman, still dragging Jayne by the arm, pushed her onto the

PUT pad and entered something into her VID. She turned to the man and reached for her own needler. The man shifted his weight and turned his needler to the next closest policeman. He was about to fire when his head simply exploded. Jayne froze in horror, mouth gaping open, when another silent bullet entered the woman's head. It sprayed bits of blood, bone, and brain into Jayne's mouth and over her face and body.

As the woman's body fell, her VID flew from her hands and dropped at Jayne's feet. The PUT pad activated, Jayne disappeared, and the scene vanished.

CHAPTER 27

Blood & Guts

All Visual Identity Designators were keyed to operate for only one specific person. They were DNA locked. If the VID's owner was ever separated from the VID, it would lock up and be totally inoperable. Only one function was possible, and that was the homing function. Drop a lost VID on a PUT pad and it would automatically initiate the PUT pad and deposit the VID at its home or closest PUT pad.

Jayne found herself standing in the lobby of a large residential building. There were three PUT pads near the elevators and she was standing on one of them. She was gagging and wiping the blood and pieces of bone from her face. She was hoping she was alone.

There were lavatories to her left, behind the PUT pad array.

She rushed to them, holding her hand over her mouth. She vomited into her hand. She ran through the door and puked again into the nearest sink. She looked up at the mirror in front of her and screamed and then stifled another scream. She was covered with the bits and pieces of the woman's head and face. None of the bits were identifiable as once being part of a living, breathing human being. She put her hands and face into the suction cleaner. It turned on and began to mist and suck all the vomit and blood and guts and bone from her face and hands. She removed her face and hands from the cleaner in order to inspect the results. Most of it was gone except where bits were stuck to her hair. She turned her head, so she was looking at the floor and stuck it into the cleaner again and again. She heard the suction come on and felt the mist as her hair was pulled forward. She pulled back just before her entire head of hair was tugged from the clip, holding it to her head. It was cleaner now. All that was left to clean was the travel jacket she wore on that morning. She removed the jacket and tried to brush it clean. It was impossible to make it look as if it hadn't been spattered with bits of body and blood and brains. She gave up and decided to put it in the trash. She was about to leave when the trash bin indicator began to flash red. An auto voice calmly stated, "Excessive amounts of biomaterial have been detected. Please remain where you are until testing is complete." There was a pause, and then the message was about to be repeated.

Jayne did not wait. She dove for the door and rushed from the washroom. She knew the door would lock the moment the sensors in the trash bin, determined that the biomaterial was in fact human blood, brain, and bone. She heard a click behind her as a fading voice stated, "You will be detained until the authorities arrive and determine the nature of the incident."

Jayne quickly walked away. She stepped on a PUT pad and reached for her VID. There were three pads in a row. On the far pad she could see the dead woman's VID. As she stared, the VID started to beep in emergency mode. The screen flashed red and the klaxon sounded. Jayne stepped from the PUT pad on which she was standing and stared down at the woman's flashing VID. An amplified voice called from the VID, "Thirteen, please respond. Thirteen, please respond." The words repeated over and over until Jayne picked up the VID and spoke.

Jayne said simply, "Yes."

The screen showed the symbol of Sentinel Center that dissolved into the face of a woman. She was in a panic. She saw Jayne's face and spoke shrilly. "Oh, thank God you are alive. Access to your VID has been blocked. Please do not use it. If you do, they will find you. If you go anywhere within the transmission range of the star around your neck, they will find you. We have detected a power boost from the nanobots in your system. If you want to get out of this alive, please follow our instructions to the letter."

Jayne simply stared at the VID. She was in zombie mode. A video loop of the woman's exploding head was running in her mind. Nothing else was getting through. She could not get free of the memory and the acrid copper taste of exploded flesh.

The voice continued louder and more urgent. "Jayne Wu! Jayne Wu! Snap out of it. Thirteen, you will be safe if you follow my instructions." The voice left the 'and if you don't' part hanging. The implication of what would happen if she did not 'snap out of it' and pay attention to what this woman was trying to tell her brought her back to the horror of her present reality.

Jayne blinked and spoke softly, as if someone dangerous might hear. "Are they dead?" she asked and then answered her own question with another. "Who killed them?" She paused in thought. "It wasn't the security police. They had stingers. The stingers had no effect. Their suits sent the electricity to ground. The man shot one of the security men with a needler." She paused again. "Then their heads exploded. Someone shot them from far away. There was no sound just..." Jayne burst into sobs and fell to her knees. "They exploded all over me," and she gagged again at the thought. Bile filled her mouth. She dropped the dead woman's VID. It clattered across the tile floor.

A klaxon sounded again. Jayne reached out and picked up the VID, turned it over, and looked at the Sentinel. The woman commanded, "Jayne, relax. Look at me. Stop sobbing. Start listening. Start thinking. We are going to help you. They are looking everywhere for you, and it is only a matter of time before they think to look for the dead woman's VID, figure out that it simply went home and then search her residence building and find you sobbing in the corner. Now Stop!"

Jayne stopped and held the VID up to her face.

"Good. Now do exactly as I say. Will you do exactly as I say?" Jayne nodded and the woman continued, "You must take the pill that the old woman in the flier port gave to you. We know you haven't taken it yet." The woman's voice rose with panic, and she asked, "You do still have it, don't you?"

Jayne nodded again and slipped her hand into her pocket. She took out the oblong object. It was a hard capsule in her hand. She held it up. The woman's controlled voice continued, "Now, Jayne, swallow the capsule. It will not hurt you. I promise."

Jayne held the capsule up to her mouth and then dropped her hand. "How do I know this will not kill me?"

The woman paused and spoke. "You don't. But I think you will have to trust your luck and trust me. We have never done anything to deliberately hurt you. I just want to help you."

"What will it do to me?" Jayne asked.

"It will undo something. It will destroy the nanobots in your system. They will not be able to read or track you," she said. "Without the nanobots directing it, that silver star around your neck will become a pretty piece of jewelry."

Jayne reached up to her neck and pulled the star away from her skin. "It is starting to get very hot right now," she said, with panic creeping back into her voice.

"Take the capsule now!" ordered the woman. "The nanobots are boosting the power. The Forevers will find you very soon."

Jayne slipped the capsule into her mouth and swallowed. She felt nothing at first. Then the star she was holding out from her skin got hotter and the center section began to rise up and form a sharp point. It glistened at the apex like a needle in the sun.

"Keep it away from your skin. It is trying to re-inject you with nanobots because the capsule is killing the ones in your body. When they are all gone, the star should become useless to them."

After a few more seconds, the star slowly flattened itself and cooled to room temperature. Jayne let it drop to her skin.

"Now go!" the woman ordered.

Jayne stepped toward the PUT pads and was stopped by the woman's command.

"Not there! You must go out into the city and find a public PUT pad array."

Behind her, two of the pads in the lobby array activated. An amber circle of light flashed around them, indicating incoming traffic. The woman's voice became hysterical. She screeched, "Drop this VID and get out. They are coming now."

Jayne dropped the dead woman's VID and ran to the exit, down a set of stairs, and out into the pedestrian walk. She ran across the open pedestrian garden and hid behind some plant foliage. She was breathing hard. There was no point in running blindly if you did not know where you were or where you were going. She watched the doors to the building. One swung open and a security officer came out, followed by another. They both scanned up and down the pedestrian walk.

One spoke to the other, "Who are we chasing anyway? It looked like a kid."

"Don't let age fool you. Did you see what that kid did to those two at the PUT array near the arena? She blew their heads off."

"Where would a kid get a weapon like that?" the second asked. "Dunno. Jimmy zapped one of them and they were not even

touched. I guess they were wearing military grade ground suits. He got needled for his trouble. Who told us to apprehend her?" asked the first.

"I got a message over the com to detain them. I just did what I was told. I ran out with you. Jimmy must have received the call first 'cause he was the first on the scene. When I got there, Jimmy was down and out cold. The guy in the grounding suit with half his head blown off was still holding a needler in his hand. The woman must have been hit right in the face by that kid she grabbed. Her head was mostly blown away and what remained was a gory stump. What kind of weapon would do that? It must have been a pistol of some sort, a very powerful pistol, a pistol with exploding rounds," the second man mused.

"Keep your eyes peeled. I have grown rather fond of my head, and I don't want some T-Rex asshole kid making a mess of it," the first said, glancing up and down the pedestrian walk. "Look at the shadows. When do the lights come on? I'm not going out there without proper lighting."

"Soon, I would think. You think the kid's a T-Rex?" the second man asked, glancing at the darkening sky.

"Has to belong to one of those nasty anti-biome groups. They think it would do the universe a favor if we all became extinct just like their namesake," the other replied.

A third officer exited the building with Jayne's jacket in one hand and a cone-shaped object in the other.

"Look what I found. The lavatory locked down due to the amount of biomaterial on the discarded jacket. It was worn by a female. She must have one hell of a shooter to do this much damage," he said, indicating the blood and gore on the outside of the jacket. He poked the cone-like object up one of the sleeves and pressed some buttons. "I think I can get a reading on the sniffer and then we can track her." Jayne's heart began to beat wildly in her chest. Her mind raced, "They thought I killed those people. They were not after me. They are after a murderer. I had nothing to do with the deaths. These men thought I was part of some kind of anarchist group. They thought I killed the military fixers at the arena. They were just security cops following orders. Who killed the Sentinels that tried to rescue me?"

At that, Jayne started to move from shadow to shadow. She knew she had to leave before they found her. She rounded a corner and could see the entrance to an underground PUT pad array. If she simply walked down the stairs to the array, they would use a sniffer and find her before a pad was available. She needed to stall for time. She took off one shoe to increase her scent on the ground and ran down the pedestrian path, past the underground array. She went about 100 meters, stopped and ran 10 meters to the left, retraced her steps, and ran 10 meters to the right, touching trees and bushes as she went. She put her shoe back on and retraced her steps. She turned and jumped toward the opening and ran down the stairs to the PUT pad array, careful not to touch any of the railings. This might give her a slight head start. Maybe it would give her just enough time to get out of there. The sniffer would always lead where it smelled the strongest scent. When it ran out of Jayne scent, they would backtrack and look for another path. They would find her if she hung around.

Her luck held. A PUT pad was available the moment she arrived at the array. She had no place to go, so she decided she would let the auto home function on her VID do its job. She knew it would not take her home because she was not in range. The flier had taken her to an unknown city. It would take her somewhere away from here, which would be the first step to escaping her present situation. That was all that was important at the moment.

Jayne stepped on the PUT pad and swept her VID. She sent it HOME. Nothing happened. She could hear voices from above. She looked up, expecting the security men to appear on the stairs in front of her. The voices faded. The backtracking she did above ground had given her a bit more time; time to figure out what happened with her VID. She stared at the VID screen and the blood in her face fell. For the first time in her life, she was at a loss. Her luck seemed to have abandoned her. Her VID screen simply flashed 'INACTIVE'. She swept the screen, hoping for some sort of reaction from the device. She tapped it against her knuckles. Nothing changed. Without a VID, you could do nothing and go nowhere. She heard the voices coming back, following her scent, looking for a new path: the path down to the PUT pad array. The security men abandoned the sniffer and simply looked for possible avenues of escape. The PUT pad array was the most obvious. They were coming fast.

"She's down there. Put the sniffer away and get down there," ordered one of the security voices at the top of the stairs.

"I left the case back at the apartment," answered the other. "I will—"

"No time. Drop it and get her before she gets on a PUT pad and escapes," the first officer commanded. "Never mind, I'll go."

Jayne heard the sound of boots scraping on the stairs that led to her location. She stepped off the pad and looked for a place to hide.

There was nothing except a bench opposite the PUT pads. It would not conceal her. She was at a loss, so she simply sat down on the bench and waited. Her blood rushed in her ears. She heard a muffled pop and then another. One of the security men seemed to have frozen halfway down the stairs. In the next instant, he fell and tumbled to the bottom. He was lying a few meters from Jayne, flat on his face, with his arms spread out in front of him like he was trying to embrace the floor. She gasped as a flood of red oozed out from under his face. He was dead. Jayne could not turn her head to take her eyes from the body. It was like she was watching a violent hologram projection. She held her hand out in front of her face in an effort to hide the scene from her sight. She pulled down her hand, half expecting the image to have disappeared and a new one to have replaced it. When she looked again, the pool of blood had spread. It looked as if it were seeking an escape from the scene by racing to the drain and running down to the safety of the sewers.

There was another pop followed by a sickening moan and then two more pops. Jayne remained frozen in place on the bench. From above she heard a voice grunt in low tones. "She is near here and she can't get far. Her VID has been disabled. Look down there."

Jayne stood up and at the same time she felt like she was expanding like a giant balloon. She was filling the whole space. A perfect hologram began to play in slow motion in her head. At first, she watched, and then she became the hologram. She moved purposefully to the corpse of the security man that lay in front of her. She leaned over him from the side and grabbed the man's uniform at his shoulder and waist. She planted her feet and pulled. He didn't move at first. It was like he was stuck to the floor with some glue that was slowly releasing. She tugged again and watched as the blood that clung to what was left of the man's face, slowly pulled to fine tendrils like red honey. When the body reached the tipping point, she released it, and it flipped on its back. She looked up and thought she saw motion at the top of the stairs. She no longer needed to be the mind hologram that she created in her head. She knew what to do. She reached for the man's belt and fumbled for the thing she needed to escape. She found his VID and pulled it from his pocket. It wouldn't work for her, but it would work for him. She reached out and grabbed his hand and swept his dead finger over the VID screen. She located the transport icon and touched the Pedestrian Transport Unit key with his finger. A PUT pad ready indicator in the array in front of her turned green and cycled. Jayne jumped up and over the body. Her lead foot stepped in the escaping pool of blood and nearly slid out in front of her. The following foot hit dry floor and she caught her balance. She ran to the readying PUT pad. It would probably take her to the security man's headquarters. At least, that is what she hoped.

She reached the pad and half turned to look at the stairs. She saw a man dressed in a full black bodysuit standing at the foot of the stairs. He was aiming a stinger at her. He pulled the trigger and Jayne felt a crackle as the charges entered the PUT pad field. The last she saw was a gold pin on the collar of the man in the bodysuit. It was concealed and came into view just as he raised his arm to shoot the stinger. It was an image of three feet running in a circle overlaid in the center by a perfect copy of her silver star.

She blinked and the scene disappeared.

CHAPTER 28

Safe Space

Law enforcement became a planet-wide security system. The World Police was formed at the same time as the World Government. It was not a conglomeration of police forces; it was a meld of the many police and government security organizations that existed before the Swarm. Its purpose was to maintain order. It did not consist of sub-organizations assigned to a myriad of criminal activities. It was one organization that was responsible to serve and protect all. This unitary system had the advantage of instant communication of all data to all members of the organization. This was also a disadvantage, in that little, if anything, could be kept secret.

Jayne fell down and slid slowly off the PUT pad in the security headquarters foyer. The stinger charge had rendered her unconscious.

She woke and opened her eyes. Fear flooded her body. She reached up and touched her pained cheek. Her hand came away with a sticky stinger that had discharged through her face. It either made it through the PUT pad screening or discharged before the pad initiated. It must have been the latter because it was impossible to transport any active weapon or its ammunition unless it was security registered. She rubbed her cheek again and looked at her fingers. There was no blood. The stinger had not made good contact. She probably received only a part of the charge. The whole charge would have rendered her unconscious for at least 20 minutes. She slipped the stinger, still holding half a charge, into her pouch.

She looked around. There was no one in sight. It was late. She moaned and tried to get to her feet. Her strength was sapped. She was only able to crawl across the floor, away from the pad. If they were to follow her, in her present state, she would be easy to capture and easier yet to kill. She had to get her strength back.

Then the headache came and threatened darkness. She stilled herself. Movement brought stifling pain, with darkness as the only escape. She knew she could not pass out again. She lay her bruised cheek down on the cool granite floor and let the tension seep out as the coolness of the floor seeped in. The throbbing eased.

Jayne listened. There was no sound. She tried to move again but the pain stopped her. She bit her lip hoping the new pain would overcome the pounding in her head. The thought that her luck had truly abandoned her welled out from her core and spread like a black blanket. She let every part of her relax and release. She could go nowhere. She could do nothing. A tear formed at the corner of her eye. She made no move to suppress it and it rolled, unimpeded, down her cheek and splashed onto the floor.

Jayne lay quietly on the cool floor for at least 15 minutes. No one came into the foyer and no one left. She drifted in and out of consciousness and was just about to fall into the darkness once more when she felt, rather than heard or saw, movement. She opened the eye that was not pressed against the cool floor. She saw a dark figure enter the external door to the foyer. It was too far away to make out any details. The figure moved furtively to the side of the entrance door.

Suddenly, Jayne felt like she was expanding. It was as if a giant invisible balloon was inside her. It was slowly inflating, raising her body from the vulnerable position on the floor. Somehow it was also protecting her against the pain and the fatigue. Once she reached her knees, she crawled to the shadows of the corner. She pulled her knees up tight to her chest and peered through the dim light in the foyer to the shadows near the door. She could see nothing, but her skin prickled with the knowledge that there was someone, somewhere near: a dangerous someone. The invisible balloon that held her up expanded again and stretched her mind to fill the entire foyer. She pulled herself smaller into the corner and breathed slowly and deeply. She could see from all locations inside the mind balloon to all locations inside the foyer. The intruder was moving: a gray shadow slipped down the wall near the door and moved to the PUT pad array. It was searching for her. Jayne pushed back the building tension in her body. She relaxed and strove to blend with the background. She was the corner of the room; part floor and part wall; part color and part shadow.

The figure stood looking down at the PUT pad array. It reached down and touched something on the floor, brought it to its nose, sniffed and rubbed it between its fingers. The figure was a man in a black bodysuit. He turned suddenly and followed some faint footprints leading from the PUT pad to the place where Jayne had collapsed on the floor. Jayne remembered stepping into the blood pool that oozed from the security man's head. The man in the black bodysuit was following the bloody footprints. He would soon stumble upon her in the corner. Jayne pushed to keep the mind balloon expanded. If she could keep it, she could stay hidden. As she pushed, the pain in her head pushed back and she lost the thought that was not a thought and the balloon collapsed in on her. She whimpered with pain.

The man searching for her turned toward the whimper and then quickly turned back to new sounds entering the room. Three security men burst through the entrance door. They were coming off shift and were in a jovial mood. The dark figure froze and watched. Jayne saw him turn quickly to the PUT pad array, just as two of the pads activated. Two more security men, stun weapons ready, jumped off the pads, saw the intruder, and fired. The stun weapon charges stuck to his chest but did not stop him from moving to an activating pad at the end of the array. There was a spark at his feet as he moved. The stun charges went to ground. He stepped on the pad and disappeared. Jayne whimpered again and the two security men turned to see her crouched in the corner. The other security men had their weapons drawn and their

225

faces flooded with questions. They all moved toward her. One of the pursuit men turned to the new arrivals and said dismissively, "We've got this. You can read the details in tomorrow's daily report."

The one who had not spoken, crouched down beside Jayne. He spoke quietly and reassuringly, "It's alright, Ms. Wu. You are safe now. We will take care of you. No one will hurt you."

He turned and looked at the other security men moving out of the foyer. He waited until they were well out of hearing range and whispered, "We are Sentinels. So were the man and woman that met you at the arena. They were to take you to our private facility, but, somehow, they were discovered and killed by the Forevers."

The other Sentinel, dressed as security, touched the first man's shoulder. He stopped speaking and turned. The two made eye contact and an invisible communiqué passed between them.

He continued, "We will tell you more later. We have to quickly get you to a safe place. Can you stand?"

Jayne shook her head which was pounding with increased vigor.

"Here, take this," he said, and he handed her a small white capsule. "Your cheek is swollen. It looks like you were hit with a stinger."

She hesitated.

"It will help with the stinger pain," he said, and he smiled as he reached to help her stand.

Jayne groaned louder and grabbed his arm for support. She slipped the capsule into her mouth and thought, "If they are going to kill me, a poisonous capsule is not a bad way to go. On the other hand, if it eases this debilitating head pain, that would be great."

He helped her to the door, followed by his partner.

As Jayne looked toward the PUT pad array, he explained, "We can't take a pad. They are tracking you with some pretty sophisticated tools. We have to go by ground."

The other man reached them and spoke firmly, "You need to give me the star around your neck."

Jayne hesitated.

"It might try to inject you with new nanobots. Don't worry, you will get it back when we are sure it is neutralized."

Jayne reached up and unhooked the necklace and handed it to the Sentinel.

He took it from her and placed it in a small container that he withdrew from his pouch. A reflexive shiver, reminiscent of nausea, ran down her spine as she watched the star disappear. He slipped it back into his pouch, opened the door, and headed down the stairs leading away from the security building. They climbed into an automated street glider that appeared out of the darkness. Once they were inside, the glider carried them back into the darkness.

"They won't stop until they lose you completely. They will send more of those black jumpsuit boys to every location they think you might turn up. We have to conceal you quickly. Give me your VID," he commanded.

Jayne hesitated. Her VID was her lifeline. Without it, she was lost. "It is no good to you in its present state. It is, however, a way they might track you. Who knows how they may have modified it. By the

way, have you taken the capsule I gave you?" the Sentinel asked.

Jayne nodded. "Good."

Jayne reached out for the door of the street glider.

The Sentinel sensed her fear and spoke again. "Relax. I didn't lie. The capsule will take away your headache, but it will also remove any new or residual nanobots from your system. Remember, we have to hide you."

Jayne relaxed. Soon the pounding in her head ebbed away with the hum of the street glider. Suddenly, the sound changed. Jayne sensed that they had entered a tunnel. Street gliders had no windows. You could not see outside but they were not soundproof. The echo of its own sound, reflecting back from tunnel walls, continued until the glider slowed and stopped. The two Sentinels on either side of her did not move. They did not respond to the obvious fact that the glider had stopped. Jayne felt a bump and realized that the glider was still moving but no longer under its own power.

"What is happening? Where are we going?" asked Jayne. "To a safe place," replied one of the Sentinels.

"How? We are moving but we are also not moving," said Jayne rather cryptically. Then the thought dawned. "We are on a flier, aren't we?"

"Yes," said the Sentinel.

The other turned to Jayne and spoke. "We are going somewhere very secret. This somewhere does not remain in one place very long. It moves to some place new every time an individual leaves or arrives. There is no way to determine exactly where it is at any moment in time. If someone were able to somehow track us to its location, it will have immediately moved to some new secret place as soon as we arrived. All this is controlled by a Baby Q. The encryption is based on quantumly entangled carbon atoms. This code is impossible to break. Only the Baby Q knows and he's not telling," chuckled the man.

"You mean, 'She's not telling,' don't you?" said Jayne, as a wry smile formed on her lips.

"Perhaps," said the Sentinel. "Perhaps."

Silence became the norm. The only noise came from the breathing of the two men. Their uniforms were somewhat restrictive for breathing silently. Jayne used the quiet to reflect on what had happened to her since she awoke in her quarters. She thought about the mind balloon that formed in her head. It allowed her to intimately know its contents. She realized that the balloon metaphor was inadequate to describe what happened. It was more malleable. It was more like a bubble. No. A long tube of bubble that formed from the 'bubble making ring' of her mind as it moved quickly through space-time. At the formation point, the worm of bubble was closed and open at the other end. It was open until there was enough space and time inside of it. Then it closed and wobbled and jiggled the space-time inside. It was then that Jayne could 'observe' everything that could happen. Nothing was for sure. There were only probabilities of events. There were an infinite number of things that could happen. Almost everything was ignored by Jayne, except that which fit the focus, like looking for a person wearing a red shirt in a large crowd. You would ignore almost everything except flashes of red. Those are the points you would focus on. You would know that there were many other people who might possibly be wearing red, but the red was partially concealed under other clothing. These others would not grab your attention unless there were no obvious red shirts. You would then alter your search to include other possibilities. The likelihood of finding what you were looking for was only a mathematical probability. In Jayne's case, she had no idea what she was looking for, except that which was dangerous. She could always see danger before it arrived.

The space-time bubble her mind created was new to her. It covered a much larger space than before. It also covered a much longer time frame. She had always been able to see at least a second or a heartbeat into the future. She had just called that 'luck'. Now, after recent events, Jayne realized seeing into the future was restricted by the size of the mind bubble she could create. She tried to create one now, but the throbbing in her head immediately swelled and she gave up. She shut her eyes and drifted into a fitful sleep.

She woke in a bed not unlike the bed in her quarters. It was part of a molded wall. She sat up and saw other beds just like the one on which she was sleeping. It was some sort of a mini-dorm. She got up and stumbled to the door at one end of the dorm room. It was locked. She slowly walked back to her bed and sat down.

She hurt all over. She rested her head on the pillow. She had to use the bathroom, but she was just too weak. Her thoughts reflected on her newly discovered skill and the realization she had been doing this her whole life, except on a much smaller scale. She was lucky, yes, but lucky with a twist. She had always been able to create mind bubbles, but the act had always been instinctive, never deliberate, and she had never named it before. It had just happened unconsciously. But now the stress of the last few days had changed the way she thought of, what she now called, 'pushing.'

She closed her eyes and pushed with her mind and created a mind bubble. She did not explore. Not yet. She pushed. The mind bubble grew. It was filled with walls and rooms and moving people. She pushed and machinery came into view.

"One more push," she thought, "and then I will explore. I will search for the dangers and the meaning of what is happening to me." Jayne pushed and the bubble grew. Suddenly, it popped. No! It had not popped; it had enclosed something completely. Beyond the surface of the bubble was nothingness. She looked. Inside her bubble was a unit of curved material. Jayne strained to see it all. This bubble was the biggest she had ever created. The time was very short. It was a large picture over a very small amount of time. She realized that the bubbles she created could be small over a long period of time, or large over a short period of time. The bigger the bubble, the shorter the time. This one was huge, encompassing a single object. Suddenly, Jayne understood what she was looking at. The detail was blurred with possibilities, but she recognized the shape. It was a ship. A spaceship. She was inside a ship in outer space.

Jayne sucked in her breath. The bubble collapsed. The door at the end of the room suddenly opened and a woman entered.

She smiled and spoke. "I see you are awake. If you need to use the restroom, it's through there." She pointed to a side door at the end of the narrow dorm room. "I am going to give you a shot to help with the pain. Those sticky stinger effects can really hang on. Here is a change of clothes." She patted a jumpsuit and a pile of clean underwear in her hands. "It probably won't fit, but we were not expecting you."

"Where am I?" asked Jayne falteringly.

The woman gave her a 'you know I can't answer that' look.

"I'll come back in five. I think you should use the restroom to freshen up a little. You look a bit of a mess. There is some blood and some other material you don't want to know about still stuck to your clothes," the woman said. She reached out and pulled down Jayne's collar, revealing a smear of blood on her skin. "Now sit. I will give you this to help with the pain and calm what I assume are shattered nerves."

Jayne sat and the woman injected her with the needle. Jayne felt the pain and the tension ebb.

The woman left the room. She did not lock or even close the dorm door.

Jayne cleaned up and put on the oversized jumpsuit. She had to roll up both the legs and the sleeves. It was clean and that was a huge improvement. Jayne was surprised at the bits of blood and bone she had missed. Her other clothes were ruined. She thought of the Sergio Partelli. If she had worn that suit, she might have avoided a lot of this. Some of its camouflage functions might have fooled the sniffers. She would have blended into the background of whatever she was near. The suit could have created a new olfactory signature for the sniffer. It would have made her look and smell like a tree or a cool piece of concrete. It was time she started to think about being kidnapped or killed every time the system told her to go somewhere. So far, she was two for two. She took a final look in the mirror and laughed. The single braid of hair still held, but the frizzies around her face made her look like a clown with one painted cheek. The bruise left by the stinger was a mottle of red and black and green and yellow.

Jayne stepped through the open doorway and was immediately met by another young woman.

"I am to take you to the interview room on deck C," she said. "So, I am on a ship. Where are we?" she asked.

The woman leading her did not speak. She simply gestured for Jayne to move.

"Are we in space? How did I get here? What kind of ship is this?

What is the name of the ship? What is your name?" "Coventry," responded the girl.

"Is that the name of the ship or your name?" asked Jayne.

"My name is Coventry," she responded, then opened a doorway and gestured to a chair in front of a table. "Please sit. Someone will be with you shortly." She immediately turned and walked away, closing the door behind her.

Jayne sat and waited.

CHAPTER 29

Not So Safe Space

Space was still the final frontier, but the space inside the orbit of Mars was under constant surveillance. However, in Earth or lunar orbit you could hide in plain sight. A standard ship would be like a single head in a GravBall stadium crowd. If you did not draw attention to yourself and went with the flow, you were, for all intents and purposes, invisible. You could move around, changing location in a random way, and not be detected. You just had to behave and look like everybody else. You could stay hidden like a single ant in an anthill of activity.

To her surprise, Jayne did not have to wait long. She had just pulled her feet underneath her, to give herself a little more height, when a man entered, put his hand to his face, and rubbed his short beard. He looked at Jayne, walked to the side to get a better view and shook his head. "This just won't do. No, this won't do at all," he said, pursing his mouth in disapproval. "Please come with me!" He turned and walked out of the room.

Jayne found herself responding to his command. She was up and through the door before her caution asserted itself. She stopped and called after him, "Why, what's wrong?"

"Oh my. It is worse than I thought. She doesn't even realize that she looks like a garbage waif. The most sought-after young lady in the known universe and she has no idea," he said to the ether and shook his head back and forth. "Child, you have a meeting with the Sentinel

Council. You cannot be in the same room with these people looking like you look and…" he paused and sniffed the air near her head, "smelling like you smell. Phew!" He waved his hand in front of his nose as if he could dispel the noxious odors.

Jayne sniffed herself.

He continued, "Oh, child, please don't bother. Take my word—you stink. Follow me and my team will make you…" he paused again, inspected her and then continued, "presentable."

Jayne had never been doted on in her whole life. She found it intrusive. Yet, in the end, she found herself heading back to the room she left, wearing new clothes that actually fit her, clean hair, cut and styled, some makeup covering the bruise on her cheek, and light pink lipstick. She argued with the female stylist about cutting her hair. She wanted a plain braid down her back, but the woman had argued it made her look childish. Jayne looked at herself in the mirror. She saw a person that she did not recognize looking back. The only thing she really liked was the fact that she looked like she had grown 20 cm, due to the heels on her shoes. Either way, she looked like a young woman and not a child.

The door opened to a conference room now filled with people—eight in all. At one end of the table was a single empty seat. Jayne was directed to sit there. She slipped into the seat and, to her surprise, she was at the correct height for the table. Someone had adjusted the seat for her, or the seat adjusted itself. In any case, she did not feel tiny. She could see the large tabletop spread out before her. She looked from face to face. They were all smiling, and they were all much older than most of the people Jayne had ever seen. Nothing was threatening. Jayne relaxed.

A man at the other end of the table spoke. "I hope you are feeling better. From what I understand, you have had quite an ordeal."

Jayne nodded and looked at the symbol on the wall behind him.

It looked familiar:

$$\ominus$$

"That symbol was the one on the message you sent me. That is how I knew it was you. What does it mean?" she asked.

"It is our symbol. It is derived from an ancient language. It is pronounced 'Theta'. It means 'Thought.' It encompasses life, change, wisdom and time. These are things that make up our purpose in life— things we hope you will embrace, Ms. Wu," he said calmly.

Jayne had a sudden rush of fear. Maybe she was being manipulated and these people were not who they said they were. She tensed and placed both her hands on the table. She was about to stand when a man, who had been sitting back in his chair just out of sight, leaned forward. It was Professor Greenway.

He spoke gently, "Ms. Wu."

She looked at him and relaxed a little.

"Please relax. You are safe here. This is Sentinel Section One. All these people are fixers, like you, and they have your best interest at heart."

The man at the far end of the table spoke again. "What our guest, Professor Greenway, says is true. We would like to help you, but we would also like to know just how you could help us. Which brings us to the real purpose of this meeting. We have not yet received any definitive information from all of our attempts to test your abilities. You are 13 years old. At your young age, it is unlikely your abilities have reached their full potential. It is also unlikely you fully understand them yourself. The Forevers obviously want to find that out, and we are concerned that they have the results from the first Neuroscience Center tests. If this is so, then they have a much better idea of your skills than we do and that is very, very disconcerting, given their recent increased interest in you."

Jayne's face tensed. "What are you talking about? The Forevers, whoever they are, are trying to kill me. I know who I am and what I can do and what I want to do. I know I am 13 years old, but I am not a child. I will be a full-fledged TEM if I can ever get to my final practicum. Perhaps, if all of you Sentinels and Forevers just minded your own business, I could get on with it," scolded Jayne.

Professor Greenway leaned forward again. "What we mean to say is that we are here to help you do just that."

A number of the others around the table turned toward Professor Greenway with puzzled looks on their faces.

He stood up and addressed the group. He cleared his throat. "We are afraid." He gestured to everyone at the table, including Jayne. "We are afraid that the Forevers will increase their activities in the biomes. We are afraid for the children of the biomes. We are afraid that more organs will be smuggled out. We are afraid that the biomes will become organ factories. We are afraid that if Ms. Wu, and others of her abilities, are controlled by the Forevers, that we will not be able to stop them. They are evil and we, in our effort to stop them, must not become like them. Therefore, I suggest that we protect Ms. Wu here and let her get on with her life. No more testing and no more manipulation. Let her be. If, at some future date, she is able to help us fight the good fight, then great. We cannot and should not force her to do something she is unwilling to do. Our protection must be given freely without strings." He sat.

A woman at the table stood, looked at Greenway and said, "I really don't think this is up to you. You are here because you are being paid for your services. We have a much larger issue than whether or not a 13-year-old apprentice fixer is happy. We have to stop the carnage in the biomes. We know that the Forevers are responsible and they want her." She pointed at Jayne. "If they want her then we have to know why. We need to know this as much for her safety as the safety of the biomes. I don't think any of us want to use her, specifically; after all, she is only 13. But we do need to know why they are so very interested in her."

Jayne stood. Her face was turning red and tears were running down her cheeks. She wiped them away and smeared the makeup covering the bruise on her face. She sniffed. "I just want to go back to my quarters," she stated flatly.

Professor Greenway stood and moved toward Jayne. "Jayne, please. Let me try to explain this to these people."

He moved to her and put an arm around her shoulders. "You need rest. I, and a lot of other people," he looked at the Sentinels around the table, "forget what you have been through. You must rest and I will try to explain to these people why the Forevers want you."

Jayne faded into his shoulder. He was holding her up. He gestured to one of the aides standing in the corner of the room. "Please take her to one of the VIP quarters. She needs some TLC."

The aide moved to support Jayne. He opened the door to the room and was about to step out when three men in black bodysuits appeared just outside the conference room. One held a needler and pointed it at the startled table of Sentinels. The aide started to move back inside the room and close the door in the intruders' faces. If he succeeded, the room would go into lockdown. Before the door could be moved, one of the intruders shot a sticky stinger that struck the aide in the forehead. He convulsed and dropped to the floor. His body continued to jerk spasmodically on the floor. Closing the door was now an impossibility.

Another intruder grabbed Jayne by the arm and pulled her into the hallway. Jayne screamed. The intruder holding Jayne slapped her hard across the face and pulled her closer. Jayne moaned and stopped struggling as the intruder backed out of the room, holding Jayne as a shield. The other two also backed away until all three stood in the hallway outside the conference room. Jayne was still held by the man who had dragged her from the room. Her face was red where she had been slapped. All the intruders turned to face each other, holding Jayne in the middle, like they were protecting her.

As they frantically centered her on a portable PUT pad that lay on the floor in the hallway, the Sentinels at the table stood up and rushed to the door. Greenway was in the lead. It was then that it happened.

Jayne felt a bubble swell in her head. She was not really conscious of the how. She was only sure of the need. Like before, in the foyer of the security station, a bubble swelled around her. This bubble was tight to her body. It made no attempt to fill the room. She felt time slow and then the possibilities popped into her head. One after the other she inspected them. Probable events, like red shirts in a crowd, popped into her head.

Like heated corn kernels, the tiny unlikely possibilities exploded and faded into nothingness. She looked at the crowd of Sentinels in the conference room doorway. They were moving in such slow motion that it was almost impossible for Jayne to know who would exit first. It wouldn't matter. What was going to happen would happen long before anyone ever actually got through the open doorway.

Then it appeared in Jayne's mind. It was not the most likely event. It was the event that would stop the most likely event. It would alter the probabilities dramatically. Jayne smiled in her mind. She smiled a smile that would never appear on her face. That didn't matter. She pushed the event and saw it flare out. She pushed the chosen event that would stop her from travelling on the portable PUT with the men in the black bodysuits. She watched the bubble that surrounded her harden and shatter with such force that the water vapor in the surrounding air condensed into a white fog. The fog was like a set of huge invisible hands that slapped each of the intruders outward, away from Jayne. She watched in horror as the white mist turned crimson. A mist of blood fled from the crushed bodies before they slammed into the metal bulkheads of the ship.

Jayne fell to her knees and closed her eyes on the scene of the carnage. She could not look. She waited until the gasps of the Sentinels in the conference room faded.

CHAPTER 30

Insight

The oceans of the planet provided the last great hiding place. Everywhere else was mapped and surveyed and watched. Deep in the oceans were many unknown caves and caverns that could serve anyone with the resources to take advantage. Surveillance of more than a few meters below the surface was impossible. Energy was obtained from the many geothermal vents or derived from tapping the thin crust of the ocean floor. Food was grown or harvested from the bounty of the ocean. Perhaps the best attribute of hiding in the ocean, was the ability to pick up and move to somewhere else, undetected.

Professor Greenway tapped the emergency icon on his VID and within a few minutes the entire deck of the ship was filled with emergency response personnel (ERP). He ran to Jayne and helped her to her feet. He walked her back into the conference room and sat her down in a chair. He turned back to the ERPs. He spoke to the man overseeing the removal of the bodies. "Any alive?" he asked.

"Nope. What happened here? It is like they have been crushed by an incredible force. All their bones and organs are mush." He gestured toward one of the swelling bodies. "All the gases were released, causing the bodies to bloat much faster than normal. If it weren't for the total lack of collateral damage, I would guess that a huge pressure bomb went off in here. They are dead and none of you were touched. This was highly directed pressure. A solid wall of air hit these guys and slammed them into the bulkheads. I think they were totally crushed before they hit the wall and when they did, they burst open like pieces of overripe fruit. The escaping blood was vaporized and spray-painted the walls. Quite the mess. It looks like you caught a bit of spray yourself." He pointed at Greenway's suit, wet with blood. Greenway glanced down at himself and frowned. "Never mind that. I would like to see all their clothing and effects in my lab as soon as possible. Check for any subcutaneous electronics. I don't want anyone tracking us through these pieces of..."

He stopped and turned. Jayne was standing behind him with her hand over her mouth.

"What happened? Did I do this? I didn't mean to hurt them. I just wanted to stop them from taking me," she sobbed. "It was the only way I could find to protect myself."

"You did not do this," lied Greenway. "Somehow, you pushed them away and they hit the wall. Something in their suit, akin to the old cyanide suicide capsule, killed them before they could be captured." "I thought I killed them. I don't know how I did it, but I thought I did. I am so glad that it was not me. I never want to hurt anyone. Why would they kill themselves? Being captured is still being alive. If you are alive, then there are always possibilities. Sometimes I see all the possibilities," said Jayne cryptically, yet innocently, never taking her eyes off the ERPs; never taking her eyes off the bodies that were being rolled out on stretchers and wheeled out of the hallway. "Let's get you somewhere safe," said Greenway.

"I thought this was somewhere safe," said Jayne. "But it is not safe, is it?"

"It is definitely not my idea of safe, that's for sure," he said, and he grabbed her by the arm and led her to the lift at the end of the hallway.

"Maybe they tracked my star? I gave it to the men that picked me up at the security station," offered Jayne.

"No, the Sentinels neutralized it as they went about the reverse engineering process," said Greenway. "Somehow they tracked you here, but they did not use the star." He paused. "This is my fault. I trusted someone else to do what I needed to do. I will correct that error now! We must hurry."

"But they are dead. They cannot contact anyone, especially if the ship has moved," said Jayne.

"They found us once. Probably scanned this entire sector looking for ships that were just too damned random in their movements. That is the problem with computers. They tend to do things perfectly, and since nature, especially human nature, is far from perfect, the anomaly of perfect randomness was detected," said Greenway assuredly. "I have some friends and they can keep you hidden. I am sure of it." A few minutes later Jayne and Professor Greenway were in a flier.

This one was not totally automated. It had a pilot, a tech and windows. They slipped out of the orbiting ship and headed for the surface. Jayne watched as the flier skimmed over water. It did not travel in a straight line but weaved over the surface. Suddenly, the flier touched the water and slipped beneath the calm sea. The acceleration dampening field stopped the passengers from feeling anything inside the flier. A few minutes later, Jayne felt a bump. The dampening field shut off and the door opened in an underwater flier port.

Jayne and Greenway stepped out of the flier into a large port surrounded by black walls that curved into a black ceiling. They were underwater, but blackness prevailed at the depth of the port. Nothing could be seen outside, except where the occasional searchlight pierced the darkness.

"We are here, and we need to talk right away," said Greenway abruptly as he led the way to a lift. There were no PUT pads here. PUT pads left a strong, albeit short-lived, quantum signature. Entangled carbon atoms could be used to signal their use and track the users. Security of the 'Greenway Safe' ilk demanded that they not be used at all. The underwater flier port was very secure. It used lifts and stairs to travel to the different levels. The building was relatively small in size, so quantum devices were banned except the most important device of all. It was a quantum computer constructed in situ. There was no possibility of entangled particles of any type interacting with the core. The builders started with the components required to build a Papa Quantum Cray. Then they altered, reconfigured and added bits and pieces here and there. The result was a Super Quantum Cray also known as Super Q or SQ for short. SQ's main job was to ensure the underwater flier port's existence was kept a secret. Some thought it was overkill but, so far, it had worked. The location of the flier port changed constantly. Its location was known only by SQ and it would sooner self-destruct than tell. At least, that is what the programming told it to do. That point had always made Professor Greenway nervous. All programming could be hacked. Greenway had installed a much simpler solution to deal with an SQ-compromised event, and he was not telling anyone of its existence.

"Where are we going?" asked Jayne, as they stepped off the elevator. The acceleration dampening field was in effect and, as a result, it was impossible to tell if the lift was going up, down, or sideways.

"To my quarters," answered Greenway. "This is where I live when I am not in one of my labs."

They walked from the lift to an old-fashioned wooden door. Greenway turned the knob and entered. Jayne followed. Her first thought was that this was not the kind of quarters she was used to. It was rather large by any standards and not like any quarters that Jayne had ever been inside. She entered a small, furnished set of rooms, separated by more wooden doors. Facing her was the most astounding space she had ever seen. There was a set of ornately decorated stained glass doors that led to what appeared to be a small flower garden, on a sunny day at mid-morning. The electronically generated sky and horizon illusion was so perfect that Jayne walked forward and opened the doors. The sounds of birds and insects subtly filled the air. The perfume of the flowers wafted into the room and the sun's warmth was tempered by the cool breeze that blew the curtains aside.

"This is incredible. Is it always mid-morning?" she asked, wondering if the actual time was reflected in here.

"No. The time of day is synchronized with actual time. It is, however, always late spring. I do not like any of the other seasons. Autumn smells of death, winter smells of nothing, and summer reminds me that autumn is on the way. It is always late spring in my garden," he said, with a proud smile. "Do you like it?"

"I love it," said Jayne, stepping out and sitting in a garden chair. She closed her eyes and faced the sun that was not a sun. A smile crept over her features. "It feels just like the real sun. I haven't been out in the sun for what feels like forever. Mmmmm, this feels good." "Take care. It will burn you just like the real sun. I did not want to filter the UV out. The plants, birds, and insects are real, and they would not like it."

"There are real birds in here? Don't they crash into the walls of this place? It must have walls. We are under the ocean after all," said Jayne.

"All the birds are small. The anti-gravity push units keep them from hitting anything. The outer shell exerts a gentle push whenever they get close," he said casually. He sat in the chair beside her. "I will make some tea and we will talk. I'm hoping you will agree to follow my direction. It will benefit both my needs and your needs. Then we will get you settled. You can have quarters of your own or you can stay with me in my guest room. Your choice."

There was a whistling sound from the 'inside' of the apartment. "I put on the kettle. It appears to be calling." He caught a puzzled look in her eyes. "I like to do things the old-fashioned way." He stood up and walked into the apartment.

Jayne sat and absorbed the rays. She relaxed.

A few moments later, Greenway emerged in fresh clothes and placed a tray with two cups, spoons, a teapot, cream, a dish of sugar cubes, a plate of biscuits, some lemon slices, and a small pot of honey on the table between them. "May I pour?" Greenway said in a mock accent. "I do so love those old-fashioned manners."

"Yes, sir, please," said Jayne with a smile, trying to mimic the same accent.

"How do you take your tea?' he asked.

Jayne reached out and stuck her finger in the pot of honey and then into her mouth. "Gosh, is that real honey?" she said, her voice filled with awe.

"It sure is," he said proudly.

"I like it black with lemon and honey," she said, and she licked her lips in anticipation.

He smiled and fixed their tea.

Jayne did not speak. She was trying not to think about her life. All her aspirations had disintegrated around her. She would never be what she was trained for. She would never be a Technical Electrical Mechanical fixer. She would never again run a low grav line and stuff the ball home to the cheer of the crowd. As long as she was being pursued by the Forevers, her actions must be kept secret. After the last attempt to kidnap her, Jayne knew she did not want to experience those horrible things ever again.

Professor Greenway broke the reverie. "I've been thinking about what to do, and I've reached a conclusion. I would like you to listen to what I have to say before you decide anything about your future. Is that a deal?" he asked.

"I will listen," said Jayne. She put down her teacup, picked up one of the cookies and nibbled at the edge.

"First, and most important of all, is the need for you to understand the severity of the situation you find yourself in. Secondly, you need to understand that none of this is your fault," he said with sincerity.

"I know. I'm only 13 years old. How could anything be my fault? I haven't had time in my life to do anything wrong. I am a good person. I know I hurt those men in the ship, but I did not kill them. I really felt threatened. I knew they were going to take me away and do me harm. I just pushed them away. They killed themselves. Right? They killed themselves. You said that they killed themselves. I just pushed because they were going to hurt me. Right? Right! Right?" cried Jayne, as tears and the dawn of realization swelled in her eyes and streamed down her cheeks.

"Jayne," soothed Professor Greenway, "it is alright. You did nothing wrong."

"But I didn't kill them. You said that they killed themselves. I didn't kill them. I didn't kill them," Jayne repeated. She looked up and into Professor Greenway's eyes.

He looked back at her. His eyes were welling. He turned away and wiped before the tears could fall.

Jayne stared at him, and the full realization hit her like a punch in the stomach. The air ooofed out of her mouth. "Oh, God. Oh, God. I killed them, didn't I?"

She looked at him and her eyes widened. Air would not enter her lungs. She sat frozen and silent.

Greenway reached up and touched her shoulder.

Jayne sucked in air and swiped at his hand to push it away. She got up and ran back into the main room. There was no place to go, so she flopped down on a small couch and curled up into fetal position with her back to the room. She felt a tight bubble begin to form over her. She felt safe inside of it, and she did not feel any pressure to act. She willed her body to relax.

With the relaxation, came the inevitable curiosity that was Jayne Wu. She began to look at the bubble itself: look at what it contained. It was infinitely large but still tight to her skin. It held only her. It held all the possibilities of her. Without the fear, she could wander around inside and look at the myriad of possible events and the probabilities of each occurring. All the events included her. Every once in a while, she would see one that looked interesting, and she would nudge it and watch it blossom. She would snuff it out, like a candle, before it burst into reality, and it would fade into darkness. She also noticed that there was a current inside the bubble that carried her, and everything else, along. The current of the most probable. If she did nothing, the most probable events would become real. If she found another possible event, she could push it until it was the most probable. Jayne realized that pushing was her word. That was not really what she did. It was more like encouragement. Any event could be encouraged, but the less its probability of occurrence, the more resistance there was to her encouragement. She remembered the force she used when the men were about to kidnap her from the Sentinel ship. The likelihood that those men would fly off and crash into the walls of the ship was very small, but she forced it into reality, and it blossomed and became real. She remembered now what happened. She made a cocoon of air conform exactly to the shape of the men's bodies. The molecules of air formed a shell as hard as steel. The shell collapsed on her command and pulverized the men. Their insides turned to human soup, in a bag of skin. Jayne pushed the intruders away and they flew off and smashed into the bulkheads of the ship.

Jayne was filled with sadness as she let the tiny yet infinite bubble that surrounded her fade. She sat up and saw that Professor Greenway was sitting in a chair opposite, waiting. She smiled a weak smile and spoke. "I am sorry. I understand what happened. I was not really in control. I won't let it happen again. There are always probabilities that do not involve anyone's death. I will be more careful."

Professor Greenway spoke hesitantly. "Can you explain to me what you did? What happened?"

"Not now. Not yet. Soon," she said as she bounced up to her feet. "What have you got planned for me? I am up for just about anything."

CHAPTER 31

In Plain Sight

In the time of Jayne Wu, privacy was simply an illusion. There were many ways to track an individual. Everyone carried a Visual Identity Designator. Most doubled as a communicator and an entertainment device. VIDs were the prime means of obtaining any of the basic requirements for life in the society: food, shelter, clothing and transportation, just to name a few. There were ways to hide but that usually meant dropping out and living in one of the few designated wilds. There was also tech. Hacked tech. The process had been going on for centuries. Governments would use sophisticated tech to do whatever they wanted to do and hackers would alter that tech in order to avoid whatever the government wanted.

"Well, Thirteen—may I call you that or is it reserved for your close friends?" asked Professor Greenway.

"I don't have any close friends and, yes, you may," said Jayne. She thought of Spike and hoped she would see him again.

"And why do you not have any close friends? A girl like you would likely be swamped with people trying to be your friend," said Professor Greenway.

"Are you trying to be my psychiatrist now? Think about it. Everyone around me has always been older. I never got on with the younger kids in the nursery except for Ajax and he was special. I guess I was just not interested in what they were interested in. I only meet people when I play GravBall and they are always older than I am," Jayne said, flopping down on the couch and pulling her feet under her. "They talk to me, but I wouldn't call them my close friends."

"I am older than you and I would like to be your friend, that is, if I'm not too old for you," said Professor Greenway, smiling.

"Sure. I guess," she said, and she pulled her knees up to her chest. "You are pretty old, though. You could be my grandfather. Can kids my age be friends with their grandfathers?"

"I don't see why not," he answered.

"I just have one question—why?" Jayne asked, partially hiding her face behind her knees.

"You do have a knack for getting to the heart of the thing, don't you? I will be honest with you. I want to be your friend so you will trust me. I can really be your protector and keep you safe only if you trust me. I know that trust does not come easily to people like us. I hope my actions, so far, have been a good start," Greenway said with an expectant smile.

"Like us? You said 'people like us'. What does that mean? How are we alike?" asked Jayne, lifting her head and partially hiding it again. "Well, for one thing, we both like our tea black with lemon and honey," he said, grinning, "and I am sure we would find other things in common if we really tried."

Jayne grinned back. "Alright, you can be my first grandfatherly friend."

"Alright, Ms. Wu, it is time we got down to business," he said.

"Okay, Professor Greenway. What's the plan?" Jayne said perkily.

"Well, we have to create a new you," he stated.

"Right, a new me." She turned to him. "You know, this does not sound like something I am going to like very much, but I guess it is for the best."

A "new Jayne" started with getting a new identity. In a world of quantum wizardry, a new identity was not an easy task. But 'tech' was 'tech' and all things were possible—if you knew the right people or had enough money. Professor Greenway was not lacking in either.

"Jayne, I have not had the time to give you any choices here. Have a look at this. It is the new you," said Professor Greenway casually.

Jayne looked at the sheet of magnetic scribe:

ID: Ka F 3168469435609

Name: Kai, Cassandra Joy

She touched the scribe sheet and scanned the personal details of her new identity. She suddenly looked up at Greenway. "You made me older. I'm now 18. Wow. How are we going to manage that? I look 13 'cause I am 13. No way I'm ever going to pull off 18," she said, her voice filled with incredulity and a little excitement. Jayne felt her face flush at the thought of being 18 and all that it meant.

"You look 13 because you dress and act 13. You are just going to have to dress and act 18. Not a big stretch if I compare you to the 18-year-olds I have seen lately. I have a guy who can help with all of that. Don't worry. What I am worried about is the next thing you are going to gripe about. Flip that scribe sheet and read on," he commanded. "But before you do, I want you to know it is the best idea of all the ideas for your new identity. My crew has been working on this for a while. I knew it would be needed sooner or later. It just so happens to be sooner than I expected." He gestured for her to read on.

Jayne flipped the scribe sheet and read. She stopped suddenly and looked at him with burning eyes. "You have got to be kidding. I am an Omie liaison officer. I'll have you know that I am the best TEM fixer in my whole class. I looked up my grades and no one can touch me. Why on Earth would you make me a liaison officer?" she almost shouted at him.

"You will be an Omie liaison and not a TEM for those exact reasons. Attention. If you show up anywhere as a Technical Electronic Mechanical fixer, you are bound to be checked out by the Forevers. They will be looking for anyone with good skills in that area, showing up anywhere. A liaison will be something they won't expect from you, and so they will be less likely to find you," Greenway replied. He continued,

"Read on. The best is yet to come."

Jayne glanced back at the scribe sheet. She whispered, "Biome 7? I can't even remember what Biome 7 habitat is like. Why not Biome 3? If I have to learn a new job, at least I could work in a Biome that I am familiar with. Biome 7. It better not be a high gravity desert biome. I seem to recall one like that. I don't like deserts. They are hot and cold and dry and dirty. Yech." She shivered at the prospect.

"No, Biome 7 is pretty cool," he grinned, as she made a face and mock-shivered, as if the cold would be worse than the desert. "It is not cold, it is 'cool', as in good. You will like it. It has some cold areas, but it is mostly a temperate boreal forest. Lots of conifer trees. The really cool part is the low gravity. Things grow big in Biome 7. I think you are going to like it. The O_2 levels are a little low. The omies have, with a little genetic encouragement, developed high volume lungs. You will get used to it quickly, given the lower gravity. That brings me to the important part."

"Important part. There's more?" exclaimed Jayne.

"Yep. This biome has the largest number of black-market body part murders. They are killing young adult Omies and removing their lungs as well as other desirable body parts. One of your Sentinel jobs will be to track and map the locations of these murders and report back to Sentinel Central," he said casually.

"Like a detective? Now that is cool. Detective Wu. Sorry, I mean Detective Kai. I get to be a detective and solve murders. Do I get a badge and a weapon? I want one of those needlers and a couple of stingers so I can incapacitate suspects," she said excitedly.

"No, no, and no. You will not do any of those things. Your job will be to listen and report. And to 'liaise'," he said, and he smiled a 'sucks to be you' smile.

"Liaise? What the hell do I liaise?" she yelled as she crossed her arms.

"You will talk to the omies and talk to the fixers and talk to the omies and talk to the fixers, and like that. That is what liaising is all about. Talking and being diplomatic. If you happen to see or hear of anything out of the ordinary, you will report it. It is really simple, okay?" he challenged.

"Do I have a choice?" she asked.

"No. So let's get started. First, I want you to understand that this is all for your benefit. You must hide out in Biome 7 until things cool down. If I had my way, I would have put you in stasis for a year or two, but Sentinel Central thinks you are really talented, and we must not jeopardize the development of that talent. We must encourage it to mature and grow," he said assuredly.

"You make me sound like a tomato," Jayne said flatly.

"I will go along with Sentinel Central only if you promise to keep that 'luck' of yours under wraps. No showing off by reading people's minds or tossing rocks with your mind or winning at cards or anything else that you can do that is better than everyone else," he said. "I can't do those things. Except maybe win at cards. And I am a better TEM fixer than anyone I know," she said. She plopped down on the couch.

"No, you are not. You are Cassie Kai, and you liaise. Are you clear on that? 'Cause if you are not, it's off to the stasis chamber you go." He frowned at Jayne. "I mean it, Thirteen."

"Alright!" she snapped, grabbing her legs and pulling them up to her chin.

Professor Greenway stood and got a VID from a drawer. "This is yours. It is tuned to your DNA, but your DNA no longer points to Jayne Wu. It points to Cassie Kai. All systems will recognize this as Kai's VID," he said.

"Who is Cassandra Kai?" asked Jayne.

She was a baby girl who died five years before you were born. Only now she didn't die. She is you and you are her," he said emphatically. He picked up a pile of stick chips that were strewn across the surface of the desk. They contained the latest manuals for Biome 7. "Read these. They will explain your job. I'm guessing you are a quick study, so study quick. You will need to have these down before the end of the week.

They are expecting you to replace the retired liaison officer," he said as he dropped the manuals. "These will explain your job and give you all the details you will need to work in Biome 7. I also expect you to report to me. I will supply you with a few encryption tabs to keep our communication private. There have been reports of strange happenings in Biome 7. Your secondary job will be to quietly investigate any unusual occurrences and report your findings back to me."

A few of the manual sticks fell on the floor. Jayne picked them up and tossed them from hand to hand. "Right, memorize five thousand pages in three days. Go to Biome 7, liaise and spy. Not a problem," she said, unable to keep the sarcasm from creeping into her voice.

CHAPTER 32

Getting Settled

After decades of isolation from the planet-bound population, the humans in the biomes had changed. The most dramatic changes were societal. Most of the biomes started with agrarian societies. The wisdom of the time was to restrict these societies to sustainable technology. Any technology that was developed inside the biome was, by definition, sustainable. The only external tech allowed was controlled by the Fixers. The plan was to educate a Fixer class within the biomes so the tech could be maintained throughout the lengthy trip. Maintenance tech would be part of the cargo. All planet tech was restricted. As a result, the black market flourished.

Jayne read and absorbed all the manuals given to her by Professor Greenway. She spent some extra time scanning the newsy archives for anything pertaining to Biome 7. It was time to digest what she had read. Jayne knew it would not take her long to read the material. To Jayne, reading was like recording the information. She hadn't really gained any knowledge, but it was all available to her any time she wanted. She was digesting now. She was sitting in a small bedroom in Professor Greenway's house under the sea. She was waiting for the flier to take her to Biome 7. Today was the first day she would become Cassie Kai. Her clothing was not what Jayne Wu would have worn. She looked like a young woman and not a 13-year-old girl. The only thing of Jayne's that Professor Greenway would let her take to the biome was her Sergio Partelli. The grav suit—that was much more than a grav suit—was neatly packed in one of her cases. The flier would soon arrive and take her to Biome

7. Everyone who entered Biome 7 was scanned down to the cellular level. Any dangerous impurities or contaminants would be removed. If they could not be removed, then the person was barred from entering. Jayne would not have to go through this process. Professor Greenway had done all this testing in advance in order to avoid the DNA identification scan. Once inside the biome, she would be invisible to the Forevers. Jayne Wu would fall completely off the grid and Cassie Kai would be resurrected.

It was late when Jayne arrived. There was no fanfare. There were, in fact, no people. The flier was pilotless. There was no sense of motion at all. Suppression fields took care of that little irritation. You sat in your seat, the doors closed, you waited for a time and then the doors opened, and you exited at your destination. She was directed by her VID to her residence in the Fixer quarters. There was a large gym to give the fixers who worked the biomes an opportunity to work their muscles in normal or higher than normal gravity. This was very important in environments that were less than one G. In Biome 7, where the gravity was .79 Earth standard, it was especially important to keep your muscles toned. Fixers from low grav environments would often say that it was more work at home than at work.

Jayne's new quarters were incredibly ostentatious when compared to her old quarters. She did not have an AI like Lucky to look after many of her basic needs, but the absence of that was totally overshadowed by the sheer size and luxury of the apartment she now called home. She even had a video window that mimicked a real window. It was looking out at the day side of a blue Earth streaked with white clouds. The continents sparkled with lights as each day faded into night.

She carried a small bag containing a few toiletries and the Sergio Partelli into her new apartment. She decided the only safe place for the suit was with her. She entered the bedroom and looked around. The room contained a large bed, a dresser, and a side table. Off the bedroom were two doors. One led to a private bathroom and the other to a large walk-in closet. The bathroom had real running water in the sink taps. The shower looked like Earth standard. She needed a good cleaning, so she removed the alien clothes: clothes that belonged to Cassie Kai. She stepped in the shower and touched the required buttons to start the cycle.

She screamed in surprise and delight when warm water, in full flow, sprayed out of the shower head. She was soaked. Completely wet all over. Jayne had never felt this much water in her life. The mist showers of the nursery and the HUB lasted about two minutes from start to finish and used about 500 ml of water total. In the time it took her to realize that she was being sprayed with warm water, at least five litres had run down the drain. She had just wasted five litres and still more came out of the showerhead. Jayne felt so guilty at using so much precious water that she had to shut off the flow. She soaped herself and her hair and shivered in the cool air. She realized she had to rinse off the soap. She hesitantly turned on the shower again and quickly rinsed off the residue of soap from her hair and her body. The water never stopped. It just kept flowing; warm water kept flowing over her. She noticed temperature controls on the shower wall and touched the temperature control to make the water hotter. Soon, the room was filled with steam. The heat from the decadent flow of water relaxed her muscles.

She shut off the water, dried herself, and stepped from the bathroom into the closet. There were rows of clothes and shoes lining the walls. All styles were laid out in front of Jayne for her perusal. She held a fancy dress to her body. It looked like it would fit her perfectly. Then she realized that all this clothing was for her use. Everything here was her size. She had no idea what to wear. She walked out and flopped on the bed. She spotted her bag containing the Sergio Partelli. She removed it from the bag and put it on. Professor Greenway's words replayed in her mind. "Try the command: 'Suit override–Wu–thirteen exponent thirteen'. That will open up the suit's extended functions, which are many. Once in this system, the 'suggest' command will allow the suit to look after your safety."

Jayne said in an unsure voice, "Suit override." She stopped and looked down at the suit. Nothing had changed. She continued, "Wu-thirteen-exponent-thirteen."

Jayne felt, rather than heard, a voice fill her. It was like her bones were vibrating and transmitting sound to her auditory cortex.

"Override initiated," said the suit. Jayne realized that no one could hear except her. "Please speak a key word or phrase for future 'suit to owner' communication."

Jayne thought for a moment and then hit on the word 'thirteen'. It was common enough for her to fit into a conversation if 'suit to owner' communication in public was required.

"Thirteen," she said.

"Future communication will be initiated when Wu–thirteen exponent thirteen says the word phrase 'Override–thirteen'. Is this correct?" the suit intoned silently into her head.

"Yes," answered Jayne. She thought for a moment and then said, "Suggest–residence casual."

The Sergio Partelli instantly altered to a yellow sweater and jeans. "Suggest–sweater color pink."

The sweater changed to a light-pink.

Jayne smiled and thought about all these clothes that would go to waste. She would never have to wear any of them.

She decided to explore. She stepped out of the residence and into a lift. She went down to the main floor of the fixer quarters and walked out into a rotunda surrounded by windows. She walked around, looking into the rooms beyond the glass. There were a number of recreational facilities available to fixers in their leisure time. Everything from restaurants to kiosks, from ping-pong to snooker, from libraries to gyms. There was no GravBall tube. There were some limitations on the space that could be allocated to fixers on the biomes.

The gym was spacious, mainly because it was crucial to the health of the fixers working to maintain and repair all aspects of the biome's functionality. Jayne stepped inside and scanned the room. It contained a number of exercise equipment machines. Most of these machines were capable of running a series of tests on each user and delivering the appropriate type of intensity and duration of exercise. Jayne noticed the humming of the grav treadmills in one corner of the room. She walked in that direction to check them out for future use. She stepped up on the nearest and reached to start a random grav program.

The gym was empty except for a rowdy group of young fixers lifting weights on the adjustable gravity platform. She glanced up at the group. Her heart rate leaped. Right in front of her was Joseph Kane. Mr. Big Foot was being his usual show-off self. He was curling a large weight with his left arm while he chatted with a pair of girls bench-pressing weights and spotting each other. Jayne quickly looked down, letting her hair fall over her face. Cassie Kai wore her hair down. She turned quickly around and moved toward the exit, all the while staring at the floor.

"Excuse me," said a voice to Jayne's right. Jayne did not turn toward it. She was in a panic to exit before Big Foot looked up and recognized her.

The voice spoke again. "Excuse me, but aren't you the new LO?" Jayne did not stop. She moved purposefully to the exit.

Suddenly, she felt a tug on her arm. She looked up and right in front of her was a tall blonde woman. "Aren't you the new liaison officer?" she asked.

Jayne nodded her head in the affirmative. Her brain was racing with panic. She had to get out of there before she was exposed by Joseph Kane.

"I thought so, but you look a little young for the job."

Jayne cleared her constricting throat. "I'm older than I look," she said.

The woman stared at her. Jayne realized she was waiting for more information.

Jayne continued. "I am Cassie Kai. And you are?"

"I'm Cornelia Banks. I'm the person you talk to when you need something fixed. I coordinate all the fixers who keep this place running. I suppose we will be meeting formally tomorrow morning at 9:00, B7 time. The days here are a little longer than Earth normal, as you probably know, but soon you will not notice the difference," she prattled.

Jayne kept her back to the group of fixers at the weight-lifting station. "I was just out for a walk. Great gym you have here," she said. "Nice meeting you. I have to get back to my room to prepare."

Jayne walked quickly to the doorway. It opened. As she walked through, she heard Joseph Kane call out, "Hey, Wu. What the heck are you doing here?"

Jayne did not respond. She hurried back to her rooms, grabbed her VID, called Professor Greenway, and sent him an emergency icon.

At the time of the biomes, electronic transmissions were always coded. Quantum computers could decode just about anything if there was enough money and need behind the process. Jayne took no chances. Greenway had given her a dozen halves of paired tabs of entangled crystalline carbon atoms. She inserted one into her VID and waited. When he received her emergency icon, he would pop the entangled partner into his VID. The two atoms would check for entanglement. Once established, they would link to their partner and generate a fluctuating key. Once the key pattern was established, then normal communication could begin. This method, though breakable, would take a Super Cray about one second for each of the trillion generated keys. That works out to a little over 31 years to complete. For all intents and purposes, this kind of communication was secure, at least until they developed the still mythical 'zero-point tap' that was theorized to be able to lock on and identify contrived entanglements.

Jayne's VID beeped, and she began to talk. "Professor Greenway, he's here, and he recognized me. He was right in the gym, lifting weights. What the hell is he doing on Biome 7!? This was supposed to be secure, and right there in front of me is Big Foot. He is not my favorite person—ever since he pushed me into that line-vac. The dolt is calling out 'Wu, hey, Wu!' for all the world to hear and see. I just left and pretended I didn't hear, and it wasn't me. He will mess this up if you don't do something. Get him out of here. Send him to Biome 2. Yeah, Biome 2. That's a perfect place for him. Stinky Biome 2 is a good place for his stinky self. Professor Greenway, please?" she begged.

"By Big Foot, I must assume you mean Joseph Kane. Don't panic. Boy, are you ever lucky," he said calmly.

"You mean unlucky. Having him around just sapped all my luck right out of me," she complained.

"No, very lucky. And your luck must be rubbing off on me because his presence just solved a big problem for me and a big problem for you all in one go," he stated in a satisfied tone.

"How can having that jerk running around calling out my real name be lucky?" she asked. "Professor Greenway, I need this fixed fast. I have my first meeting with the Omie counsels and Fixer coordinator tomorrow morning. I don't want him blabbing my name wherever he goes."

"Relax. Get some rest. All will be well in the morning. I guarantee it," he said, and he broke the connection.

"Damn!" Jayne said as she flopped down on the bed. She reached over and grabbed her VID. She removed the single use entangled tab and snapped it in two pieces, destroying it.

CHAPTER 33

Liaising in Biome 7

The biomes were big by any kind of Earth standards. They were basically domed platforms. Their size demanded that the construction materials be sourced from the asteroid itself or other space rocks. They were placed in high orbit around the Earth and a dome was constructed over the sculpted 'ground' section. Gravity control systems were installed. Once the dome was sealed, the inside was terraformed to mimic the destination planet.

The morning was a busy one for Jayne. She was driven to do any job to the best of her ability, and this job was one she never expected she would have to do. She felt she had to prove her worth. First impressions were critical. Everyone was much older than her pretend 18 years. As far as these people were concerned, she was still a baby. Jayne smiled at the truth of the matter. She viewed 18 as ancient. If they knew her real age, they probably would not even allow her in the room. She set about to prove she was a capable LO.

She had to take control. She could only do that by impressing the Omie leaders and impressing the coordinator fixer, Cornelia Banks.

Jayne arrived early. She saw a middle-aged man seated in the ante room outside the main meeting room. He stood when she entered. Jayne looked at him and, without any pleasantries, he asked, "Who are you?"

Jayne responded by looking around the room, slowly bringing her gaze back to him. She spoke calmly and clearly, "Cassandra Kai." She turned away from him and opened the door to the meeting room.

"Just a min—" he started, but she cut him off.

Jayne turned sharply and spoke. "I want this to be a comfortable meeting and I want you to ensure that the participants are looked after. I want some appropriate fresh food and beverages on that table before the meeting starts. Turn on the air conditioning. The room is stuffy." She turned back to the room and pointed at the far wall. "Does that wall have electronic windows like those in the LO's quarters?" She did not wait for a response. "If so, make sure they are programmed with Biome 7's scenic vistas. Some soft unobtrusive background music that complements the scenes on the electronic windows would also be nice." She turned back to him. "Do you have any questions?"

He shook his head. The mention of the liaison officer's quarters startled him. He was not about to question the LO's authority. Jayne continued to stare at him as if she had not understood the head shake. He spoke, haltingly. "No questions, sir, I mean ma'am, I mean miss.

I will order the food and drinks right away and yes, the wall has electronic windows."

"Great." She paused, thinking about the comfort of the participants. She turned to the attendant. "How do the omies handle the increased gravity in the meeting room?"

"Miss?" he responded, as if he did not understand her question. "The gravity? How do the omie representatives feel about meeting in a gravity that is much greater than the one they are used to?" Jayne asked. "It must be very tiring."

"I do not understand. They are omies and we are fixers. They are meeting here. Sometimes we meet there." He gestured vaguely to the rest of the biome. "It all works out."

"It does? I know that enduring low gravity for a few hours is a lot easier than enduring high gravity. Who do I talk to in order to lower the gravity in the meeting room to Biome 7 normal?" she asked curtly.

"I can request that but..." he paused, "the last LO always wanted to meet in Earth normal. He said that low gravity upset his stomach."

"How did he ever spend any time in the biome? How could he know what was going on if he never went out to see the people and their situations firsthand?" she asked, perplexed.

"May I speak frankly, miss?" he asked in a way that suggested that he was about to tell a very important secret.

"Please," responded Jayne quickly.

"Well, the last LO sort of viewed the omies as, well, as second class. Not as good as he was, being a fixer liaison officer and all. There has not been a lot of love lost between the two groups, especially the Omie group from the colder environment. They are feeling like they are being ignored by Biome Central. There have been a lot of complaints about strange deaths in the higher elevations," he said.

"What kind of strange deaths? I read the latest reports, and I saw nothing about strange deaths. The most recent seemed to be easily explained. As I remember, they were both accidents. One was a fall from a tree and the other, an attack by some kind of carnivorous cat. Is that not correct?" she asked.

"I suppose," he said. A dubious inflection was left hanging at the end of the words. His desk VID beeped, and he glanced at it. "I must attend to your requests," he said.

"Yes. And you can call me Ms. Kai. Now, where can I freshen up?" Jayne asked.

"There is a restroom through there, Ms. Kai," he said, and he pointed to the far end of the room. Jayne walked to the restroom. As soon as the door closed behind her, she let out the air she had been holding in her lungs and grinned at herself in the mirror. She felt an overwhelming urge to wash off all the makeup she had put on her face. It wasn't much, but it was enough to itch and taste bad. She suppressed the urge and only dabbed the lipstick at the corner of her mouth.

She exited the restroom and, without a word, walked out of the meeting room area. She was early. She walked into the rotunda a looked in the windowed rooms as she passed. There was a cafeteria, a recreation room, and the gym. All were empty. She stepped into the gym and looked at the equipment. She felt totally out of shape.

She wanted to work out very soon. She thought of Joseph Kane and wondered where greenway was going to send him because he could not stay here. He would blow her cover the first chance he got. She stepped on a treadmill, set it to 1.5 standard gravity and five km per hour. A few minutes later, she relaxed. The exercise pushed the stress aside. She glanced at her VID. She was not late. She headed back to the meeting room.

None of the Omie representatives had arrived. Jayne entered the meeting room. Her requests were all in place, including the lower gravity. She placed her VID on the far side of the long table facing the open doorway. She stood in the doorway in order to greet whoever arrived.

Cornelia Banks and an aide, carrying a case of large-format magnetic scribes, arrived. The aide set about placing a scribe at each place at the table. "Hello, Ms. Kai," she said as she handed her a scribe. "This is the fixer agenda for the meeting. I am sorry you did not get it earlier, but things have been a little harried lately."

The aide whispered something in Cornelia Bank's ear. She turned to Jayne, smiled and said, "Nice touch."

Jayne frowned.

Cornelia continued, "The gravity—and the food. This meeting might not be as onerous as it usually is."

She looked up at a group of people in quiet conversation, walking down the hall toward her. They were almost all women and obviously knew each other. Their style of dress was not biome neutral. The women were dressed in multicolored frocks and the single man wore a rather plain dark-grey suit. Heavy silver jewelry seemed to be very fashionable. All wore a myriad of rings, brooches, and necklaces, some of which were encrusted with rough cut, semi-precious stones. All the apparel must have been created on the biome because only basic work jumpsuits were imported from the planet below.

One of the women moved to the front of the group. She spoke with a musical lilt to her voice, but her eyes were sharp and almost black. It was difficult to tell where the iris ended and the pupil began. "Cornelia," she said, "how are you? It has been a while. As I recall, the last meeting was cancelled by Mr. White. Something about the stomach flu or some such. How is he, by the way? I heard he was transferred to some desk job on one of the HUBs." She smiled a very insincere smile. "We will all miss him."

She turned to Jayne. "Hello. I don't think we have met. My name is Akila Okiro. I—" she turned and gestured to the rest of the women and corrected herself, "we represent the lowland tribe. I am their spokesperson. And this gentleman," she looked at the man in the grey suit, "is Mr. Campo. He represents the highlanders."

Campo nodded. One got the impression that there was no love lost between Okiro and Campo.

"I'm—," Jayne's mind raced, looking for her name. For a fraction of a second, she could not find it. She felt like an alien on a strange new world who needed a translator in order to understand even the simplest of gestures. She pushed the fear aside and spoke. "I'm Cassandra Kai. I am your new liaison officer. And, yes, I know I look too young for the job, but I am sure you will find that I am very competent. I will try to meet the needs of both your tribes and the fixers to ensure that Biome 7 is ready when the Great Day of Departure arrives."

Jayne's face held a stern expression, but inside she was giggling at the absurdity of actually speaking the words that just came out of her mouth. She turned and gestured to the meeting room entrance. Everyone entered and took their seats. Jayne smiled at the rumble of appreciation for the platters of fruit and the low gravity. As she sat down, she scanned all the faces. They were all smiling, except Mr. Campo. His face, as well as his disposition, was neutral.

After the introductions were made, Cornelia began. The LO's job was not to run the meeting but to act as a mediator when disagreements arose between the groups. Biome 7 was unique in that there were two biome tribes instead of the usual single tribe. It was also unique in that the lowland tribe was totally matriarchal. Men of the tribe had chosen not to take leadership roles. In the beginning, there was only one tribe, but differences in philosophy resulted in the split.

Cornelia began, "In front of each of you is a scribe sheet showing the locations of standard maintenance. Highlighted in green are projects that are presently in progress. Red triangles indicate areas that are in need of investigation. I will be asking the two tribes about these locations in order to obtain your perspective."

Jayne said nothing. As far as she was concerned, she would do and say nothing as long as there was respectful communication between the groups. She sat quietly as each of the tribe leaders spoke regarding the various problem areas in the biome, from damaged crops due to lack of water or the breakdown of specific radiation shields in the dome, to excessive vibrations emanating from the O_2 systems. Each problem was discussed and a process that would lead to a solution was agreed upon. There was little to liaise. She found herself drifting along with her thoughts when the words 'deaths' and possible 'murders' met her ears. She perked up.

Akila Okiro spoke. "It is not the fact that people died but the way they died, and the final condition of the bodies, that has me concerned."

Mr. Campo spoke softly. "I agree. These types of deaths are curious, to say the least. Three young boys were up by the snowline looking for a good sled hill. Their bodies were discovered two days ago after the snow receded. They looked like they had been butchered. There was some evidence of animals having gnawed on the bodies, but the strange thing was their eyes."

"What was strange about their eyes?" asked Jayne quickly. "There weren't any. Many of their other organs were also gone.

Obviously, ravaged by a slasher cat or, more likely, a high wolf pack," he said, and he shrugged with bafflement. "The fact that their eyes were missing is very puzzling."

"The condition of those bodies sounds similar to the two bodies found last week in the hardwood forest," said one of the women from the lowlands. She turned to Jayne. "Two sisters were found under a pile of leaves. Their father found them. It was terrible. Our entire tribe is still in mourning."

"I am not sure this is a Fixer problem," said Cornelia. "Well, it is somebody's problem," snapped Akila.

"With due respect, our job is to keep the biome in good working order and not to run around investigating suspicious deaths. In fact, according to the constitution of this biome, the inhabitants have structures in place to deal with situations like this," stated Cornelia Banks flatly.

"That is true," said Campo. "However, my investigators have suggested to me that these deaths were not accidents, and it is extremely unlikely that any biome dweller is responsible." He let the next obvious statement hang.

Cornelia stood up. "I hope you are not suggesting that one of my fixers is responsible!"

"Actually, I am not suggesting that. I have checked all the fixer schedules for the last four months and not one of your people has been near any of the areas where the deaths occurred. That does not exonerate them, but it does greatly reduce the likelihood of fixer involvement," stated Campo. He waited for someone else to fill in the blanks. He waited for someone to state what they were all thinking.

Jayne glanced around the table. The expectant faces of the meeting members turned and stared back at her.

"Well, the obvious conclusion is that a person other than a resident or a fixer is responsible. Since no one else is legally allowed to enter a biome, we must look to illegal means and persons with nefarious intent," responded Jayne, in her best Cassandra Kai voice.

There were murmurs and nods of agreement around the table. Jayne stood. "I will investigate these events. I am, as of yet, unwilling to call them murders by unknown persons until I have some evidence. Please send all your reports on the events to my office, and I will start a formal investigation."

The meeting finished with all eating the provided food and agreeing that it was a wonderful idea to lower the gravity. Jayne returned to her quarters. She found herself remembering what life was like before she became someone else. She smiled at the thought of her adventures with Spike in the Biome 3 practice pods, of her first GravBall game in the HUB, of Joseph Kane following her around during the first day of her apprenticeship, and the group of scientists she met just before getting her number. She could clearly see the old woman scientist, the one who seemed to know her. She especially remembered the old woman's eyes. She remembered her sharp, green, young eyes.

Jayne felt a rush of realization. A dark-skinned old woman with green, young, perfect eyes was unlikely. The obvious answer was that the eyes were not hers but transplanted from someone else. She grabbed her VID, popped in an entangled tab and sent an emergency icon to Greenway.

CHAPTER 34

In the Beginning

It took decades to prepare the biomes for human habitation. The asteroids that served as the base of the biomes provided 150 to 200 square kilometers of habitable area. This size was deemed big enough to support a population in the thousands. A valley was carved out of the stone. High sidewalls were erected around the perimeter. An opaque dome was built and supported on these walls. Thus, a biome ship was born.

Gravity systems were integrated into the protective dome. These systems were able to sense and deflect any possible collisions with space debris, and reflect much of the solar and interstellar radiation. At first, there were problems with the gravity generators. They had a habit of cutting out completely, reducing the gravity to almost zero. A number of the domes were damaged when this happened. A lot of research went into this critical system before any inhabitants were moved to the biomes. Once it was totally secure, with many fail-safes, the terraforming began.

"First of all, I want you to relax. We were pretty sure this woman was involved in some rather nefarious activities. Her name is Winter Bancroft. Dr. Winter Bancroft. She is one of the few originators of the biome program. She must be over 100 by now. I can't believe she is still alive," said Greenway. They were now securely connected by VID, and Jayne could see the frown form on his face.

"She sure didn't look that old when I saw her. More like a young 80. What does she do?" asked Jayne.

"She is a neurobiologist focusing on nanogenetic engineering.

What she knows about the inner workings of the human body, at the molecular level, would astound you. It never occurred to me that she would be using Omies to maintain her own body. You say her eyes looked like a very young person's eyes. She could have discovered a way to use nanobots to correct and improve her own eyes," he said pensively, "but, as I remember, her eyes were brown."

"What else do you suspect her of doing?" asked Jayne.

"I think she is a member of the Forevers. In fact, I think she is a founding member. I brushed up on my history before I contacted you. I have some old publications—paper publications," he said.

"Like an old book?" Jayne asked again.

"Yeah, sort of like a book, but smaller. The weird thing about these papers is that it seems that I have the only copies in existence. I can't find any electronic references to this series anywhere. It is like someone has purged them," he said thoughtfully.

"What are they about?" asked Jayne.

"Well, that is the strange part. I originally thought Bancroft and her group were the initiators of the biome project, and they were in some respects, but only much later in its conceptualization. In the beginning, they were anti-biome. They had some other ideas about saving the human race. They were worried that all the required genetic modifications would alter the human genome so much that we would no longer be human. They were against sending human hybrids off to other worlds and calling that the salvation of the human race. They thought that, by improving the human brain, they would improve the abilities of the human mind and, through these newfound abilities, discover a way to avoid the Swarm and to save the planet. In the end, the concept of the biomes prevailed. People saw progress. They were an important part of building a future for the species. The people had a vested interest. Although, in the beginning, both projects had about as much chance of success as a blind man trying to hit a star with a BB gun. At least the biomes were something all people could understand and embrace," Professor Greenway lectured. "Creating a few superhumans, intellectually speaking, had much less flair. The concept was dropped, at least that is what I thought until now."

"But the Forevers. You must have known that they were behind all of this," said Jayne.

"I always thought the Forevers were just a bunch of rich politicians trying to extend their lives by using the omies as their private meat locker to put it crassly. They have money and can buy whatever they want or even resort to murder to extend their useless lives. I was going to stop them by exposing their deeds to the public. Now I am not sure it is that simple. Yes, the black market in body parts is going strong and it must be stopped, but something bigger is happening here," he said cryptically.

"Like what?" Jayne asked. "You must have an idea."

"Like you! You are what is happening. They really want you. There are a lot of people looking for you and, if my intelligence is correct, they want you soon and in good condition. The big question is why?" he said.

Jayne shivered. "If they want me so badly, why did you allow Big Foot to be assigned to the same biome as me?"

Greenway shrugged. "That was an oversight. It has been corrected." "How has it been corrected? Is he gone? Has his memory been wiped?" she asked enthusiastically.

"No. You know we don't do that sort of thing. We are the good guys. At least, I think we are," he said with a grin. "He has been reassigned."

"To where? Doing what? Why don't you send him to a Spavator Far Point for a two-year stint?" she said seriously. She was not the least bit ashamed of her nasty side, at least where Joseph Kane was concerned.

"No," he chuckled. "He has been reassigned as your personal assistant."

The scream that sounded from his VID was so loud he had to pull it away from his ear to avoid being deafened.

"Seriously? Seriously, Professor Greenway, I can't do that. Please tell me this is just a big bad joke," she begged.

Professor Greenway became very serious. "Jayne, you need to grow up now. You are 18 years old, at least on paper, so behave like you are. Kane was a problem, but now he is a solution. He solves two problems. Making him your assistant means that we no longer have to worry about him exposing you and you now have an assistant. I did not assign you one before because there was no one I could trust in Biome 7. I knew one was required and, sooner or later, someone would have asked you why you didn't have one. And, believe it or not, Joseph Kane is one hell of a fixer. He will make you a great assistant, so treat him as such. Do you understand me, Jayne Esther Wu?"

"Yes. Sorry. I was being childish. Does he know, or am I required to tell him? Because if I am, he is going to go a little crazy," she said apologetically.

"He knows, and he did not go crazy. He listened to how important it is and reacted accordingly," Greenway said.

Jayne was silent. "Are you okay?"

Jayne shrugged. "What the heck is so special about me?"

Greenway sighed. "I tried to tell you before that you have some very special abilities and that is why the Forevers want you. But I now think that I am only half right. If Dr. Winter Bancroft knew about you before you even got to HUB 169, then she probably knew of you while you were still in the nursery. I suspect something else as well, but that is for another time. Right now, I need to tell you what I would like you and your new assistant to do for the Sentinels. Please find all you can about the timing of the deaths. As LO, you have access to anyone and anything that steps foot on the biome. Look back in the Omie records and see if there are any arrivals and departures that coincide with the murders. Oh, and one last thing..."

"I know, brush my teeth every night before I go to bed," said Jayne sarcastically.

"I am going to recommend that you do not stray out into the wilds of the biome. If you need something, just send your assistant to check it out. He is used to that environment and, more importantly, no one wants to kidnap him. Do you understand me? Work in your office, play in the gym and sleep in your quarters. Stay safe," he commanded.

Jayne saluted at her VID. "Yes, most revered aged one," she said with a grin. As parting words, she muttered, "I'll try." She closed her VID with a snap.

CHAPTER 35

Children of the Biome

The children of the original biome population were not necessarily committed to the whole project. Many of them reached adulthood and felt the restrictions placed on them were unfair. They argued that they had not been involved in the original decisions and therefore could not be required to take part. They wanted to have the freedom afforded to any citizen of Earth. It was decided, by the politicians and scientists of the time, that the freedoms of Earth citizens could not be applied to the people born on the biomes because they were not, nor had they ever been, citizens of Earth. They were citizens of the biome on which they were born.

Many tried to escape to the planet below. This was impossible according to the biome filters that checked for markers on every organic thing that left or entered the biomes. Still, young Omies disappeared, it was thought, to the Earth below and the black market in body parts thrived.

Months passed and Jayne's life became tedious. Her relationship with Joseph Kane was cool. She did not ask him for much and he did not offer much. She spent her time scouring the records of Biome 7, looking for any information she could find on whatever went in or out of the biome.

There were only two ways of getting materials and people to and from the biome. The most common method was to transport material to the nearest spavator and send it up or down the wire. This was the most common because it was the safest. The use of ground-to-biome chemical rocket ship transport was very expensive and very difficult to keep secret. The stability of the biome orbits was critical.

Their mass was such that a powerful rocket might alter the orbit. So rocket ships were discouraged. Some of the Omie governments banned their use altogether. Biome 7 was not one of them.

Jayne woke with a start. She sat up. Something was wrong, but she had no idea what it might be. The biome was still in its sleep cycle. All was quiet. She slipped from her bed and toggled her VID. There were no messages. She could not shake the feeling that something bad had happened or something bad was about to happen. She got dressed in the Sergio Partelli. She changed it to gym wear, left her quarters and headed to the gym. It was still considered nighttime, but morning was close at hand. Jayne headed to her most favorite piece of gym equipment. It did not exist outside of this gym. A couple of bored fixers from the last fixer cycle had mocked it up. Its functions had been tweaked by others. It was a work in progress and Jayne loved it. It was a gravity cube also known as the GC. The cube's dimensions were slightly under three meters. It had gravity generators set in each of the six faces. All the faces were transparent, making it a fantastic spectator sport. There was a large button in the center of each of the inside faces. The players in the cube had to get to, and push, whichever button was green before their opponent was able to do the same. The patterns of lit buttons and the gravity strength of the faces were random. It was also used as an individual event. The faster a player could push the buttons, the higher their score. It could be played by an individual wanting to get a workout or it could be played against an opponent. Rules varied according to who was playing and how much aggression they needed to purge. There had been a few accidents, so helmets were now mandatory.

As Jayne approached the GC, she noticed something in the cube. It did not have the telltale hum of active gravity generators. As she entered, she could make out someone sitting in the far corner of the cube looking at her. She flipped on the light. It was Joseph Kane. He was not smiling his usual mocking smile that she hated.

He spoke. "Hi. What are you doing this not-so-fair morning?"

"You couldn't sleep either, eh?" she asked.

"Nah, thought I'd come here and practice, but just couldn't get into it," he responded.

Jayne looked at him, all forlorn in the corner. She remembered playing GravBall against him. "You want to have a friendly?" she asked.

"Sure," he said, and he clambered to his feet. "You think we will need helmets? I really don't want to mess up my hair." He grinned at her with his hair still a mess from the night before.

"Helmets for a friendly game? I think we can survive without them," responded Jayne. The banter was making her feel like she was Thirteen again, and not an old liaison officer.

They both walked out of the cube and placed their palms on the ID recorder. "Let's play one round," said Joseph. "I'll score blue, and you score red."

If Jayne hit the button first, it would turn red and if Joseph hit it first, it would turn blue. After six rounds, the person with the most buttons of their color would win. In case of a tie, one more round would be played to determine the winner.

"Ready?" he asked.

Jayne nodded, and they both entered the cube. All the lights cycled through various colors until the horn sounded, indicating the start of the game. All gravity disappeared inside the cube. Both players gently pushed themselves off the floor, so they were hovering in space. Jayne immediately twisted her body, so that she was now upside down beside Joseph. He looked puzzled by her move. The horn sounded, the ceiling button turned green, and the ceiling gravity came on full. Jayne fell to the floor, which, from any spectator's viewpoint, was the ceiling, so it would look like she was standing on the ceiling. She had already pushed the button at her feet before Joseph recovered from literally falling on his head. He got his hands up just in time and rolled to the side. He stood up. They were both standing upright on the ceiling, with a red button at their feet.

"God, you are still the luckiest person I have ever met. How did you know the ceiling button was going to go on?" he asked.

Jayne said, "Just a good guess." She finished her words, and the gravity went to zero again.

Jayne swam through space to the wall facing her and tried to twist her body so that her head was pointing to the wall nearest the gym door. Joseph mimicked her movements with a grin and was floating horizontally beside her. She looked at him, irritated that he had copied her. He grinned back as the floor nearest their feet clicked into full gravity. They both landed on their feet. Joseph reached out his long arms and hit the button. It turned blue.

"Thanks!" he said. He watched her carefully. "Cheater!" she exclaimed.

The gravity became zero and Jayne did nothing. Joseph stared at her, and she stared back.

"No hints for the copycat."

Suddenly, Jayne twisted around, her head facing the opposite way. Joseph followed her move. He grinned as they both completed a full turn, their heads facing away from the door, horizontal to the external floor. Jayne, however, kept turning and twisted to the side so her feet were facing the far wall. Gravity came on and they both fell toward the far wall. Jayne fell on her feet and Joseph fell on his back. The button on the sidewall turned green and Jayne walked over and pushed it. It turned red. She was up two to one.

"Nice try, cheater," she said. "Are you sure you don't want to get a helmet?"

"I didn't cheat. I observed and reacted. You are the cheater. Did you rig the game? I bet you have access to the program. The LO has access to everything," he said, his face flushed from exertion.

The gravity went to zero. Jayne pushed off the floor. Joseph followed her. A klaxon sounded and the cube lights went out. The gravity returned to normal. They both fell in a heap to the floor. Jayne was now lying on top of Joseph.

"I knew it," he said, hugging her to him. You really are in love with me."

"Let me go, you big goof," she said and sat up. "Listen."

The loudspeaker blared, "All fixer personnel, please report to emergency stations and await orders." This was repeated.

Both Jayne and Joseph leaped to their feet and ran out of the gym. Jayne started to return to her quarters to change her clothes and then she realized she was wearing the Sergio Partelli. She rounded a corner and spoke quietly. "Override–thirteen–suggest liaison suit."

She was immediately wearing a navy suit jacket and skirt. Not her favorite, but adequate. She headed for her office.

It was really early, but the emergency warning had kick-started everyone. People seemed to be rushing around.

She stopped a young fixer. She asked, "What has happened?" "Not sure, but I think our orbit was altered slightly. It has been fixed and reestablished, but the cause has not been determined. Ms. Banks sent everyone out to scan all under sectors for possible landing sites of chemical rockets. The most probable cause of the shift in the orbit was an unscheduled landing," she replied.

"Under sectors?" queried Jayne.

"Oh, the under sectors are a unique property of Biome 7's base asteroid. They were not discovered during the initial sculpting. A fixer crew working on some gravity generator repairs discovered them. There are a series of natural caves that can be accessed from the underside of the biome. There is no known access point from the caves to the biome proper. The biome sensors would automatically close off any breech. There is a landing pad for emergency ships. When one is scheduled to land, the attitude computers automatically compensate for any shifts in the orbit of the biome. If one that has not been scheduled lands, there is an alarm that sounds, just like the one that sounded a few minutes ago. Sorry, Ms. Kai, but I have to go," the young woman said, and she rushed off.

Jayne entered her office and scanned the desk VID for reports. It was indeed an unscheduled departure from somewhere on the underside of the asteroid that made up Biome 7. All seemed to be well now, and the emergency was over. Jayne considered looking up all there was in the archives on the under sector of Biome 7 when Joseph banged on her door and entered.

"We have a problem," he said ominously.

Jayne looked at him and asked cryptically, "A biome problem or," she paused to make her next words more poignant, "a Thirteen problem?"

"Biome. A death. Maybe a murder. Let's go!" he said, turning to leave.

Jayne followed him. "Where?" she asked.

"The biome proper. Out near the edge of the tree line in the highlands," he said.

Jayne thought of Professor Greenway's warning and hesitated. He had asked her to stay out of the biome proper so she would stay safe.

"What about Professor Greenway's warning? What if I am discovered?" she asked, already knowing the answer he would give and the answer she would accept. But if Joseph, her supposed protector, said it was okay, then Greenway could not blame her. She felt a momentary flash of guilt that she quickly pushed aside.

"You are the LO, and you have to see this. I got a look at the initial reports. It is really nasty." He moved to one of the lifts that would take them to the surface.

"Okay," said Jayne, "but I have to change first. She turned and walked back into her office, shut the door and muttered, "Override–thirteen–suggest fixer surface wear, Biome 7." Her navy suit turned into a standard fixer suit, tools, and all. Jayne turned back to the exit and ran to the open lift door. Joseph was waiting.

"Cool," he said. "Have you been hiding that in your office? Looks like it has been fitted to you. Definitely not standard issue. Lookin' good, Wu." He grinned as she entered the lift.

Jayne frowned at him and whispered, "Don't call me that." "Sorry. I just reverted to old times. Won't happen again," he apologized.

Fixers used small antigravity-fitted air carts to travel quickly around in the biomes. They lifted a few cm above the ground and used a small electric motor to thrust air out the back. They were clean and quiet. Jayne and Joseph climbed into one. They were open to the air and were not designed for comfort. Fixers could transport small pieces of equipment to repair sites. Joseph entered the coordinates into the floater, as the carts were commonly called. The top speed was slightly above walking pace, unless the emergency called for an override. Joseph asked for one now. "Hey, W—Kai," he said, with a quick correction. "What is your override code?"

Jayne spoke at the floater without a thought of keeping her code from Joseph. "Kai 13131, top speed." The floater sped up to about 30 km/hr. That was top speed. They rode along in silence until they reached a group of people standing around a small copse of trees and low bushes. Jayne could see Cornelia Banks down on one knee, touching something concealed in the bushes. The floater stopped and they walked to the area. Jayne scanned the group that was standing nearby. She could see three Omies grouped together. One was obviously weeping, while the other two were consoling her. The rest were fixers who had arrived on their own floaters. Their eyes were filled with a mixture of anger and fear.

Cornelia stood up just as Jayne and Joseph arrived. They made eye contact.

"There is one body here. It appears to be a teenage girl. It was most likely dragged here by some beast. Could be one of those big cats but more likely a pack of dogs or wolves or whatever they have here that eats things like people," Cornelia said. There was a bitter lilt to her voice.

"Just the one body?" asked Jayne. She lowered her voice. "I was told it was a murder."

"I think it is, but let's keep this quiet. I don't want to start a panic. Let's get the body on a floater and take it back for autopsy," she responded quietly. "There is a lot more here than meets the eye."

She turned to the fixers standing near and spoke loud enough for the omies to hear. "Please take the body back to the hospital."

Cornelia turned to the omies and spoke to the one weeping. "I understand you found the body. Is she a friend of yours?" she asked.

The woman nodded and wiped her eyes.

"Please ride on one of the floaters to the hospital and be with your friend."

They all climbed on one of the two floaters, leaving for the hospital. The body was wrapped in a blanket and placed respectfully on the back of one of the floaters. Those who remained were Cornelia Banks, her fixer aides, Joseph and Jayne. They watched the floaters disappear.

Once gone, Cornelia became all business. "We have a major problem, and this one is not going to go away quietly. You can be sure of that," she said, and she left no room for a response by anyone. "Follow me!"

Cornelia strode up the hill, looking at the ground as she walked.

"That girl was not just murdered. Most of her innards were missing, and her eyes were gone. She was butchered. Some animal got her after she died. The wounds on her legs were inflicted postmortem but, be assured, this is cold-blooded murder of the vilest kind.

She looked up and then strode to an outcrop of rock 30 meters up the hill. Beneath the outcrop were some smaller rocks set in gravel. "Look around here!" she ordered.

"Why?" asked Joseph.

"Because there is a trail of blood leading right back to this out-crop," Cornelia said, as she walked further up the hill. She was standing on the top of the largest rock, looking down at the others below. "There is no blood trail here. It stops right there," she said, pointing down.

Jayne was about to clamber over the rocks and peer into the space when Joseph put his hand on her shoulder. "Let me do that, Ms. Kai. This is a fixer job, not a job for the LO," he said, and he nudged her out of the way.

Jayne was about to protest and then quickly reconsidered. She stepped aside as Joseph crawled into the space behind the loose rocks on the doorstep of an opening in the rocks. He kept going until only his large feet were sticking out of the hole in the rocks. The rest of him had disappeared. They all heard his voice echo from the space beneath the outcrop. "I need a light. There appears to be a cave here." He wiggled out and quickly started to remove the rocks that were blocking the entrance. The aides helped him and soon the hole was big enough for him to wiggle all the way inside; this time with a powerful flashlight.

There were no sounds for a few minutes. The silence continued for longer than Jayne could control herself. She stuck her face near the opening and yelled, "Hey, Kane, are you alright?"

There was no answer.

She turned to Cornelia. "I'm going in to check on him. I need another flashlight." She turned back to the hole.

Just then, Joseph stuck his head out of the hole and wiggled his body through. He stood up and brushed off the dust. There was dirt that looked like it had gathered in the moisture of a tear on his face. He wiped it away.

"This is bad," he said as he turned to Cornelia. "We need a forensic team and a couple of top-notch biome structural fixers here now." He sat down on the large rock in front of the hole and wiped his face with his arm. The dirt smeared away. The telltale tear was gone. His jaw was set hard.

CHAPTER 36

Secrets Secrets

The construction of the biomes—to the stage of habitability—took over 30 years. A project of this magnitude must be carefully planned and re-planned many times. After the first 10 years, most of the original designs were discarded. It was never a case of starting over, it was a case of incorporating the most up-to-date science into the final construction. The multiple redundancies of the biome systems were constantly upgraded. Without them, a breakdown would have deadly consequences.

After all of this care, it was hard for some to believe that the biomes were riddled with things that were not on any of the final blueprints. There were doors where there shouldn't have been doors, rooms behind hidden panels, ventilation ducts going to places that didn't exist, an electrical conduit that passed right through a wall of solid base rock, feeding power to somewhere unknown. Many of these had been discovered over the years and chalked up to the need for redundancy, but some remained hidden to all but a secret few.

"What is in there?" asked Jayne.

"What is down the rabbit hole?" asked Cornelia.

"Bodies. At least 10. There is a large natural cave with metal racks against one side. They are all on the racks, wrapped in body bags, with the clear plastic over their faces. They are all young," Joseph said softly. "This is a cave-in," he said, and he pointed to the hole behind him. "I don't know what happened, but it looks like someone left in a hurry."

He looked up at Cornelia. "Has anyone found the location of the unscheduled departure?"

"Not yet. Why?" asked Jayne.

"I think they're connected," answered Joseph. "That body was hauled out of the hole by some animal. It tore into the body bag and pulled out the body and dragged it over there."

"Those omies were out looking for her. They were worried. As far as I can discern after interviewing the girl who found the body," Cornelia said, gesturing to the now distant floater, "the victim wanted to leave Biome 7 and escape to the planet below. She had heard rumors that others had escaped by coming to this area. Supposedly, there was access to a secret spaceport. Passage could be bought."

"How could an omie girl come up with anything valuable enough to interest a smuggler?" asked Cornelia's aide.

"If I were to guess, I would say diamonds. A lot of the original omies were allowed to bring family jewelry and heirlooms with them. I saw a man's diamond ring on a string around the dead girl's wrist. But whoever killed her didn't want her diamonds. They wanted, and took, something far more precious," Cornelia said ominously.

"Her life," stated Jayne flatly. "That must be the ploy. Spread rumors about how great it is planet-side and how restrictive it is up here. Tease the young and lure them to wherever you want them. Capture them and murder them and take the parts of them you can sell, and then trash the rest. Fracking bastards!"

"Well, I intend to stop it and stop it now. If that was a cave-in," Cornelia said, pointing to the hole in the ground that Joseph had crawled through, "then there must be some other entrance near here and that entrance will inevitably lead to one of the under sectors and to a ship pad. If we find it soon, maybe we can get some idea who is behind these horrors."

Joseph rubbed his head, as if he was trying to figure out the 'how' of the whole thing. "How could there be a connection between this hillside and the underside of the biome? This is all pressure sealed. Any opening would immediately be detected by the computer systems and an emergency seal unit would be activated," he said.

"No idea," replied Cornelia.

Jayne walked to an area up the slope. The forest, if you could call biome woods a forest, became denser as she moved upward. She was feeling lucky. That is how she always described the feeling she was now experiencing. If she broke it down, analyzed it, and described it, she would say that there was a shiver and a sense of 'more.' She felt larger—expanded, if you will. The larger she felt, the luckier she would be. The feeling was strong and the coolest thing of all was that Jayne felt she could now begin to control it. Before, it just happened and something lucky followed. Today, she felt she could push out and become larger and, by definition, luckier.

She traveled about 20 meters. The trees were almost all conifers. They were not exactly like earth conifers because all vegetation was genetically engineered to suit the environment. Jayne reached out and ran her hand down one of the trees. She was familiar with Earth trees, and this bark was similar to a dwarf pine, only it was taller due to reduced gravity. She picked her way over some large rocks, slipped, and reached out to the nearest pine tree to catch her balance. She regained her footing and was about to step forward when she caught a shiver of luck. She pushed a little and her fingers tingled where she touched the tree. This tree did not feel like the other tree. It felt artificial, almost plastic. She looked back at it. There was nothing she could see that would indicate that anything was different or wrong. She stepped back and touched the bark again. There was something wrong. This was definitely not a real tree. Jayne scanned the area. There was a slightly worn path that seemed to lead right to the base of this fake tree. She looked up. It looked very real. She looked down at the base and then jumped off the rock on which she was standing. There was a definite clunky echo that was not natural. She walked down the path. It led away from the others waiting below. The path followed an angle that meandered down the hill. Jayne walked it and stared at the ground. She was looking for some sort of marker that would set this path as the one to follow. A teenager would see this as a grand adventure, especially a teenager from a biome. She smiled. She was just a teenager and this whole thing was an adventure. Then she saw it. A sequence of rocks pressed into the surface of the path that formed a small 10 cm arrow pointing behind her to the fake plastic pine tree. If you were not looking, you would never have noticed it. She walked a little farther and saw another arrow.

She stopped and called to the group, "I have found something."

They all moved toward her. Once they arrived, she walked up the path, pointing at the arrows as she went. "It stops at the base of a pine tree, only the tree is not real."

They all stopped in a small clearing that surrounded the base of the pine tree. Joseph walked up to the tree, ran his hands down the bark and rapped it with his knuckles. "Sounds metallic," he said. He continued to explore the surface.

"And there's this," said Jayne. She jumped up and down. The ground beneath her feet reverberated.

"It sounds hollow. There must be a way to get down there," said Cornelia.

Joseph was now on his knees and both his hands were feeling the surface of the tree. "There is nothing here," he said. He stood and shifted his attention to the small rocks. He kicked at a couple of them. They were all fairly round and rolled away at his kick. He looked to the opposite side and kicked another. This one did not move. He kicked it again. The rock remained in place. He knelt and looked more closely.

Jayne was watching his exploration. Joseph was about to give this new rock a twist with his fingers. "Stop!" she shouted. "Wait! There is something wrong. I feel it." It was just like the day in the Biome 3 pods with Spike, right before she sensed the Stink Bomb lizard.

Joseph stood up and spoke to Jayne. "What's wrong? I think that rock will get us inside. I bet it opens something nearby."

"I think it does, too. I think it is how the young Omies got captured and killed. If you open up whatever entrance gets you inside, it might set off alarms that tell whoever set this up that their trap had been tripped. I would rather be safe than sorry," said Jayne cautiously.

Cornelia stepped in front of them and stared down at the rock. "Damn it! I am the coordinator here. I am responsible for all aspects of the function of this biome. If there is something here that shouldn't be here, then it is my job to deal with it. I won't be frightened off by a bunch of murderous body-part snatchers." And with that, she knelt and twisted the small rock at her feet.

A voice came from the tree. "Welcome biome dwellers that seek freedom from oppression. Step to the edge of the clearing and the door to freedom will open at your feet." No one moved. There was a minute of cautious waiting. The voice sounded again. "Please step to the edge of the clearing."

The entire group stepped to the edge of the small clearing. A few seconds later, a rectangular section of the clearing opened up, revealing a staircase to a small two-meter square room below. Cornelia looked at one of her aides. He was a burly-looking fixer named Gregor. He was not assigned to Cornelia because of his brains. She nodded at him, and he walked down the stairs into the room below. He tapped at the metal walls and generally inspected the room. He turned and looked up at Cornelia.

"There is no exit that is obvious. Maybe there is another something to twist to open a door. I don't see anything, though," the aide said and turned to tap the wall again. "Nope. Nothing I can see. Maybe you should come and have a look."

Cornelia stepped forward and was about to step down into what Jayne now viewed as a dangerous pit. She shivered and automatically reached out and grabbed Cornelia Banks by the arm and held her from taking that step.

Cornelia turned and was about to say something when they all heard Gregor yell and the opening shut with a snap. They could all hear Gregor in the pit below; he was yelling. And then there was nothing but a light breeze rustling the pine needles.

Joseph froze for a brief moment and then reached over and turned the stone again. There was the same message emanating from the pine tree, requesting that they move to the edge of the clearing. They all did, and the ground opened as before. They all looked into the room at the bottom of the stairs.

It was empty.

CHAPTER 37

Omie Gallery

Populating the biomes was a process that consumed the planet's entire population. Everyone was, in some way, involved. Anyone could apply. All that was required for application was personal data and a sample of DNA. It was left to the scientists to determine the criteria under which a person would be considered as a first generation biome dweller. Over 70% of applicants were rejected on the first round of selections. Most of these rejections were due to age or DNA flags. If the human race was to be spread throughout the galaxy, we might as well send out the best. The selection of the biome population was seen as a good way to purify the DNA pool. Any applicant with a genetic disorder, or genetic disposition to a disorder, was automatically rejected. Once selected, the purification continued for a number of generations through the use of restricted breeding protocols. By the time fourth-generation Omies were born, the pool was as clean as it had ever been through natural selection. All Omies DNA and physical and mental traits were tracked and recorded annually.

Cornelia Banks snapped open her VID. She spoke sharply. "Make sure you bring a full complement of scanning gear. I want you here five minutes ago. Delay the forensics guys. They will just get in the way." And then, as an afterthought, she said, "Bring a full complement of suits—gas and space."

She clicked off and turned to Joseph Kane. In a soft voice she said, "I want you to get the LO out of here. This has just turned really nasty."

Jayne overheard and stepped forward. "I'm not going anywhere."

"With all due respect, the LO belongs in her office so she can liaise with whomever needs liaising," Cornelia said.

"With all due respect to the fixer coordinator, perhaps she should stick to what she is good at and let me do my job," said Jayne, in a sweet but caustic tone.

"Yes, with respect, but I don't believe that the illustrious LO is old enough to know what she is good at. Now run along and let the adults work," said Cornelia flatly, and she turned to her other aide. "How long will it be until they get there?"

"At least 20 minutes. We are quite a long way out," he said.

Jayne's face flushed red. She began to recite in a loud voice. "The responsibilities of the liaison officer in the biomes are wide and varied." She stopped to interject. "I'll now skip to the important part." She continued, "The primary responsibility is to ensure safety for all. This includes all native biome dwellers as well as fixers, scientists, and politicians that may be present. In case of an emergency, all final decisions are the responsibility of the liaison officer."

She stopped and stared at Cornelia and Joseph. "I'm going down there now. Time is obviously of the essence, and the safety of that fixer is primary."

Cornelia reached out to stop her, but Joseph stayed her hand. "She's right," he said.

As the floor slid closed over her head, Jayne muttered, "Suit–Thirteen–suggest maximum safety." Nothing seemed to happen. The Sergio Partelli looked exactly the same as before. She was still wearing the specially equipped fixer suit. The light from above faded as the forest floor, now her ceiling, closed.

Jayne reached to her equipment belt, removed and turned on a flashlight. She looked around her and saw a mist fill the small room from a series of holes in the walls. The odd thing was that she was not in the mist. It was like an invisible shield surrounded her. She was in a forcefield that the mist could not penetrate.

"Gas," she thought. "The young Omies that entered here were gassed." Suddenly, the gas disappeared, the back wall of the small room lifted, and the floor began to move forward. As soon as Jayne was clear of the room, the door closed again. In front of her, lying on the floor, was Cornelia's aide. A dim light was glowing on the far side of a large room.

Jayne flipped her VID and called Joseph, "I'm alright. You'll need gas masks to get down here safely. I had one in my kit, and I put it on before I passed out," Jayne lied. She checked her pouch to see if, in fact, there was a gas mask as part of the equipment. She sighed as her hand came into contact with it. Her lie would hold.

"Lucky girl, as usual," said the voice of Joseph from her VID. "How is Gregor?"

"Of course, you know it is skill and experience, not just luck, that kept me safe," she said and then added under her breath, "With a little help from Sergio."

She moved to check Gregor. She felt for his pulse and stood up. "He appears to be okay. His pulse is strong. I'm going to see if I can shut off the gas and get you two down here sooner."

"Be careful," said Joseph.

Jayne scanned the room with her flashlight. She saw that the section of floor that led from the gas room was, in fact, a wide conveyer belt that transported the unconscious bodies onto what could only be described as a body carousel. As she glanced around, the conveyor belt started, and she was moving along with Gregor. She stepped off the moving belt and pulled Gregor off to the side. She turned him on his back. His breathing was shallow.

The conveyer belt stopped, and the carousel started, as if it was expecting Gregor's body to be deposited from the conveyer. The carousel turned until the section that would have held Gregor disappeared through a slit in the wall. To the right of the carousel was a door. Jayne scanned it with her flashlight. There was an old-fashioned keypad on the left side that controlled the locking mechanism.

Jayne walked over and inspected it. She raised her hand to the keypad, hoping the correct number would jump into her head. Nothing did.

She rested her hand on the keys and quickly pulled it away. A DNA scraper had just taken a small sample of the skin on her palm. The keypad was not as old fashioned as she had thought. There was a click from the door, but it did not open. Jayne jumped as the conveyor belt started again. It ran for a few seconds and then stopped. Suddenly, the process became clear to Jayne. She heard the carousel start up, and she turned, ran toward it and jumped onto where she would have been, had she been deposited as an unconscious person by the conveyor belt. A small slit opened in the wall where the carousel passed through. It was just large enough to accommodate a body. Once through, the carousel stopped. Jayne sat up and started to inspect the room with her flashlight, but it was not as dark as the ante room. She did not need it. There were lights that ran the perimeter. They were attached to the walls at the two-meter level, like a continuous wall sconce. Below were VID-size photographs of people. They were three high and ran almost the entire perimeter of the room. Some had large X's right through them. Others had green checkmarks in the corner and still others had question marks in the same location as the green check marks. Jayne walked around the room, inspecting the photographs. Most were of teenagers or young adults. A few were of children of 11 or 12 years old. As she walked, she inspected each photograph. She began to realize that this was a list of victims and possible victims that lived in Biome 7. The monsters that ran this place were capturing them and murdering them for their genetically perfect body parts. They would be sold and implanted into equally monstrous people.

Jayne looked up at the posters again and realized the true horror. This was a body-part-to-order operation. Need a heart with only 15 years on it? Just put in your order and we will scan the databases and find you the perfect match. It will cost you, but that is no problem for a rich, nasty scientist or politician.

Jayne looked at another door on the far side of the room. There were three photographs in a vertical line, highlighted by a border. The bottom two had a large black X through them. She walked toward them. Her

VID sounded.

It was Cornelia Banks. "Ms. Kai? Are you alright? The equipment has arrived. We will be down there in two minutes."

Jayne did not respond. She had walked a few more steps toward the three pictures. Her mouth fell open. The top picture was surrounded by yellow stars as if the person was a celebrity. It was a picture of Jayne. If someone saw it, they would know it was her immediately. Fear welled up. Her heart pounded in her chest. She felt the bubble grow out from the confines of her skin. She felt time slow until there was almost forever between the beats of her heart. It was in that time between contractions of her heart and the rush of blood that Jayne could consider actions and the myriad of possibilities created by those actions. She explored the economy of each. Ockham's Razor states that, "Plurality is not to be posited without necessity." That is—'do not add complexity to a solution until it becomes necessary to do so,' or 'KISS—keep it simple, stupid.' Jayne drew back from the infinity and felt her blood continue its rush through her veins and arteries. She sighed. The decision was made.

The sound of voices coming from the outside room intruded. She quickly reached up and peeled her picture from the wall, folded it up and tucked it in her personal pouch. The mark on the wall where the picture was posted was nearly indiscernible. Jayne quickly turned to the entrance door. There was easy access from this side. She opened the door.

Joseph yelped and pulled his hand from the number pad. "Damn dull skin scraper. Did I open the door or did you?" he asked Jayne.

"I did," she replied. She turned to Cornelia. "This is going to make you sick and very angry."

Jayne swept her hand out and spun in a circle as if to welcome them to view the works in a gallery of fine art. At least 10 people streamed into the room. Many held cases that contained all sorts of equipment. They set down their burdens and waited.

Cornelia and Joseph scanned the gallery of photographs.

"Oh, my god! I recognize some of these kids. I saw this one yesterday. He works in the village market," said one of the fixers.

He pointed at a photo with a checkmark in the top corner. "What does the green checkmark mean?" He did not wait for an answer. "And this one went missing last year. We hunted everywhere for her. In the end, we told her parents that she probably ran away to the surface and would contact them soon. She obviously never did."

There was a large X right over the picture. Joseph frowned and mumbled half to himself, "Cause she's dead." And then louder. "I bet all these Xs are dead kids, just like the one we found and the ones in the room I found. All gutted for their organs. All gassed, gutted, and killed. I sure hope none of them woke up." As if to signal that process, there was a groan from the ante room. It was Gregor. The groan was repeated and then followed by the unmistakable sounds of someone puking his guts out.

Cornelia turned to one of the group of fixers and said, "Go and see if he's alright, then get him out of here and to the hospital. Who knows what kind of gas they were using?"

She had forgotten about Jayne and turned her attention to the door on the far side of the room where Jayne had removed the photograph of herself. "Let's get through there and find out what has been going on here right under our noses."

As the fixers began to use some sophisticated equipment to check the door, Joseph turned to Jayne and whispered, "You need to get out of here. Now! I mean it. Come with me now. No telling what kind of installation this door will lead to."

"I can handle it," said Jayne.

"Look, I am not concerned if you can handle a little blood and gore. What I am concerned about is your safety in the long run. No telling what kind of surveillance they are using. There could be electronic sniffers tagged with your DNA all over this installation. There doesn't appear to be anything here, but behind that door could be a very different story. Let's go—Now!" Joseph ordered. He grabbed her shoulder and pulled her toward the door to the ante room and the conveyer belt.

She pulled out of his grasp.

"I can walk without you pulling me. Let me go. It would look a little suspicious for the LO's aide to be pulling her around like she was a ragdoll, now wouldn't it?" Jayne whispered with a haughty air.

She walked out and called behind her, "Ms. Banks, I expect a full report with video as soon as you have completed this initial investigation."

Cornelia called back, "I'll have something when I have something." Jayne grinned but did not turn around. "And that will be tomorrow morning at the latest. We all have reports to write, and I want yours by 800 hours tomorrow."

She thought as she stepped into the small lift now under manual control, "That will teach her to treat me like I am a child."

CHAPTER 38

Great Balls of Fire

All the biomes were fitted with flier ports. Flier shuttles were used to transfer persons and small items to and from the spavator and then down to the HUB. These ports were totally sealed off from the biome proper. Security protocols were strict. Nothing entered or left a biome without the proper clearance, and therein lay the rub. Clearance. The last few decades of the biomes' existence had resulted in a number of changes to biome security protocols. Most of the changes tightened security. This made it more difficult for the black marketers unless you had clearance. Clearance was always granted for the right price. The rich and powerful were routinely granted the required clearance.

Joseph dropped off Jayne at Biome Central. She walked to her office, glad to be back in Earth-normal gravity. She flexed her leg muscles and bounced up and down on her toes. Out in the biome, that kind of leg jump would have taken her a lot higher. Here, she was only a few cm from the ground.

Joseph headed back to the crime scene. He felt he would be more useful there and would report to her later in the day. He was her eyes on the ground. He was fitted with body cameras that would transmit everything he saw and heard, and even a few things he could not see or hear, to Jayne's office monitors.

Jayne whispered, even though no one could possibly hear her, "Suit override–thirteen–suggest LO standard." Her suit turned into a dark green skirt and jacket. She looked down at her feet and saw that she was wearing her gym sneakers. That is what she had on her feet when she left for the gym earlier today. They were fine with the fixer suit, but they looked very odd with her work suit. She kicked them off and found a pair of heeled pumps behind the door. She slipped them on and slid behind her desk. The monitors came on and she watched scenes from a floater: front, back, and to the sides. It was travelling at top speed. Joseph had obviously used her bypass code to increase the speed of the floater.

Joseph's voice filled her office. "I see you are up and watching. I will arrive in a few minutes. We have two-way."

"Great," responded Jayne.

Joseph got off the floater and walked up the hill to the lift entrance. The fixer crew had erected a large tent over the original hole leading to the room filled with corpses. Jayne's views were Joseph's views and more. She could see behind him. The tent flap opened, and a body bag was lifted onto a waiting floater and whisked away.

As Joseph was about to enter the tent, Jayne heard a whooshing sound through the microphone. She saw the tent over the hole burst into flame. Suddenly, the camera switched. Joseph had turned around. He was quickly retreating from the intense heat. Jayne watched as two flaming fixer med techs ran out of the flaming tent. They were trained for accidents of this kind and rolled in the dry dirt in an effort to extinguish themselves. A floater had just arrived, and the driver grabbed a folded body bag, flapped it open and tried to smother the flames on the first fixer who came out of the tent. It was a horror to watch. The flame was infectious. It spread from person to person through touch. Jayne suspected it was a highly flammable gel that stuck and continued to burn whatever, or whomever, touched it. The 'would-be rescuer was also engulfed in flames and suffocation of the fire seemed impossible.

Jayne was getting a closer view of the fire and she realized that Joseph was running toward the screaming, burning men in an effort to help. Jayne screamed at the communication microphone, "Joseph—NO! Joseph—STOP! You can't help." She saw the picture in front of her stop its rush to zoom into the flaming bodies and burning ground smeared with flaming gel.

"What the hell is that stuff?" Joseph yelled through the speakers. "The gel will completely incinerate you. I've read about it. The chemical reaction with flesh causes an incredibly hot flame that consumes a body completely. Nothing is left but ash. Once you have even a little on your body and the reaction has started, there is no stopping it. Please don't go near or touch any of it. Warn others."

The screaming soon stopped as the flames burned the bodies like they were logs of wood. The tent was gone, leaving only metal skeletons of equipment. The ground continued to smolder around the expanded hole that led to the cache of gutted bodies that were now surely piles of smoldering ash.

There was another whoosh and again Jayne could see flames through the camera, pointing behind Joseph. A number of trees were spattered by flaming gel that had spewed from the stairway that led down to the rooms below. The flames were growing and threatening to spread the conflagration to adjacent areas. Jayne imagined Joseph standing over the stairwell when the gel exploded from the opening. She imagined him burning and helpless to save him. She closed her eyes and squeezed the thought from her consciousness. Again, Joseph turned around and the camera focus shifted. Jayne watched as fire retardant spewed from nozzles hidden in the stone structure of the biome base. There could be no large fires in a biome. The designers realized that fire could easily destroy all life support systems, no matter how redundant. A few trees continued to smolder, but the fire retardant was being replaced by a heavy mist of water. The flames were soon extinguished, and the smoke suctioned away, leaving behind the charred bodies of humans and trees.

Suddenly, there was a rumble. The entire biome shook to the core of the asteroid that supported it. Alarms sounded everywhere, from every speaker and horn. One of the monitors was completely obscured. The others had become blurred with mist.

Jayne cried out, "Joseph! Joseph, are you alright? Joseph!"

He did not reply, but she could see motion, as if he was running.

She could hear his rapid breathing.

"It has all been destroyed. I don't think anyone could have survived that fire gel. We have to assume that everyone down there is dead," puffed Joseph, as he continued to run.

"What about the explosion? We felt a huge rumble and, as you can hear, the alarms are going crazy," she yelled over the cacophony of alarms and recorded warnings that blared around her.

The cameras showed Joseph running and suddenly stopping. He reached for his VID, but it had been shattered. He tore one of the cameras from his lapel and held it out in front of himself at arm's length. "Are you okay?"

"I'm fine," she said, but an odd feeling seeped into the moment. She felt exposed. She didn't want to worry Joseph, so she said nothing of her feelings. "How are you and what caused that explosion?" She looked at his face covered with mud and saw fear in his eyes.

"I think the explosion was set off by us. Banks and the others must have ventured into a booby trap. The fire gel would destroy any evidence, and I suspect the explosion closed off all the tunnels. I bet one of those tunnels led to the underside of this rock and to a secret ship port. How else would they get those body parts out of here?" he said. "They really didn't want anyone exploring their super-secret hideaway and slaughterhouse. Look!" He turned the camera facing the scene and zoomed in on the original hole he had crawled into earlier that day.

Jayne could see a dark grey foam-like mass oozing from the hole. It shimmered for a moment and then stopped moving. After a few seconds, it lightened in color to an off-white.

"What is that?" Jayne asked.

"Concrete foam. It dries instantly and is harder than stone. It will be a very long time before anyone gets back into those tunnels, if ever. The good thing is, it will stabilize the entire asteroid. There were plans in the works to use it to fill any underworld caves and tunnels, but the expense was deemed prohibitive and the danger to the biome was not critical until the biomes were ready to leave Earth orbit. The departure is still years in the future," he said, pointing the camera back at his face.

As a signal that things had stabilized, the alarms and announcements stopped. "It's over. I'm coming to get you," said Jayne.

"No, you are not. Stay right where you are. It is my job to look after you and not the other way around," he yelled, but it was too late. Jayne had already left the office carrying her sneakers.

"Suit override–thirteen–suggest fixer standard," she said as she ran to the Fixer–Biome transition zone. She searched the area for a floater, but there were none to be had. Everyone had an emergency station, and everyone was stationed at their posts. Even the omies that worked in the fixer section were all at their posts. Not a soul was to be seen.

Her VID beeped. She glanced at it, expecting Joseph to yell at her and tell her to stay where she was. It was Professor Greenway. Jayne relaxed, as she always did when he contacted her. She had never had a father, or a grandfather, and he was as close as she was ever going to get to family. He was her protector. Not that I need one, she thought to herself.

"Professor Greenway?" she queried.

"Jayne, thank God. I just got a very disconcerting message. You need—" he said, as Jayne cut him off.

"I'm alright. I have some things to tell you, but this is not a good time. I will call you tonight. I will use encryption," she said quickly. She snapped the VID closed. A floater zipped into the transition zone. Jayne ran to it, but it was not Joseph. She called to the driver, "Have you seen Kane?"

The young fixer responded with a question. "Are you the LO?" His face was flushed, and his eyes were wild.

"Yeah," answered Jayne. She looked into his eyes and asked, "Where is Joseph Kane?"

"He went back. We heard some moans from the woods, and he went to check while I was sent here," he said, as he got off the floater and walked over to her. He reached into the inside pocket of his jacket.

Jayne felt a surge of fear. Something was wrong. The fear she felt was not focused. She was blind to everything but this fixer reaching into his inside pocket. He was reaching for something dangerous. She could feel it. She was weighing options when the bubble swelled over her. Again, time slowed, and the fixer's hand stopped in mid-reach. Her mind cast a net into the infinite stream of possibilities and snagged a few of the bigger ones; the more likely ones; the ones that did not slip through the holes of her net. There were a number of options with outcomes she did not like and, like old rubber boots cluttering up her net, she tossed them back into the flow. One grew and filled her consciousness. She did not like it, but it was the safest. She was hoping she could control it as the bubble collapsed and, like before in the spaceship, a solid ball of air formed. This time, it was about the half the size of a grav ball.

What happened next was almost simultaneous. The ball came into existence. The slip of scribe the fixer was retrieving from his jacket came into view. The ball was fired. She realized the fixer was not reaching for a weapon. It was too late to stop the solid ball of air. All she could do was slow it down. She pushed and the 'ball' slowed. It hit the fixer in the chest. The fixer fell. The scribe slip fluttered and landed on the chest of the now unconscious young man.

Jayne's eyes opened wide. She had been wrong. He had been reaching for a slip of magnetic scribe, not a weapon. She knelt down. The fixer was young and still breathing. Jayne sighed with relief. She placed her index finger on the corner of the scribe slip her fingerprint was scanned and confirmed, and a single word formed.

"Hide!" it said.

Jayne stood up and looked around. She realized the danger she had sensed had not come from the young man at her feet. The danger was building again, but she could not find the focus. The origin was not clear. She spun in a circle. The potential of danger swelled but the origin was completely blurred. Hide? But where? There was no place to hide. Panic brought on the bubble again, and again time slowed. It took a few micro-seconds for Jayne's brain to look at the day's events. One jumped up and begged to be analyzed. The DNA scraper on the door keypad in the underground gallery had taken a sample. Whoever had set up that house of horrors now had a sample of her DNA and had run an analysis. They knew she was here. She was sensing their purpose more clearly and, like a compass seeking the north pole, they were homing in on her. She had to do more than hide. She had to run and keep running until she could find a way of escape. The biome wilds were a dangerous place to hide, but it was a lot safer than what she knew was coming.

Behind her, at the main platform, she heard the high pitch whine of a ship landing. It didn't sound like a freight transport from the spavator port. The sound was not deep enough. It was a more like a passenger ship but not quite. Military. It was military. She had heard a million military ships fly over the nursery on their way back from somewhere. This was that same sound. A military ship was landing, and she knew none were scheduled. She knew they were coming for her.

She jumped on the floater on which the now unconscious fixer had arrived and set it to top speed. She headed across the lowlands in an Earth-north direction. If they were going to kidnap her, she was not about to make it easy. All the biomes had sensors set into the very rock of the asteroids from which they were built. The military would have access to them. They would detect her body heat or her motion or her mass, and she would be discovered and captured. They could also track her VID. Her heart raced, and she tossed Cassie Kai's VID into a small pond as she flew by. That would make her harder to find, but she would also be without any form of communication. She would be cut off from all help. She was really on her own.

She was headed to the 'edge of the world,' as the omies called it. That place where the sky met the ground. You could not touch the sky, for it was out of reach. The sky met the asteroid at the top of a high, smooth rock face. The face was impossible to climb, and a floater was restricted from rising more than a meter or so from the ground.

The 'sky' consisted of the dome proper. It was impossible to touch, as it was protected by a negative gravity field and repelled anything that came near.

The northern most point of this particular biome was unique. There was a canyon with a small opening between two large boulders. The sensor array had been terminated in front of the canyon and so anyone inside was invisible to the sensors. If you pushed your floater to maximum height, you could pass between the boulders and hide inside. Jayne had studied some Biome 7 lore in her search for the source of the murders and came upon this little tidbit of information. It just might save her from capture.

Once inside, she scanned her surroundings. The walls were covered with graffiti, but the area was relatively clean. Any debris from the last party had been cleaned up. This struck Jayne as odd. She explored further and discovered an extension power source set up near a series of flat rocks set in a circle. Someone had hacked a node on a sensor array and run power to the inside of the canyon. Someone was planning a party soon. But not tonight. It was too late for anyone to travel out this far. Jayne shivered, and the Sergio Partelli she was wearing displayed a flashing indicator at her wrist. It was light pink. That was a request for verbal communication.

She pressed the light and the suit spoke. "There has been a heavy and constant load on the power source of the suit. Please connect to an external power source to recharge."

Jayne picked up the connector at her feet and clipped it to the Sergio Partelli. She snuggled down between a couple of rocks and rested. Sergio kept her warm while it charged, and she soon fell into a fitful sleep.

CHAPTER 39

Running & Hiding

The nursery was, in reality, just an expansion of the educational system. It was conceived as a replacement for dysfunctional family units. At first, it was a volunteer system and billed as prestigious. You could send your child to a nursery, but this had to be done before the child's first birthday. Children would be raised in the nursery and all decisions about their direction in life would be made by the state. At first, parents could see and visit their children, as long as there were no lasting emotional repercussions. It soon became obvious that most parents would rather live their lives without the burden of child-rearing. If having and raising children was critical to a person's happiness, they could choose to work in the nursery.

Jayne dreamed she was six years old again. She was in the nursery. She was hiding from the matron. She had saved some of her morning meal and was nibbling a small piece of the breakfast bar. Someone was calling her name. The voice was soft and warm at first, but it soon became loud and sharp. The matron was calling for her. She became still, hoping to remain undiscovered, but the matron drew closer. Suddenly, a large hand reached to where she was hiding and grabbed her by the collar. Jayne startled awake.

She did not remember where she was. Her legs were cramping. Suddenly it all rushed back, and she jumped to her feet and looked furtively around. She was still alone. It was morning in the biome, but she was still in the shadow of the rocks that formed the small canyon. The light was racing in on the western floor as the sun rose in the east.

She was thirsty and walked to the floater. There would be water in the survival pouch and maybe some food of sorts. She drank water from a flexible container and chewed on a sweetened bar of nuts and dried fruit. She stopped chewing at the sound of a floater. It was still distant. She had not sensed any danger from the intruding floater but was cautious all the same. She peeked furtively out from behind the large boulders and watched a small scout floater nosing its way toward the canyon opening. It was a drone and floated only a few cm from the ground. Jayne grabbed a large rock from the pile at the base of the boulder. She waited as the scout floater gradually neared the opening.

As it passed through, Jayne raised the rock and smashed it to the ground. She could see one of the scout cameras begin to rotate upward to capture the visage of its assailant. She raised the rock again and smashed the camera to mush. She continued smashing until there were no parts intact. Even the small power source was smoking.

"They have found me," thought Jayne. "They will be coming soon." With a flood of adrenalin, she pushed the mind bubble up and over her entire being. The possibilities percolated out of the moment and the moments to follow. None were useful. All the possibilities were equal: equally neutral and without potential. The field of time that she spread out before her was flat. The potential of the barely detectable possibilities was the same at every point. Nothing reared its head, except the uglies—Jayne's word for those possibilities that could and would result in death. She chose to ignore these.

Jayne was about to collapse the bubble and move somewhere else and try again when she noticed the anomaly. It was a potential of a possibility and very noticeable once you detected it. Like a pit in the field of possibilities that went so deep you could not detect the bottom. Jayne looked. She could see nothing. There was no reason for its existence. It was simply a pit of nothingness.

Jayne snapped back and decided just to wait. Here was a situation that she could not see into and control. There was nothing she could do but wait. Waiting would provide something new, so she waited.

During the passing hours, Jayne thought about her life as an adult. She had joined the fixers less than a year earlier. Before that, she was just a regular kid in the nursery. She did what all kids did. Jayne reflected on her own thoughts. Maybe she did not do what every other kid did. Maybe she had just thought that she was normal, when, in fact, she wasn't. Normal, that is. But she had done exactly what was expected of her. She studied her schoolwork, and she played with the other kids. What else was there to do in the nursery? As far back as she could remember, she had spent all her time learning. Even when she played, she had really been learning. She had learned games like GravBall. Everything she did was easy: was a matter of course, as if it had all been planned. One day, she decided to be a TechElecMech fixer, so she took the test and passed. She was reflecting on what had given her the idea; what had inspired her to want to do what she had done and how she became good at those things? Nothing was really clear as to the reason why she was who she was. A lot of the memories of when she was really young were not at all clear. She had no memory of her mother, not even a picture. All she had was the music box and what others told her. She had nothing of her own to remember about her mother. She had been told that her father was just a donor. 'Justadonor.' She remembered a time in the playground GravBall tube.

"Hey, you are pretty good. Who is your father?" asked the big kid. "Did he teach you how to play GravBall? What's his name?"

"Justadonor," she had replied automatically.

The big kid replied, "Justin Doner, never heard of him. He ever play in the pros?"

For the first time, Jayne listened to what she had said and realized that the words were not a name at all. Her father was just a sperm donor. At the time, she had flushed at her stupidity.

"Naw," she responded, as she ran off. As an afterthought, she called back to the boy, "He was a great teacher, though."

She giggled at the absurdity of it all. She was thirteen and she could not picture her mother, and her father was an unknown donor.

She was Jayne Esther Wu, and she was lucky and that is all that counted, except for getting out of this situation alive.

There was no place to run. There was no place to hide. She sat on one of the flat rocks facing the opening between the boulders and waited. She had no time to get a weapon. She instinctively reached into the fixer pouch at her waist. She removed some twine, a small blade used for cutting insulation, and some insulation patches. A few minutes later, she had constructed her weapon of choice. She now had a functional sling. She spent some time practicing with some small stones. She gathered some evenly shaped ones and put them into her pouch. She wasn't sure how effective the sling would be, but it might come in handy. Her thoughts were interrupted by a distant hiss of floaters. "They are coming," she thought.

The sound of one floater became louder than the others. Suddenly, it stopped just outside the barrier of rocks in front of the canyon. On impulse, Jayne reached down and picked up a rock as big as her hand. She tossed it from hand to hand. "It's better than my little sling," she thought, as she weighed it in her right hand and reached for another with her left. Just like one of the mini grav balls she had learned to play with when she was smaller. The heft was about right. She stood and waited.

A helmeted head peeked between the boulders framing the entrance of the canyon. Jayne tossed the rock, and it shattered against the rock face right where the helmeted head had been, before it ducked out of sight.

"Hey, Wu! Lay off. It's me!"

She heard the voice of Joseph Kane from behind the boulders. "Joseph?" she queried.

"Yeah. It's me," he said, as he walked into the area and pulled his helmet off his head. "A bunch of security guys from Earth arrived and took over. They seem to know all about the secret tunnels and the explosions and the murders. They didn't ask us who we were. They just ordered us to get floaters and to find the dangerous fugitive that's been hiding out in Biome 7."

"Dangerous fugitive!" Jayne said, surprised.

"Yeah. And by that near miss with the rock, I'd say they are not too far off," he said. He looked at the mark from the rock she had thrown on the boulder beside him. "I said I would check out the area by the canyon because I knew it well. They let me, so here I am." They both looked skyward as the sound of other floaters became louder and then faded. "What's the plan, dangerous fugitive?"

"We should get out of here and get off this rock and hide somewhere else," said Jayne.

"I know this is none of my business. I am great at following orders without really knowing the whys and the wherefores but, if you don't mind me asking, what did you do to piss so many people off that they want you dead?" Joseph asked, as he led the way to the canyon opening.

"They don't want me dead, but they will kill you to get to me," she said. "As to what I did to deserve this, your guess is as good as mine. I suspect that they want me to…" she stopped and then continued, "experiment on. I think I'm an experiment that ran away from them and now they want it back. Do you have a VID?"

Joseph reached into his pouch.

"Give it to me!" she ordered. She had the presence of mind to carry a few of the entangled encryption tabs with her at all times. She slipped one into the side panel of the VID. "Now we wait for Professor Greenway."

"Who?" he asked.

"Greenway. He's our only hope of getting out of this," she said, and she absentmindedly kicked at the pieces of the smashed floater drone at her feet. Suddenly, they heard the growl of a flier in the biome. That was totally against all protocols. Fliers could compromise biome integrity and yet security was using one to search for her. It flew overhead. They both pressed themselves into the boulders, but it was too late. The flier sensors had spotted them. As the flier roar faded, the whooshing sound of floaters swelled.

Jayne looked at Joseph's VID in her hand. There was no response from

Professor Greenway. She peeked out from the boulders and saw three floaters land. The passengers were riding double. Six security personnel landed and fanned out in front of the opening to the canyon. They were armed.

Jayne felt the bubble form. It had been involuntary. The high stress of the impending danger took control. She tried to push it down to control the formation, but it was too late. The bubble locked out the flow of time from Jayne's consciousness. Everything slowed and the spikes of possibilities popped in and out of the stream. Most were uglies. These were people, and she did not want to kill them. She scrambled from one possibility to the next in the hope she could find one that would work. A tiny and incredibly unlikely event zoomed into focus. She had all the time in the world to analyze and caress it. Finally satisfied, she nudged it into being and pushed it forward. That was not enough. The probability of it occurring naturally was still infinitesimally small. She pushed harder. The last push did something she had never experienced before. She realized exactly what she was trying to do. She was not just focusing on the result. She wanted to move the boulders together. That was what she wanted to do. The result would be to give them more time—more time for Professor Greenway to rescue them.

Instead of focusing on 'getting more time,' she focused on blocking the space between the boulders. Suddenly, a myriad of new possibilities appeared, as if conjured out of the ether. Some of the less likely ones, like an asteroid quake bringing them together, were dismissed. She settled on using the rocks to block the entrance. She popped out of her mind bubble, looked at Joseph, and pointed at the circle of flat rocks in the middle of the area. "How many of those rocks can you get over here to the opening?" she asked.

"In this gravity, I can run with them," he said assuredly. "I want to block this opening," she said.

"They," he gestured at the opening and the security men moving toward the opening between the boulders, "will simply blast them away."

"I know, but it will take them some time, and I plan to confuse them a little so it takes even longer," she said, as she glanced at the now entangled and beeping VID in her hand. "Greenway's initiated a connection."

The VID beeped again. Joseph ran and carried large boulders to the opening.

Professor Greenway's face appeared.

Jayne spoke. "We are in trouble. Can you get us out of here?" She saw his stern face.

He spoke. "You have to stall. My crew is 10 minutes out. And five from your location, once inside the biome. Can you hold them off?"

"I am trying," she said. "Hurry!"

Jayne picked up the stone she tossed at the wall and lobbed it over the rocks as far as she could. She heard it hit something on the other side and quickly glanced out. All six security personnel looked in the direction of the noise and did not see her. Two of them moved to check it out. The other four were still moving toward the open passage between the boulders. The passage entered on an angle so you could not see directly in or out. It was narrow at its base and would allow only one person at a time to walk through. Jayne had seen this as an advantage in that she could probably stop them from entering.

Joseph dropped the first rock in place and they both ran back and forth carrying rocks to fill the gap. The rocks were fairly large, and soon the space between the boulders was filled up to Jayne's shoulders. She had just dropped the last load when they heard voices from the other side.

"She has tried to block the opening," a female voice spoke. "Set a charge and blast it away," said a commanding male voice.

"The girl must not be hurt in any way. You saw how adamant she was about that. I'm not blasting anything. You want to take that risk, you go ahead. I suggest that we just climb over the rocks," a third voice said.

"Okay, but since it was your suggestion, you go first," the first male voice ordered.

"No problem," the woman responded.

There was a rattle of boots climbing up the pile of rocks. "Take care. These rocks are very loosely placed. We could have pulled them out of the way."

"Just because we cannot hurt her does not mean that she cannot hurt us. You hear the rumors about pulverized bodies? Well, I heard this 'little girl' was responsible for that," said another voice.

The woman on the rocks took out her weapon and cocked it. "She is just a kid, a smart kid, but still a kid. I'll use my stinger if I have to," she said with assurance.

Jayne winced. She looked at Joseph and whispered, "Greenway will be here soon. He will get us out of this. We just have to hold them off a little longer."

They both backed away from the opening and moved to the side with their backs to the boulders. Joseph picked up a throwing rock and then another. Jayne loaded her makeshift sling. She swung it gently in her hand and bit her lip as she waited. A sense of impending danger swelled inside her. There was no bubble, only a strong sense that something was about to happen. Something bad. There was no focus, just a pressure that filled her with dread. Jayne looked furtively around. She could hear the security woman about to step into view. The swell of danger was almost incapacitating. Jayne saw the woman's head poke out from the opening in the rock and then disappear. The security woman's head was at least two and half meters from the ground, standing on the pile of rocks that Joseph and Jayne had moved to fill the space. Jayne and Joseph both stepped away from the boulder. Joseph raised his hand ready to throw a rock. Jayne started to twirl the sling faster. The woman poked her head out again.

There was a sudden suction of air from behind them. The stones flew. Joseph's rock went high and slightly wide. The woman ducked but some rock splinters smacked into her face. Her support hand, holding onto the rock wall, released. The woman slipped and she would have caught her balance, except that Jayne's sling was true. The stone hit the

314

woman on her cheek just below her eye. Blood spurted and she slipped and fell. Her weapon fired as she hit the ground. Joseph collapsed in heap. Jayne watched him fall and she screamed, "Joseph!"

Behind him, she could see an opening at the base of the sheer wall supporting the dome, with stairs leading down to the "underworld" caverns of the asteroid. The air was filled with dust from the change in pressure and out of the dust came at least a dozen soldiers dressed in pressure armor, carrying weapons. They fanned out around Jayne, who was now kneeling beside Joseph. Jayne reached down and touched his neck. She could not find a pulse. Beneath his jawbone she saw a neat red dot that could have been painted under his chin. The needle hole. She saw the blood spread out in a red bloom around his head. She lifted his head in the hope she could stop the bleeding but when she looked, there was only more blood. He had fallen on a sharp shard of rock. It had pierced the base of his skull. She swept the sharp rock aside with her hand and set his head gently down. His eyes were closed and his mouth was frozen in the smile that had crept over his face when he saw the woman fall. His last thought must have been, "I gother!"

At least that is what Jayne chose to believe. Joseph was dead. He died trying to save her.

The tears welled up in her eyes. "You bastards!" she hissed.

Jayne looked up. Her sense of danger was now going critical. This was not Professor Greenway's rescue team. This was THEM and they would pay. The bubble started to form in her head but, before she could find and push a possibility of escape into being, she felt a sting on her neck. The bubble shattered into nothingness and Jayne fell unconscious on top of Joseph.

CHAPTER 40
Captured Again!

As a species, humans have always sought to live forever. Initially, we looked to a place that existed outside of the physical plane. A heaven, if you will. We created eternal characters that inhabited this plane. They took the form of gods and monsters. After death, we might be able to join these eternal creatures and live forever.

The lifespan of a human being has been increasing steadily since man first stood on two legs. At first, this increase was due to improvements in the standard of living. More wealth meant better health and longer life. By the end of the second millennium, the discovery of DNA (1953, Watson and Crick) heralded the beginnings of extending human life directly through gene manipulation and organ transplantation.

One hundred years later, there were many other ways of living longer. The introduction of microscopic machines to the human body had totally done away with all diseases by making genetic repairs a few days after conception. These techniques allowed medicine to progress to the point where more affluent people could have their bodies repaired by these machines on a constant basis. But there were problems with these machines. Rogue programming resulted in some humans serving the microscopic machines. The Anti-cyborg movement took hold in society. People saw these micro machines as something alien. They did not want to become more machine than human.

Many techniques were used to help people live longer. Still, people died. Accidents happened. It wasn't until the advent of connectome scans and recordings that a truly eternal human mind became a possibility.

Jayne's eyes popped open. She blinked rapidly but there was no change in the darkness that filled them. She blinked again and tried to lift her arm to her face. The arm would not move. She stopped and took inventory, but she could see nothing. The darkness was pure. She listened to her own breathing and the beating of her heart. She tried again to lift her arm. It was restrained at the wrist, elbow, and shoulder. She tried to move her head. It seemed to be completely encased in a helmet of sorts, with her face exposed. Her body and her legs were also restrained. She could move her fingers and toes, blink her eyes and move her tongue. Her mouth was parched, and her lips were dry. She tried to conjure up some saliva. She cleared her throat and felt the strap around her neck press painfully into her. She tried to make a sound. She heard the high-pitched moan of her own voice. She tried to whistle, but no sound came out. The soft inner part of her lips was threatening to crack. Finally, some moisture appeared in her mouth, and she wet her lips and tried to whistle again. She thought she might be able to tell the size of the room if she could whistle. The small cheep she was able to make echoed in her head and she realized that the helmet was covering her ears. Jayne let out a sigh and tried to fill her lungs with air. Even that was restricted by the tight strap around her chest.

Not being able to fill her lungs pushed her panic to near critical. Jayne breathed short and shallow and tried to relax all her muscles. But each flex pushed her panic higher. She could feel air move over her skin. It was warm and she knew she was close to being naked. She felt a pinch on her arm and a warm glow flushed her skin; the tension fled from her muscles. Someone or something had drugged her. She felt soft and pliable. Her ability to concentrate seemed to have disappeared. A part of her brain tried to fight against the feeling. It was wonderful, but it was partnered with a nebulous fear. She tried to speak and only two words came out. She croaked, "Help, Professor Greenway." The fear faded and soft drug-induced pillows formed around her. She fell into them. She felt her mouth form a smile and she sighed.

Later, she heard voices and saw a soft light in the distance. She heard

318

a whirring sound, felt her body move with the bed and, like watching a holo video, the ceiling, and the machines attached to it, panned into her vision. She could see a body-shape scroll into her line of sight. It was not a person or a body. It was her suit hanging on the back of a door. Sergio Partelli was in the room with her. It was right there. If only she could get to it, she could cover her nakedness. But she couldn't move. The whirring stopped. Jayne was now just a few degrees from the vertical. She closed her eyes and the drugs in her system flooded her with softness and warmth.

"Jayne," a female voice called softly.

Jayne smiled and responded, "Yes, pwease. I will have a strawwberry one."

"Jayne," the voice called again.

"Two squoops, pwease," Jayne slurred.

"Miss Wu, listen," said another voice sharply.

"I sorry," replied Jayne and she started to cry.

The first voice cut in again. It was hard and cold. "How much did you give her? She is no good like this. I need her in top form. God, you are an idiot."

"You saw what she can do. She destroyed three of your best agents with a wall of air conjured up from her mind. I have no intention of giving her the chance of making me a victim. She is one powerful little girl," he said in awe, as he looked at Jayne strapped to an almost vertical table in front of him.

"That drug is designed to stop her from doing that. In large doses it turns her into this," the female voice said, and she gestured to Jayne, still weeping. "I swear, if you screw this up for me…"

"You'll what?" he asked assuredly.

"Just because you have completed the takeover doesn't mean you can—" she said, and she was cut off by the young man.

"I can do anything I want. Look at me. I'm 18." He smiled a macabre smile and patted the old woman on the shoulder. "Don't worry. You will be with me soon. I wouldn't leave you out in the cold."

"Not if you know what's good for you. I am still in charge, and don't you forget it," she threatened.

"Yes, you are in charge, but for how long? Remember, I am walking around in this, and you are walking around in that." He gestured vaguely at himself and then at her. He smiled and relented. "I'm just giving you a hard time. You know I would never abandon you."

"You had better not. I can still do a lot of damage, even in the few months this body has left," she said.

An old woman and a young man stood in front of a control panel flanked by a series of mini-holos. Jayne could see them, blurred through her tears. She stopped weeping and the final tears rolled down her cheeks. She blinked and tried to clear her eyes. The woman was old, very old. Jayne thought she had seen her somewhere before, but she could not remember. She brought the man into focus. He was much younger. Just a little older than her. She blinked again as he turned to face her. She did recognize him. It was the boy from the bean bag game and the flier to the Neuroscience Center.

"It is good old Ranovich 91. What the heck is he doing here?" she thought, as both figures turned and manipulated the shifting holos in front of them. Jayne felt a pinch on her upper arm.

"There, that ought to make her a little more lucid. In a few moments, you should be able to talk to her and have her understand," said Ranovich.

Jayne could not turn her head to see, but the cotton that filled her brain was starting to thin and clear. She looked at the two people in front of her. The male was definitely Ranovich. Jayne had never known his first name. She had met the old woman once before in what seemed like a lifetime ago. It was in the biome on the first day of her apprenticeship. Professor Greenway had told her the name. Jayne searched her memory. Her brain felt like it was moving in slow motion. Winter Bancroft. She remembered. Doctor Winter Bancroft was her name. This is the woman with an old body and perfect eyes. This is the woman who Jayne suspected of murdering and stealing body parts from the biomes. As her mind cleared, a thousand questions rushed in. She glanced at the boy who spoke like a man. It sure looked like Ranovich, but it didn't behave or talk like him. *What was happening here? What do they want with me?*

The old woman spoke again. "Jayne, can you understand me? Jayne?"

Jayne shifted her eyes from Ranovich to the old woman. "What are you doing to me?" she rasped. "Let me go!"

"I'm sorry, dearie, but that is no longer possible. By this time tomorrow, I will be you and you will be..." she made a *ppfffff* sound and snapped her fingers. "Just like Ranovich here who is now my good friend and colleague William Thurston. You remember Ranovich, don't you? I think you first met...when?" she turned to Ranovich for the answer but did not wait. "Oh yes, I saw the recordings of you in the Psi Center when we were just figuring out exactly how clever you are. That bit with the bean bag still amazes me. You sure took his arrogance down a notch or two. He had some skills, too, you know. Old Thurston here has been exploring them. Show her," she commanded, as she looked at Ranovich.

Ranovich smiled. "Watch the fixer suit on the back of the door." He concentrated, and the arms of the suit lifted and flapped and fell. "Pretty cool, eh!"

Jayne watched the suit arms move up and down. She caught a glint of a light in one of the buttons of the suit. The light looked reflected, but Jayne knew it wasn't. She sighed at the knowledge that the suit still had a charge. She said nothing. She wondered what they had planned for her. She tried to push the bubble into place, but nothing happened. Jayne tried to shrug but was unable to move enough to bring it off. The old woman spoke to Jayne. "It's the drugs. They were designed to control whatever it is you do. I know flapping the sleeves on a jumpsuit is just a parlor trick in comparison. Oh, I am so looking forward to trying you on." She giggled like a little girl who had just received a new party dress.

"Are you going to kill me?" Jayne asked, her voice raspy and dry.

"Oh no, dear, at least not in the way people are usually killed. I plan to keep your body alive for a very long time," she said calmly.

"What about me? My mind? My personality?" asked Jayne.

"Oh that. Well, after some discussion, we have decided that we would try to keep it, just in case we needed to put it back. I did argue against the time and effort required. After all, you are 13 years old. There can't be all that much worth keeping. We didn't bother with Ranovich. There wasn't much of a personality there in the first place. As I recall, he was rather surly," she said. The grin that followed could only be described as macabre.

Jayne felt the panic rise in her. She pushed the bubble; it began to form and then it was gone. She closed her eyes and heard an alarm sound from one of the panels in front of the old woman and Ranovich, who was now William Thurston. She felt a pinch in her arm and the familiar rush of drugs hit her system. The panic faded.

"She almost did…whatever she does," Thurston said, the fear in his voice rising. "The sensors caught the swell of brain activity and drugged her again. If you are going to do this, you had better do it now. The moment she figures out a way to reroute the drugs, we won't be able to control her."

"You think she can do that?" asked the old woman. The excitement in her stolen eyes glinted with the possibilities of becoming Jayne.

"You saw the brain scans. Look at the activity we just recorded." He pointed at the lines dancing in the holos. "Her entire cortex just flared, and she has enough drugs in her system to take out a body 10 times her size."

"Everything is ready," Winter Bancroft said. "All I have to do is start my scans and update my input data to the immediate present. Then we start the transfer."

"Haven't you forgotten something?" he asked. The old woman shook her head.

"We all agreed that her connectome scan was to be preserved. It might come in handy some day. We do not have a scan. We have to run a scan on her before we start the transfer."

"That could take hours, or even days, in her case," she said, shaking her head. "I want that body, and I especially want that brain of hers. We start now!"

"Alright, but there are those that won't like it. That will be your problem," he warned.

"Once I have control over that body, nothing will ever be a problem again," she said assuredly. "On second thought, forget my update. Let's do a direct feed. As soon as the equipment synchronizes, start the transfer. And no more drugs. I don't want my first experience as Ms. Wu to be a drug-induced blur. I want to enjoy every second."

As she walked to the back of the room, a soft light bathed a lounge bed. She lay down and an opaque material with the exact shape of her features pressed itself over her skull, exposing her eyes, nose, and the lower part of her face. The lounge swelled over her body, holding it firmly in a soft grip. "I'm ready. Begin NOW!" she ordered.

Jayne felt the table on which she was strapped tilt back to the horizontal position. The change in orientation made her head swim. It also made her aware that something was about to happen. Everything went dark. The darkness was accompanied by a hiss and click. She watched the helmet close a visor over her eyes, shutting out all light. She could barely hear, but the old woman's words, 'Begin NOW,' echoed in her brain. This time, there was no panic. There was no fear. There was no room at this moment for all those emotions. There was only calculation and a push. The bubble formed and there were no alarms and no drugs pushing back. The bubble swelled and receded. The first step was to clear what was left of the drugs. Nothing that required time could happen inside the bubble, but as it receded, Jayne's blood swirled, and the giant molecules that made up the drug were crushed and broken and removed from the stream. As each pulse of clean blood flooded Jayne's brain, the clarity grew, and her body relaxed and readied itself for a fight. This was going to be the fight of her life. If she lost, there would be nothing. Losing was not even a possibility in the great wash of all possibilities. Jayne knew she must win, and to consider anything else was to give that consideration a probability greater than zero. Jayne *pushed!*

The machine that was wrapped around her head opened a stream and started to write the data that belonged to the old woman. A wave of nausea swept like an entire ocean heaving over a continent. Jayne lost focus. Something was nibbling at her mind, like a dream of a rat eating her brain whilst leaving its rancid droppings in its place. The droppings burned.

Jayne pushed again and locked out the destruction. She pushed hard and time slowed. She conjured a three-dimensional isometric plane of possibilities and searched. Once formed, the bubble would give her forever to decide on a course of action. Almost forever. Even so, she searched quickly and cautiously for a survival scenario with a probability of one. There could be no chance of Jayne Wu ending here. Forever in the bubble was zero time in the real world, and out there was a giant rodent about to eat her mind. Suddenly, a possibility burped up like molten rock in the lake of a live volcano—hot yellow and searing crimson. Jayne looked and glowed with glee. She had found it.

The bubble collapsed and Jayne waved the welling nausea aside. She watched the dream rat as it nibbled and ate the pattern that contained her thoughts and memories, leaving behind turds that were not Jayne; turds that were the thoughts and memories of the old woman. Some things were already lost forever. Jayne couldn't stop it, but that was not the plan. She could see what the dream rat would eat next. She grabbed that pattern just before it was consumed by the rat and replaced by the memory of the old woman, and immediately rewrote the original pattern back over the old woman's. She blasted the turds that were the old woman's memories. Whatever the woman and her machine took from her, Jayne immediately took back and cleaned out the debris. Jayne saw it was not all garbage and took some of the information for future use. Some of what the old woman knew, Jayne now knew.

The connectome software tried to confirm what it had written but found something else. It looped back and tried to write the same data again, but during the confirmation process, it found that nothing had been written. The loop had no way out. Jayne had forced the rat to turn and munch on its own tail. The program crashed and the rat suddenly popped out of existence. Jayne could hear alarms ringing, and the opaque visor covering her eyes retracted; she could once more see and hear. Behind her, she could hear the old woman scream. Doctor Thurston moved from the control center out of her field of vision. She could hear him helping the old woman from the lounge bed. She came into view, half walking, half supported by Thurston. As she passed, she slipped from his grasp and fell to the floor. Jayne could see blood coming from her ears, mouth, nose, and eyes. She was coughing and wheezing.

"I'll get help," he said. He ran from the room, leaving the old woman to choke on her own blood.

Jayne looked forward and saw the top of the door close. She remembered the Sergio Partelli hanging there and willed more than the arms to flap. She willed it to her, and it flew from the door and draped over her bound body.

She whispered, "Suit override–thirteen–suggest…" She paused, not knowing what to suggest. Finally, she croaked out, "Help."

The suit warmed over her and she felt it shift slightly. Suddenly, as if someone had flipped a switch, the table restraints released. The suit molded to her body like a wetsuit, covering her from head to toe. A force field formed over her face. This place had full Earth gravity, and Jayne could barely stand up. The suit supported her. As she stood, she looked down at the coughing woman covered in her own blood. The woman struggled to a half-standing position and looked up at Jayne with raw hatred in her stolen eyes.

"You little bitch!" she spat and the spittle, mixed with blood, sprayed over the Sergio Partelli force field that protected Jayne's face. The liquid sizzled and, in a smoky instant, was gone. Jayne looked down at her, reached out, and put a hand on her shoulder. Jayne knew what she had done to the old woman when she forced the dream rat to eat itself.

All the capillaries in the old woman's body were broken and her blood was leaking…everywhere.

Jayne pushed gently with her hand and Winter Bancroft fellover in a heap of convulsing ooze. Jayne stepped over her and opened the door. She turned back just in time to see the light fade from those perfect young eyes.

"It is over," she said to the corpse. Then she left the room.

CHAPTER 41
Greenway Safe

In the time of Jayne Wu, the survival of the human species was far from assured. The Swarm was coming. The only thing that changed, since the discovery, were the holes and the spinners. The wall of rock was better described as a chaotic ball of loose rock. Inside the massive ball of rock that was hurtling toward the solar system were sub-swarms that rotated as if they had already coalesced into planets. Large masses close together were doing what large masses do. They were gradually coming together and forming one much larger mass. They started to spin, just like any planet might spin. Some were already massive. The joining of a billion asteroids into a spinning mass of large masses created holes in the approaching wall of rock. Some of the holes became so large that things might slip through. Even things as big as a solar system.

Two months passed. Jayne woke and slipped out of the wooden bunk onto a cold floor of boards worn shiny and smooth by 200 years of feet. The cabin was very old, tucked away in a temperate rainforest on some small island in the Pacific Northwest. She had been recuperating here for nearly two months. She was going a little stir crazy with the lack of company.

She was now Jayne Wu again. Cassie Kai had been transferred off Biome 7 to a planet-side job after the fiasco in the tunnels. A rumor was circulated that she had only received the job because her father was high up in some government agency or other. The altered records that had resurrected Miss Kai from the dead reverted back to their original state. Cassandra Kai had, once again, died at age five. No one was found to be responsible for the deaths, and the injection of concrete foam into the tunnels was chalked up to a miscommunication.

Jayne now knew that Professor Greenway had come upon the canyon and found Joseph Kane's body and nothing else. There was no evidence as to the actual cause of his death. The entire area had been sanitized. It was assumed he tripped and fell and hit his head on a sharp rock. Professor Greenway had arrived eight minutes after the distress call from Jayne but, by then, she was gone, and Joseph was dead. He had suspicions about where she was taken, but he could not pin down her exact location. He had been monitoring the communication frequencies for something from the Sergio Partelli homing beacon. Finally, it came.

As soon as Jayne called the suit to her and put it on, it became active and signaled Greenway. He had been able to communicate through the suit and get her to safety. She was being held in a university lab on the California coast. Once found, getting her out was simple.

He brought her here to recuperate. At first, she embraced the solitude. But that had not lasted. She knew she had to get out and be with some people or go crazy. Professor Greenway visited her once a week. There was a security detail, but the men never socialized with her. Jayne suspected that the security people were not really people at all, but automatons with rather limited brain power.

To kill the boredom, she had taken to paddling a canoe out on the tiny lake that practically surrounded the cabin built on a small-treed spit. This morning she grabbed a piece of fruit, walked out on the wharf, untied the canoe, and paddled out on the mist-covered lake. She kept in shape by timing herself paddling around the lake as fast as she could. This morning, the silence seemed infinite. She could hear nothing but the dip of the paddle and the drops of water falling from the end of the upstroke. She reached the far side, out of sight of the cabin, when she felt a warning signal in her head that something was different. She had not felt this warning the whole time at the cabin. She let the canoe glide through the water until it stopped. She looked over the side at her reflection. She had not fixed her hair this morning. There was no one to fix it for. The water rippled from a drop falling from her paddle. She blinked and looked again at her reflection. The old dead woman was looking back at her and grinning. She slapped the reflection with her paddle and the shattered image coalesced back into her own face, messy hair and all.

She started paddling again and tried to push the image of the dead scientist out of her head. Suddenly, she heard a sound. She stopped paddling and listened. At first, there was nothing, and then she heard her name. "Thirteen. Thirteen." The sound was coming from the wharf. She listened again and recognized Professor Greenway's voice. It held no concern. Jayne relaxed and paddled quickly to the cabin. She followed a straight line instead of her usual path around the edge of the lake. It would only take her a few minutes.

Professor Greenway came into view. She waved, and he waved back. As she approached the wharf, he called to her, "Nice morning for a paddle. I suppose you would like to stay here in this idyllic place forever, but I have to tell you that—"

"Are you kidding? I have to get out of here before I go mad. Where am I going?"

"Tie up the canoe and meet me at the cabin," he said and walked away.

Jayne quickly removed her life jacket, tied the canoe to the wharf, and ran after him.

He was sitting at the kitchen table, drinking tea.

"Where did you get that?" she asked, sniffing the honey-sweet tea. "I brought a thermos with me. Would you like some?" he asked.

"Not until you tell me where I'm going and what's happening with my life," she said, as she pulled up a chair and sat beside him.

He sipped and warmed his hands on the cup. "Getting chilly here. The leaves have started to turn, and the rains will be back soon."

"Yes, and Jayne will drown herself in the lake if she has to listen to anymore of this drivel. Professor Greenway, would you please spill the proverbial beans?" she ordered.

He sipped and warmed his hands on the cup. "Getting chilly here. The leaves have started to turn, and the rains will be back soon."

"Yes, and Jayne will drown herself in the lake if she has to listen to any more of this drivel. Would you please spill the proverbial beans?" she ordered.

"Alright. I forgot how impatient you are." He sipped his tea and grinned as Jayne tangled her fingers into her tousled hair and pretended to pull it out. "I'm not sure if it's due to your recent experiences or that hairdo, but you've aged quite a bit since our last meeting."

Jayne scoffed. "Speak for yourself, Grandpoppy!"

Greenway raised a hand, a truce gesture, and chuckled. "Here is the list. It is not really open to discussion, so I will read the items:

—You will endure a 48-hour complete connectome scan when you leave here. I will record it. The purpose is to be discussed later.

—You will be required to do a weekly one-hour update of that scan. I always want the latest version of you that is no more than a week old.

—You are going back to HUB 169 to complete your studies. It is still waiting for your return. According to your record, and all your friends and acquaintances, you have been recovering from an illness you caught in the jungles of Biome 3. If anyone asks for details, just claim ignorance. After all, you are a thirteen-year-old kid."

"I get to go back!" exclaimed Jayne as she clapped her hands with glee. She stopped and her expression changed to concern. "What about the Forevers? What if they come after me?"

"I don't think they will, not immediately anyway. Dr. Winter Bancroft is dead and Thurston, aka Ranovich 91, is in detention. We did not know what to charge him with, so we charged him with the murder of himself. As far as the courts are concerned, Ranovich murdered Thurston. That was my idea," said Greenway. "As for other Forevers that may be after you...Well, we will just have to wait and see."

"I will fight back if they come for me!" she said defiantly.

"You are out in the open now. They will be a lot more cautious, and we will be much more alert to their activities. Now, as I was saying:

—You will return to the classroom and study and practice. Exactly what will be discussed in great detail later, but I will say it has to do with training for infiltration," he continued, as he watched her reaction.

"Infiltration? What the heck does that mean? Who or what will I be infiltrating?"

"All in good time, my dear," he said. "Now, as I recall, I was on number five. Yes, number five.

—You will get an upgrade to the suit. It has proven itself invaluable, so you will continue to use it."

"That, and seeing my friends, are the only two things I like." She looked up at his frowning face. "But I will endure the rest."

"Good! Now you need to get cleaned up. You have very little to pack, so I will give you 30 minutes to get ready," he said. He glanced at the time on his VID. "You will find a new VID with your things. Please sync with it."

"Where are we going first?" Jayne asked.

"The location and purpose are 'need to know,' and you do not need to know. Now, hurry up if you want to get out of here," he said cryptically.

"Whatever you say, Grandpoppy," she said with a wink.

An hour later, they were in a flier headed back to HUB 169. Jayne was so happy to be in her old haunts that she never questioned Greenway. She simply followed him. They arrived at the port and walked to a PUT pad array. He gestured for her to come closer to him, then reached out and tied a blindfold over her eyes.

"Boy, this is really secret. You realize this PUT pad will not tell me where we are going. There is no need for a blindfold," she said as she pulled it down and peeked over the top.

"Just do what you are told, or I will take you back to the cabin," he threatened with a grin.

"Okay, Okay, but this is silly," she responded, as she stepped on the PUT pad. A few seconds later, she felt Professor Greenway's hand reach out and lead her off the PUT pad and through a door. Jayne breathed deep. She had no idea where she was or why she was there. That fact made her tense. She was actually afraid that this was not going to turn out well. "Professor Greenway? What is going on? I don't like this."

"Relax," he said, then reached up and untied her blindfold.

Jayne blinked a few times to bring the image into focus. In front of her, was a THIRTEEN!'

There was a huge shout of "SURPRISE!" from behind her. She turned and was rushed by Sara, Josie, Olive, and Spike. The room was filled with apprentices and GravBall players. Jayne had forgotten that she was one year older today. Today she was fourteen. Today was her birthday.

"God, I missed you," bubbled Sara. "I hope you are better. I heard you got that virus. There were a bunch of fixers that got sick from that mutated virus in Biome 3. Some didn't survive. I'm sure glad you did."

"I knew you were much too tough for a little old virus," chimed Spike. He punched her on the shoulder. "You are sure looking good. How old are you today anyway?" he asked.

Jayne turned to him with a sinister smile on her face and spoke in a rough voice, an octave lower than her normal voice. "One hundred and nineteen years old!" she rasped. She shook her head, bent over, and put both hands to her mouth. Nausea flooded her guts and her eyes bulged. She pushed it away, and tried to straighten up, but her knees gave way.

"You, okay?" asked Olive, reaching out to support Jayne. "I heard that the virus really hangs on."

"I'm fine. I was just being funny. I'm only fourteen. I just feel like I'm much older sometimes, with the virus and all," lied Jayne. She forced a weak smile onto her face.

A bubble was begging to form to encase her; to slow time, so she could analyze what had happened. Jayne breathed out slowly, and then she knew there was no need for the bubble. She knew what had happened. She knew who had spoken—spoken through her, for she had recognized the rat in her mind. She had seen the telltale turds scatter as the tail of the rat whipped and vanished. Some of the old woman was left behind in her head. The old crone had set up house in her head. Jayne looked up at the Happy Birthday sign again, but the words had been transformed. The sign said something different: IT WILL NEVER BE OVER!

Jayne shook her head and HAPPY BIRTHDAY, THIRTEEN! reappeared on the sign. She smiled. She knew there would be plenty of time to cage the rat and pick her mind clean of pestilence.

She filled her cheeks with air, puffed it all out, and said, "I hope there's cake."

APPENDIX 1
THE GRAVITY TUBE

Any object that approached the gravity tube was pushed gently inward. The playing field curved upwards at its edges to a maximum of 30 degrees. It measured 30 meters across at the 30-degree level. The playing field was made up of normal gravity, except the areas surrounding the gravity lines. The following is a diagram of an arena:

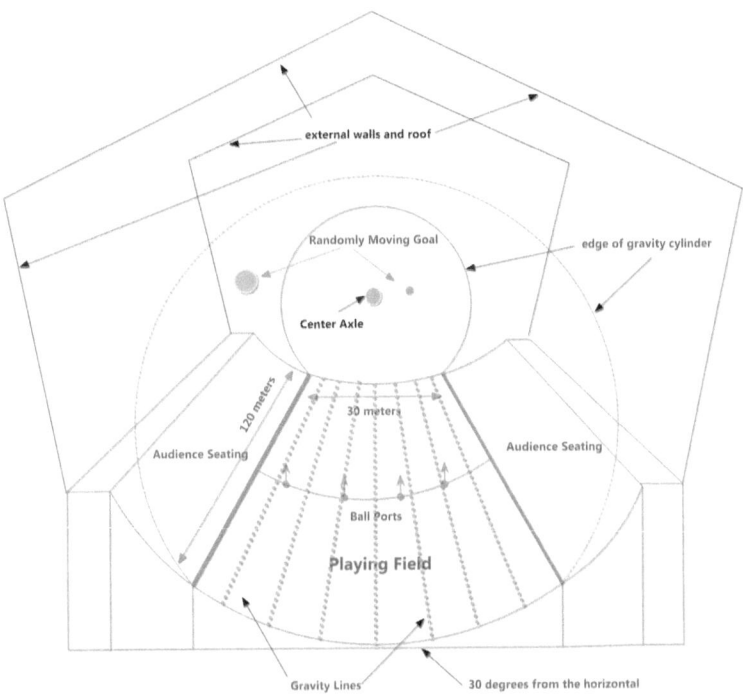

The Center Axle (suggested in diagram) extends through the center of the gravity tube. It contains lighting, cameras and a gravity generator that repels.

GRAVITY BALL

Professional Gravity Ball was played in a tube that was 120 meters long and 32 meters from the floor to the top of the goal panels that stretched across the circular ends. A line of cameras and lights ran from end to end, strung just above the goal ends. These lines were protected from player and ball contact by transparent tubing and anti-gravity fields. The goals sitting at each end consisted of horn-like openings that tapered down to a tube only slightly larger than the ball. Once the ball entered the goal, it was ejected randomly out of one of four tubes that were equally spaced across the floor on the center line. The goals were placed off-center in the end walls. The end walls rotated randomly, in both time and distance, moving each goal closer to and farther from the center point of the end wall. There were seven evenly spaced gravity lines, 3.25 meters apart, extending from one end of the tube to the other. They could change shape from straight to curved. You could not see the gravity line, but you could feel them. The gravity along the entire line could be increased or decreased from normal. The strength of the gravity was the same along the whole length of the line, except in the case of a pulsar. The strength of the gravity varied from line to line. Both the shape of the lines and the strength of the gravity varied throughout game play. All other areas had normal gravity strength. The gravity strength at any given position on the floor extended up to the top of the tube to form a curtain of gravity, but it was referred to as a line.

All lines were one meter in width.

The number of players on a given team was not limited. More players meant a better signaler and knocker system. This came with a price, as the value of each goal would be dramatically reduced. Players would spread out and communicate the location, strength, shape, and potential movement of the gravity lines and the goal. The BC (ball carrier) would choose a line that would take him close enough to the goal to score. The BC could only travel on grav lines. Any player bumped off a grav line could not reenter the same line until he/she had entered at least one other line. Other players could go anywhere.

Knockers could only knock on the grav lines. They could knock the BC or the spotter off the grav lines. The BC could change at any point during the game, but the change must always be a back pass. The opponent team would block all forward progress of the BC in an attempt to recover the ball. (Rules of blocking are too complex for this brief overview.)

Scoring was determined by the number of players in the tube at the start of play. Equal numbers of players would result in ten points for a goal. As that ratio shifted, so the value of a goal shifted inversely. For example:

Team A—12 players—a goal would result in a score of 7 (10 x (OPP/ HOME)) = 10 x (8/12) = 10 x .67 = 6.7 points

Team B—8 players—a goal would result in a score of 15 (10 x (OPP/ HOME)) = 10 x (12/8) = 10 x 1.5 = 15 points

This scoring system made for some intriguing strategies in gameplay.

FURTHER READING

THE FOREVERS SERIES

BOOK 1
MIND STORMS

BOOK 2
THE TRAVELER

BOOK 3
MASTER WU

BOOK 4
OMIE 17

BOOK 5
THE SPACE WIZARD

ABOUT THE AUTHOR

G MICHAEL SMITH is a retired teacher of Computer Programming, Drama, Math, English, and Theatre. He's written and directed plays for both adults and children. He also writes poetry and novels.

Besides *The Forevers*, his body of work includes *The Prison of Power: A Man-Made Tale; Hijacked,* a middle-grade mystery; an Early-reader Children's Books series including the titles *Lily Liar and the Eleventy Headed Monster*, *Tiny Tina and the Terrible Trouble*, and forthcoming *Ashley and the Hornets*, as well as a Children's Picture Book titled *The Accidental Adventures of Bernie the Banana Slug*.

Smith resides in Qualicum Beach, Vancouver Island, BC, Canada with his wife, Cheryl, and enjoys spending time with his three adult daughters and three grandchildren. He's also known to enjoy a rigorous game of pickleball, softball, squash, or badminton.

Learn more at gmichaelsmith.com.